UNEQUIVOCAL MALICE

UNEQUIVOCAL MALICE

A Novel

Michael Parker

iUniverse, Inc.
New York Lincoln Shanghai

UNEQUIVOCAL MALICE

A Novel

iUniverse books may be ordered through booksellers or by contacting:

iUniverse
2021 Pine Lake Road, Suite 100
Lincoln, NE 68512
www.iuniverse.com
1-800-Authors (1-800-288-4677)

ISBN: 0-595-33137-8

Printed in the United States of America

With appreciation
to my family and friends
for their assistance
over the past three years.

Contents

Part I: TROUBLE IN CENTERVILLE

PART II: THE PAST

PART III: FINDING THE KILLER

PART I

TROUBLE IN CENTERVILLE

PROLOGUE
CHAPTERS ONE THROUGH NINETEEN

PROLOGUE

His breath coming in short gasps, Marsden's victim looked down the black barrel of a loaded twelve-gauge shotgun.

"I was only kidding," the hostage pleaded, his blond hair matted with perspiration. "The...arguments...and your problems weren't your fault."

"I know that," Marsden said, with mounting irritation in his voice. In the yellow moonlight seeping between the tall pine trees, his coarse face, with a long mouth and sunken eyes, bore a light resemblance to a skull.

Marsden said nothing for a few moments before resuming the conversation. "You kept me in such a terrible situation," Marsden continued. "For so many years. And all you've got to tell me is that it wasn't my fault."

He raised the shotgun.

"I needed the money," Marsden's victim said. He was afraid to make the slightest move, never taking his eyes off Marsden's shotgun. "It was the economy," he offered furtively.

"I don't have any sympathy for you," Marsden said. The pupils of his eyes were hard and black against the white pigment.

Marsden looked away, into the unlighted woods. No one seemed to be around. *He's one of them,* Marsden told himself in black-and-white terms. *He's the enemy. No matter what I did, the poor bastard never took my side.*

Unable to control his rising panic, the man shouted, "For crying out loud, you've got to trust me."

Not far away, a raccoon padded unevenly toward a clearing. In the moonlight, its gleaming eyes half visible, it was frightened by the desperate voices of the two men. To the creatures of the forest, the men were intruders.

"Like the old saying goes, it's a cruel world," Marsden explained. "I don't trust anybody. Not you, not the sheriff, not the media."

Marsden slid his hand over the smooth butt of the shotgun, placing his finger behind the trigger. The wind whispered, kicking up dust from the dirt road behind him.

"Oh, my God!" the man yelled, thin tears streaming down his sagging cheeks. He was on the verge of breaking down. "I feel grief…for what I have done," he admitted.

"Grief isn't good enough," Marsden snapped. "You told me about this place," he said, turning his head toward the dirt-crusted walls of the empty building. The sounds of shifting tree branches and the bubbling river floated on the breeze.

"You don't understand reality," Marsden accused, as if he was standing in a courtroom. "You're the one who is to blame for whatever happens."

Tonight, he believed the forest possessed evil qualities. However, this spot was an exception to Marsden's unreasonable theories about the brutal side of nature. Since going through a turbulent period over two decades ago, he had occasionally found solace in this isolated place, and he was accustomed to its vacant buildings and underground caverns.

Like the victim's exhausted wheezing, Marsden's acrimony was reduced to incomplete fragments. "Urban sprawl," he mouthed out loud. "Tourists."

Marsden formed a picture in his head: *Each tourist double-checking the time. Every motorist impatiently pressing his foot on the gas pedal, plowing down the highway at top speed. Vans and sport utility four-by-fours, passing in the left lane and passing in the right lane, rushing past the dull lives of the lazy degenerates.*

Prank phone calls. Junk mail.

"He filled out complaint forms and nothing happened," Marsden declared, wrapped up in his own thoughts.

"Shut up!" the terrified man protested, as if to ward off hysteria.

"Her boyfriend filled out complaint forms and nothing happened," Marsden repeated.

"Everyone experiences…setbacks," the victim pointed out, a pleading tone in his voice.

"Setbacks!" Marsden swung his head around, looking from the edge of the woods to the old building. Marsden noticed he had left his laptop running, and the dim light from the screen was barely visible. It shined through the building's dusty windowpane. "You call this good-for-nothing place a setback."

"That's not what I meant," the man answered nervously. "I can't think straight," he trembled.

"Don't try to explain," Marsden warned. "Don't try to console me. None of that will work."

With tension showing on his face, he studied the captive. Marsden licked his lips. *He might try to get away,* Marsden told himself. *When I'm done with him, I can find another one. They're all the same.*

"They read headlines," Marsden said, without further explanation. "You were in the newspaper."

Behind his sagging cheeks, with a sickly look, the man called up mental images of the past: paint-peeled gutters, gasoline fumes from the tractor, white lights from the helicopter, the guards screaming in agony, the stories in the newspaper. He felt a heavy weight creep over him, the pressure of being trapped.

Grotesque shadows spread across the wooded property.

The man shrugged, exposing the wrinkles in his face. "What do you plan to do to me?"

"We have to go someplace else." Marsden glanced at the wood-planked walls of the weatherbeaten structure. Then he looked down the winding road, which intermingled with skeletal outlines of pine trees.

He was groggy and he felt sweat matted against his undershirt.

Squirming, the victim continued. "Please put the gun down. Killing me isn't going to solve anything. The sheriff will have you arrested."

Marsden stepped forward, making a low noise in his throat. "Nobody will miss your rotting corpse," he scowled.

CHAPTER 1

"Jason, I can hear scary noises coming from the woods over there, just off the highway," Sheryl Peterson said. "They're definitely a turn-off. Maybe we should leave. What if there are wild animals such as bears back there?" she giggled. "What if there's a depraved stalker after us?"

Jason Wells shrugged, and Sheryl glanced at his bewildered expression. His dark eyebrows were knitted together. In the radiant starlight, he looked modestly handsome, with lively blue eyes, a wide face and well-groomed black hair. Having grown up in farm country, he had a muscular build.

"Everybody needs some rest and relaxation," Jason advised. "It's refreshing to be out here tonight."

"So far, it's been a romantic evening under the clear night sky and distant stars," Sheryl agreed. "But I wonder about us being here alone."

Jason and Sheryl, his attractive girlfriend, had taken an evening drive down U.S. Highway 46 to the Waubeka National Forest, about thirty minutes north of Centerville. They had been stargazing from the scenic overlook, which offered a panoramic view of the woods. The observation point was a breathtaking spot where five nature trails intersected. It included a modern visitor center, which was closed for the night.

"Jason, I've never known you to be such an optimist," Sheryl said. "Jason Wells, the friendly human bear. A journalist who writes about dread, but doesn't let it stop him from getting away from it all."

"Sheryl, if something happened, I'd take care of you," Jason said.

"I know you would, Jason," Sheryl moaned.

Jason squeezed Sheryl's hand reassuringly, planting a tender kiss on her welcoming lips. As he pulled away, he noticed something.

"What's wrong?" Jason asked.

Sheryl leaned her trim figure against Jason's taut chest, brunette hair flowing over her shoulders. She continued in a warm, particularly feminine tone of voice. "When I started working as a reporter three years ago, I didn't know much about the town, the woods or the newspaper. Although Centerville has become my home and you were raised here, I worry, sometimes."

"About what?"

Sheryl sensed the vacuous timberland surrounding the observation point. "About things people worry about—forgetting to pay a charge card bill on time, urban sprawl…the cell phone slipping out of my pocket."

"The phone's taken care of," Jason said. "I charged it up at my place. It's in the cup holder on the front seat."

Feeling an uncomfortable chill creep up her spine, Sheryl blurted out, "One night, we'll take a spin out to the forest. And then, as in crime stories, something bad will happen."

"Don't be ridiculous," Jason responded, flashing a charming smile.

For a moment, he stopped himself. "I don't mean to shoot down your theories about news angles on high-profile crimes, but the forest is safer at night than you think. I doubt there's anybody around here except woodsmen, hunters and fishermen. They're usually amiable folks. When there's trouble, it often comes from impatient tourists scrambling down the highway and outsiders unfamiliar with the wonders of nature."

Wearing a lightweight cotton blouse, a snug, hip-length summer jacket and navy-blue slacks, Sheryl shook her head. Her outstretched, brown strands of hair flapped in the night breeze.

"What do you think?" she asked, pointing to her hair. "I went to Angel's Hair Salon yesterday."

"Your hair looks gorgeous," Jason responded.

Sheryl returned to the subject of tourists, telling Jason there had been an incident at Angel's. "After I walked into Angel's, I noticed a woman with a startled expression on her face," Sheryl explained. "She was seated in the waiting area. We got to talking, and it turned out she and her boyfriend were tourists. Before I arrived, another customer who had been waiting behind her boyfriend to get his hair clipped lost his cool. He yelled to the stylist that the tourists were in his way, that her boyfriend should have gotten an expensive eighty-five-dollar haircut downtown."

"What happened next?" Jason enquired.

"I guess the hair stylist threatened to phone the sheriff's department," Sheryl continued. "And the irate customer left Angel's without a haircut."

Just then, a pair of dim headlights appeared out of the night far down the highway. They came into greater and greater focus, resembling the brilliant lights of a locomotive reaching a railroad crossing. A clanging semitrailer truck, a sixteen-wheeler, whooshed down the asphalt strip, leaving Jason's Chrysler Sebring, not far from the gravel shoulder, vibrating like a motorboat on the white-capped surface of a windy lake.

A few minutes later, another vehicle, a green Ford Ranger pickup truck, slowed down. The pickup pulled into the parking lot, near the spot where Jason and Sheryl were standing. The driver, a lank, dark-haired man, leaned across the front seat and lowered the window on the passenger's side. The man had placed the gear in his pickup truck in park and the engine was idling.

"Do you need any help?" the stranger asked. "Is your car stalled?"

Jason answered quickly. "No, there is nothing we know of wrong with our automobile. We don't need directions."

He paused. "We just look lost because we don't come out here very often. I was fishing a few weeks ago at Crater Lake, so I'm not especially familiar with this particular spot. We're just having a pleasant night looking at the stars."

The driver nodded. "Yes, it is a pleasant night," he yelled from inside the cab of the pickup truck. The man reminded Sheryl of the subject of a mug shot she had seen in the newspaper morgue. She couldn't remember the person's name.

"I'm heading to my lake cabin. I store my fishing poles and tackle boxes there. I didn't mean to bother you. I just thought I'd ask, make sure everything's OK, and see if your car was stuck. I've heard of tourists getting lost in the woods for as long as a week. I'd panic like hell if I had to go without food and water for a week."

"What do you mean?" Jason asked, following his news reporter's instincts. "Is someone missing?"

"No," the man stammered. "The last case I remember took place two years ago."

"Tell me about it," Jason said quickly.

"It involved a resident of Crater Lake, a man named Lester Jenkins. His canoe got caught in the rapids, and he was swept down river. He lost one of his oars, and the rocks and strong current fractured the hull. He was missing for three days—tired, delirious and wandering around the forest. He survived on bottled drinking water and a package of uncooked hot dogs."

"Wait a minute," Jason interrupted. "We work for the newspaper, and I vaguely remember reading about that. A local farmer, Brian Johnson, found him lying on the ground near the edge of the forest. Jenkins was taken to Memorial Hospital, where he was treated for the injury to his arm. The Observer did a big write-up on him. He said he wasn't sure he'd make it out of the woods, and was relieved the farmer had spotted him."

Jason added, "That was a harrowing adventure. In fact, when I wrote the headline, that was how I described it—a harrowing adventure."

Irritated by Jason's know-it-all bluntness, the man shot a hostile glance in his direction. "I guess it was." With a sudden jerk, he rolled up his window, and Jason and Sheryl listened to the tires crackle over loose pebbles in the parking lot. The pickup turned onto the highway and sped away, the taillights becoming a red blur.

"You don't have to tell strangers about our jobs," Sheryl corrected. Although Jason was a sweet person, she thought that below the surface of his congenial personality were two distinct halves—a caring boyfriend and, at times, a detached journalist. Despite the fact they had begun dating five years ago in college, she had a few doubts about Jason.

Jason studied Sheryl's countenance. "What?" was all he said.

"That man looked familiar," Sheryl said. "I couldn't place him."

"You mean from the newspaper?"

"I think so."

Jason was more nervous than he cared to admit. Without explanation, he reached into his pants pocket to make sure his keys were still there. Tracing his fingers along the familiar metal grooves left him feeling reassured.

Jason took Sheryl's wrists in his hands. He brushed his lips against her cheeks, planting another soft kiss.

Sheryl looked at him with appreciation. "Let's get going," she repeated.

"OK," Jason answered. "We'll have a good time tomorrow night. It should be more than just a party."

They strolled from the scenic overlook to Jason's car. He unlocked the doors, they slipped quietly into the front seat and pulled out of the narrow parking lot. Jason steered the maroon Sebring west on U.S. Highway 46 toward Centerville.

CHAPTER 2

Trent Purnell tried to start the outboard motor in the charcoal-grey rental boat. Again and again, he tugged on the pull-cord connected to the gas-powered motor, but there was no mechanical sound. Only the smell of gasoline.

"What happened?" his girlfriend, Jean Kirchner asked innocently. Tall and slender, she had fluffy blonde hair flowing over the shoulders of her turquoise sailing jacket.

"I don't know," Trent answered. "I checked the gas tank, and it's three-quarters full." Trent pounded his fist on the motor in frustration. With his thin nose and eyebrows pushed together in confusion and beads of sweat dripping down his long blond sideburns, Trent appeared worried.

"Damn!" he said, the irritation mounting in his voice. "I don't know what the problem is. I've been trying to start the thing for the past fifteen minutes," he said, shining the flashlight on the motor compartment.

"That doesn't sound good," Jean said impatiently.

"What do you want me to do?" Trent snapped.

"I'm not sure," Jean replied. She leaned dejectedly against a wide tree trunk, her slender body forming an S-shape. "When we decided to come out here, I thought you knew how to operate the motor boat."

"I can pull-start a working engine," Trent said. "The motor must have malfunctioned. Something's wrong."

"We can't stay here forever," Jean said.

"No, we can't." Trent dug into his backpack, and removed a plastic compass and a black flashlight. He watched the red directional needle inside the compass float into place. Trent also studied the shoreline with the flashlight, his white corduroys visible in the darkness. Beyond the mighty rock formations, the waves lapping against the riverbank and carrying the odor of rotting fish carcasses, the shoreline resembled an emerald-green wall of brush and trees.

"I guess this should be very simple. After we left the boat launch, we headed east from Crater Lake down the river. All we have to do is follow the shoreline west, the way we came. That shouldn't be too bad. We can take the thermos, flashlight and food from the boat. I doubt we're more than five miles from the harbor."

"Trent!" Jean yelled loudly. "You mean we have to hike back to the resort. I'm tired. That will take all night. We don't have a cell phone or a map. We shouldn't even be out here at this time of night. We were supposed to have the boat back two hours ago."

"I've tried starting the motor," Trent said. "We'll probably run across a hiking trail. Portions of the Knob Rock Trail run parallel to the river. We've got a chance of finding it."

Before the entire night was wasted, they decided to head back in the direction of the resort. They couldn't be far enough from the Bay View not to make it back on foot, they reasoned, even if it took them hours. They began tramping through sparse foliage, pushing low-hanging branches out of the way and finding openings between tree trunks. Elm trees dotted the riverbank, and the wind had tossed patches of bark and branches onto the ground. Fallen trees and hollow logs lined each hillside. The incongruent shades of green shrubbery resembled mismatched socks, shirts and pants strewn all over a messy bedroom. It was easy for them to lose track of exactly where they were located.

Smooth water-sanded stones, jagged rocks and a carpet of pine needles made up the bulk of the forest floor. Shafts of moonlight cut in between bushes, exposing flying insects such as mosquitoes and bees. The wind cried down the river valley, disturbing the stillness.

After hiking for twenty-five minutes, the Marengo River, the hazy waterway they had sailed down in the early evening, had disappeared from sight. They were on the eastern slope of a steep ravine.

And on the other side of the ravine, Marsden had heard Trent and Jean, strangers, approaching. The couple at the overlook hadn't appeared to pose a threat. Trent and Jean were another matter.

Now, as in the past, bad memories had driven Marsden to seek solace in the woods. Not too far from him, Jean and Trent were arguing. Marsden was both surprised and angered by outsiders snooping around his place. In the gloomy light, a raccoon dined on a chunk of hamburger left behind by campers. Frightened by the odd man, Marsden, in the maze of trees, the raccoon finished eating with uncharacteristic haste.

Rather than pass the summer simply working, Jean and Trent had decided to get away from the headaches of the city. When fall rolled around, they expected to return to the sedentary lifestyles of undergraduate students at Lydell University. They needed an escape, so they found Centerville on an Atlas travel map. On Trent's computer, they had booked a room for a week at the Bay View Resort, located on Crater Lake thirty miles north of town.

They had driven Trent's used 1995 Olds Cutlass up to the resort from Milwaukee. Trent had left work early to join Jean for the start of their one-week vacation. By Thursday, he and Jean had gotten a sun tan on the beach, and in the afternoon, there had been the run-in with the weirdo in the barbershop.

Earlier on Friday, they had cruised for over an hour on a boat tour around the lake and down the river. The tour guide had repeated local lore about 19th century settlers, Indian reservations, sunken ships and forest fires. He had claimed there was once a fountain of youth—a system of underground springs that produced water so pure it slowed the aging process. In the early 1900s, tourists, including celebrities and politicians, had flocked to Crater Lake to receive the medicinal benefits of the water.

Since then, residents and tourists alike drank bottled spring water and bathed in it, expecting their health to improve. Some people believed the water protected their health, but others met with disaster, dying in hotel fires, drowning mysteriously and disappearing in the woods.

Even if the stories were pure fantasy, they gave Jean and Trent interesting subjects to talk about. On impulse, they had decided around dinnertime to rent their own motor boat for a romantic evening.

They had planned to return by 8 p.m., but had ended up venturing farther down the Marengo River. They had stopped, and had gotten off the aluminum boat to take a stroll down the shoreline. Trent had found himself admiring Jean's beauty—her small firm breasts and her gorgeous hips. Telling Jean about her sexy smile, the young couple had engaged in a series of long kisses. Losing track of time, they had spread out a blanket and undressed quickly and made love. After returning from the trip, they had planned to have sex again later that night in their room at the resort.

However, as the evening wore on, the sun had gone down, and hours later, they were lost. Now Marsden listened to them bickering, first, about how much money the vacation would drain from Trent's cheapskate budget, and second, about turning up missing.

"Your not really thinking of hiking all the way down this river," Jean protested.

"There should be a trail coming up."

"Not along the river," Jean replied. "There's nothing here. We don't know our way around."

"That's why we should follow the river," Trent replied.

"We won't be able to make it down the rocky shoreline," she said, becoming very upset. "Don't you understand what a terrible mess you've gotten us into?" she said, her face red with embarrassment.

Trent fumbled for words. "Just settle down," he advised.

"Settle down! Are you nuts?" For a moment, Jean stood still. If there was a long-distance trail, she realized, most of it wouldn't run parallel to the river. "I'm going to take a look this way," she said, marching away from the jagged shoreline. "Just stay there, Trent," she commanded.

Trent started after her. "Don't go yourself," he yelled, feeling frustrated by his loss of control. "We'll make it back. Don't give up."

But without realizing it, Jean had lost her patience. She left Trent along the shoreline, finding narrow lanes between the pines until she came to what appeared to be a grassy footpath. She was astonished. Other people had really been out here. Now she had something tangible to report to Trent.

Before turning around to get Trent, she decided to explore just a little further. After all, that was one of the reasons they had come out here. Jean started down the slope of another wooded hill into a deep ravine. Marsden squinted his eyes, as she made her way around a jumbled pile of decaying logs and a rock outcropping, closer to to his hostage, to the spot he assumed belonged to him.

It's the city bitch from the hair salon, Marsden thought. *I don't even need the gun. This will be a piece of cake.*

A muted screech shot through the dusky woods. "Trent, is that you? Where are you?" Jean looked around suspiciously and walked faster, losing track of where she was going. "Is someone there?"

With reluctance, she pushed aside branches obstructing her view and determined she was standing on a steep bluff. Looking at the jagged hills and dirt access road below, her heartbeat skittered to an accelerated pace. Tracing the road along her line of sight, she made out the dark outlines of several buildings.

"Trent," Jean mumbled. She had found a sign of civilization, yet the unlit buildings were far below her position on the bluff. Even worse, no one seemed to be around. Not even Trent.

She recalled her childhood. When she was nine years old, her neighborhood friends had pretended they were sailing across the ocean, like ships of pioneer settlers anticipating the barren shores of the New World. The children conducted sword fights along a narrow two-by-four on a neighbor's white picket fence. Once, Jean had toppled off the fence, and on the way down to the ground, two layers of skin were scraped from her knee by a hard wooden picket.

She remembered Trent hugging her only a few hours ago. Distracted, she barely heard the shallow breathing and muddy debris crunching maliciously underneath someone else's work boots.

Suddenly the flashlight beam burned through the darkness, and then Marsden spotted her—climbing to her feet, at first, and then running. With Trent she had been lost and without him she suddenly felt deathly afraid. She should have been kinder to Trent and given him the chance to follow her. She had lost her cool.

Marsden was intent upon stopping the intruder from learning anything about him. He ripped apart a handful of dead brush and threw it into the racket caused by the rising wind.

"Somebody, please help me!" Jean yelled, a note of defeat in her voice. She heard a muffled response, probably Trent, judging from the direction. He would likely come looking for her, but someone else was there, also.

She stepped on a tiny, sharp object, and after she slipped onto the ground, reached over to pick it up. She stared silently at the absurd-looking child's ring in her hands, which had a white skull mounted on a silver band. She tossed it away, and after it landed, Marsden seemed to be standing there, his countenance pale in the moonlight.

Jean was terrified. Marsden's head, with vacant eyes and an oval-shaped mouth, looked like it was chiseled on a rocky cliff along the river.

"I'm sorry," Marsden mumbled. "You shouldn't be snooping around here."

"Trent and I have been lost for hours," she explained desperately. "Can't you do something?"

Marsden disappeared for a moment behind a stand of trees, and Jean could have sworn she had seen a hallucination. When she tried to move her feet, the ground seemed to shift uncomfortably. She planned to run to the buildings she had seen. And when she ultimately returned to her home, in her bedroom, she would pass out underneath the warm comfort of soft blankets piled on her canopy bed.

Although she was tired and disoriented, she felt the blunt force of Marsden's work gloves dig into the flesh on her neck, beginning to choke her. With Marsden pushing sharply, Jean flopped helplessly down the steep ridge, her head slamming against a mass of hard boulders.

In a matter of minutes, the scene of Jean's unexpected murder dissolved into the murk of Marsden's twisted perceptions. There was still little color in Marsden's chalky face, and his eyes were virtually emotionless, revealing only a trace of remorse. Marsden heard rustling in the brush, and stood still, while another figure approached.

Through a break in the low-hanging branches, Trent spotted the dark figure. But his survival instinct had told him to shut up, not to call attention to himself, that the other person wasn't Jean.

Marsden lunged at Trent's nylon jacket with his crude oversized work gloves, twirled him in a circle and tossed him onto the ground. Trent landed on his back against a tree trunk. With his head swirling, Trent staggered to his feet and grabbed a branch that was lying on the forest floor. He thrust it against Marsden's midsection, but it snapped in half.

"There's nothing you can do," Marsden taunted from the shadows. "Your girlfriend is dead. After arguing with her, you got carried away and you lost control."

A trickle of blood rolled down Trent's right cheek. Trent squinted his eyes, Marsden's gaunt visage remaining only partially visible.

"Fighting me won't do any good," Marsden said. "Why not leave things the way they are? A jail cell isn't so bad."

"If you've hurt Jean or anybody else, you're the one who's going to end up in jail," Trent responded.

"Can't you hear? Your girlfriend's dead, buddy," Marsden teased. "I saw you slam her head into the rock. Now you're going to have to go without it."

"You bastard!" Trent shouted. "I've never done anything to you."

Trent picked up another thick oak branch and clutched it with both hands. From the highway, headlight beams flashed through the shroud of nature. Adrenaline rushed through Trent's weary body, and in self-defense, he pounded the branch off Marsden's shoulders. A sickening thud echoed, while Marsden issued a wretched groan.

Trent heard another person walking through the woods and a truck's engine humming slowly on the highway. Courage welled up in Trent, and he swung the branch again, striking Marsden's retreating figure.

Trent turned away, dropped the branch and staggered toward the highway. Then, to his utter relief, he saw the semi-truck's headlights. He gasped and passed out.

CHAPTER 3

Clayton County Sheriff Roger Weaver stood near Trent. Weaver was a husky man with thick arm muscles, a middle-aged paunch and black hair turning grey at the temples. He had the serious look of a county sheriff in the prime of his career, not to mention the department's most experienced member, a veteran of twenty-plus years.

The blinking lights of two sheriff's squad cars parked on Highway 46 filled the embankment with sporadic flashes of light. Sheriff's officials told Trent he was approximately two miles from Crater Lake and the Bay View Resort. He had been found semi-conscious, in a daze.

A sixteen-wheel truck was idling in front of the squad cars on the gravel shoulder. A deputy informed Trent that the truck driver, Ken Fielding, had spotted him laying in a field. Trent had passed out. The truck driver had used his CB radio to call for help. While Fielding was waiting for the sheriff and a deputy to reach the scene, he had seen Jean's motionless body inside the shallow perimeter of the woods, near Purnell. She was dead, and the truck driver was terrified.

Weaver lifted his cap and wiped the perspiration out of his hair. "Can you tell us what happened?" Weaver asked.

"When we climbed out of the boat, we were together," Trent told the sheriff and deputy. "We were scared. We tried to head west, along the river and in the direction of the lake. It seemed like the harder we tried to find our way out of the forest, the more we lost track of wear we were.," he muttered shakily.

When Trent had regained consciousness, he hadn't felt like himself, he said. Although his head ached badly and his ears were plugged, he remembered struggling with a stranger. And he recalled that he had been separated from Jean.

"A stalker was after us," Trent continued. "I fought him off with a branch. The fucker killed Jean."

"Do you think you could describe the suspect or identify him from police photos?" Weaver asked, studying Purnell's reaction.

His head ringing, Trent hesitated. "He was Caucasian, with dark hair," Purnell volunteered. "In the shadows, I couldn't see him clearly."

With a wide nose and a dark mustache, it wasn't easy for Purnell not to notice the quizzical expression on Deputy Dennis Balton's face. "What weapon did the perp use?" Balton interjected.

Almost in a state of denial, Trent didn't wish to acknowledge that his girlfriend was dead. "I think he jumped me from behind. He was wearing work gloves. As you can see, I don't know my way around these parts very well."

Ray Morehouse, the manager of the Bay View Resort, believed he had seen Trent and an unidentified person, presumably his girlfriend, Jean, struggling in the shadows. He had heard the shrill screams. He told the sheriff and deputies, who, for years, had known him to be a demure, law-abiding citizen, that he had been conducting a nature investigation with his camcorder. He wasn't sure if the tape had picked up evidence of what had transpired, and he was relieved to learn the truck driver had contacted authorities.

Morehouse recognized Trent as a guest at the Bay View Resort. Trent and Jean were vacationing, and had checked into Room 205, he told authorities. Morehouse had also tried to contact the county sheriff's department using his cell phone. Due to a weak battery, he wasn't able to reach 9-1-1.

"Away from the city, we thought we were going to find some peace of mind," Trent babbled. "It never would have occurred to me to harm Jean."

Judging from the skeptical expressions on the faces of Weaver and Balton, Trent figured out it had crossed their minds that he might be the killer. The gash splitting Jean's head was covered with blood, and there were small bruises on her neck, as if the assailant had attempted to strangle her. Trent also had marks from a scuffle.

He continued his description of the ordeal. "It wasn't much of a boat trip. We got lost. The engine on the boat went out. We were exhausted," Trent said.

"We went a long time without using a bathroom," he added. "We began arguing about money and getting lost." Trent's eyes opened wide. "The asshole must have heard us."

Weaver interjected, "After quarreling, you became separated, is that correct?"

"After I was separated from Jean, I couldn't figure out what happened." Trent closed his eyes, and thinking of Jean's tragic death, tears streamed down his face.

He returned to his account of what had transpired. "I was out of place. Someone else was in the woods. I'm sure of it. He murdered Jean."

Trent added, "As the hours ticked away, I became more frightened. I couldn't wait for the first streak of daybreak. I tried to run to the highway, but it was useless."

Then Trent forced himself to the spot where Jean was found. He examined the corpse, verifying it was Jean. Then, slowly, he staggered away.

Weaver and Balton decided to hold Trent in custody for further questioning. Apparently, they would have to wait for the report from the coroner's office and watch the contents of the tape from Morehouse's camcorder. Unless they found conflicting evidence, Trent, for the time being, was someone they needed to talk to.

CHAPTER 4

Sheryl received a telephone call at her apartment at 8 a.m. Saturday morning. Matthew Merteau, the city editor for the Observer, had received news about a death on his answering machine. He told Sheryl about two tourists who had been piloting a rented boat when the engine died, and how Kirchner had turned up dead and Purnell had been discovered semi-conscious. A torn piece of Purnell's shirt had been found hanging on a branch near the murder victim's corpse, and as a result, Purnell had been taken to the county sheriff's building for further questioning.

Meanwhile, sheriff's officials continued to inspect the crime scene. Their suspicions about Purnell stemmed from the fact that the investigation was in its early stages, Merteau said. Since the couple were from out-of-town, deputies hadn't had time to locate anyone else with a motive.

"I realize you were supposed to have today off," Merteau told Sheryl. "I'm kind of shorthanded at the moment. Would you mind running down to the sheriff's department to do a write-up for tomorrow morning's Sunday edition. I'd like to read the story in my computer file by 3 p.m."

Sheryl accepted the assignment, and added, "This is short notice, but I didn't have anything else planned for this afternoon. I'm at my apartment. I'll try to find out what I can about the death and finish at least one story by 3 p.m."

"OK," Merteau said abruptly. Sheryl hung up, planning how to arrange her schedule. With Sheryl's busy schedule, even though she was a reporter, she existed, at times, like the contacts she interviewed for her news stories. In fact, that was one of the factors that had attracted her to work in the print media: She would be able to write about the world's troubles. And hopefully, she wouldn't end up contributing to them.

She sat down on her plaid couch. It was the centerpiece of her two-story apartment's living room, which was colored beige and decorated with contemporary wall hangings and furniture. She glanced at yesterday's Observer, which was sitting on the glass coffee table.

Sheryl had also anticipated attending the Centerville Symphony tonight with Jason. The performance would mark a landmark seventy-fifth year of noteworthy local classical music. It was included in a season series, starring soprano Jenny Warveren, who was part of a canon of mezzo-soprano singers visiting Centerville.

The concert was to take place at the Performing Arts Center, located in downtown Centerville on Main Street. In addition to the Performing Arts Center and the Clayton County Courthouse, Main Street was home to the sheriff's office, the Centerville Banquet and Conference Center, and a dozen industrial factories such as the Pollard Steel plant. There were several banks downtown, including the Centerville State Bank, the M&I Bank and the U.S. Bank. And there were hotels such as the Ramada, the Best Western and the Centerville Hotel.

Sheryl had scheduled an interview with the singer before her performance for a human-interest story, which would appear in the Observer's Music Section. When Warveren was sixteen years old, she had had a run-in with her grandmother, who presumed she was wasting too much of her parent's money on private singing lessons. Her grandmother, Arlene Warveren, had once threatened to have her arrested for shopping with her mother's charge cards.

After the performance, she and Jason planned to arrive late at a party at the Bay View Resort. It had something to do with an acquaintance of Jason's, and Sheryl knew little about it.

She glanced at the oak wall clock. She would be on the go. After grabbing a fast breakfast and tidying up her apartment, she would head down to the sheriff's department. If it was necessary, she could shorten the feature story about Warveren.

At the sheriff's department, she needed to verify that Trent was the primary suspect and ask police what they believed the killer's motive was. Attempting to set up an interview, she dialed the sheriff's number. She was told law enforcement authorities had sketchy information at this point in the Kirchner case, so there would be an abbreviated press conference at noon.

After she hung up, Sheryl found herself to be nervous. Nights were calm in Centerville. It was a typical Midwestern community. But now an apparent homicide had taken place. Kirchner was young, Sheryl reflected, and she had been out with her boyfriend Friday night, the same night Jason had driven her to the overlook.

Instead of turning out to be wrong about leaving the overlook, Sheryl's worst fears had been confirmed—something terrible had taken place. As a general assignment reporter, she wasn't necessarily an expert on crime. She worried that her coverage would be insufficient.

It was early, but she picked up the phone, anyway, and dialed Jason. She told Jason about the murder case. As soon as he heard Sheryl relate Merteau's description, he reasoned the story would be covered by several reporters, not just Sheryl. She felt at ease.

"I'm sorry to hear about it," Jason said. "I guess all of the people in Centerville aren't as clean as I thought."

Sheryl paused. "Doesn't that shock you, Jason?"

Jason seemed dumbfounded. "You bet it does," he answered reluctantly. "The story will probably be all over the media."

Sheryl suggested Jason meet her after work for dinner. Then they would both proceed to the concert, followed by the party afterward. Jason readily agreed.

CHAPTER 5

Sheriff Weaver walked into the press room. Growing up in a big family with seven siblings—four brothers and three sisters—he had experienced a wonderful childhood, filled with plenty of talk and plenty of competition. As sheriff, as chief of the department, it was time for Weaver to talk about the Kirchner case, with both print and broadcast journalists competing for Weaver's attention. Weaver stepped behind the podium, and gestured to the room of seated reporters, telling them they could begin asking questions.

Sheryl knew the basics of the case, but she needed to find out if the sheriff had gotten a confession or a statement of innocence from Purnell. She didn't assume the investigation had remained unchanged since she had spoken with Merteau. "Have there been any other suspects arrested so far other than Trent Purnell?" she asked Weaver.

"No. At the present time, Purnell is our only suspect in the death of Jean Kirchner." Then Weaver repeated background information about the case. He was a law-and-order man, and an organized person who wanted to know the hard facts. Although reporters and deputies had criticized him, at times, as a condescending speaker, he liked the idea of laying out the groundwork for each case.

"We've sent a search party to locate the missing water craft from Captain Moore's," he added. "They're scouring the crime scene to locate additional evidence.

"How many people are in the search party?" another reporter asked.

"We sent out ten local citizens from the Centerville area, including three volunteer firefighters and three deputies."

Sheryl shrugged, feeling lost without the mantle of protection that Jason and other reporters in the newsroom offered. With her pocket tape recorder running, she looked up from the white notepad she had been writing notes on. "Are they looking for anything else? A specific suspect or witness?"

"I think you understand they're seeking all kinds of evidence, including statements from potential witnesses and suspects," Weaver said, his eyes pinched. "Of course, we hope no other bodies are discovered. Killers do illogical things. We don't know what results a search, coupled with further community-wide investigation, will yield. We certainly hope to find the rental boat."

Kimberly Hastings, a reporter for Centerville radio station WKBJ, asked, "Is that the only place deputies are investigating? If the coroner rules the death a homicide, do you suspect the killer was a tourist such as Purnell or a local person?".

Weaver spoke with a trace of irritation in his voice. "We try to investigate as many leads as we can. At the moment, we want to determine where the missing boat is located. We're in the process of contacting relatives of the couple. We're asking citizens in Centerville who might know anything about the death to contact the sheriff's department.

"In addition to that, members of the investigative team have instructions to follow the Knob Rock Trail through the Waubeka National Forest."

Occasionally, news sources lost track of time. Sheryl didn't like rudeness, but she interrupted. "What are they doing there?"

"Based on an oral statement from Purnell, they're looking for additional proof of a third party," Weaver said. "Purnell has told sheriff's authorities he was involved in a struggle with a stalker, someone he has been unable to clearly identify, whom he believes murdered his girlfriend."

"Are you saying you've arrested the wrong suspect?" Sheryl asked.

"I'm saying we have to look at this from all of the different angles," Weaver answered. "Purnell says a Caucasian man with dark hair assaulted him, probably after Kirchner was killed. He believes this assailant took the life of his girlfriend, though he said he didn't witness the incident and has denied committing the murder himself. We have to research the possibility that other parties, even accomplices, may have been involved."

Tom Sowinski, a reporter for the Bad River Gazette, lifted his hand. "If the death resulted from murder, do you have any reason to suspect it was premeditated? In other words, was money involved or did the assailant trap the victim?"

"We haven't had an opportunity to fully investigate, to gather all the facts or to reach many firm conclusions," Weaver exhaled. "A killer might murder a person he doesn't like. Or simply kill to steal cash. Or two lovers may have gotten out of control in a violent quarrel."

"Is that what you think happened, that the couple had been arguing and Purnell invented the scenario involving an unknown assailant?"

"I can't comment at this time," Weaver said. "I can only reiterate that we're taking the matter very seriously."

Suddenly Sowinski blurted out, "Roger, my sources have told me the autopsy of Kirchner will fail to show conclusively that a weapon was used. You haven't told us how the perp killed Kirchner. What weapon did he use?"

Weaver's facial expression widened. "Without the benefit of the autopsy findings, the victim appeared to have died from a blow to the head caused by contact with a mass of boulders located next to the victim's body."

During another round of questions, Weaver told the media there were signs of a struggle, detracting from the likelihood the death was accidental. Purnell had also told sheriff's investigators about the argumentative customer at the hair salon. Since the customer had failed to sign in, and Angel's was a brand-new shop, deputies didn't have much of a lead. Purnell hadn't gotten a straight-on angle of the angry customer at Angel's, Weaver said. He'd only glanced at him in the mirror.

Judging from the questions and answers, it didn't sound to the reporters as if the victim was a person who was asking for trouble. It could have been an emotional squabble between boyfriend and girlfriend, since no obvious weapon was apparently used. Or a vicious killer might be on the loose.

Questioning Weaver further, Sheryl and other reporters explored additional possibilities. The search taking place at the crime scene coupled with the coroner's findings might shed light on the case, Weaver finished.

Sheriff Weaver stood inside County Coroner Lewis Grinnel's examination laboratory with the door closed behind him. He was worried because he had gotten caught in a bad traffic jam after lunch. He had listened to the car radio, and in between songs, a disk jockey had joked that a dead body might turn up in his yard. With the mountain of paperwork at the office, the sheriff was concerned about getting behind schedule.

Although Weaver had taken a phone message from the coroner, he wanted to have a look at Kirchner's body himself. With preliminary test results in his hands, Grinnel left his glass-walled office and greeted Weaver next to the examination table. Behind Grinnel's concerned expression, his thought processes were a combination of medical and police training. Grinnel paused a moment, and pulled back the white coroner's sheets.

Weaver looked with inquisitive eyes, noticing the contrast between the sterile gleam of the steel lab equipment and the sensitive flesh on the corpse. With consternation, he observed the bruises in the midsection, and the gashes and swollen spots on the head and neck.

"How long was she dead?"

"Not very long," Grinnel answered. "The body was still warm when it arrived."

Weaver arched his back. "Can you give me an estimate?"

"From my preliminary exam, I'd say an hour at most."

"Have you found any prints?"

"Just Purnell's," he said, adding he needed more time to double-check.

Like the coroner, Weaver said he considered the theory an unknown assailant may have used work gloves to cover up his identity. To Weaver's mindset, the random appearance of the wounds was an argument against premeditated murder. It looked like Kirchner had been killed in a spontaneous act of rage. Judging from broken branches and traces of footprints near the body, it looked like someone, possibly her boyfriend, had lost control.

However, there were contradictions. What if Kirchner's boyfriend wasn't guilty? Why weren't there bloodstains on Purnell's clothing? What was his motive? What would additional fingerprint results reveal? What would make the victim's boyfriend violent enough to murder her?

"It's not likely she simply stumbled," the coroner said. "The severe trauma indicates she was pushed with a great deal of force."

Weaver maintained his composure, and Grinnel slipped the white medical sheets back over Kirchner's head. "What about the suspect?" the coroner asked.

"No confession," Weaver said. "During interrogation, he said he was attacked by a nondescript man, a rugged individual. We showed him a series of mugs, but he said it was too dark to make out the perp's face. Other than that explanation, he had no alibi."

"Do you know anything else?" Grinnel asked.

"Judging from the position of the body and the blood on the boulders, we're pretty certain it was a homicide," Weaver answered. "No money or personal belongings appeared to have been stolen from her purse."

Grinnel told Weaver he'd turn in his complete findings as soon as possible, and escorted Weaver to the door. When he emerged from the coroner's offices,

Weaver glanced down the busy main hallway toward his own office. The sheriff listened to the drone of automobile engines idling in traffic along Main Street.

As the sheriff walked from the white-brick Clayton County structure to his cruiser in the parking lot, he ran into Deputy Drew Campbell in the parking lot. Campbell's short-cropped red hair was tucked neatly underneath his cap, but his long mouth and thick lips slanted across his face. "How'd it go?" Campbell asked, referring to the press conference.

"Same as usual," Weaver sighed. "More questions than I'm able to answer. One thing I'll say, if this Purnell guy isn't the murderer or if he had an accomplice, we have to be concerned about other bodies turning up. Whoever the hell the killer is, he used a lot of force."

For the time being, Campbell kept his own opinions to himself.

"The media story looks like it will get a lot of play," Weaver said. "Including the Observer's reporter, the press conference was heavily attended. The reporters asked a lot of questions."

Instead of returning to his office, Weaver decided to take another up-close look, this time to the Waubeka National Forest and the Bay View.

"I'll hang around the office," Campbell said. "I'll stay on the phone. I'll also keep track of the TV and radio broadcasts in case the media uncovers something we don't already know about."

Campbell watched Weaver drop snugly into the upholstered front seat of his sheriff's cruiser. In his department report, Weaver would state that although Purnell was being held on suspicion, sheriff's officials were still probing the possible motive. The sheriff remained worried that an unidentified maniac might be on the loose.

Driving toward the crime scene, he lifted his eyes from the black ribbon of highway. Along the route was a lakeside golf course, two campgrounds, and numerous rural and farm properties interspersed with woodland. Over the years, Weaver had noticed virtually every kind of house and building somewhere in the farm country. And not just in Clayton County, but all around the nation.

There were even abandoned buildings, as well as brand-new industrial facilities, tract neighborhoods, and gas stations adjoining convenience stores.

In the early afternoon, through the branches of the elm trees in the front yard, he saw a white, wood-frame farmhouse at the top of the hill. Vernon Stonehill's place. Weaver knew that many years ago Vernon's wife had run away, either to New York or Las Vegas. Vernon's adult son, Nate, had remained on the farm.

The farm was a small two-man operation, a contrast to full-scale farms in parts of Illinois, for instance. There was only half a dozen cattle and a modest barn.

Vernon and Nate tended a cornfield, which appeared to be work that was both quiet and invigorating. They also took odd jobs, seasonal work, to supplement their low farm income.

Bordering Stonehill's place was Elm Road, which wound through a portion of the forest and led to summer homes on the lake. Across the road was Hector Lowell's farm. Weaver saw Lowell riding his tractor in the cornfield from time to time. He remembered one of Lowell's kids attended technical college in the summer.

Sometimes sheriff's investigations seemed overwhelming. Dozens of residents near the woods might be potential witnesses to the events of Friday night. It was incumbent upon the sheriff's department to canvass the area.

The world had all kinds of people in it. A sheriff's search was a matter of separating the bad apples from the good ones, Weaver theorized.

"Weaver to dispatch," the sheriff announced on his radio. "I'll return to headquarters in a couple hours. I'm driving to the crime scene to take a look around."

Weaver had figured out when he joined the sheriff's force, that simply flashing his badge was insufficient. He needed to stop the case from getting out of control.

CHAPTER 6

It was the day Morehouse's guests, Doug Hilton and his 14-year-old son, Kevin, would arrive at the Clayton County Airport in Centerville. And Morehouse, wearing a sailing cap over his silver-streaked hair, looked like a tourist himself. His maroon-striped sports shirt accented his light-colored pants.

Gone was the shoulder-length coiffe Morehouse had displayed in his gambling days. He no longer punctuated his sentences with "man" and "dude", as he had done in the 1970s. Gone were all-night rounds of poker at the gambling table. And gone were his bouts with binge drinking while shooting billiards for hundreds of dollars.

Since buying the Bay View and fixing it up, the resort had yielded palpable results. Time had erased his gambling habits.

On Saturday afternoon, Morehouse had driven to the airport, saving Doug and Kevin the trouble of calling a taxi. Morehouse would let them use one of his cars up at the Bay View Resort. Why should friends have to supply their own automobile?

Morehouse expected the Bay View to project congeniality. And he gave careful consideration to business decisions. The Bay View earned Morehouse a steady income. It wasn't exactly opulence, and it wasn't a repetition of Morehouse's high-roller background in New York, but it kept his wife and daughter living comfortably.

The Bay View was a family vacation spot on Crater Lake that Morehouse had refurbished five years ago. The resort's restaurant, the Treasure Chest, had kept Morehouse's guests and friends satisfied.

Aside from advertising periodic travel specials and reserving blocks of rooms for tour groups, he had scheduled occupational conferences and symposiums. With grounds totaling twenty-five acres, the main lodge and resort hotel, maintenance buildings, and Morehouse's two-story lakefront home, he had bills to worry about, as well as profits. Compared to the money-loser the Bay View had been when he bought it in 1995, the hotel and restaurant complex was definitely up and coming. With steady customer traffic and visitors using Crater Lake, it had built up a reputation as a relaxing vacation spot.

Morehouse recalled the first time he sat down behind the manager's desk. He had pulled open a door and browsed through several papers from the previous ownership. He found a weekly bank deposit statement for the modest sum of $1,555. He reasoned if he went ahead with a full renovation, even though it meant going into debt, he would come out a winner in the long run.

In part, he had used the lake retreat to escape from the mercurial atmosphere of the city and the misery of prison. Morehouse had grown up in a lower-class New York neighborhood. Even though he had served time for burglary, he hadn't brought his misguided obsession with gambling with him to the tranquil countryside surrounding Crater Lake. He had escaped from the depression of urban poverty, street crime and tough neighborhoods.

Now in his middle-aged years, he wasn't too old to work the guest check-in desk or too young to make a sound business decision, as had been the case when he tried to cover his executive ass by essentially stealing money, sending him to a state correctional facility for two years. He wasn't controlling a downtown skyscraper or responsible for a posh vacation complex, as he had hoped might one day be the case. Yet the Bay View was a dramatic improvement over his days of working as a desk clerk at the downtown Clarion, asking prostitutes not to disturb the other guests and checking the elevator to make sure no one had been mugged.

Guilt, denial, anger, confusion. Those were factors not mentioned on Morehouse's resume. Sure, the 1970s were electric—electric music, electric sports, electric cities. But there were also street people, gang wars, drug addicts, rape counselors and murder victims. Plus Morehouse's compulsive gambling and the resulting nervous symptoms—sporadic insomnia and repeated swallowing in his throat. Morehouse no longer had to tell police each weekend that the shit smell in the Clarion's first-floor bathroom came from shit sometimes, rather than marijuana. The Bay View was a respite from all of that.

Morehouse had escaped the tyranny of poverty. Now he was able to show guests to their rooms and arrange rides from the airport. He put in his workday, and no longer followed current fads in big cities.

Tourists could take that much-needed vacation. Eight-year-olds to eighty-year-olds, wearing sunglasses and looking for the key on check-out day. Guests at the Bay View looked forward to an enjoyable stay in a clean, modern hotel room, offering a delightful view of Crater Lake or the Waubeka National Forest. Half of the one hundred rooms and suites overlooked the lake and the other half offered a picturesque view of the pine trees in the woods.

Moreover, visitors could stop in for drinks or dinner at the Treasure Chest, which was next to the banquet rooms and kitchen. And the hotel's entrance lobby and living room, located just beyond the check-in desk, was a place to chat and meet guests. The centerpiece of the living room was the striking fireplace near the adjoining outdoor deck. Just down the main hallway was a full fitness center and a children's game room. Aside from the indoor swimming pool, guests could lounge in a hot whirlpool, a separate children's swimming pool, a steam bath and a sauna bath.

Several miles away on Highway 52, which slanted north on the west side of the lake, was the Indian-managed Waubeka Casino. It featured dozens of different kinds of slot machines, totaling nearly five hundred in all. Casino guests played table games, including blackjack, poker and bingo. The casino had progressive jackpots reaching into the millions of dollars.

After Morehouse had been released from prison, he quit gambling. In his case, it had become an obssession that cost him his job and his freedom. However, the Bay View sponsored promotional contests, some in connection with the casino. The Bay View awarded prizes such as free hotel stays and restaurant visits, jewelry, apparel and CD players. The hotel had a convention center with two banquet rooms, covering 7,800 square feet. They served business conferences and holiday parties. The Treasure Chest served breakfast, lunch and dinner, everything from hamburgers to butterfly shrimp.

Up and down the shores of the lake, buttressing the wilderness, was a curious mix of tourist-related facilities, residential homes, farm land, lake cottages and forest. The combinations ranged from poor to middle-class to wealthy, depending on the location. There were highways, country roads and dirt back roads in the woods. There were towns, rural areas and the forest. There were houses, farms and nondescript buildings.

Interspersed between towns and patches of the winding forest and lake were beaches, gas stations, convenience stores, motels and resorts, bars, churches, shopping centers, schools, commercial manufacturing and storage facilities, and municipal government buildings. Spread over an area of about 2,500 square miles were summer hiking trails, snowmobile trails, golf courses, boat tours, guided fishing excursions and scenic helicopter rides.

As Morehouse waited in the airport lobby, sitting down, he pulled out the letter Hilton had mailed him. He had received the letter earlier in the summer. It explained that Doug and Kevin, would arrive for a two-week vacation. It also mentioned that Doug had spotted a property in between a farm and the woods that he might be interested in buying as a summer retreat.

Morehouse read the letter a second time.

Dear Ray:

I hope you and Adrienne are doing OK.

As far as I know, Jill's sister, Jody, has finished her daily treatments for stomach cancer at St. Joseph's Hospital. I think she had treatments for a month and a half. Her health looks better. However, following her morning treatments, she appeared tired in the afternoon. I think she had difficulties sleeping during the treatments because, at times, her face looked pale.

Most of the time, she has looked healthy. Now that the treatments have ended, she seems stronger and well rested.

Greg and Rita like their new house in Green Meadow. It is a modest one-story ranch home with a spacious yard. Their dog, Harry, looks more comfortable because the backyard is fenced in. There is a small incline in the yard. It is sunny because there are not many trees on the property.

I don't know exactly why they moved. I think they got tired of renting. They probably wanted to buy their own home. I suspect Jody, the homeowner, was complaining to them. Their dog chewed up a window sill in the house and the blue carpeting in the living room is very dirty, with dog tracks and footprints all over it. I don't think a carpet cleaner will do the job. If Jody is serious about selling the house on Howell Drive, someone, either Jody or the new owner, will have to install new carpeting in the living room.

I went up to Centerville last spring, in April, as I recall. Outside of town, I saw the beautiful lake, forest and farm properties.

I also noticed a few rundown properties off the main highway. I might be in the market for real estate. I likely don't have enough funds for an upscale property.

I drove by a mailbox on Highway 46. It was at the end of a dirt driveway leading to a small family farm. I turned left on Elm Road at the edge of the farm field. Driving down a secluded dirt road, I spotted several properties.

Just next to the field was a rundown rural property. It's not on the lake, but I might be interested in purchasing it. There was a "For Sale" sign—Garson Realty, 867-9905. It could make a good summer place.

The lake property was overrun with vegetation and wild grass. The trees and bushes had blocked off the driveway to the garage. Two paths had been chiseled through the property. The wire fence on the neighboring farm field looks like it is no longer electrified.

In other words, we weren't able to immediately tour the property. When I got back home, I made a phone call. Apparently, a lawn crew hasn't mowed the property since the late 1990s, according to the real estate agent, Theresa Bernard. Since the owner, Ralph Lukavich, has been living elsewhere and was not well for years, no one mowed the property or kept up the maintenance.

As a result, Rod Herman, a next-door neighbor to the north, who used to attend Centerville High School, offered to buy the property for $65,000 two months ago. I think that was back in April. Jill talked to relatives or read a book or something and concluded it was worth an asking price of at least $75,000. Part of the reason for this is the antique car trapped in the dilapidated garage, and then two or three boats that are on the property. That's why it has been up for sale for months.

I suspect it might be a good idea for me to get permission from the real estate agent and look at the place soon. Gary, my brother, was up there a few months ago. He told us the yard was overrun by the wildgrass. He didn't tell us how bad it was. Clumps of brush reach the top of the garage roof. Somebody would have to use a scythe machete to slice a clearing near the garage just to get into the old building.

About nine years ago, Mr. and Mrs. Koller, Jill's parents, said they were willing to help us buy a lakefront property as a home. That was a long time ago. As you know, we live in Illinois. I haven't asked them since then about helping us buy a summer place.

I asked the real estate agent on the phone, and Jill and Gary at a birthday party two weeks ago, if they thought it was legal to leave the property in disrepair. They understand that the owner has a problem with an illness. They all said it was acceptable to leave the growth on the property. It would be a big job, but they thought it could be cleaned up by a lawn crew.

I talked to Herman, who is in his sixties and is retired. He said if he bought the place, he would spend several months cleaning it up in his spare time. Then he would sell it.

Anyway, I have a feeling Jane and I might make a decision to put out an offer on it soon. Since Herman isn't going to live there, we might buy it and have it cleaned up.

Rita likes her new house. She and Greg plan to get married next year, and I think they wanted the fence in the backyard for their dog. They must feel like they fit into the neighborhood atmosphere in Green Meadow better than Kobbs Corners.

There are many homes for sale here. The Wicklands, who live down the street from us, put their home up for sale a month ago for an asking price of $279,000. The average home goes for about $240,000, according to a recent newspaper article. The Wicklands haven't sold the home yet, and have been staging open houses every Sunday. Home buyers have time to browse on the weekend.

Jody has been slowing down due to her treatments. She also wanted to visit you at Crater Lake for a week. I don't think she feels well enough.

Now that her treatments are finished, my son, Kevin, and I might stop in. We would rent a room at your resort motel, the Bay View. We would let you know in advance. We would not visit long, only a week or so. I would like to visit Centerville and go fishing on the lake. Jill is busy and has no plans to stay at the resort.

If this letter is too long for your on-line mailbox, I will mail you and Adrienne a written copy. I hope you kept the letter I mailed you a few months ago. Don't throw it away.

I decided to use the spell-check on my computer for this letter. Hopefully, there won't be too many spelling errors.

Cordially,

Doug

"It will only be about ten minutes till we get to the Bay View because of the heavy traffic," related Morehouse, with his shoulders slightly hunched and his hands holding the steering wheel. Morehouse, Doug and Kevin, had just come off the exit ramp from the freeway, where they had an excellent view of downtown Centerville from Morehouse's Chevrolet Caprice. Morehouse had picked them up at the airport and was driving them to the resort grounds.

"How long has it been since we moved out of Centerville?" asked Kevin, his blond hair, which was streaked with shades of brown, ruffled by the draft blowing into the open car window.

"Oh, I'd say about five years," answered Doug, his father. Smiling, he turned toward Morehouse. Doug's short reddish brown hair and neatly trimmed goatee gave him a business-like appearance. "In addition to the remodeled hotel lodge, something else, the grounds possibly, looks a little different. Considering the amount of money you've sunk into the place, it looks good. But I see you've maintained the original atmosphere. In other words, it seems the same, yet improved."

"I'm glad you feel that way. But you say you can't put your finger on the upgrades. In the photographs I mailed you, didn't you notice the other new buildings—the storage and equipment sheds, for instance?" asked Morehouse, with a sense of anticipation in his voice.

"No, I didn't," said Doug jokingly. "I remember what it was like when we lived next door to you and your family—your wife, Adrienne, and your daughter, Sarah. Let's see. We moved out of the neighborhood four years ago. Not an extremely long time. We'll always remember you coming over to borrow blenders, card tables and all sorts of things. Where did you get the money to buy the Bay View and remodel the resort—the addition of the Treasure Chest Restaurant, refurbished hotel rooms and new furniture?"

"Well, through business contacts. We saved money on appliance costs over the years, you know," Morehouse snickered.

"I know," said Kevin's father. "You borrowed our stuff so you wouldn't have to buy your own. If we'd known you were such a cheapskate, we would have moved out of the neighborhood much sooner than we did. It's not as bad as having to deal with the devil, owing an arm and a leg in interest."

And with that, Kevin's dad and Morehouse, his former neighbor and father's friend, broke out into polite laughter. Kevin was busy sticking his head out the car window to experience an effect similar to a strong wind, the curls of his hair pasted flat against his ears, flapping over the back seat.

His father corrected him. "Kevin! Don't stick your head out the window. That's dangerous."

Kevin objected. "I don't think it's dangerous. You think my head might bounce off a sign? If it gets knocked off, just screw it back on."

"Kevin, just do what you're told. Keep your head inside the car. OK?"

"What if we drive underneath a bridge and it collapses?"

Doug said, "Bridges rarely collapse. Semi-trucks drive below them all the time."

From his spot in the back seat, he watched Centerville spin past. There were manufacturing plants, banks, taverns, grocery stores, drug stores, department stores, and doctors' and dentists' offices.

Kevin was aware his parents and the Morehouse family had kept in touch, exchanging holiday cards, letters and phone calls from time to time. Scenes of his old neighborhood brought back a sentimental memory or two. He had lived in Centerville until he was nine years old, and he knew times from the past didn't necessarily repeat, as reruns of movies and TV shows did.

Kevin's parents, Doug and Emily, had bought a new home in Skokie, Illinois, a suburb of Chicago. At the time, they were very excited about it. Like an automobile in a body shop, the house was populated with new furniture purchased within Doug and Emily's limited budget. The situation was similar to Morehouse's. Kevin and Doug looked forward to seeing the Bay View. They enjoyed making a return trip to Centerville, visiting again with the Morehouses and seeing Kevin's old neighborhood.

After leaving the airport on the southwest side of Centerville and passing through the downtown, they headed north on the highway. Crater Lake was located a half hour north of Centerville on Highway 46. The highway and the Marengo River both ran south to Centerville.

As soon as Morehouse, Doug and Kevin entered the Treasure Chest, a chorus of "Hello, Doug and Ray," greeted them. Kevin was surprised, but he kept in mind the fact that the patrons shouting were old friends of his father's and Morehouse's from down in Centerville. Whenever a family moves, the uninformed neighbors wonder where they went and how they're doing.

A mental circuit connecting visual images in Kevin's brain had changed since they had flown to the Clayton County Airport from their home in Skokie. Aside from tourists, it was, once again, local people from Centerville and surrounding towns—workers, farmers and friends of Morehouse's—who lined the bar stools.

His father and Morehouse said hello and shook hands with people they knew. They exchanged pleasantries for five minutes.

Doug and Kevin sat down at a table near an impressive bay window overlooking Crater Lake. They read through the dinner offerings listed on the laminated cardboard menu.

"What do you want?" asked Doug.

"I'll have a milk and a hamburger," Kevin said.

"So will I," said his father blankly.

About fifteen minutes later, the waitress served them. They had a hard time eating. It was Happy Hour, and the patrons at the bar, on the opposite end of the restaurant, were calling for Morehouse to serve them more food and drinks. While Kevin was eating, he overheard various conversations at dinner tables and kept his eye on Morehouse.

"Hey, Doug," said a husky man calling across the restaurant. "Did ya hear about Tom?"

Doug shook his head. "No, I didn't."

"The sheriff's department found him sleeping it off yesterday in an alley near the corner of Sixth Street and Greenbriar Road. They could smell booze all over him."

"Oh no! That's terrible," Morehouse said. "I tried to get him to stop. I wasn't even going to serve him any more drinks."

"It's not your fault, Ray. He would have gone to some other place anyway." Kevin could see the look of astonishment mixed with concern on Morehouse's face. Morehouse immediately joined them at the table when a young-looking woman in a waitress uniform approached them. She was accompanied by a middle-aged lady with a round, puffy countenance who appeared to be her mother.

"Hi, Ray," said the waitress. "I'm sorry we're late. We got up late this morning, there was a lot of traffic on the highway and we've been running behind all day. I'll start washing the dishes right away."

"Oh, that's all right," Morehouse said. "I want you to meet Sally."

Morehouse asked, "How old is Kevin?"

"Fourteen," Doug said.

"Not as old as Sally," Morehouse said. "She's eighteen. She and her mother, Nancy, work for me. They just drove in from Waldwick."

"Hello," Doug and Kevin said in unison. As soon as Sally and her mother had left, a tinge of guilt, an uncontrolled feeling, came over Kevin. When Morehouse introduced him to Sally, he felt callow, and guessed it was because she lived in Waldwick, a poor township in between the resort and Centerville.

Kevin and Doug resumed eating. Later, they noticed some of the folks at the bar, who were mostly people heading home after their first-shift jobs, staring at them. Kevin and Doug were tired from traveling and, having flown in from O'Hare Airport in Chicago, somewhat out of place.

Dressed in black casual pants and a striped sport shirt, a thin-faced farmer was sitting at the bar. A grey-haired man wearing farm overalls was next to him. They both looked like they had been drinking.

Kevin and Doug sat down, read the menu and placed their orders. Morehouse was busy, taking care of a variety of business. Doug was hungry and gulped his food. Kevin ate less and took in his surroundings. After a relatively short time frame, they both finished eating dinner. They were eager to get to their hotel room. "All right, we better get going," suggested Kevin's dad.

As they got up from their chairs and started for the exit, the man wearing blue-jean overalls jumped off his stool and lunged out at them, knocking down a thin-legged oak chair and an empty dinner table.

"I wanna go, too," he yelled as he staggered toward them. Everyone was staring. Doug rushed to help the man off the floor. After he climbed to his feet, Morehouse and Doug helped him sit down in a booth. His face was red from drinking too much alcohol. He looked as if he had been walking around outdoors in January.

Wiping beer off his pants, the man sitting next to the drunk lost his cool. "You spilled your drink on me. What planet are you on, asshole?"

Morehouse recognized the intoxicated man who had lunged off his stool—Ted Jenkins, the brother of Lester Jenkins, who had been reported missing from his woods home. Morehouse didn't think it would be a good idea to let Jenkins drive home, so he phoned for a taxi.

Other patrons who remained seated had observed the scene with a mixture of angry trepidation and delight. They likely didn't relish embarrassment, and were relieved that the onus had fallen on Jenkins, that someone else had stumbled into the table.

As Kevin and Doug walked down the lobby to Room 210, Kevin saw customers leaving in the parking lot. He wondered what happened to adults who drank too much. These were the contemplations of an older child trying to make sense out of the world. He figured the bartender had to earn a living, as Doug had once told him, and that customers must have a place to unwind.

CHAPTER 7

When Sheryl returned to her apartment, she took a break from her hectic schedule. She climbed the circular stairway from the entrance hallway into her spacious bedroom loft. She sat down at her dressing table to put on mascara for the Saturday evening concert. As she was applying makeup, she glanced sideways at the doll sitting next to the mirror. She had brought it with her to Centerville from her mother's house. Her parents had bought it when she was five years old. When she walked into the living room one Christmas morning, it was sitting underneath the tree.

The plastic baby doll was supported by baggy legs that drooped over its grey slippers, and was dressed in a light pink smock that extended from the shoulders down to the kneecaps. It featured rosy cheeks, ruby lips, a wisp of golden hair curled over the forehead, fleshy arms bent at the elbows, and chubby hands and fingers. Below its upturned plastic nose, its lips were parted, exposing two front teeth. The doll's flattened ears were plastered against the shining round head, which had B.P.W.J. Inc. imprinted in plastic, skin-colored lettering in the back, below the baby's amorphous, wax-like neckline.

Sheryl grabbed the doll and the light blue eyes flipped open. With her finger, she pushed the eyelids closed, then flipped them open again. She put the doll back in place next to the mirror. Tired, she walked to her bed and lay down to take a nap. As she rested her head against a small mound of several pillows, she glared at the doll. When Sheryl's heavy eyelids blinked together, it appeared as if the doll's eyes also closed. She rested a few moments. When she looked at the dressing table, she noticed the doll's eyes had fallen closed.

When Sheryl's headache wore off, she propped herself up in bed, and noticed the doll's eyes looked like they had sprung open. She asked herself how that could have happened. The breeze from the open window must have pushed the doll's plastic eyelids open.

The room was cheerful in the sunlight, in spite of Sheryl's overworked condition. She got out of bed, began walking and stopped in her tracks. She heard voices, and strode to the window. Outside, in the park across the street, several children played on a swing set. A mother sat on a nearby park bench next to her baby carriage. Staring across the rectangle of light flowing through the window onto the flowered wallpaper, Sheryl heard a voice call, "It's time for dinner."

Trying to hear better, Sheryl slid the glass window open wider, exposing more of the screen. The girl on the swing made a face at the boy standing in front of her.

"It's getting crowded here," someone said. "We must go."

Sheryl pressed her face against the window. The woman remained seated on the park bench and the children continued playing on the swings. With trepidation, Sheryl turned around. The doll's head had flopped over, its eyes were closed...and its face was pressed against the mirror. Sheryl felt a chill run through her body. Although the breeze from the open window had caused the doll to flip around, it was as if an intruder had snuck into the apartment and spun the doll as a prank. Sheryl's mind was stressed out.

She closed the window and saw the reflection in the glass image of the doll's good-natured face staring coldly at her, its cherry mouth smirking.

The doll could not have been watching her, yet she felt a tinge of paranoia. It must have been her imagination playing a trick on her. Sheryl was running out of time. She had to get dressed for tonight's concert and party.

She walked toward her dresser and noticed that paperwork she had brought from the office had been blown across the carpeted floor. Sheryl was in the habit of using a metal letter opener to rip apart sealed envelopes, going through them in assembly-line fashion, one after another, and reading them when time permitted.

Among the papers, Sheryl picked up what she thought was a press release that had been blown out of an envelope. The typewritten message caught her eye:

Dear Muckraker:

Why don't you print the whole story? We were cheated out of our place in the world. Something had to be done.

You're an invader from the outside. You've violated the law.

Don't waste your time going to the newspaper office. You deserve the mud-crusted heel of his work boot.

The universe will collapse.

Marsden

Some press release! Sheryl examined the envelope. It was addressed to the newspaper and her name was on it. It was missing a return address. Sheryl didn't know anyone named Marsden, and doubted that was the letter-writer's real name. Sheryl placed the hostile complaint letter and the envelope back on her dresser. She planned to show the note to the staff at the newspaper, including Jason.

Outside Sheryl's window, in the park, Marsden watched from a thicket of trees and bushes in Stafford Park, located on the north side of Centerville next to Sheryl's apartment complex.

Marsden waited in the park, where a jogger went past. Marsden had not lifted his feet from their position for a long time. In his mind, the park was a TV. Fleshy older people were sitting on benches. A woman's body was bulging out of her cotton dress, and the man sitting next to her had his tie unknotted. Sitting at the brown picnic tables spread around the park were couples with kids. One man was sitting on the ground reading a newspaper, probably a story about the murder case.

Marsden was wearing another ring with a skull face. Marsden moved halfway down a ravine, standing on a hillside. He was standing behind an elm tree. He glanced at the children on the swings and the woman with the baby carriage.

Scrutinizing Sheryl's apartment window, he knew she had heard the sounds from the park and had gazed out her window. Standing underneath the elm tree, Marsden realized she had failed to spot him.

Chapter 8

With the front windows open and summer breeze filtering inside, Jason's Sebring held the gondola-like feeling of a convertible with the canopy rolled down. The highway outside the city limits of Centerville slid away.

Jason and Sheryl were deliberately late for the party, later than they had anticipated, in fact. They had enjoyed the concert, and Sheryl had told Jason about the vindictive letter. It would, no doubt, be shown to Merteau. But for now, they had things to talk about, and their daytime responsibilities were gone.

Jason's friend, Jeff Fergus, was a supervisor for the Clayton County Parks and Recreation Department. Jason had met him at a newspaper interview about county programs, and following the interview, they chatted and got to know each other. Jeff, who had rented a banquet room at the Bay View Resort, invited Jason and Sheryl to the department's annual party.

As they pulled into the parking lot, Sheryl wondered about Jason. Like Sheryl, Jason was a fellow writer, and taking his young age into consideration, he was a well-read person. His lighthearted jokes could degenerate into biting sarcasm, yet it was impossible to imagine what her world would be like without him. Although they argued periodically, she was probably in love with him.

Jason and Sheryl had first met each other when they were unsullied sophomores in college, within three months after the fall semester had begun. Sheryl ran into Jason on the dormitory elevator several times, before they exchanged phone numbers. Jason's dorm room was located on the seventh floor of the Parkview Dormitory Building and Sheryl's was on the fourth floor. When the elevator hummed, they had begun talking, and it turned out they were both interested in the esthetic challenge of understanding literature and writing for the news media.

Neither of them had declared a major. Jason was considering a broadcast reporting sequence in the journalism school, and Sheryl ended up choosing English literature as her primary course of study.

Sheryl had been determined about her reporting pursuits for the student newspaper, the Daily News. She had been self-directed and disciplined about her academic studies. In her junior and senior years, she had put in twenty-hour weeks at the newspaper, covering general assignment news.

As a cub reporter, Jason had not worked as strenuously. He freelanced for the News, contributing a limited number of feature stories when he found ample time. To earn a weekly paycheck, he had driven an immoderate-sized food delivery truck part-time, transporting meals from a campus kitchen filled with jabbering dishwashers to innumerable university buildings, where meetings, conferences and banquets were held.

Jason and Sheryl dated off-and-on for two years at the university, sometimes studying together in the mammoth, book-lined library building. Occasionally, they ran into each other at the busy campus newspaper office, and afterward, they went out to dinner and movies together.

In class, the professors had fired information at the seated, note-taking students so fast that Jason joked he might not make it to graduation. At times, Sheryl rehashed the memory of her first day on campus, the day her parents drove her up to the college. Being away from the protection of her parents had left her feeling both independent and sentimental, as if her years as their precious daughter had ended.

In high school, Sheryl had analyzed a dozen university campuses before she chose Lydell University. She had wanted to attend a college where she could gain worthwhile newspaper experience. And she had intended to go to a community where her parents would not worry about her.

Jason paid for his lack of dedication to print journalism in terms of a staggered employment record. After graduating, he more or less disappeared for six months. He and Sheryl exchanged a couple phone calls every month, and Jason wasn't very specific about what he was up to. Sheryl knew he was still delivering meals for the university, and she was inclined to think he was searching for permanent work at a broadcast station.

Six months after graduating, he had favorable employment news. He telephoned Sheryl, telling her had been hired as an entry-level news announcer for radio station WJYX in Markstown. It was the only radio station in the community of 12,000, which was located merely seventy-five miles down the highway from Centerville. Unlike Jason, Sheryl had been hired as a reporter at the Centerville Observer when she graduated.

After three months at the radio station, sitting behind the microphone as news announcer, meeting with advertisers and covering news outside the control room with a tape recorder, Jason had begun looking for newspaper work. He and Sheryl saw each other from time to time, and kept in touch through the mail, on the phone and over the computer.

To Sheryl's surprise, after only a year in Markstown, Jason had been offered a general assignment reporting position for the Centerville Observer. Centerville was his hometown, and he returned to his parents' rambling two-story country home just outside of the city limits. His first year on the job, Sheryl had been a palliative helpmate, assisting Jason in his quest to learn standard newsroom procedures, including how to handle his schedule and use the company's computer.

Sheryl was in her third exciting year at the Observer and Jason was in his second. Covering breaking news, the time had flown by since Sheryl had initially lent a hand to Jason with his homework in the university library.

Now the social graces were beckoning. After exiting the car, Jason and Sheryl smelled the sweet scent of evergreen trees. Despite the fact that it was getting late, they had been psyched for the weekend when they left work. Sheryl rubbed her wet lips seductively against Jason's lower neck and lifted her face parallel to his. The pair pulled their arms around each other, caressing during a pleasing, sustained kiss in the dark parking lot.

As they gently moved away from each other, breathing with anticipation, Jason heard the automobile engine hissing. He had forgotten to turn off the ignition and remove the key. He looked with concern at the driver's door, and noticed he hadn't locked it. When he finally shut off the idling engine, a car shot past on the highway, kicking up an echoing burst of dead leaves, which fluttered across the hood of Jason's Sebring.

They left the car and walked across the parking lot to the resort clubhouse. Evergreen and spruce trees had been cleared from the west end of the grounds to leave a path for the wind, which usually blew down from the northwest, slapping against the ample picture windows in the hotel restaurant. An open entryway with a teepee-shaped, shingled roof led into the guest lobby.

Along the way to the double-door entrance, Jason and Sheryl heard visitors chatting outside. Amid the animated talk, they walked through the entrance lobby. They hung up their coats and entered the rented banquet room, which had a black-and-white tiled floor and scattered dining tables. There were rings of smiling people around the room and scant pockets of conversation were audible.

Once inside, they didn't immediately recognize anyone. Not having planned to attend the entire event, dinner had already been served.

Jason spotted Jeff, who was talking to a group of his friends. They were in the back lefthand corner. Jason and Sheryl made their way through the crowd of married couples, and single men and women..

Jeff extended his hand. "I didn't know if you were coming," he said. "Glad you made it." He introduced the folks in the circle. "This is Bill, Phil, Nick, Tricia and Claire." They said "hello" in unison. "Phil and Claire are married. Claire is an assistant manager at Smitty's Restaurant and Phil is a greaser auto mechanic at the Amoco gas station. I just met Bill, Nick and Tricia tonight. Is that confusing?" Jeff quipped.

"No," Jason answered, putting his hands on his hips. He enjoyed moments when he could get a fresh start by meeting new people.

"Actually, I took a course in auto mechanics at Centerville North. That was about nine years ago. I had a used 1983 Chevrolet Camaro, and got tired of the engine conking out. I couldn't afford a brand-new car back then, so I did my own repairs. That was a long time ago. As I recall, I got a B in the class. Frank Luntz was the teacher."

"I don't remember Luntz," Bill sighed. "But I graduated from Centerville North in 1991. I didn't take auto mechanics.

"I remember an industrial arts teacher named Jim Anton. He had us watch videos about home repair. One day someone called him a nerd in front of the class and he blew up in a fit of anger. It was one of the students, a troublemaker named Nate Stonehill. They got in a big argument and exchanged insults. Stonehill got so mad he grabbed three industrial arts projects—students' wood carvings, bird houses, clay statues and glassworks—and hurled them out an open second-story window. One after another, they smashed into pieces all over the cement sidewalk."

"That's pretty serious," Jason interjected.

"Yes, it was," Bill said. "He was suspended for a week. Stonehill didn't talk to Anton much during the remainder of the spring semester. I don't remember what happened to Stonehill or Anton. I think Anton retired recently, a few years ago."

"Anton retired after thirty years with the school district," Sheryl said impatiently, after waiting for the conversation to wind down. "His picture was in the newspaper in the Community Section."

Standing at the party, Sheryl noticed the romantic longings in Jason's eyes. They both listened to the muffled sounds of the four-member country band, Briar Ridge, playing a contemporary version of "I Feel The Heartache". Even though Jason could play the role of hard-nosed reporter, he was sometimes a quiet, reserved person.

He held the opinion that he might be more competent at placing sophisticated wire stories in the newspaper, than he was in covering local news events. Theoretically, he believed it was easier to dummy pages than to drum up stories from scratch. Tonight, Jason was discerning, keeping his professional worries to himself.

Jeff asked, "Would you like anything to drink?"

Sheryl looked at Jason. She ordered a Coke, and Jason, a beer.

Jeff, who was wearing an oversized purple sweatshirt and blue jeans, jockeyed through the crowd.

"I volunteered for the newspaper," Nick said. "I delivered papers when I was a kid. They have a rural address out on Highway 46. My folks still have their place out there. That was where I grew up.

"About ten years ago, when I was in college, there were some bad traffic accidents—cars demolished and drivers trapped. I ran out on the highway a dozen times and snapped photographs for the newspaper. Several made the front page," Nick said.

"The worst one I ever heard about took place three years ago," Jason said. "It was a twenty-vehicle pileup at the rush hour. Fifteen drivers and passengers were killed, and eleven vehicles were totaled. The unusual thing was, when emergency workers showed up to direct traffic, they detoured drivers traveling around the accident in the wrong direction."

As he spoke, Jason's eyebrows were knitted together and the tone of his voice was quizzical.

Nick said, "The workers are not always familiar with the highways. Over the years, road signs get blown down in rainstorms. From time to time, drivers get lost and tourists are reported missing in the forest."

Nick stopped talking. "Are you entertained by ghost stories?" he asked.

"No, not all," Jason said. "I work at a newspaper. I don't believe in ghost stories. There's no truth in them, but you can try one anyway."

"In the 19th century, settlers believed that whenever a local resident died, a mysterious figure wandered the forest, announcing the death," Nick said. "If people tried to communicate with the ghost, they died also. Yet they could catch glimpses of it moving through the forest, reminding everyone of the last death. Residents claimed it visited their doorsteps at night, telling them a relative had died."

"How did this story originate?" Jason asked.

"The ghost was supposedly an Indian, Shadow Walker, who was wrongly accused of murdering settlers," Nick said. "He reputedly crept up on townspeople at night—men, women and children—and strangled them to death as they slept. Citizens in the town were outraged. They tracked Shadow Walker down and hung him without a trial. As retribution, they also killed his family—his wife and three children.

"It turned out they accused the wrong person. A year later, there was a series of unexplained deaths, which took place at night. The police arrested a farmer, Byron Hallanger, who admitted to randomly murdering two dozen citizens. After the trial, they hung him in front of the courthouse. The murders stopped. However, witnesses claimed they saw the image of the wrongly accused man screaming in the woods every time a resident died."

Jeff returned with a glass of seltzer, several Cokes and two bottles of Miller. He removed each drink from the tray he was holding, disbursed them and put the tray down on an empty table.

"Thanks," Jason said, taking a sip of his beer. "I'm glad we're at the Bay View Resort."

Jason had cursory knowledge of the layout of the resort. The Bay View was on a north-facing slope overlooking Crater Lake. The banquet rooms and conference rooms were in the rear of the main lodge. There were hotel rooms in the two-story central building and rustic fishermen's cabins to the east.

The expansive banquet room had been the long-lasting restaurant before the Bay View was remodeled eight years ago. There were wooden booths and tables, shaded bronze lights hanging from the ceiling and a billowing dance floor in front of the stage. A new restaurant had been added to the main hotel building.

Jeff pointed to a maple dish cabinet against the wall on the other side of the busy room. "See that?" he asked. "We have a metal storage cabinet resembling that one at the park that's filled with permits. I rented the banquet room after daytime hours for the party. Many of the guests here work for the park and forest system. The first impression a park worker makes is the one that lasts the longest. It's what they say in our training manuals—an open recreational area like this, a big forest and spacious parks, creates a fish-bowl environment in which employees think the public is scrutinizing them."

Jeff looked across the room again. "If you're interested in that type of thing, there are legal notices hanging on that bulletin board. We posted them tonight. We'll take them down tomorrow. They give explanations about subjects such as eating during working hours, illegal drug abuse, jury duty, personal belongings, tuition loan funds, cash handling, attendance, work schedules, employee training and equipment maintenance. Mostly, we take care of the public, watch park grounds and keep the equipment running."

Jason and Sheryl usually followed a rule of not asking too many newspaper questions off the job. "It sounds like you don't have many serious problems with suspicious people."

"You mean vandals trashing picnic tables? We find a few tables down in various ravines after the winter season has ended, probably caused by both vandals and slippage due to the wind, ice and snow."

If Sheryl was on the job, she would have asked more questions and put together a feature story. She didn't like asking questions without preparation. She shrugged and gazed across the party to a conspicuous picture hanging next to the bulletin board. It was a framed black-and-white photograph of Buddy Holly. His curly black locks were neatly combed at the top of his meaty forehead. He wore oversized glasses at the bridge of his big nose and smiled politely at the crowd. Blue lettering below the picture read, "Golden Oldies Hour" and "Radio Station WKBJ".

Despite the thin layer of fat wrapped around Jason's midsection, invisible underneath his sweater, he took a long swallow of his beer. He smelled the dinner grill in the kitchen. A group of people walked to the door and said goodnight to each other.

Like Sheryl, Jason sensed the late hours closing in. He glanced at his watch, and noticed it was after midnight. It had been stimulating to listen to the folks chattering around him. Jason talked to Sheryl briefly, and they decided to take off.

As they drove back from the Saturday night party to Sheryl's apartment, Jason was still thinking about the woman's body that had been found near Highway 46. How long had the suspect, Trent, known the victim? he wondered. Jason told Sheryl about a previous case involving a killer, Arthur Chalker, who had murdered his wife and parents, and buried the remains in a shallow grave in the woods. Under questioning, he had explained to authorities his missing relatives had failed to return from a weekend camping trip.

Using the samples of scent from Chalker's clothing, the buried bones of the victims were discovered by two police dogs near the Bay View Resort. In that case, it had been Balton who had shot and killed Chalker.

Returning to the Kirchner case, Jason remembered the newspaper photographs of the crime scene involving Kirchner near Highway 46 that Sheryl had shown him. He recalled the yellow police tape marking the spot where Jean's corpse had been found. "Jason, you're kind of quiet," Sheryl interrupted.

"I was thinking about the gruesome shot of the corpse," Jason said. "It ran on the front page."

"I certainly remember the pitch-black night hanging over the woods," Sheryl started. "And from the photograph, we can only imagine the initial chaos the discovery of the body caused," Jason finished.

Only several hours after Jason and Sheryl had left the overlook on Friday night, sheriff's deputies had carried away the body and cleaned up the crime scene. Jason saw the image in his mind of emergency lights flashing from the highway, casting a faint glow over the feral woods.

Sheryl left the bedroom and returned with a couple drinks. She plopped herself down next to Jason, gave him a drink and slipped the fingers of her free hand through the thick tangles of his black hair. She nestled her head against his shoulder.

She rubbed his shirt above his chest, and heard him breathing. He murmured a few romantic lines, and concluded with, "Let's make love." Following a surge of pleasure, they moved to the bed and began kissing and undressing. Jason unbuttoned Sheryl's beige blouse, and she pushed herself up with her elbows and sat on the side of the bed. She unbuttoned her cotton bra and slipped it off. Then she unzipped her blue jeans, pulled them past her ankles and dove back under the covers. Jason went to the bathroom and urinated. He undressed down to his underwear, and placed his cable-knit sweater and corduroy pants on the back of an armchair.

When he was done, he joined Sheryl in bed. Jason grasped her in his arms, and the springs in the mattress groaned. She rubbed his shoulder tops, and heard him breathing. After they had both reached orgasms, Jason murmured a few more romantic lines. Without much thought, he rolled onto his back and fell asleep. Sheryl listened to him snoring, feeling Jason's warmth in the dark room.

Sheryl worried about tomorrow, and when she woke up it was tomorrow morning. The morning brought her usual walk. When she and Jason went down the tree-lined streets, Sheryl sensed that the atmosphere in her neighborhood and in Centerville had been made worse.

When they returned from their stroll, she glimpsed the doll propped against the mirror, and, in the back of her mind, realized that someone had seen them, and that he was absorbed not with them, but with death. With the hostile letter, the stories at the party and the recent Kirchner death, Sheryl sensed fear tightening around them, returning intermittently like a sick hospital patient to a doctor.

In her mind's eye, she had caught a glimpse of his face, the patches of unshaven growth on his cheeks, like globs of mud in a municipal sewer pipe. His dreadful anger shined like sunflowers in his eyes. The malicious stranger was becoming more desperately wicked with each passing moment. Sheryl could cover the case, but she didn't know who to share her fears with, other than Jason.

Sheryl's news story about the apparent murder Friday night stood in contrast to her emotional feelings off the job. Sheryl tried to keep the report objective. The story about Purnell's arrest appeared in Sunday morning's Centerville Observer.

Man held in apparent homicide

A 25-year-old Milwaukee man was taken into custody in connection with an apparent homicide early Saturday morning in the death of Jean Kirchner, a tourist from Milwaukee staying at the Bay View Resort, after her body was found in the Waubeka National Forest by the resort owner and a passing truck driver on Highway 46.

Clayton County Sheriff Roger Weaver said authorities did not have any suspects other than Trent Purnell, Kirchner's boyfriend. Purnell was being held for further questioning.

Sheriff's officials believe Kirchner was killed by trauma to the head following a struggle with an unidentified assailant. Unusually severe bruises and gashes were discovered on her head and neck, according to sheriff's deputies.

She and Purnell, had rented a motorboat from Captain Moore's Boat Rental Friday evening. The motor apparently malfunctioned, and the couple hiked through the woods in the direction of Crater Lake, where they had rented the motorboat, authorities said.

Sheriff's officials have not determined why Purnell might have killed his girlfriend.

Kirchner's body was found by Ken Fielding, a truck driver for Dawes Metal Tube Co., and Ray Morehouse, the manager of the Bay View Resort, 300 feet from Highway 46 in the woods. Purnell was discovered unconscious in a clearing in between the highway and the spot where Kirchner was believed to have been murdered.

Fielding contacted sheriff's officials with his CB radio.

The couple were believed to have been drinking alcohol on the boat.

"They were on a one-week vacation at the lake resort," said Anthony Kirchner, Jean's father, from his home in Milwaukee. "She was a wonderful daughter. I can't imagine why anyone would want to harm her. I don't know what happened. I was terribly shocked to learn that she had died."

Kirchner refused to comment on the possibility that Purnell was the assailant. "I don't think they had any enemies. I think it's a tragedy."

"I want to express sympathy for the victim," Morehouse said. "When they checked in at the Bay View on Friday, they indicated they planned to use the indoor swimming pool, to take a trip down the river and to hang out in Centerville."

Fielding had spotted Purnell unconscious in a field near Highway 46 from the cab of his sixteen-wheel truck.

"I caught a glimpse of a dark figure crawling in the clearing," Fielding said. "I was driving slowly around a turn. I slowed the truck down. I was sure I got a view of the person in my headlights. The figure was too large to have been a chipmunk. Deer occasionally watch the truck on the highway, and I can make out their eyes, even at night."

Morehouse told deputies at the scene Friday night he heard loud noises during nature taping with his camcorder.

Morehouse said he makes video tapes of forest scenes of interest to nature lovers as a hobby, and has shown them to tourists and friends at the resort complex. Morehouse didn't immediately know if the tape had recorded screams from a struggle between Kirchner and Purnell.

According to sheriff's deputies, Morehouse believed he heard a woman screaming and the sounds of people fighting in the woods.

"I was relieved Fielding came along when he did," Morehouse said. "He was alert enough to spot Purnell in the glare of his headlights. He had the presence of mind to use his CB radio to call for help."

No other bodies have been discovered.

Chapter 9

The next day was Sunday, and Kevin and his dad visited Morehouse at his place on Crater Lake. The home was located east of the main hotel lodge on the resort grounds. It was a lakeside cottage-type dwelling with steep gables and sufficient space for four second-story bedrooms. It was facing the lake and angled toward the northwest. The shingled roof hung over the front porch and was supported by four columns. A stone path led from the beach to the porch.

Doug and Kevin accompanied Morehouse and his wife into the house. The screen door swung readily, making the comforting sounds of a lived-in family homestead, and they pulled up chairs noisily in a half-circle in the living room around the coffee table and couch.

"What do you think of the sheriff's deputy, Balton, stopping in here last night?" Adrienne asked. Her brunette hair was parted stylishly down the middle. When she talked, her eyes revealed concern.

"I think the murder case was weighing on his mind," Morehouse responded. "He didn't seem to know much, though. He asked us a lot of questions, but didn't hint at any answers. You would think he would have gathered more evidence against the victim's boyfriend. Balton didn't seem to have a list of suspects."

"The deputy was tight-lipped, and asked us a dozen questions. He didn't tell us much about the investigation," Adrienne said. "He didn't make much of an impression. Don't you think so?"

"They're not supposed to tell us much, other than the information released to the news media," Morehouse said.

Margaret, Adrienne's white-haired, eighty-year-old mother who also stayed in the house, was planted firmly in a hulking cushion chair on the opposite end of the coffee table. "You're too demanding, Adrienne, plus you're naive. If Balton knows anything sensational about the case, he isn't going to tell us. He's keeping the evidence to himself. He has no reason to tell us anything. He might even suspect us."

Morehouse snickered. "I have a children's cap gun in the attic. We should go up there and make sure nobody has stolen it."

"Ray, Deputy Balton didn't ask you about your past...about your record."

Morehouse said, "They already know about that. They had that in their sheriff's files when I bought the Bay View. I had to get permits for liquor sales and remodeling. They ruled me out as a suspect Saturday."

Morehouse halted. He felt mildly ashamed. After years of perpetual gambling in New York, where he had grown up, one thing led to another. That was years ago, back in the 1980s, and was a part of Morehouse's life he had left in the past. He had rebuilt his career at Crater Lake.

"If I was a deputy, like Balton, I would also have to be careful in order to get the facts straight," Morehouse said. "Shoddy investigative work causes the system to break down. When that happens, citizens don't trust the sheriff's department. They run into a wall. The Sam Shepard case is a known example. The authorities were convinced he murdered his wife, and he was found guilty and sentenced to prison for murder. But there was too much conflicting evidence."

"I remember that," Margaret cut in. "He maintained until his death he was innocent. That he was sleeping downstairs on the living-room couch when an intruder murdered his wife upstairs."

Morehouse said, "The family goes through an ordeal—the tragedy of murder, the shock and finality of death, and then learning a close relative may have been the killer. Over the years, witnesses die, people forget the circumstances surrounding the case at the time it took place, and the whole thing gets thrown down a time tunnel."

"No, it doesn't," Margaret said impatiently. "It doesn't get thrown down a time tunnel. Folks my age remember the Shepard case."

Morehouse fumbled for words. "What I meant was, the society keeps moving forward, while the victims are left with terrible memories. Apathetic citizens remain uninvolved. They aren't willing to risk jobs and social status. They don't want to grapple with complex issues. What if the Shepard case was mishandled by judicial and law-enforcement officials?"

Morehouse looked disconsolately through a living room window at the rough grass in his yard. A bird was camped on a tree branch. It tried to spring from the branch, but its wings pinwheeled inexplicably after it miscalculated the opening and flew into a utility wire. Instead of cutting a straight line, the hungry-looking creature, flapped its wings helplessly in a web of branches, and eventually tumbled into the vegetation below.

While his father and the Morehouses were holding a conversation inside the house, Kevin had wandered outdoors. Kevin studied the murky water from the end of the pier. He wasn't expecting to experience anything frightening.

He walked off the pier by accident, and fell into the nippy waters of the lake, and, panicking and falling into hysterics, believed he was drowning. But he was not drowning. He only thought he was drowning, and it was a matter of perception. Of course, his father, Doug, had been in the house, talking to friends. Now he was chatting on the pier. There wasn't a lot of room on the pier, and the guests were engaged in conversation.

It was a sunny day, with white cotton-ball clouds floating across the summer-blue afternoon sky. The wind ruffled their eardrums, and there was other distracting hubbub: motor boats, water skiers, swimmers and fishermen. When Kevin accidentally plunged through the frigid surface of the choppy lake waters, a spray of water stung his eyes, squirted up his nostrils and climbed into his mouth.

He erroneously believed he was drowning. Gravity was pulling him into the weed-tangled, fish-infested bottom layers. Despite his panic, he saw it resembled the pockmarked surface of the moon. Tiny bubbles were swirling around his head. In the silent water world, he saw a vision of an indistinct figure on the lake bed.

It was his father who spotted him floundering just below the surface of the water. Anxiously, Doug watched Kevin disappear, down and down and down, like a heavy anchor heading for the bottom. Doug had ripped his shoes off and plunged into the lake.

Kevin's throat was clamped shut and he struggled to breathe. Suddenly Doug's large hand pulled him upward. He tugged Kevin back to the surface. A small group of Morehouse's friends stared at Kevin, while Doug swam him back to the pier. When Kevin was thrust out of the slimy lake, he spit water out of his mouth and gagged repeatedly.

After fifteen minutes on the pier, Kevin's arms and legs moved with ease. Kevin was feeling like himself again. His father had been watching, and without hesitation had come to the rescue. Kevin had believed he was surely going to drown, and, fortunately, had been wrong. Was there a shadowy figure in the lake? Kevin doubted it.

After Kevin was out of the lake for awhile, the reassuring sounds of conversation returned. He had accidentally lost his footing, as if he had been skating on glassy ice and tripped into the lake. An hour later, things looked the same. People at the lake wanted something in return for the time they had invested. In this case, they were treated to the spectacle of a kid falling off a pier. The child engaged in the incident was too embarrassed to dwell upon it, even though it was important to the guests, who talked about it for the remainder of the day.

Once out of the water, Kevin realized he could use the story to impress his friends at home—that he had experienced a vision in the lake when he felt like he was drowning. There had been a shaft of light from the sky slicing through the lake shrubs. Site, sound, touch. Past, present, future. The brain absorbs millions of pieces of information from its surroundings every hour—sixty seconds of snapshots in every minute of an hour. Bad memories were locked behind the mental door leading to the subconscious.

Kevin's cotton shirt and blue shorts were soaked with the mucky odor of lake vegetation. Kids are told not to go anyplace alone because it's unsafe. Yet Kevin was amazed. His father had found him in the middle of the muck.

CHAPTER 10

Weaver was scheduled to work the Sunday night shift. Following an evening thunderstorm, rainwater flowed heavily through the gutters of the white-brick sheriff's administration edifice and other buildings in downtown Centerville. Pedestrians were returning to the sidewalks and traffic was resuming on the streets, which were slick from the downpour. A utility crew sent by the electric company scaled a telephone pole and reconnected a broken power line.

As Weaver strolled into the considerable, three-story Clayton County administration building, muddy-looking rainwater spun down a vertical gutter pipe on the house across Main Street and gushed like the overflow from a stuck toilet onto the concrete sidewalk. He didn't want the rubber soles on his sable office shoes to become saturated with muck, so he strode gingerly over the stunted islands of puddled rainwater. As he passed between the glass doors of the imposing police building, he left muddy footprints on the checkered tile floor.

The sight of Weaver coming into work brought a smile to Campbell's lips. "I'm on the street tonight, and Balton is in tomorrow."

"Good."

"I reviewed Morehouse's tape," Campbell said. "There's nothing visual on it. Just screaming on the audio. I couldn't make out who it was. I left it on your desk."

'You know what they say—every piece of the puzzle counts," Weaver related.

"It sounds like a fight. It was too dark to see who it was."

"I gathered as much," Weaver responded.

Campbell slipped his deputy's cap on. "I'll stay out of your way. If you need anything, give me a buzz."

Weaver, growing impatient with the investigation of the Kirchner case, paced down the hallway to his office. His desktop was littered with open folders and loose paperwork, plus the tape. Potted sunflowers and mayberry plants were standing on the windowsill. He had apparently forgotten to water the orchids at the end of the row, and the leaves were pockmarked with rust-colored holes from the dry, indoor atmosphere. He picked it up and tossed it into the wastebasket.

He took off his sheriff's jacket and tossed it over the back of the cobalt office chair behind his desk. He was not as neat as Deputy Balton, whose wife kept his uniform freshly ironed.

Weaver followed his standard procedure of skimming over forms and filing them in metal cabinets. In his overall approach to law enforcement work, he didn't think he was as conventional as the preceding social class of Clayton County sheriff's officials who had occupied the building. Floyd Coleman, the county sheriff in the 1940s, had worn well-ironed, sharp-looking pants and a stiff white shirt each day. As time passed, sheriff's officials, like the society in general, relied to a greater degree on changing technology such as computers. Known as a serious, unpretentious sheriff, Weaver strove to maintain unbiased thinking regarding either old or new crime-detection processes, assuming there was necessarily a significant difference between them.

Aside from the cluttered paperwork on his desk, was a book about firearms. It was next to framed photographs of his wife, Tammy, and his two children, Rick, 12, and Sandy, 18. Plaques and glass photographs of former Clayton County sheriffs hung along the wall. There was also an aerial photograph of Centerville, population 20,000.

Weaver started his computer, the screen on his desk lit up and he searched through off-line records within the county department's own filing system. As the screen hummed unabatedly, Weaver searched files and leaned against the soft cushion on the back of his chair. In his search for evidence, he allotted time on each workshift for browsing through folders. He moused through onscreen files, highlighting and saving pertinent information.

Weaver shifted gears, studying the Marsden note the Observer had forwarded to him. It was a threatening one, that was for sure.

Weaver dialed his phone and reached the Observer's answering machine. "This is Sheriff Weaver at headquarters. I received the Marsden note. If you learn anything more, please contact us."

Weaver examined another letter. He was to make an appointment for a state examination of the county's jail facility.

He telephoned and greeted the state patrol office, asking a captain he knew, Harvey Smith, if he would pass a message along.

"I'd like to show the inspector around, give him a tour of the grounds," Weaver explained. "However, I'm busy this week, and there is little flexibility in my schedule." He set an appointment with the inspector for two weeks from Tuesday.

"We've gone through a nerve-racking week here," Weaver said. "Got a volatile case going. In any event, I hope our jail system will live up to the state's fine standards," Weaver said confidently. "We keep the jail facility in first-rate condition. I'm sure the state guy would like to make the inspection fast and thorough. If I'm not in, Deputy Balton will show him around."

Smith asked him about the Kirchner investigation, and a bleak grin spread across Weaver's face. "This is the umpteenth time I've been asked about it. I prefer Sherlock Holmes cases myself. So far, we have little to go on—a body in the woods, a young tourist. Her boyfriend might have gotten out of control, but I'm not so sure. I don't think this will turn out to be *Friday The Thirteenth*, but nowadays, you never know."

Weaver paused, listening to a question. "Nothing was stolen," he answered. "I'll get back to you."

After wrapping up the call, Weaver was overcome with fatigue, and his head became as heavy as a chunk of metal. He had previous experience with headaches in the office and was prepared for them. He walked to the office closet and pulled a pillow from the top shelf. He laid down on the couch, thinking he would take a nap.

A dim nightmare began. At first, it was impalpable, but pulled Weaver along in fervid detail. A prison official, on a statewide circuit of inspections, had inexplicably arrived unannounced at a vacuous prison. Weaver had fallen into a sound sleep, snoring, receiving replenishing rest, while the inspector chatted with him. Weaver's work routine had been changed, and he was no longer the sheriff. He was now warden of a suppositious prison that didn't exist.

In Weaver's nocturnal imaginings, the whole prison was in perfect order. A speck of dirt could hardly be found. The inmate beds were neat, with fresh blankets and sheets from the laundry, and each individual cell was more than sufficiently supplied with toiletries. It was as if Weaver held an irrational fear of imperfection. As a local sheriff, Weaver was used to the food smells and sloppiness of having a microwave oven in the dispatcher's office, and the occasional old lamp at home that refused to work.

In the silent fabric of Weaver's subconscious mind, the trek past wooded land supporting ramshackle properties seemed to race by. Weaver and the inspector marched in the cold air along a deserted road, which offered little to see other than the skeletal outlines of trees. Finally, they came to an old graveyard elevated along a sloping incline. Weaver believed that law enforcement was the bedrock of any community. But the graveyard was filled with ashes and debris caused by a fire, and even in his subconscious sleep, Weaver felt the anguish of death.

In a state of internal confusion, with the agitated prison inspector shouting, Weaver struggled awake from the uncharacteristically terrifying nap. Throughout his career, he had placed an emphasis on tangible facts. He was familiar with stories about the woods and he found little evidence to support superstitions, which sometimes placed disrepute on people who foolishly announced any belief in them.

As Weaver lifted himself off the couch, the fictitious words of the agitated prison inspector lingered. Weaver, feeling as if he had emerged from another world, sprawled off the couch and ambled toward his desk.

The nightmare was the most unusual Weaver had experienced. On occasion, Weaver had trudged through other fears stemming from his responsibilities in law enforcement. Early in his career, he had weighed the possibility of being harmed in the line of duty. He had once dreamt about a murder suspect pulling a gun on him. He had worried about his sheriff's cruiser crashing during a chase. And now he had undergone a bad dream that he was unable to understand.

Later that night, Morehouse also experienced a bad dream about death. A shadow wriggled over his body in his bed, and crawled inside his head. He saw the piece of cloth tighten in the man's hand and heard screaming. The man vanished and reappeared in a squad car, and a sheriff's gun was laying on the ground, outside the open door. He had already strangled the woman in the forest, Kirchner, and now he was shooting at Balton in a parking lot.

Morehouse raised his head off the pillow and sat on the edge of the bed. With Morehouse talking in his sleep, Carol had come awake, realizing Morehouse was babbling to himself, the inside of his head floating back into his skull. Carol jumped out of bed, flipped on the nightlight, studied Morehouse, who was still under the covers, and flopped back into bed next to him.

"The woman was clutching her throat," Morehouse said. "She saw the killer's face, even in the darkness. She thought she might be able to get away. A deputy captured the killer, but he escaped from a squad car."

Carol was exasperated. She stared into Morehouse's bloodshot eyes. "Why are you fabricating these elaborate lies? To feed your ego? You're going to get both of us into trouble."

"I'm trying to get myself out of trouble."

"It's like you're in a trance half the time," Carol said.

"I can't just lay there at night, and watch a murder in my head without doing anything about it," Morehouse said.

Morehouse picked up the cordless phone on the night table and dialed the sheriff's department. At 3 a.m., the dispatcher answered, and Morehouse's call was forwarded to Weaver. When Weaver started on the night shift, he never thought he would receive a call reporting the contents of a bad dream. Weaver believed he had heard every conceivable type of police call. Maybe that had something to do with his receding hairline and bad indigestion after meals. Tonight was slow-going, and Weaver had fallen into a kind of trance. Now Morehouse was on the phone, telling Weaver about his nightmare, how Kirchner was strangled in the forest.

Morehouse said, "The man was a farmer. I'm pretty sure he killed the woman in the woods...his face resembled a skull. It was an indistinct image in the shadows. The man left the body in the woods and returned to his farm. I don't know exactly where the farm is located. I couldn't see it clearly in my mind. I think it's near here."

"You were sleeping?" Weaver asked.

"Yes. What do you think I'm doing at this time of the morning?"

"Have you been drinking?"

"No."

"Have you seen anyone? A doctor?"

"No."

"I also had an unusual dream, but it doesn't sound as serious as yours. It's difficult to put much faith in them," Weaver added.

"You can believe whatever you want," Morehouse said. "I don't expect you to believe anything. I'm only able to tell you what I saw."

Morehouse said, "We might be in danger...my wife and I...here at the Bay View. That brutal man—I don't know who he is or where he is? Somehow, I think he knows about me, about my place here. He knows I might figure out his name. One of our guests was killed. He could go after someone else."

Weaver asked, "Is that what you see when you're trying to sleep?"

Morehouse ran his fingers through his greasy hair. "You'll keep a record of my report, won't you?"

"Yes," Weaver said. "Is that it?"

"That's my report," Morehouse finished, and hung up.

Carol glowered at Morehouse, her frowning lips long across her face. "You're just worried, Ray. You want this imaginary man to find you so you can get your name in the newspaper."

"No, I don't," Morehouse yelled.

"You want to read about yourself in stories and headlines, and see your likeness on TV. Who the hell are you to call the sheriff at this time of the morning? You have no genuine concern for other people! You don't care about the sheriff's department or care what the deputy thinks about you. You just want to make a name for yourself."

He said, "If this was only a dream, do you think both of us would be awake right now? That nightmare is trying to tell us something. That person in the woods might come after me. I was out there that night."

"You're nuts!" Carol yelled, looking at the clock. "You're suffering from delusions stemming from stress. Me, me, me. That's all you ever think about. Can't you get your mind off yourself and your problems. Nobody cares about you enough to chase after you. You just want attention."

"I know someone who doesn't want the sheriff's attention," Morehouse said.

"Who?"

"The person who committed the murder. I think he might kill again."

"What do you want to do now?"

"I'm going downstairs to get two glasses of red wine."

Carol buried her head in the pillow.

CHAPTER 11

The pickup truck skidded to a stop in the farmyard. The driver flipped the headlights off, allowing the darkness to descend on the small farm. The unshaven man, Marsden, rigidly hauled a thick burlap bag out of the rear storage compartment of the truck and dragged it along the ground to the barn, doubling back to pick up something. He wore blue jeans and a drab T-shirt.

The original structure of Marsden's barn followed the Pennsylvania style of exterior architectural appearance. It was a combination pole frame barn and grain silo, a type that is common in California. Existing barns that had been refurbished reflected present-day trends, while traditional barns in Europe showed the historical roots of the peasants who had built them.

The barn was an architectural form that was in the middle of those two extremes. Underneath the gambrel roof, the frame was built of rough-hewn timbers. Patches of the siding were weathered and gray. Despite a decorative cupola, the eight-foot, ground-level stone foundation below the siding made the exterior appear rustic and almost medieval. There were thin slots between sideboards for ventilation. Half a dozen decorative hex signs had been painted on the exterior wall of each side.

Located at the end of a dirt entrance drive leading to Highway 46, Marsden's farmhouse and barn were tucked into a shadowy hillside. The wide, hinged doors at the entrance to the barn faced Marsden's farmhouse, and the long side of the building was pointed south toward the highway.

Behind the barn, toward the hillside, it was shady, providing relief for cattle on bright, sultry days. Farther back was an old-fashioned pump well, which hadn't been used in years. The paint was peeling.

Rusting metal sheds used for equipment storage were also located in the rear of the farmyard. Three ample sheds housed mechanical equipment such as tractors and threshers. Two moderate-sized sheds were filled with dirty shovels, rusted rakes and other aged, rotting implements. A barbed-wire fence cut between the overgrown trees and vegetation and the wooded hillside, which stretched into the Waubeka National Forest.

Even if a potential buyer was interested, only a fool would have placed a bid on the real estate without checking the deed to validate the name of the owner. Marsden was an alias, a nickname he had concocted to cover up his identity. His dilapidated property didn't make him seem like a responsible landowner.

Over the years, following the disappearance of his mother and the death of his father, the deteriorating property had not been well-maintained. Islands of knee-high grass cut through the backyard. The livestock, which amounted to six dairy cows, grazed behind the barn, sporadically taking care of Marsden's lawn-mowing chores. The backyard, bordered by a cornfield on one side and the farmhouse on the other, was overrun with prickly foliage, seven-foot bushes, weeds and ferns. Yung trees pushed against the paint-peeled gutters of Marsden's farmhouse. Although Marsden had maintained the front yard, the back yard was out of control.

On the way to the barn, Marsden paused to catch his breath. Then, smiling to himself, he continued dragging the bulging sack into the barn. Once inside, he swung the extensive wooden doors together and double-checked that they were latched shut.

He yanked the cumbersome bag to the back of the barn, where there was faint lamplight. He propped the bag against the rotting barn wall. He began fumbling for the button on his flashlight when there was a piercing crash. Drooping against the wall, the sack had toppled over and ripped along the side, its contents spilling out.

Breathing slowly, Marsden studied the mess of yellowed newspapers, single sheets of lined white paper, pamphlets, and paperback and hardcover books. He had accidentally smashed the sack into a horse stall, breaking a decomposing partition in half.

He smelled the stench of cattle and uttered curses to himself. In his work shirt and jeans, he cleaned the mess up. Far above the barn roof, Marsden heard aerial noise—a propeller airplane.

He checked the window and saw only rows of corn flourishing in between the water-enriched furrows. Pushy, gas-pedal tourists were speeding down the highway past the farm. Even though the baby boom had ended, an increasing number of outsiders were moving into his area and destroying it, he concluded.

A stainless steel tractor stood in the lamplight. Rakes, shovels and a handful of farm implements were propped against the cobwebbed wall. A tiny dirt-brown spider inched across the lines of its cobweb.

Marsden walked to the tractor. The gauge on the dusty dashboard indicated a quarter tank of gas. In the darkness, the headlight beams of passing vehicles reflected off the decaying wood of the barn walls. When he pulled the key out of the ignition, the tractor's CD player snapped on in the middle of a rock song.

Flicking his eyes back and forth, Marsden swallowed. Through the window he observed the headlights on the highway, which in the abstract fringe of his mind, appeared to hesitate momentarily. He turned off the CD player.

He left the barn and walked toward the farmhouse. The piles of loose junk behind the barn and puddles from recent rainstorms, gave the lackluster property a light resemblance to a war-torn village building in the Vietnam War.

Marsden let himself into the farmhouse through the back door. In the thin light, his eyes took in the lambent country kitchen, including the black-and-white framed photographs hanging on the walls. Jerome Tallmadge, a freelance nature photographer, who traveled to scenic wilderness locations around the world, had taken the photos. He sold his detailed photographs to magazines in the 1960s, and he favored black-and-white shots of congenial country people.

Marsden and his parents were pictured in them.

Marsden went through the kitchen and entrance hall, and up to his bedroom. He laid the following day's wardrobe out on the bed. It consisted of a pair of blue-jean overalls, a saffron sport shirt, white farm socks and clean underwear. In the tingling ribbons of moonlight, his pasty face was visible.

When he had undressed, he considered himself to be like an ancient creature observing humanity from a black forest. Moon-reflected solar light traveling millions of miles cut through the splotched windowpane. Inside Marsden's head, the room whirled slowly in wide arcs. Marsden's eyes glittered with mad rage, like flaming coals in a grill. For now, the corrupt behavior Marsden blamed on the tenebrous woods had receded. Overcome with fatigue, he flopped onto his bed.

Citizens in the town of Waldwick failed to see Jenkins grocery shopping every second Wednesday, as he normally did. No one had seen him in Waldwick for two weeks—the longest time frame he had been missing. On two previous occasions, he had disappeared from his rural farm for three days at a time. In each case, it turned out he had gone on a drinking binge, failing to tell anyone his whereabouts.

For instance, after going to Jackson's Bait Shop one morning three weeks ago, he appeared at Freddie's Tap, a local tavern, at 3:30 p.m. He had gone fishing, slept in a drunken haze on the bank of the Marengo River, and hadn't reappeared until Thursday. He showed up staggering and suffering from heat stroke on the porch of Emma Hennberry's house that morning. She promptly telephoned the sheriff. While she waited for the squad car to arrive, she refused to feed him. Lester was taken to the hospital and treated for exposure to the elements. He returned to his ramshackle home near Waldwick.

A month later, a similar incident took place. Jenkins was spotted by deputies in his boat, floating near the shoreline of Crater Lake. That was after a farmer, Miles Giffin, called sheriff's authorities. When Giffin had gone to the barn in the early morning to milk the cows, he had found Lester sleeping in the hayloft. Tired and crabby, Lester climbed down, wrangled with Giffin and grouchily marched off into an empty field.

Authorities didn't relish chasing after missing people like Lester, especially when swarms of irritating flies were out. In the fall, they could see more clearly between the leafless trees. The flies were gone, and aside from hunters, fewer people were in the woods.

In summer, inexperienced campers rented lake cabins and set up tents. Bike riders, motorcyclists and hikers found little-used trails that were too remote for automobiles. Motorists who spotted unfamiliar vehicles parked along the gravel shoulders of area highways, stopped to offer assistance.

Reserve National Guard troops trained at Camp Fairfield from May through September. Military-green personnel carriers and open-roofed jeeps kicked up dust on dirt roads during practice exercises. It was easy enough to follow their tire tracks through a wooded lot because the noise from the engines gave them away. Sometimes a pair of hikers on a solitary walk would come across the Sixth Battalion climbing through rocks on a steep hill. The military encampment was behind a line of trees just south of the lake.

Tourists trying to sneak around the area at night ended up running into other folks—fishermen driving boat trailers at 3 a.m. in preparation for a dawn boat launch, all-night truck drivers traveling straight down the highways to evade daytime traffic, and vacationers and third-shift workers driving frantically.

At least that's the way Marsden viewed things. After sleeping only a few hours, Marsden had gone downstairs to his living room. Sipping a beer, he sat quietly on his couch, contemplating matters. He knew, of course, that Jenkins was missing.

He also knew that Vernon Stonehill hadn't been seen in weeks. It wouldn't be long before authorities figured that out.

Marsden saw a brochure sitting on the coffee table. He snatched it up, and in the scrawny light filtering from the kitchen, he started reading the first paragraph. It began: "*Welcome to the Bay View Resort where guests enjoy country living—swimming in a spacious outdoor pool, chatting in a family lounge with a fireplace and dining at the Treasure Chest Restaurant. Private social gatherings are held in the Bay View's banquet room, which features dining booths, a grill restaurant and live entertainment. The region around the resort offers nearby activities, including recreational swimming, cross-country hiking, winter skiing, camping, and tennis and golf. Located in the Waubeka National Forest, the resort stands atop a hill overlooking Crater Lake.*"

The brochure went on to explain the Treasure Chest Restaurant served breakfast, lunch and dinner seven days a week. It showed an aerial photograph of buildings on the property, ranging from the main resort hotel to metal equipment storage sheds. It also depicted the swimming pool, and camping and fishing cabins. Nearby were tennis facilities and a golf course. The photograph also showed woodland, rivers, creeks and hills on the resort grounds.

Marsden tossed the brochure onto the coffee table. In the deserted hours before dawn, he looked through the living-room window at the blurry shapes of fields and wooded hills. He mulled over the shabby state of his house as compared to the refurbished resort, the place where his last victim, Kirchner, had been a guest. Marsden was making plans. For now, it felt good to sip beer and look at his shotgun, propped against the wall.

CHAPTER 12

As Deputy Balton made his way out of the sunshine and into the sheriff's office on Monday morning, his mood lightened. After working on the investigation of Kirchner's death by skimming over legal files of pending cases at the Clayton County Courthouse, he decided it was time to meet his fellow deputies. Following the late-morning meeting, he planned to break for lunch.

When Balton was initially hired, he saw himself as a trainee who was hanging onto his job. But he found a niche within the department. He developed personal contacts with the bureaucratic staff at the county courthouse, and discovered written files of pending police cases. The folders were in between a substantial amount of material about active cases and cold cases. They were in metal file cabinets in a windowless, lighted basement below the first floor of the marble county courthouse building. Initially, a county clerk Balton met, Rachel Oswald, had ushered him into the lower recesses of the courthouse building. The clerk had shown him rows of filing cabinets containing records of Clayton County police and sheriff's matters in various stages of progress. Underneath a bank of florescent ceiling lights, the compressed room reminded Balton of a vault.

Once he decided to do an unauthorized, in-depth check of the records, he realized there was more to Centerville than met the eye. There were folders containing material about persons missing in the Waubeka National Forest. Balton's interest was piqued by the case involving the fifty-two-year-old farmer who was fishing alone on the Marengo River. In July 1998, he lost control of his canoe, which rushed past a shoreline pier. The canoe continued sailing downriver out of control until he reached the shoreline. Jenkins wandered through the forest before he made his way to a nearby farm, according to information in the folder.

Skimming over the contents of the folders, Balton believed he found patterns. Back in the late 1980s, for instance, dozens of fires spread throughout the forest during a dry, blistering summer. Back in the 1970s, there was a serious collapse at a mine.

He had read about a major blaze that took place five years ago. An elementary school in the small town of Waldwick, population 1,100, was engulfed in flames on a Wednesday night. The scant number of employees in the building, which amounted to several teachers and the janitor, were evacuated. The public school burned to the ground, and had to be rebuilt from scratch. A similar case took place three years ago. A high school in Waldwick, population 6,400, caught on fire. The community was not so fortunate. Fifteen students, six teachers and two janitors were killed in the blaze.

Balton was surprised. There was information in the files that deputies could use about unresolved cases—murder, missing persons and arson. There were also files covering legal proceedings. A typical deputy remembers specific facts about police cases off the top of his head. But Balton was not content with this, and read through the judges' decisions for each case in a chain of court dates, struggling to understand the arguments and evidence presented by attorneys.

Without informing his colleagues in the sheriff's department, Balton read them in his spare time underneath the glow of the florescent lights in the courthouse basement—the black ink and small type slurring through his overworked mind. He often left the building at closing time. One case, it seemed, led to another, and Balton detected evidence linking one crime to another crime. This gave him leads to follow when he wasn't working on assigned cases. Nobody could remember, but Weaver mentioned Balton's avid interest in reading courthouse files, and word of Balton's zeal for research spread amongst other officers in the department.

Balton headed to his desk in the office.

He had decided to join Deputy Campbell for an informal meeting in a sheriff's conference room. He sought to pick up leads on ongoing investigations.

Law enforcement work was traumatic, and the meetings were places for deputies to voice concerns about work in the sheriff's department. When the talk became animated, Balton imagined other people, listeners, witnessing deputies exchanging secrets during their conversations about developments in the department.

Balton entered the conference room and closed the door behind him. Deputy Campbell was already seated at the table. "Sit down and make yourself comfortable," Campbell said, sliding into an office chair.

Balton spoke impulsively. "The spot in the forest where the woman's corpse was found was not the exact place where she was killed," he explained assuredly. "I know that's not what the responding officers think, and that's not what the obvious evidence indicates. They're likely to conclude Purnell is the prime suspect, and that he murdered his girlfriend. I know that's what Deputy Upton suspects, but I believe Kirchner was chased by someone."

Campbell, who prided himself on balanced judgment, studied the emphatic expression on Balton's face. "You suspect the victim was stalked by a stranger who knew she and her boyfriend were lost?"

"The wounds and contusions on the neck and head aren't proof that the murder was committed in the exact spot where the corpse was located," Balton said. "What weapon did Trent use to puncture the skin on Kirchner's neck when he supposedly bashed her head in? Why would he have been so hot under the collar?"

"How do you know there were puncture marks on the skin?" Campbell asked.

"I talked to Carol, the coroner's secretary."

Irritated, Campbell cut in. "Were you authorized to contact the coroner's office without waiting for the official findings to be released?"

"I've known Carol for years. I expect the coroner's report might be confusing. There will be contradictions. The report will indicate the perpetrator had to have possessed greater strength than what Purnell was capable of."

Campbell studied Balton in silence. Although Balton had acted confident, his babble about the murder was strange. Campbell asked, "Do you know of any other suspects who had a motive?"

Balton contemplated for a moment. In the back of his head, there was a trace image, crude, shabbily dressed man. "Offhand, I'm not aware of any specific suspects," he said. "Morehouse stumbled upon the body entirely by accident? That's difficult to believe," Balton said. "There are hundreds of acres of timber. What was Morehouse doing in that part of forest?"

"He claims he was on a routine nature walk," Campbell said, brushing his hand over his neat, short-cropped hair. "He goes out with a camcorder, even at night. When he's off his job at the Bay View, he tapes birds, deer, beavers."

Balton interrupted. "He's the owner and manager. True. But he also has a record. Why does he say he tapes nature?"

Campbell answered, "When he finishes his shift as desk manager, he goes out into the woods in his spare time, as a hobby."

Campbell opened a folder of forms and personal notes pertaining to the case. He placed it on the Formica conference table. He studied the contents for several moments, flipping through the pages. "He had his camcorder turned on. I looked the tape over for evidence. There was light, from both the camcorder and Fielding's truck. There was garbled, indistinct noise."

Balton said, "Another person has phoned in reports that she has spotted a green pickup truck in that general vicinity over the past year. I've heard the dispatcher on duty, Janet, take the calls. Later this afternoon, we can look over more information on the matter. Since there were at least half a dozen wounds on the corpse, and other tourists may have been in the vicinity, we have to thoroughly check anyone who has the slightest chance of being a legitimate suspect."

"You're probably on the wrong track," Campbell said smugly, with a slight smile that irritated Balton. "When the search is finished, the boat Purnell described may turn up downstream. The couple were exhausted, possibly at odds. I agree with you on one point: The forest can do strange things to people, especially tourists who are lost. You know that, Dennis. Purnell might well have lost control, gone berserk, and in his rage, delirium and exhaustion, killed his girlfriend."

"Unless there is…" Balton said, a tinge of desperation in his voice. He waited for Campbell to proceed.

Campbell suddenly became animated, anticipating Balton's thinking. "You suspect an unknown assailant, somebody who' spotted an easy target," Campbell suggested. "Do you think the suspect is possibly an alcoholic or a drug addict? Or are we looking for a Jekyll-and-Hyde type?"

Balton waved his fingers over the table. His voice sounded deeper, like Weaver's. "First, the sporadic nature of the crime. That might indicate the guilty party wasn't somebody who knew the victim. Or that it might not be one person working alone. You still haven't answered my questions. Where would a tourist like Purnell find the nerve to deny such a brutal killing and to try to cover it up?"

Campbell said, "The perpetrator feels important precisely because he is able to cover up the callous nature of the crime."

"That's your personal opinion."

Campbell interjected, "The families of loved ones in custody hope everything will turn out all right. I plan to contact Purnell's parents again. If I press them, I might come up with a motive."

Balton rehashed Weaver's dream and Morehouse's phone call. Based on his reading, he had a hunch Kirchner had seen something that triggered the murder. Balton planned to talk to residents not far from the crime scene.

Balton said, "The picture in my head is a blur. There were few people known to be in the area. Right now, it's just a feeling I have, that Purnell's telling the truth. I was nauseous and sweaty when I woke up. Even though I had been sleeping, I felt like I had jogged five miles. I took a long, hot shower to calm my nerves."

Campbell recalled other instances in which he had heard hyperbole from Balton. But like his fellow deputies, he had gotten used to it. The deputies traded information about the incident at Angel's, Morehouse's resort and missing persons. As they ended their discussion and rose from the conference table, Campbell half believed Balton's hunch, yet he also had a queasy feeling in the pit of his stomach.

"Once a person resorts to crime, and gets away with it, he becomes desensitized to it and tries the crime again," Balton explained. "That's why we have to stop him. A neurotic killer is compelled to complete the rituals of murder and sacrifice."

The coroner's report to Weaver stated that Kirchner's thyroid arch was not intact, another sign that the perp had attempted to choke her before pushing her down the incline into the mass of boulders. In addition to that, the coroner determined she had been killed by severe trauma to the head. Weaver did not know if Purnell was strong enough to have attacked Kirchner in such a short time span. The body had been discovered face up outdoors in the brush, and there was no evidence the assailant had tried to transport the body to another location. If Purnell had killed Kirchner, it seemed as if he had acted spontaneously, without premeditation.

Weaver loaded a disc into the CD compartment. The plastic shelf automatically slid from view, disappearing into the inside of the computer unit. With all the billions of bits of information and extraneous data, the computer was a valuable tool. It was too bad the computer didn't just solve the case for him, Weaver told himself.

Weaver studied the flow of computer information worriedly and issued a snort of disgust. He typed a sequence onto the keypad, and information about Morehouse flashed across the screen. For Weaver, it was sort of a ritual. He had known Morehouse for years, and had few reasons' to suspect his friend of wrongdoing. Yet he put Ray's record on the screen to keep himself humble, in case he had missed something.

Weaver discovered a minor point, that Morehouse had recently received a traffic citation. Although he had complained to Deputy Balton, who issued the traffic ticket, he had been found guilty, anyway.

Weaver switched gears, calling up information about missing persons. He was already familiar with Jenkins' periodic disappearances. The woodsman would likely surface drunk again.

Weaver looked up Stonehill. Oddly enough, sheriff's records didn't reveal much. He had been cited five years ago for disturbing the peace, an incident involving public drunkenness. He had also received a drunk-driving citation.

Something scratched at Weaver's memory, something the computer didn't call up and something he couldn't put his finger on, like the nightmare about the prison inspector. The next time he saw Deputy Balton he would ask him about Morehouse's citation.

Chapter 13

Morehouse drove to the Centerville Library, where he rented a classic black-and-white movie video called "Monkey Business", starring Cary Grant, Ginger Rogers and Marilyn Monroe. After watching the humorous tape at home, he drove it back to the library. He also planned to find books and news stories about crime in the Waubeka National Forest, hoping they would give him a clue about Kirchner's brutal murder.

As Morehouse entered the library, two dark-haired women walked so close behind his heels that had he not jumped to his right he would have been pushed into another patron exiting the busy cement-block building through the narrow two-door entrance. One woman disappeared into an office room, and she reappeared behind the circulation desk, checking the computer screen. She was a red-haired circulation-desk worker in her early twenties. She was dressed in hazel corduroys and bore a light resemblance to a hip broadcast announcer named Gina Madison, who hosted a PBS TV show about motorcycles called "*Cycle Highway*".

"You almost ran me over in the entrance lobby," Morehouse fumed. "What's your problem? Don't you have any respect for library patrons? My name is Ray Morehouse, and I run the Bay View Resort. What's your name?"

The bourgeois library worker swivelled her head from side to side, self-consciously. She was used to ignoring distractions. For a hasty moment, she pondered Morehouse's hostile reaction. "Gabriella," she answered coolly.

Morehouse was still fuming. "You must have been late for work. When I walked through the entrance doors, you walked past me very swiftly like you were going to run me over. I had to jump out of the way. If I hadn't gotten out of the way, you would have stepped on my shoe. I could have hurt my foot...or even wrecked my back."

Morehouse was still upset, so he marched up to the main librarian's desk to complain. The squat, black-haired woman sitting at the large desk identified herself as Chloe. Morehouse repeated his concerns, but recommended the library not take any action against Gabriella. Chloe suggested he describe the incident in writing and submit it to the library complaint box on her desk.

"I've seen library workers walking impatiently through the carpetted building before," Morehouse responded. "I have written other complaint letters to the Centerville Library Board about strangers stepping on my shoes, touching my clothing and charging into me like encroaching football players," Morehouse said. "As head librarian, you're supposed to remind them not to bump into anonymous patrons."

A year and a half ago, Morehouse had written a short note that he placed in the library's cardboard complaint box about the boisterous workers and piles of books near the checkout desk. Since then, the library had hired quieter, more efficient workers and the stacks of books had been reduced. Chloe's suggestion that he put another complaint in the box seemed redundant.

It wasn't on the grand national scale of past injustice, such as racial bigotry. Yet it was one of the minor infractions that wrecked Morehouse's day.

"Another problem I've experienced is a circulation worker who I believe has made sarcastic remarks to me when I have been in the process of checking out books. He looks a little like a famous Hollywood B-movie director. If his rude behavior continues, I might report him in the future."

Chloe stared at Morehouse, who didn't seem to mind spending his time making a library staffer squirm. "Several weeks ago, I told Deputy Balton and a central-desk librarian that a small number of local residents have followed my car in the morning down Rancho Avenue to the library and to the Piggly Wiggly Grocery Store. Since describing these types of weird episodes to law-enforcement and library authorities, there have been fewer of them," he explained.

"Your name is Ray Morehouse, isn't it?" Chloe enquired.

"Of course."

"On behalf of the clerk who bumped into you, I'd like to apologize," Chloe said. "She was probably late for work."

"So."

"Mr. Morehouse, you don't want to take it personally," Chloe said. "We deal with the public all day. We can't respond to each incident."

"What do you mean?"

"We're concerned about public safety," Chloe explained. "You haven't got a substantial complaint. Let me give you an example of what I mean." Chloe slid open her top desk drawer, pulled out a wrinkled white piece of notepaper and spread it over her desk so Morehouse could see it.

The typed note read:

Dear Librarian:

I'm out for blood. Burn all of your books, bitch.

Marsden

"Do you know anybody named Marsden?" Chloe asked.

"No."

"We get bogus notes in our complaint box from time to time," she said. "This one bothered me, so I saved it and showed it to the staff. I mentioned it to the sheriff's department on the phone."

"For goodness sakes, that's the kind of problem I'm complaining about," Morehouse said.

Some of Morehouse's babble had made sense and was even compelling. Having calmed down from his state of agitation, Morehouse resumed. "This is highly interesting because these hateful pranks and road rage incidents are described in a small percentage of the general fiction paperback novels. They're on a bookcase located in the middle of the library."

Like other readers, Morehouse sometimes found curious imbedded statements in novels that were intended to preserve law and order. He earnestly informed library habitues such as Chloe that he had been reading to overcome compulsions involving work and gambling.

"In the past, I have worked as a successful businessman," he finished haughtily. "So I would suggest the library's clerks avoid charging through the cramped entrance doors with too much celerity, especially at the earthshattering speed of sound. Maybe the library director would like to replace the clerks with scorekeepers."

He had used the word "celerity" to irritate Chloe.

"However, I'm glad you reported that complaint note to the sheriff's department," he finished, smiling politely.

Morehouse wished to dispute a citation for "Failure to Stop/Improper Stop" at a stop sign issued at 11:43 p.m. Thursday, April 4, by Deputy Balton. The deputy alleged the defendant, Ray Morehouse, violated Ordinance No. 1823 under State Statute No. 352.43. In response, Morehouse had gone through the trouble of researching traffic violations at the library.

Morehouse had entered a plea through the mail of "Not Guilty" to the traffic charge of "Failure to Stop/Improper Stop" at a stop sign on North Burnham Avenue. Morehouse really believed he completed proper stops at all the stop signs on North Burnham Avenue even though he had consumed a few drinks.

That night, there were two other vehicles, a pickup truck and a car, behind Morehouse with bright headlights shining in his rearview mirror. One of them was tailgating Morehouse's 1994 Ford Taurus station wagon.

Deputy Balton's citation didn't indicate how he was able to single out Morehouse's automobile from the two other vehicles, whether his sheriff's squad car was following Morehouse's Taurus, if the street Morehouse had been driving down included a hidden speed trap or why he suspected Morehouse failed to stop properly at an intersection. Moreover, it didn't show similar incidents that had taken place in Centerville since 1991 in which police decided not to issue a ticket. As a resident of the Centerville, Morehouse believed it was his duty as a citizen to report this controversial traffic case to authorities.

If Deputy Balton's information on the pink traffic ticket was accurate, he suspected Morehouse had failed to stop properly at the second stop sign among a series of stop signs on northbound Burnham Avenue. He suspected Morehouse was drunk. Morehouse believed he had stopped properly at the stop sign—and at all of the stop signs—for a sufficient time frame and was driving within the speed limit.

After Morehouse had rolled down his driver's side window after proceeding west on East Hampton Avenue following a left turn from North Burnham Avenue, Balton walked up to Morehouse's car. He asked Morehouse if he had exceeded the speed limit and if he had made a proper stop at an intersection. Morehouse told him he had stopped sufficiently at all of the stop signs and had been driving within the speed limit. Morehouse communicated to the sheriff's deputy he had been heading northbound to his home at the Bay View Resort north of Centerville.

When Balton returned from his idling, humming squad car, he did not issue a ticket for driving under the influence. However, he went ahead with a citation for

"Failure to Stop/Improper Stop" on North Burnham Avenue, costing seventy-five dollars in fines and totaling three points on Morehouse's driver's license.

The incident had taken place around midnight and there had been few, if any, pedestrians on the subdued neighborhood streets. As Morehouse recalled, possibly from wishful thinking, he had stopped properly at stop signs and had not exceeded the speed limit. It was an old complaint that traffic officers heard often.

As a former Centerville resident, he was familiar with north Oakfield and east Hampton avenues. Morehouse had seen brave police officers join other members of the community in lowering the rates of certan types of street crimes.

However, Morehouse didn't understand how Balton could have seen the rear of his automobile unless Balton's squad car was the vehicle tailgating his car or the vehicle behind that one. As Morehouse recalled, at least one and presumably both of the vehicles behind him had turned left off of Burnham Avenue before heading west.

He was not aware of any witnesses. Even with bright, glaring lights shining in his rearview mirror, he genuinely believed he had stopped properly at all intersections. He also didn't know why Balton had been following him, other than to issue a citation.

The ticket didn't state why the patrol officer thought Morehouse missed a stop sign. Typically, there were visibility obstacles at night, so Balton might have mistaken another vehicle, which turned left off of North Burnham Avenue, for Morehouse's. The other car, Morehouse believed, had been the speeder. Balton's ticket did not inform Morehouse how the deputy had been able to spot his car and isolate it from other vehicles on the road.

Morehouse did not know what street Balton had been watching his automobile from, or why Balton suspected he had not stopped adequately.

The deputy's car had been one of the vehicles behind Morehouse's car. Why would Balton provoke him into violating a traffic law? To score traffic points with the sheriff's department? As Morehouse understood it, entrapment, or provoking a citizen into violating the law, even in a minor traffic-violation case, was against the law.

The public court system understands that a citizen is considered innocent until proven guilty, ignorance of the law is no excuse, one crime isn't necessarily insulated from other crimes, and that both traffic violators and sheriff's officials make mistakes.

Morehouse knew of related incidents. Since 1991, Morehouse had placed phone calls to local police departments and the State Highway Patrol regarding tailgating, road rage, and irresponsible drivers accidentally crossing the center line in the oncoming lane. He had telephoned deputies regarding his vehicle getting singled out in 1991, 1992, 1993, 1998, 1999 and 2000. At the other end of the phone line, sheriff's authorities told Morehouse to drive defensively. They had to witness road-rage violations, and a deputy likely wouldn't issue a ticket anyway because it would cost him a day in court.

At one point, a Centerville deputy on a government-recorded phone call had told Morehouse it was unlawful for a motorist to pull off the road, even if he is tailgated. The deputy said Morehouse should drive faster, with the flow of traffic.

Had Morehouse put his numerous traffic complaints in writing, he would have placed the term "average driver" in quotation marks because he believed people in town who knew he had served time for theft had singled his car out for road rage. In fact, Morrison had contacted sheriff's officials so many times that deputies could describe the make, model and color of Morehouse's car from memory.

It was easy to understand why deputies had ruled out Morehouse as a suspect, and on the night of Kirchner's death at that. Somebody who had been reporting minor traffic incidents for years wouldn't hang around a corpse if he had been the one who had committed the crime.

Morehouse believed in coincidences. No government police official had ever indicated any reason for giving him a ticket over the years other than the information stated on the citation. Morehouse claimed that, dating back to the 1980s, he had noticed unusual, mysterious, unexplained coincidences on several occasions in which there was a connection between his videotaping and minor infractions such as burned-out headlights. Now a murder, of all things, had taken place.

In casual conversation, he was asked several times by sheriff's officials pulling him over on the street what books and videos were in his car. Even though they were innocent, good-ole-boy questions, in an unreasonably distrustful frame of mind, usually late in the afternoon, Morehouse had cause to wonder. Was this George Orwell's *1984*, with Thought Police patrolling the streets? He believed sheriff's officials were supposed to enquire about weapons!

And then something terrible occurred to Morehouse. What if Kirchner's killer had educated himself in the gruesome art of murder through literature? In part, that would explain why street deputies like Balton were on edge.

Though he was not an expert on the law, it was Morehouse's understanding that deputies were to issue tickets for the violations written on them, and not for other reasons. It was against the law to single out for mistreatment certain occupations, educational backgrounds, intellectual levels, religions, geographical locations, personality types, and racial and ethnic heritages.

Morehouse was concerned about community safety. He included in a complaint letter descriptions of other unresolved street incidents involving Centerville sheriff's deputies on the south shore of Crater Lake.

One that was fixed in his memory took place in 1991. He was pulled over late at night by Balton, who eerily stared at his car from the street like a zombie, did not say a word to him, frightened him, and drove away without explanation and without the squad car's emergency lights flashing. In another similar 1993 incident, Balton stopped his car in the middle of the night and asked Morehouse where he was going. He told the deputy he was returning a video to the Blockbuster Video Store in Centerville. Morehouse had spare time on his hands due to the seasonal fall slowdown at the resort. Failing to give any additional explanation, the deputy disappeared into the night without the squad car's emergency lights on.

In an incident in 1998, Balton began talking to Morehouse through his driver's side car window in the parking lot of the Centerville Library. Morehouse didn't remember what transpired in the brief moments of conversation, but Balton became visibly agitated, sauntered back to his squad car, slammed the door shut and drove away. In yet another unusual 1998 incident, a Clayton County squad car followed Morehouse's vehicle, which he was driving home from a Centerville shopping trip for as many as several blocks on Hibiscus Road with the squad's brightly-colored emergency lights flashing. The squad car made a frightening U-turn at the Franklin Elementary School and sped off southbound on Magdalena Road.

There were many other incidents like these over the years since the late 1980s involving different police officers, especially Balton, and private citizens following Morehouse's vehicle. In the spring of the year 2000, Morehouse wrote a handwritten letter to the Clayton County Sheriff's Department about two off-duty deputies, Balton and Campbell, who tried to order him to drive his vehicle away from a traffic-accident scene on Oakwood Road that was not properly marked for motorists with emergency road cones and traffic signs. Balton and Campbell, who both looked visibly upset, had attempted to order Morehouse to somehow drive his car backward through a completely fogged-up rear window. Morehouse couldn't see the roadway because there were no traffic officers with glowing night batons directing him from behind his car.

Another weird traffic incident took place in July 1999. Morehouse was driving near Rancho Avenue eastbound on Montana Drive in Centerville in the daytime.

Balton stared at his car and waved at Morehouse to drive over what appeared to be a race course for a July Fourth bike race. Morehouse decided to drive away from the race course and did not follow Balton's hand gestures to drive in the direction of what looked like a bike race.

He took a longer route back to the resort. He learned through broadcast news reports later that evening that a Centerville fire engine driver returning from an emergency call had driven onto the Rancho race course and accidentally struck and killed two bikers. It was a terrible mistake. Morehouse did not understand why the fire truck driver could not wait half an hour for the bikers to go by, radioed the dispatcher that he would be available for emergency calls out on the street, and would not return to the fire station until the bikers were finished using Rancho Avenue.

Morehouse read in the local newspaper the driver was later terminated from his job. This was another reason for Morehouse to spend time reading about traffic and police matters. A month later Morehouse received a response in his mailbox. Balton's citation stood. Morehouse was guilty of the traffic violation. He wrote out a check for seventy-five dollars, put it in the envelope and mailed it.

CHAPTER 14

That afternoon, Morehouse got off his couch, and drove down the congested highway to Jimmy's Buick to have a replacement drive shift lever attached to the steering wheel of his 1994 Ford Taurus station wagon. He had been zipping around town several weeks ago during the internationally televised summer Olympics, and accidentally ripped the deteriorating plastic knob off the metal lever, which was attached to the shaft. But he found a cheap, makeshift answer: He reconnected the knob to the lever with, of all things, several three-inch lengths of Scotch tape. However, the problem resurfaced. When Morehouse was driving the old car, the knob tore loose from the silver handle again.

Morehouse was getting like his late father, Harold, who had bought a 15-year-old turquoise Buick Le Sabre in 1988, the year he died. When Morehouse finally traded it in five years ago, the dashboard was covered with a layer of grime, and the aging relic resembled a collector's automobile.

Yet the Le Sabre, which his mother was used to driving, remained in acceptable running condition over the years without many repairs. The burgundy carpeting in the front driver's seat had substantially faded away. An amber luminescent light on the old-fashioned dashboard read, *"CHECK ENGINE"*, for several years before she got rid of it.

But the new Caprice looked impressive! It was a rich dark blue, a deeper color than the lighter blue outdoors on her home on Centerville Road.

After Morehouse finished his work the day he bought the 1998 Caprice, he jumped inside the car and studied the tape player, horizontal headlights that turn on automatically in the daytime, a glowing radio clock, and up-to-date modernized dashboard readings. He cruised down the congested rush-hour freeway to

Jimmy's Buick to turn in the shining set of spare car keys on his silver key chain for the '88 Le Sabre.

Traffic was heavy downtown in the late afternoon, and Morehouse felt uneasy. But the Buick salesman, a diminutive, elderly man named Don, wanted a duplicate set of Le Sabre car keys. He was a polite man, with a thin, healthy-looking wrinkled face and stick-like legs, whose desk was located in an open, wall-less space at the west end of the modest automobile showroom. They chatted. The salesman bought bagels for a group of his Lake Avenue neighborhood friends who stopped in when the sales floor wasn't busy. There was another salesman, Buck, in his office. The salesman had much to say when Morehouse visited them on Thursday night.

Morehouse's mother supposed this would be the last new car she would see her son purchase. She believed it was possible that within two years her deteriorating eyesight would be so terribly out of focus, that she wouldn't be able to drive much. She still experienced cloudy vision in her right eye. She had been driving throughout the area, as she normally did, to the Piggy Wiggly grocery store, the Lutheran church on Sundays, the small social gathering with her five remaining sorority sisters from Garfield College, and to the urban Jimmy's Buick car dealership, which had a sizeable auto sales lot.

She looked like she was in good health, and doctors hadn't told her of any additional eye difficulties. But during the daytime and the nighttime, she was half-asleep sometimes, which was common among elderly people.

"My mother has been thinking about traveling, maybe even visiting relatives in Florida, suggesting I visit Worland Harbor, or possibly take a drive up to the cottage property in Orfordstown," he said. "I recently received a season-ticket promotion from Great America, so maybe I'll head down to the Gurney, Illinois, this summer."

Ironically, Southtown Mall, once a bustling, thriving shopping mall, was becoming a ghost town, like the Rosston Mall. "Sears is pulling out of the mall and a number of other specialty small stores already have left, rendering one-third to one-half of the mall empty. It makes for easy shopping because there aren't many people there," he said.

"The Southtown Mall is on the fritz because of nearby giants such as Wal-Mart, Stein-Mart, and Logan Plaza, all of these being outdoor shopping areas. I get my haircut around there and browse at a used bookstore. The Southtown Conrath's Grocery Store closed down, as did the Sears Auto Center. I suspect part of the reason for the closings is that some people moved out of the area, and headed to other nearby localities such as Waldwick, Clementsburg, Orfordstown, West Creek, Rock Falls, Worland Harbor, Sunbeam and Bingham have some big new shopping complexes," he said.

"Well, I'm growing tired and it's getting late," he said. "I was watching "Batman", "Twilight Zone", a Vincent Price haunted house movie, and an unheralded science fiction movie called "Species" about a half-human genetic-error creature trying to become impregnated through humans. The mad scientists think they destroyed the creature, but the evil spreads to rats in city sewer system toward the end of the movie. I'd like to talk longer, but I'm running out of time."

When Morehouse looked out the showroom window, he saw a stranger walking down the sidewalk in front of the showroom. The man looked familiar. He jumped in his pickup truck and pulled away. Morehouse put his right hand into his coat pocket to double check. His car keys were still there.

"That's a great-looking car," Jason told Morehouse in the parking lot of the Treasure Chest Restaurant. They had finished their lunch date, and Morehouse had told Jason about the new turquoise Caprice he bought last week. Morehouse, who was in his late forties, had gone through a dozen different cars over the years. His last car, an economy car, had piled up 122,000 miles on the odometer. The interior was coated with dust. The muffler and the four-cylinder engine were objecting vociferously every time Morehouse turned the key in the ignition.

He had to buy a new car, so about three weeks ago he began scouting the classified ads in the Observer. After a few phone calls and in-person test drives, he was still undecided. A week later, he dropped in at Jeffers Chevrolet, and picked up the two-year-old Caprice, which had 20,000 miles on it. He put a down payment of seven hundred dollars on the six-cylinder, four-door car, and agreed to the monthly payments.

He had met Jason on a newspaper interview two years ago. Jason was putting together a series of stories about local employment and interviewed Morehouse about the job hurdles he had overcame. Morehouse was one of many subjects used in the series. Following the interview, the two had become acquaintances and met occasionally for lunch.

"I'm going to take a spin to the marina and go fishing," Morehouse explained. He was to meet with Hilton, his son, Kevin, and Justin for a few hours of fishing on Crater Lake. "Why don't you come along?"

"I've got plans for this afternoon," Jason said. They exchanged pleasantries and the conversation ended. He watched Morehouse head east down Highway 46.

CHAPTER 15

Wednesday morning came, and Sheryl, who still felt awkward writing about serious crime, skimmed over a folder of articles from the newspaper morgue. The newsroom was in a state of tension, with reporters jumping at computers and answering telephones on deadline. Sheryl was looking for a new angle on the unexplained death.

She checked a schedule pinned to the newsroom bulletin board to see if a press conference had been set for the afternoon. Nothing was scheduled.

As she turned away, Sheryl's eyes met the gaze of Merteau's. He was walking down the middle aisle between rows of reporter's desks. Sheryl returned to her messy tabletop desk and sat in front of her computer screen.

When she began her career in print journalism, she had expected the city editor to be a different sort of person—surly, opinionated, dynamic. Instead, Merteau was diminutive and polite. Yet he had hauled in a major newsroom prize—the city editor job. Merteau, whose hazel eyes and pure-colored ties matched his clean dress suits, made a professional impression answering readers' questions on the phone and giving reporters directions at staff meetings. But his diffident confidence left aggressive reporters yearning to see more than just the subdued side of his personality.

To deflect a lengthy conversation that would interfere with deadlines, Merteau, in his typically abrupt manner, walked to Sheryl's desk with little fanfare and looked directly at her. "I have several sources you can call for a weekend story. They'll give you more information about the crimes. You've been turning in too much background material. I want the story for the front page of tomorrow's edition by ten o'clock tonight at the latest."

He handed Sheryl a sheet of lined paper listing names of news sources, and immediately walked back to his office, located just off the west end of the newsroom.

Merteau's unexpected visit left Sheryl worried. On the list, along with Weaver, was Jarvis Oliver, the city attorney, and Sandy Ryan, a private investigator.

Sheryl began typing on her computer keyboard. Her desk was cluttered with paperwork, mostly loose notebook pages, unopened press releases that had come in the mail and news photographs. She glanced around the office, listening to a group of reporters making small talk.

"Jason received a tip," she told Lori Phillips, a reporter. "He was subbing on the police desk during the Saturday night weekend shift. Through his general assignment reporting, he knows deputies in the sheriff's department. He got a message today on the phone, and drove to the sheriff's office to do a follow-up on it. Before he ran out of the newsroom, he muttered something about sheriff's officials releasing more information."

"They did that already, didn't they?" Phillips asked.

"Not exactly. They haven't provided a complete description of the case," Sheryl said. "They haven't found enough evidence...or put everything together. I don't know why. Maybe that's what Jason went to find out."

"Why didn't the sheriff's department phone with the information?" Phillips asked, with a beleaguered expression on his face. "Why didn't they schedule a press conference?"

"They don't want to lose Jason's business," joked another reporter, Luther Trask.

Sheryl chuckled at the quip. Silently, to herself, she pondered possible reasons why the sheriff's authorities didn't immediately release additional information over the phone.

Sheryl leaned across her desk. "I didn't ask Jason if he knew why a press conference wasn't scheduled. He charged out of the office right away, and I didn't have time."

"Maybe he'll find a story," Trask said. "If nothing else, he can get a decent cup of coffee. It's a good thing he doesn't have any kids. If he did, the trip to the cop shop would interfere with changing diapers."

"He probably won't get substantial information from the deputies other than what the sheriff reveals at a press conference," Phillips interjected.

Sheryl shifted her gaze to the computer.

She stopped scrutinizing the text on her screen, halted her copy editing work and placed a phone call. On a reporter's notepad, she jotted down notes from the news source. With a concerned look in her eyes, she hung up the receiver. Her fingers returned to the keyboard and she resumed her writing work.

A few minutes later, the phone rang again, and she picked it up. It was Jason, calling to confirm that sheriff's deputies had not located the missing boat. They found evidence that a struggle had taken place in the spot where Kirchner's body had been located. Jason's story would include a description of broken tree branches on the ground in the woods and information about loud screaming on Morehouse's videotape.

Sheriff's officials also had received reports of two other missing persons, Lester Jenkins and Vernon Stonehill. Both had a records of previous disappearances. Since Jason wasn't the regular crime reporter, he wanted to know how much time he had to turn in the story about the murder case.

Worried about the deadline, Sheryl looked at her watch impatiently. "Jason, are you all there? It's eleven-thirty in the morning. You have half an hour to drive back here and write the story." Sheryl hesitated. "I'm not very busy at the moment. Why don't you give me the story over the phone? I'll type it up for you and submit it to Merteau."

With the receiver squeezed between her ear and shoulder, she typed hurriedly on the keyboard. Ten minutes later, when she put the receiver back in the cradle, she seemed confused. The name, Stonehill, sounded familiar, and Sheryl vaguely remembered the stranger who had told the anecdotal story about Jenkins. The man in the pickup truck she and Jason had met near the highway Friday night had mentioned Jenkins, not Stonehill. Sheryl recalled fragments of the conversation—that something had happened to Jenkins, that the hull of his canoe had cracked on the Marengo River and he had been missing for three days.

Sheryl also remembered how weary she had been Saturday when Merteau had phoned about the sheriff's press conference...and that she thought she had heard voices...voices coming from outside her apartment window...and that she had stepped up to the windowsill and gazed at children and their parents in the park...and at her doll in the bedroom.

Standing behind Sheryl, Merteau tapped her lightly on the right shoulder. "What are you working on?" he asked.

"Jason phoned in a story about the murder," she answered defensively. "Sheriff's deputies found more evidence—blood on the ground, footprints, broken branches, screaming on Morehouse's videotape. They told Jason about it and I took the story over the phone. I can put it in your file in ten minutes, in time for the deadline."

"Before you do that, I want you to phone Weaver back and double-check the facts. Who was screaming on the videotape? Whose footprints did they find? Are there any other leads or suspects? That type of thing."

Sheryl's eyes popped wider. "I won't have time for all of that," she protested. "The deadline is in fifteen minutes. What if Weaver's not in his office?"

Merteau flicked his wrist impatiently, glancing at his watch. "Weaver's probably in his office. If not, I have his home phone number. I'll go to my desk and get it for you. You must verify the information Jason gave you. Make sure Purnell is still the only suspect. There were other people near the crime scene…a truck driver. I don't remember his name. And Morehouse, the owner of the Bay View. What were they doing there? Put the story in my city file and we'll use it in today's edition. Then when Jason gets back, both of you can work on another story about the murder for tomorrow's paper. I'll look for today's story around noon."

"OK," she said meekly. Merteau walked back to his desk, and Sheryl phoned Weaver. He answered his phone. Sheryl explained briefly about the deadline rush and went through a checklist consisting of half a dozen questions. After Weaver responded to the questions, she returned to the computer and wrapped up the story. She sent it to Merteau's computer file at 12:10 p.m.

After checking it over, he placed it at the bottom of the front page.

Following an hour lunch break, Sheryl returned to the newsroom. She realized she hadn't included any part of the information about Vernon Stonehill or Jenkins in the article she worked on earlier. Someone, either she or Jason, would have to find an existing article about Stonehill in the newspaper's library. Or someone would have to phone the sheriff's department to request that a deputy get back to the newspaper with background material about Stonehill's disappearances.

As she strode past the open door to Merteau's unoccupied office, she noticed an internal sample edition of today's newspaper on Merteau's desktop. Drivers were loading today's edition into delivery vehicles on the loading dock. Readers wouldn't receive the newspaper for several hours.

She entered Merteau's empty office and read the headline over Jason's story at the bottom of the front page: "Sheriff's Officials Uneasy About Case". It described how deputies had gathered more evidence at the crime scene and how they were concerned about finding a plausible motive involving Purnell.

The story Jason had dictated to Sheryl over the phone began, "Despite the relaxed atmosphere in Centerville, sheriff's deputies were noticeably uneasy about not finding additional evidence in last Friday's apparent murder of Jean Kirchner.

"The twenty-year-old Milwaukee woman was believed to have been sailing down the Marengo River with her boyfriend, Trent Purnell, when her body was discovered by two local people early Saturday morning. Purnell was found unconscious near Kirchner, who apparently died from a severe blow to her head after being choked and thrown against a large boulder. Purnell, who told authorities she was killed by a stalker, was taken into custody by Clayton County sheriff's deputies."

The story mentioned that Morehouse's videotape failed to unravel the case. However, the audio portion of the tape picked up Kirchner screaming and loud snapping sounds from branches breaking. As she read further, Sheryl figured out the story was missing an explanation that spelled out the reasons Morehouse was taping in the forest at night. She remembered reading an article yesterday saying Morehouse recorded nature.

Authorities were checking up on Kirchner and Purnell, interviewing their friends and relatives. So far, they hadn't found information indicating why Purnell would have murdered his girlfriend. Neither Kirchner nor Purnell had a record. Deputies also didn't know why an unknown assailant would have been following the couple.

Jason's story made another point, a factor that had likely led deputies to think twice. Although authorities suspected Kirchner was killed by Purnell, whose blood had stained the brush in the forest? If there was blood loss from wounds to Kirchner's head and neck, were there finger prints?

Working on deadline made Sheryl's frazzled adrenaline flow. She and Jason had put the story together on the phone, and she had turned it in only ten minutes late. Merteau hadn't said anything about missing the deadline.

She reached one conclusion: The person who committed the murder might still be at large. She left Merteau's office and went back to her own desk.

Jason marched into the newsroom with a sense of importance. He muttered a greeting to Sheryl and sat down. Jason started his idle computer and browsed through his files. With the screen glowing, he found a column he had been in the process of writing. He began working on it. He moused up and down the text on the screen until he found a spot to add information.

"When I finish my feature column, I want you to call it "A Reporter's Day" and insert my mug shot into the text," Jason said.

"What? Have you freaked out? You don't write a column," Sheryl said.

"I won't be deterred by complaints or ridicule," Jason said. "After today's front page story, I deserve to be promoted to columnist," he said, apparently joking.

Feeling the early stages of a tension headache, Sheryl put her right hand over her temples. She considered the questions the story hadn't answered.

"Since you're so smart, who committed the murder?" she asked Jason.

"Lester Jenkins," Jason replied snidely. "Jenkins was mad because he was alone and out of money. When he saw a victim in the forest, he attacked her. He had nothing better to do."

"Jason! I don't think that's funny. You shouldn't be flippant about a serious matter."

In bad taste, Jason continued. "I'm not supposed to crack jokes about serious matters in newspapers, especially at the Centerville Observer. Maybe you're right. This place is too good for snide remarks."

"Jason, I think we've both been working too much," Sheryl said. She paused. "Part of the story I took from you over the phone didn't make sense. If authorities suspect Purnell, why wasn't there blood on his hands?"

"I told you. Jenkins did it, and ran away." Jason continued. "Like a creep, he hid in the shadows."

"How did Jenkins know Kirchner was lost in the woods?" Humoring Jason, Sheryl tried to show sarcasm. "How did Outer Space Jenkins know there was a human on his planet?"

"He just knew," Jason pleaded. "It's like in Bigfoot books. That's his forest. He senses when his enemies encroach on his territory. He guards the woods and thinks he owns the land. It's like old-time Mafia families. Even though they claim they went legitimate, they left spies and guards behind. They tell the don who controls the territory about intruders."

"Why didn't you tell me that the other night when we were in the forest at the scenic overlook?" Sheryl asked.

"I didn't think of that," Jason admitted. "Like other people, I assumed it was safe. The odds of being victimized by crime out there are low."

"Jason! We could have been attacked and possibly killed," Sheryl responded.

"I guess I didn't think of that," Jason said. "I was concentrating on the big picture. I guess we should ask the deputies if anything was stolen from the victim. They've indicated the possibility of alcohol abuse. When we have time, we can get more background information. The deputies still haven't found the rental boat."

"Jason, I think what you meant is that newspapers have come a long way since covering gangland shootings from rolled-down car windows in city streets."

"Yea, there is some truth in that, but there is also room for disagreement," Jason said. "If Purnell murdered Kirchner, machismo was still an issue. On a psychological level, whether he knew it or not, the killer was showing his physical superiority over the victim. He was like a gangster from the 1930s."

"That might reflect bad judgment—to include in a newspaper story opinionated interpretation that claims the murder case reminds you of mobsters, brute strength, physical superiority and Bigfoot," Sheryl said.

"You're right," Jason said, a touch of resentment in his voice. "We're not supposed to be giving opinionated lectures in a newspaper story."

"Unless you really think you're a columnist, Jason. I know you were only kidding," Sheryl said. "If you mention something like that to Merteau, he'll take you seriously."

Considering this, Sheryl stopped talking. Sheryl observed Jason's mannerisms, trying to anticipate his reactions. He was writing at the keyboard on his desk. She hadn't been working in the newsroom for a long time. She often wondered how much stress spilled over into their personal lives. She decided to ignore Jason's weird remarks, and his proposed column, and work on the story about the Kirchner death.

"When we get the chance, we must put together a feature story about the community's reaction to the death. For a while, at least, that might replace your column idea."

"OK," Jason said. "I won't mention anything about broad crime angles, unless the sheriff's department finds evidence to support that line of reasoning. We can describe it as a standard murder investigation, possibly even an isolated death, unconnected to other cases."

"We'll find out," Sheryl responded.

Jason sensed Sheryl sizing him up. Their reporting work provided an emotional bond between them despite the frustrations of working together.

"I must be on my way," Sheryl said. "I'm going to cover Purnell's hearing."

As she left, Jason looked at her and smiled, but felt a pang of tension.

Sheryl had gone back to her apartment. Jason sat in the newsroom, with only a handful of staffers. He had stretched his legs lengthwise under the desk, working on his computer, but came alert when he heard the phone ring.

From time to time, Jason had received prank pornographic phone calls. The anonymous callers breathed heavily into the phone and made weird sexual statements.

These callers did not state opinions about anything except sex. They did not describe themselves other than in references to their private parts and romantic matters. They simply mentioned sex quickly, and then they hung up.

Jason picked up the receiver, expecting news. Instead, he heard a sensuous woman's voice. She said, "Young men, attorneys, factory workers, farmers, college professors, doctors, even old men stand in line for me."

As far as Jason knew, the caller, if it was a conventional caller, was anonymous. The voice sounded mechanical, leading Jason to believe it was a tape. "They're astonished," the caller on the tape said. "They can't wait to come to me."

There was a pause, and the woman laughed. "Men of all ages—they can't wait to fire their lasers and save the planet."

"It sounds like you've been reading the Observer. Is this some kind of a joke?" Jason asked earnestly.

It turned out to be a tape, and Jason's question was ignored.

"Try me at your convenience. You can join the Space Sex Challenger Club, and become a player in Space Sex Challenger, an interactive fantasy game for adults, at my web site. I'm easy to win over."

Jason became indignant. "I don't like prank calls. What do you want?"

All Jason heard was, "Marsden". It sounded garbled, as if it was a tape that had malfunctioned. Then there was a click on the phone line followed by the dial tone. Jason didn't know what Marsden meant, whether it was the name of a company or a web site. Or a person.

It was the first sex call Jason had received in the newsroom. Jason realized sex calls ran in cycles. There had been a flurry of them last fall, about six in all, yet the calls were made to his home. Then they had stopped until the springtime, when Jason received another half dozen.

Jason had filled out a complaint form and mailed it to the telephone company. He believed the calls had come from another reporter at the Observer who was nervous about his work abilities. He didn't know exactly who it was. Now he had received another one, contradicting his theory that they came from a newsroom source.

CHAPTER 16

The dawn sunrise was beckoning, and realizing she couldn't sleep as late as planned, Sheryl flipped on her reading light on the night table. She groped the contents of the drawer, feeling several books. She pulled out a hardcover with a grainy texture, her *Bible*. She opened at the bookmark to the section she had been reading about the three wise men. In the literary realm, the *Bible* is considered a classic. She read the passage about how a prophet had told the chief priests and scribes to search Bethlehem, in the land of Juda, for a ruler of the people of Isreal.

She flipped through more pages, until she came to Isaiah 40:3. She read, *"Prepare ye the way of the Lord, make straight in the desert a highway for our God."*

Contemplating the passage, she climbed out of bed and stared blankly at the backyard through the window. There were two oak trees in the yard, and tangerine sunlight was streaming in columns between the low-hanging branches. She had been too impatient to just lie in bed, and too fatigued to concentrate on her reading. She cast a vacant stare out the window, gazing at the back yard and the rising sun.

She was uncertain about whether the Marsden note or her unusual conversation with Jason in the newsroom yesterday had caused her uneasiness. She considered the murder story she and Jason were covering. Was it a coincidence that a death had taken place near the overlook Friday night?

They had been sitting in Jason's car. Maybe Jason had been right—that the forest was usually safe and the suspected homicide was a tragic aberration. Somehow it had crossed her mind to warn Jason that it wasn't always safe out at night. Her judgment had proven to be correct.

She plucked a romance novel out of the drawer. Her face was drawn and tired-looking. Her musings drifted to the early-morning hubbub on Regents Avenue, where the traffic was in slow motion. As she began reading faster, her mood brightened.

Like a person under the influence of a hypnotist, she laid her head back on her pillow and fell into a waking dream. In the isolation of the forest, she saw the woman, Kirchner, running, her clothing caught in the dense brush, with Marsden in pursuit. She had never knowingly met Marsden, and did not recognize his face. When she perked up, she was left feeling confused. Like the residue of lightening following a thunderstorm, the tendrils of the troubling dream faded away.

Sheryl had drifted off at four o'clock in the morning and woke up again in earnest several hours later. After going to sleep, her slumber had been punctured by dreams about the forest and visions about talking to Jason in the newsroom. She went down the circular stairway to the kitchen. She began fixing coffee and assembled the ingredients for a strawberry waffle. After slicing fresh strawberries and tossing them into the batter, she tossed the mixture into her waffle iron.

Sheryl sat at her kitchen table, sipping steaming Jamaican coffee, which was more than enough to keep her going. Sheryl peered through the kitchen window, staring at the frozen-looking summer landscape. The hard-packed rows of grass highlighted the clear blue sky. She saw animal tracks, probably from a deer, and even though it was summer, visualized a magical Christmas reindeer tugging a sleigh through the pitch-black night. The wind rattled the window.

When the buzzer sounded, she rose from the table, smothered her waffle with butter and syrup, and returned to her seat. It was too early to think straight, and there was something claustrophobic about the summer greenery. She contemplated small animals, such as raccoons, that traveled through the yard at night. Storms were becoming a weather phenomenon that was changing with global warming. But the morning coldness was still there.

Even though it was early, she flipped out her cell phone and punched in Jason's number. After all, he was her boyfriend. It was one of those days where Sheryl felt like getting out of her apartment if she could talk to Jason first. Instinctively, she sensed Jason's laugh and his voice on the other end. Jason gave her some encouragement about her writing work.

Jason had been thinking about going to Waldwick Saturday to visit a friend of his. "You've got a better chance at the newspaper, if you stick around Saturday, Jason," she said.

She didn't like monopolizing Jason, but she reminded him, "You'll get a better handle on the case if you stick with the facts."

"If I hang around, I could work on my computer, then drop in at your place," he said.

"OK. We should go over notes. I'll clean my apartment up and make it feel like a home."

Listening to Jason babble about his work, Sheryl felt a warm feeling come over her. It went through her mind how Jason had become more responsible since college, and how her advice had helped him. Looking at the serene park outside her window, and thinking of the countryside around Jason's parents' home, where he still resided. She couldn't really imagine not trusting Jason, and it was probably just a matter of time before both were certain about their future together.

"Don't ever let go of the story," she reminded him, gazing at the all the books and office materials, such as staplers and notepads, in her apartment. Peace and quiet? She likely had more peace and quiet with Jason's arms around her.

Jason had complained in college he resented Sheryl dating anyone else.

Jason mentioned vacant land and homes for sale along Highway 46 on the way to Waldwick, admitting that was part of the reason he wanted to take a spin to Waldwick.

He kept several changes of clothes at Sheryl's apartment, and Jason's parents were friendly to the young couple. "We're going to have to take a serious look at homes for sale," he said. "It's just a matter of time before I...we...can come up with the down payment."

They had been saving money, and though they didn't spell out their plans, that was why. Neither were economists, but it had been rumored for six months the staff would get a raise soon. The management had purchased four weeklies last month, adding to the company's chain. The Observer, competing with larger urban media outlets due to an influx of new residents, was scheduled to expand the Lifestyles and Entertainment sections, and add another education reporter to the staff.

In an old-fashioned manner, Jason had lived at home, with his parents, and Sheryl had her own apartment. Jason had been bringing up the subject of their own house, and when the opportunity presented itself, they would settle on a place.

Sheryl pushed her cup aside, and told Jason to come over this evening for dinner. He agreed to stop in after work and to forget about Waldwick on the weekend.

"Money is power," Jason philosophized. "I've been so busy writing and stopping over at your place. I haven't gone shopping much. I've drained your grocery budget. I'll feel like a jerk if I don't bring groceries, especially champaign and flowers."

The park next door led into the Waubeka National Forest, and likewise, Sheryl realized her relationship with Jason was becoming permanent. Next spring they could move into their own house.

"Shall we look at a few places?"

"Two weeks from now we'll both have the weekend off. We can look around then."

"That's great."

"I plan to work on a few stories today. Jason, when you go shopping, pick up a few lined notepads."

"Sure. As your resident knight in shining armor, I'll be more than happy to pick up supplies. I need to buy an adaptor plug for my computer, anyway."

Sheryl continued, "I had trouble sleeping. I was worrying about the threatening note. I don't understand it. Since it wasn't handwritten, if the sheriff's department takes it seriously, they'd want to check it for finger prints."

"So that's what's bothering you."

"Yes."

"The screwball who wrote it was trying to scare us," Jason said. "I'll meet you for dinner."

Sheryl hung up.

Scarcely was Jason's voice off the phone, when Sheryl began checking the kitchen pantry for preparations. She pulled out the ingredients for meat loaf in onions and sauteed spinach and carrots. Later, she would leave the news office around lunchtime, start preparing dinner, and return to work with meatloaf baking in the oven.

Before leaving for work, she flipped on her computer, connected to the internet and looked up the newspaper's crime briefs. Three boys playing outdoors on a farm were viciously attacked by a pack of dogs. One, a fourteen-year-old boy, died in a pool of blood in the farmyard. The two other boys, a ten-year-old and a twelve-year-old, were taken on ambulance stretchers to the hospital emergency room, where the media was waiting for further reports. Another brief described a fifteen-year-old teenager who gave birth in a high school bathroom. There was additional news, including a light feature story about a small-town man who collected hundreds of stamps over fifty years. In another story, amid taxpayer objections about spending, the city council was debating additional budget reductions. The community received a forestry award.

Sheryl walked across the living room and stood beside the window. A drift of leaves covered the path to the mailbox. She speculated over the birds nodding on the tree branches and listened to them chirping. She wondered what birds would do without their wings, with just a pair of scrawny legs to support their meager weight. She shifted her gaze to the patio and spotted more animal tracks, likely caused by a raccoon. She gently slid her hand down the windowpane and felt the pulse of the wilderness.

She had taken pride in the orderly world she had created for herself. Jason's matter-of-fact demeanor added to her sense of uncertainty about the chaotic nature of news reporting work.

When she was a little girl, she had dreamed of one day becoming a ballerina, of performing on stage. When she had first met Jason at the college union, he had encouraged her to join the staff of the campus newspaper. At first the newspaper work frightened the hell out of her. She was self-conscious about everything—speaking up at end-of-the-week news meetings, asking the city editor for serious reporting work, exposing her writing in public, trying to compete with reporters who had firm news contacts. Within a year, she had put together a credible biweekly column about student government, and suspected she had a promising future in the print news media.

She recalled when she had started at the Observer, she had tramped around Centerville with a sloppy loose-leaf notebook and had lost film in the messy front seat of her automobile. When she was on the run, she drank soda and ate potato chips for lunch in her used automobile. There were fast-food wrappers strewn around the inside of her car. She had found out that even at a newspaper, a polished professional image mattered in tracking down breaking news stories. She got in the habit of talking to Jason in the newsroom and joining him for lunch at Roscoe's, a trendy restaurant where she could find leads for behind-the-scenes feature stories.

Her relationship with Jason was like a flower blossoming. He introduced her to friends and relatives, and she gradually became a fixture in Centerville's hard-to-crack social structure. Her list of news contacts, from police officers to local politicians, had increased. She broke the story about the Centerville mayor's anticipated divorce after years of marital strife and alcohol problems. She also made the front page with an extensive series about Centerville's business expansion, including the Bay View.

Sometimes Sheryl helped out in the newsroom, writing headlines on election night and putting together popular special editions that profiled dozens of local candidates. Dashing around the newsroom, sorting through piles of stories and photographs, having to work so close to the editors and drinking an occasional cup of coffee made reporters like Sheryl nervous. In fact, when she returned to her apartment after work, it took her awhile to settle down. She ended up living like a news junkie, sorting through news magazines and surfing cable television channels. She had mixed feelings about her occupation. She liked the adrenaline rush, but she also worried about the future of her career and her social life.

Jason's good humor had erased the narrow lines of worry that might have consumed Sheryl. His spontaneity and her command of factual information removed some of the unknowns. If their work schedules matched, after wrapping things up, they would meet in the springtime at a pier offering a panoramic view of the Marengo River and hold long conversations into the evening.

Sheryl was ready for a shower, and she tore her bed clothes off. A pink plastic shower curtain was hanging from the silver overhead crossbar. Blue wallpaper with multicolored flower bouquets, which were framed in white squares, stretched across the room. The shower stall was tiled in white, and the wall mirror was positioned on the west side next to the door.

As she walked into the shower stall, her eyes were fixed on the gleaming faucet handle, but her mind was elsewhere—analyzing her work at the newspaper.

One thing Sheryl could count on, however, was keeping her body clean. So even though she couldn't get a grip on the murder case, she intended to maintain her hygiene by taking a shower. Sheryl stopped thinking and flipped the handle to the "hot" setting. Warm droplets of faucet water cascaded down her scalp, face, chest, waist, legs and feet. The prosaic newspaper world, haunted by crime, had been kind to her. She had few reasons to expect trouble of any sort, other than Jason showing up late for dinner.

As the rising steam in the shower opened her blood capillaries, she became relaxed. The atmosphere in the shower stall was suffocating as she writhed and undulated under the spray of hot water. She looked down the towel rail at the line of towels, the frosted glass of the bathroom windows, the amber-shaded ceiling light and the humid steam floating upward.

She stepped out of the humid stall, dried herself off and returned to her bedroom. While getting dressed, she sprayed "Flower Petal" perfume on her neck.

Alone in her bedroom, Sheryl stared at her reflection in the dresser mirror. In childhood, she assumed love would be easy to find, like her high grades and scholastic accomplishments. In college, viewing her appearance as plain, despite Jason's compliments about her looks, she had succumbed to her desire to find a serious relationship. She had found someone with whom she was compatible, and hoped she had chosen wisely.

The shrill chirping of birds could be heard coming from the dim corners of her yard, and robins and their friends were flying up hilly, tree-studded streets such as Delaware Avenue. The restless oak and willow trees in the yard behind her apartment complex had sprawled considerably over a period of years, with the tangles of leafy branches reaching the building's roof and the black asphalt entrance drive.

Summer was a wonderful time to lighten up and try new outdoor activities. Typically, Centerville experienced moderate temperatures and sunny skies. A year ago, there had been heat waves in July and August, with temperatures reaching ninety-six degrees and the town taking on the atmosphere of an Egyptian desert.

Undoubtedly, Jason had not been ridiculing her in the newsroom yesterday, Sheryl believed. That didn't sound like the sweet, good-natured Jason she had known for years. He had been on edge, become insensitive. Parts of her collective memory were bottomless pits, and she tossed Jason's unusual remarks down them, figuring he was stressed out.

The day passed, with Sheryl returning to her apartment a couple times to check on dinner.

Shery realized it would be foolish to ever give up easily on Jason. Idle reservations crossed her mind, none that were serious. It would be a matter of time before they had enough money to buy their own place. Jason loved her, though he he hadn't outwardly spoken the words. He needed more encouragement.

After dinner, Jason took her hand in his. "During the past five years together, we've gotten our feet on the ground."

In college, low on cash, they had only had each other. They didn't know they would end up in Centerville. She remembered Jason trembling after a lecture class, wanting to get outdoors.

Sheryl's parents had never fully understood her devotion to Jason. Why did she want a boyfriend in the same unpredictable occupation? Inexperienced journalists didn't necessarily have established careers. Why didn't they develop the wherewithal to get married and buy their own home? her parents wanted to know.

Wouldn't Sheryl be better off returning to college to study for a master's degree or law school? She had gotten straight A's a few times in high school and elementary school. For a moment, she was afraid, recalling how she had chosen to stay in Centerville, to trust Jason and his friends, and to turn down the career potential that a post-graduate degree offered.

Leave the Observer and Jason? His B grade-point average hadn't been high enough to qualify for graduate school. Right or wrong, Sheryl had decided to keep her present job and her boyfriend.

It was a lucky break, a very lucky break, that Jason had been hired at the Observer. When Jason had moved to Centerville, back to his parents' home, she and Jason had reunited. Neither had seriously dated anyone else. And here they were, spending all of their time together.

Early in both of their careers, each lacked the staying power of an experienced editor. But they had energy and drive, plus a foot in the door. The each drank a glass of champagne, and Sheryl wrapped up cleaning off the dinner table.

Later in the evening, they watched a movie on TV, *The Tommyknockers*, about a disgruntled writer who confronts evil. Then they slid into bed. "Tomorrow morning you can use the shower first," Sheryl told Jason.

She exchanged a decidedly sexual glance with Jason. She felt the joy of Jason's embrace and of lying naked with him. He rubbed his hands over her warm breasts, probing her lips with his tongue. Jason brushed his legs between Sheryl's thighs.

Jason's eyes searched hers, and the worries cleared out of her mind. He buried his face in her neck and the loose strands of her clean hair. His controlled thrusts and her wet acceptance created more than enough excitement for both. Jason felt his surge of power penetrate Sheryl's warm flesh, her orgasm receiving his like a vessel. When they were finished, Jason moved to his side of the bed, and they fell asleep.

CHAPTER 17

"Let's catch lots of fish," Doug said, sitting behind the wheel of the fishing boat he had rented.

Kevin stretched his legs. He was enjoying his vacation, but he remembered his home. His mother had decided to hang around the house.

Justin quipped, "Just think, Kevin. If you had stayed home, you would be experiencing the thrill of feeding your goldfish, not to mention playing softball."

As the boat moved farther and farther from the shoreline, and from Captain Moore's, Kevin became less concerned about his routine life around the house. The mild lake breeze tossed the boat gently on the waves.

Justin, Weaver's son, and Kevin sat on a passenger bench along the gunwale. Kevin knew Justin from when he had been a resident of Centerville, and had invited he and his father to go fishing with Doug and Morehouse. In the headwind, Kevin's bangs flopped onto his eyebrows and over his ears. When the throttle was turned up, and the boat sped through the water, he smelled the gasoline stench coming from the fuel tank.

Justin, who was wearing navy blue shorts and a white cotton sport shirt, cleared his throat. He said, "Since were on Crater Lake, do I get a prize for spotting a chunk of meteor, or for catching an alien, rather than a fish?"

"Don't be silly," Doug replied, his voice rising. He couldn't determine if Justin was trying to be funny. "Nobody will believe there's an alien around here unless you bring back evidence. You won't find a meteor in the lake."

"OK," said Justin, his brown hair blowing across his forehead. "I guess you don't think we'll find a space suit hanging on a tree branch. What if there are alien bodies cryogenically frozen in the icy water at the bottom of the lake? They could rise to the surface and pull down victims like the monster in "Creature from the Black Lagoon".

Morehouse answered, "The next time we come out here, we can buy laser guns at Sears. Or I can bring my camcorder. As far as I know, trout, bass, perch thrive in the lake. The fish are truly amazing."

From the boat, scraggly trees dotting the landscape and antenna dishes on rooftops looked like they were rolling by in slow motion. A freight train crossed a harbor bridge. There were dozens of boats in the harbor, and along the nearby shoreline were clumps of trees, open farm pastures, a golf course and tennis courts.

The boat, named the Sharkey, was equipped with an electrical fuse box and voltage regulator, heater, automatic window washers, mounted binoculars, and a small galley with perishable food.

As waves scraped against the hull, Doug steered from the helm station in the front captain's cabin. Even though Morehouse had his own boat docked at the Bay View, Doug had rented this one from Captain Moore's.

While Doug maneuvered the boat between navigation markers in the channel leading out of the bay, the others felt the vibration from the propeller shafts underneath them. Perhaps it was only natural, but Kevin and Justin worried about the boat sinking and cracked jokes about it.

Although Weaver was enjoying the outing, he still felt a sense of unfinished business dogging him. Since he'd worked the Sunday night shift, he was off on Wednesday afternoon. Holding their rods, they chatted idly.

"What made you decide to go into law enforcement, sheriff?" Morehouse asked innocently.

"It's funny you've never asked before," Weaver said. "I joined the sheriff's department over twenty years ago. I had to support my family. I was able to make a contribution to a lower crime rate. After a trial period as a deputy, I decided to stay on with the department. I didn't know I would become a candidate for sheriff."

Morehouse had the feeling that during his time as a deputy, Weaver must have demonstrated leadership.

"I wanted to preserve order and decency in society," Weaver said. "I was given the honor of serving as sheriff."

Characteristically calm, he tilted his fishing cap and wiped the sweat off his forehead. "Criminals find ways to prey upon the innocent. They play off the victim's weaknesses."

Weaver had been raised by decent, upright parents who valued justice and order. "My father was a deputy in Washington County. He never made sheriff. I'm the first one in our family. My brother's down in New Orleans. He works as a private detective.

"It took me awhile to develop the patience to sit in the sheriff's office. When I was a young deputy, I wanted to get out into the community."

Kevin interrupted, "Ever have trouble with unbelievers?"

"What do your mean?"

"You know. With criminals who don't believe you're for real."

"I try to get them behind bars—with the facts, with solid evidence, especially in the courtroom. Footprints, guns, eyewitnesses. The sheriff's department tries to convey that crime doesn't pay."

"So far, I haven' seen anything…real suspicious," Kevin related.

"Good, Kevin," Weaver said. "If I'm not able to prevent most types of crime, or at least take action and find the perp, successfully prosecute him and put him behind bars, where he belongs, then I'm not doing my job."

Morehouse interjected, "Sounds like cop work is pretty rough, eh boys?"

"A sheriff is like anyone else," Weaver said. "I think all of us like getting away from it all."

"Out here, you can be one with the universe," Morehouse added.

Doug jumped in with a question. "How about you, Ray, how's the Bay View holding up?"

"We get our fair share of tourists," he said. "It won' be long before the lake's filled with cyberbookers."

Kevin looked at Doug. "Say, dad."

"Yes."

"You did it again. You forgot to bring your electric shaver."

"Don't worry about it," Morehouse advised. "Crater Lake belongs to the customer. I've got plastic blades and shavers at the main desk. We've even got remote-control lanterns. At some point, I'll figure out how to get a remote on your shaver."

"Good. What comes next?"

Morehouse answered, "Time to pay our respects to the fish—trout, perch, bullheads."

"What kind do you prefer?" Weaver asked.

Morehouse leaned sideways, a sneaky look on his face. "Don't tell anybody this. I like shrimp sauteed with fresh vegetables and sliced almonds."

"I meant around here."

"You can't beat the fresh trout."

"We better get going," Doug said, accidentally bumping his toe into the side of the motorboat. "Kevin and Justin have to learn about handling fishing rods."

Awhile later, they were listening to talk about fishing.

Kevin kept his eyes on the minor turbulence in the water, the lake winds caressing his face. An unexplainedly morbid image flashed through his mind. It was a sunken vessel sitting on the lakebed. Laying on the deck of the indistinct boat was the body of a dead man.

"I don't see you setting up your fishing gear," Doug interrupted. "You don't look happy, like something's bothering you. What's the matter?" he asked innocently.

Kevin responded reflexively. "I was thinking about the boat sinking—and us drowning. There have been people who have died on the lake. There might be a dead body down there," he ventured.

"We'll be all right," Doug answered defensively.

"When was the last drowning?" Kevin persisted, a disturbed expression on his face.

"Last summer," Weaver answered. "Ralph Barriasco was in his speedboat and it flipped upside down. A rescue attempt was made. It was too late. He got caught in rough water. He drowned, and his body was retrieved from the lake."

Doug wheeled around on the deck. "That was a freak occurrence. That doesn't happen very often. Don't worry about it. As far as I'm concerned, the lake is off-limits when there is strong wind and rain."

After Doug guided the Sharkey into the eastern portion of the lake, and Morehouse found a good fishing spot, the five cast their baited hooks into the water. Justin could see a few groups of sunbathers scattered along the dry ivory sand on the beach.

A fish tugged on Morehouse's line. Morehouse reeled in a long trout, with its tiny gills opening and closing. Against the strength of the lure, it foundered for a few minutes before starting to give up. The ferocious trout splattered lake water noxiously in the pit of the boat before it died and was tossed into a pail of water.

"Ooooo," Doug said. "Look at that."

"Great catch," Weaver said.

Morehouse, Weaver, Doug, Kevin and Justin spoke to each other for a few moments. Kevin handled the task of cleaning the boat of slimy fish water. The boat tilted this way and that, foamy mist spraying over the side. The additional fish they caught were wrapped in foils and stored in Styrofoam ice chests with other provisions.

In the steady current, the boat jerked up abruptly in the stuttering waves and fell softly down the crest of each one. Doug stood up on his feet, and while he dusted his cotton pants, he gazed at the open water.

As they occasionally drifted closer to shore, the whitecaps gave way to small rolling mounds that were easy for swimming. Morehouse's black hair looked stringy, like spaghetti noodles, in the breeze.

After two hours in the boat, the shoreline changed gradually from the appearance of a faraway, slender shadow, to the sight of lake homes and oak trees coming into focus. Massive stones were embedded in the barren foothills in between lake properties, shoreline buildings and wilderness.

"If my memory serves me correctly, you thought we would fare better than a catch of only three fish," Doug said.

As one of the smooth, dead fish floated harmlessly in the pail, its wide, cracked, unmoving mouth resembled a sick smile. Its gills were frozen in place. Kevin noticed the creature's tiny marble eyes.

"Isn't it cruel to destroy fish?" Kevin asked Doug. He studied the tender meat on its fragile bones and the faint colors on its scaly epidermis.

"Most people don't think it is," Doug said, irritated. "It leaves room for other fish, and other fishermen have them available all around the planet."

"You have to be optimistic," Morehouse said. "The stinking fish would eat you, if it could."

"Wouldn't it be better to let them go on forever?" Kevin insisted.

"That's impossible. And you know better than that," Doug growled. "Folks like us have to use them for food."

"Doesn't a fish experience a lot of pain with a hook jammed into its mouth?" Kevin asked. "Like going to the dentist," he said, shivering in the cold breeze.

Doug looked impatient. "They don't have well-developed brains," his father said. "They don't feel pain as much as people do. Dinosaurs could have ruled the entire planet if the ice age hadn't stopped them. The human race had to fight off predators such as dinosaurs, lions and tigers, even sharks and other fish."

"I wouldn't want trout running the planet," Justin said.

Kevin gazed at the terrain behind the lake. He saw the cave where he and his friends had pretended they were pirates.

"We haven't disturbed the ecosystem," Morehouse cut in.

"Forget about the fish," Justin advised. "At this point, they need to be cleaned."

"The trout should taste delicious," Weaver said. "Thank God, it's safe to fish."

Kevin saw the pattern within the pattern. None of them had taken out aggression on the fish, as a criminal does. Weaver and the others had gotten some time away from worrying about another murder.

Still, the woods on the distant shoreline reminded Kevin of a remote island, where 18th century pirates were left stranded when they were caught stealing. In the centuries of the pirates, the chalky island beach competed with the gloom of the castle dungeon, as far as pirates' hostages were concerned.

Kevin's eighth-grade teacher, Mrs. Jill Compton, had given him a talk once about how he was not always disciplined. He had faced obstacles concentrating on schoolwork, and she chastised him for a snowball fight in which he lost his temper.

Last winter, he had sat on top of Spike and pinned him down in a cold snowdrift. He had washed Spike's face with snow, until it turned as crimson as the January sunset.

Spike had lost his temper. "Are you on drugs? What in the world is wrong with you?" he had asked.

Kevin realized he had gotten carried away. He tried to remember what the teacher had said about not being patient and controlling his anger. To retaliate, Spike had thrown him onto his back in the snow, and, shaking with fear, he had apologized to Spike.

Spike had still fumed. "I'm getting away from here," he had said. "I'm not afraid of you. As far as I'm concerned, you can freeze in the snow like an ice statue and get frostbite."

Back in the warmth of the classroom, Spike told Mrs. Compton what had happened. She kept Kevin after school, launched into a speech about his bad behavior and telephoned his parents. After Kevin had gotten home, his father asked him why he had given Spike a face-washing.

"I don't know," he had told Doug.

"Yes, you do," his father had said.

This had made Kevin think some more. "I wasn't very careful and got out of control. We were playing. I was jealous because Spike got an A minus on today's math test and I got a C minus. I threw some snow in his face. I won't do it again."

"Why don't we get away from here?" Doug had said. "That was inconsiderate to throw snow in Spike's face. You've apologized to him. I plan to go fishing on Crater Lake this summer and visit a friend of mine from Centerville, Ray Morehouse. I want you to get permission from your mother to go along. We'll go out on our fishing boat in July and you can bring your old friend from Centerville, Justin, along."

"No problem," Kevin had said.

"You and Justin used to get along with each other most of the time. This will give me some hope for you," Doug had said.

Kevin had defended himself, telling Doug he wasn't as bad as some kids.

"I don't think you are. You better not get into trouble again," Doug had said.

Kevin recalled this incident leading up to the fishing trip. Now that they were actually spending the day on the lake, there were a number of matters he had concerns about. Again, he bothered Doug by asking him another question—whether fish and birds are afraid of people?

"We keep them in the freezer, cook them and serve them on plates," Doug said. "Birds are smart enough to stay away from us unless we feed them bread crumbs. They know we're the enemies, and that we might hurt them."

Justin interjected, "Fish miss their relatives."

Doug looked perplexed. "I don't think so. A fish has no idea what's happening to it."

Kevin and Justin watched Doug pick up some fishing gear. Kevin didn't entirely believe what Doug had said—that a fish didn't intrinsically know the difference between a lake and a pail, especially when it had a metal hook jammed into its throat. Why was the perch struggling so much if it didn't know it had a hook stuffed in its mouth?

Doug studied Kevin and Justin. "I'm not convinced fish such as perch are in danger, just yet. Whales are closer to extinction. There are enough perch are in the lake. They get in each other's way half the time. We can have perch for dinner tonight. The next time we go fishing, we can throw the fish back in the lake."

Doug placed his hands on Kevin's shoulders. "Come on. Let's get going."

Kevin, Justin, Morehouse and Weaver reeled in their fishing lines. Doug braced his legs, as he stood erect and walked to the stern. He started the motor and steered toward the shoreline. As the porcelain-green shoreline came into view, Kevin thought he saw the man near the lakebed, the current swirling above his boat.

Justin said, "Sixty-five million years ago, uncharacteristically, sheets of frozen snow and hard ice crept across the landscape, changing everything. Even the dinosaurs, if there were any in the neighborhood, didn't last."

Doug guided the boat through the glassy waters of the harbor to the dock. They disembarked and secured the Sharkey to the pier. Morehouse, who was in a hurry to go to Centerville, got off first and drove away. Weaver, Doug, Kevin and

Justin packed up their things, including their fish. Doug listened to the rusty metal poles shake as the three walked down the pier to his rental car in the parking lot.

CHAPTER 18

It was late afternoon when Morehouse left Captain Moore's Boat Rental and began driving down Highway 46. On a day off from work, Adrienne expected him to go to Centerville to shop for groceries and clothing.

An unexpectedly sharp turn on the highway brought Morehouse to attention. From behind the wheel, Morehouse looked over the verdant farmland and the Marengo River valley. The ribbon of highway continued to wind down the ridge. On Fridays, Highway 46 was typically clogged with tourists—fishermen hauling small water craft on car trailers, water skiers who had driven up from a big city and tourists looking for a motel, lake cabin or campsite.

Steel and concrete barn silos jutted above the lush, rolling hills, the traditional white farmhouses, and the sea of green landscape. Morehouse checked the gas gauge. The red needle indicated the tank was one-quarter full.

In the 1960s, the gravel shoulder of the highway held sporadic clusters of litter—soda cans, beer bottles, cigarette butts, and fast-food garbage, including white hamburger wrappers and Styrofoam coffee cups. By the 1990s, the level of debris had been reduced. Morehouse had occasionally contemplated what caused the lack of concern for road litter in the first place. He remembered the roadside pollution problem was rectified when fines were enforced, and tourists tossed less junk-food garbage out of the car window to flaunt the authorities. He wondered why workers ran out of time to pick up the litter, preferring, instead, to enforce the law with stiffer penalties. Despite his connection to gambling, Morehouse never viewed himself as a tough negotiator, and years went by before he realized that the government wasn't going to clean up the highway trash without making the public pay fines.

Morehouse drove on. It was a crisp, sunny day, but the meteorologist giving the radio forecast said it could change dramatically, and that a thunderstorm from the northeast was on the way.

Morehouse didn't see much traffic on the highway, and he wanted to return to the Bay View in time for dinner. As he pushed down on the gas peddle, hitting seventy-five miles per hour, a rear tire slipped on an uneven patch in the highway.

Morehouse was closing in on a tanker truck, which was transporting a cargo of liquid gasoline and struggling up a shadowy pine-covered ridge top. The steep incline accounted for a long stretch of the upcoming highway. If he waited too long to pass the massive, sixteen-wheel truck, it might end up right behind him a few minutes later going down the steep hill. This happened to Morehouse on rural highways: He would pass the truck too late, and the impulsive truck driver would blow right past him on the way down the hill. Once, a lumber truck barreling down a twisting curve was so close to his rear bumper that he pulled over onto the gravel shoulder. Better to be cautious, than to be run over by an angry truck driver, he had speculated at the time. Yet Balton, the sheriff's deputy, had disagreed, arguing it is a minor violation not to keep pace with the normal flow of traffic, a technicality the sheriff's department isn't able to enforce.

Morehouse recalled another occasion ten years ago when, after a night on the town in Waldwick, he had an unexplained panic attack. His heart was palpitating into his throat and his upper body was petrified. He had never previously suffered a panic attack, so he pulled over to calm down. Morehouse had failed to reach a gas station bathroom, and carelessly resolved the dilemma by taking a shit in his pants.

Suddenly a green pickup truck pulled up behind him. He hadn't seen it, and wondered where it came from, and was concerned about getting caught in traffic between the vehicle behind him and the slow-moving truck in front of him.

Morehouse began passing the sixteen-wheeler, and the pickup truck followed his Caprice. The pickup truck should have allowed Morehouse to complete the pass. Instead, it was tailgating him, and was so close, in fact, that, looking in his rearview mirror, he saw the shadowy figure of a man in the front windshield. A trouble-making tailgater, Morehouse thought, double-checking the narrow lane ahead to make sure there was no oncoming traffic.

He pressed his foot against the gas pedal, but it was too late. The pickup truck had moved alongside the rear of Morehouse's car. Morehouse picked up speed, but the pickup truck gained momentum, and the tanker was on the right, its horn blowing in the confusion. Morehouse felt like the Caprice was trapped in between the two vehicles.

The green pickup truck charged wildly at the Caprice. The Caprice accelerated, like it was racing through a red light in an intersection. The engine puffed, Morehouse jerked the steering wheel to the right, and the frame of the Caprice rocked and vibrated. Insanely, the pickup truck rammed the side of Morehouse's Caprice. With beads of sweat clouding his vision, he fumbled for the steering wheel and slammed his foot on the brakes. The pickup truck grazed the Caprice's front bumper, and both vehicles spun rapidly in circles. The Caprice almost became entangled in the wheels of the tanker truck. The truck had made it safely over the bridge. The driver tried to slow down and the tanker's brakes squealed.

The green pickup truck had disappeared at high speed down the highway.

Morehouse jammed his foot on the brake pedal and swung the steering wheel sharply to the right. The car churned up dusty pebbles as it careened out of control. A stab of pain cut through Morehouse's midsection.

He heard stiletto popping sounds similar to machine-gun fire. Through the haze of smoke puffing into the front seat from the engine compartment, he was able to see the door on the passenger's side. Inexplicably, it appeared to Morehouse as if it was riddled with dents and holes. While he scrutinized the door, the car left the ground, flipped over and landed upside-down on the exterior roof. He heard broken glass, plastic and metal fly past his head as the car tumbled. The undercarriage gleamed in the sunshine, and two passenger-side tires were punctured. The front axle was bent and cracked. Gaping holes pockmarked the windshield. The rearview mirror had snapped off the interior foam ceiling, and the starter key was missing from the ignition slot.

Morehouse had felt his body press against the dashboard during the crash. He opened his eyes momentarily, and black smoke swam across the windshield. He ran his hand across his sweaty forehead. He began gagging and his lungs were choked with smoke from the fire. The highway had vanished, and he was someplace else, presumably at the bottom of the embankment.

Morehouse's car had somehow traveled hundreds of feet from the roadway.

The headlights had been smashed into broken pieces, and the flames lingered. He raised his aching legs, slid from underneath the crushed steering wheel, and tried to open the driver's door, pounding his fist against the vinyl and glass. He yanked the door handle and nothing happened. He applied more pressure, but it was glued shut. He pounded against the glass window as if it was a cage.

As he tugged on the plastic handle, it flew off the melting door. The car was very hot, like an incinerator.

He groped frantically. He figured out where the plastic lock button was, and unlocked the door. The window was painted with clear, spidery cracks and glass cobwebs from the accident. He grabbed a chunk of hot metal from the damaged steering column and punched a hole in the window. With the piece of metal, he gouged through the glass. His hands burned like hell and he screamed.

Pieces of glass flew into the knee-high grass. He curled his hand through the broken window and opened the door using the exterior handle.

He spilled out into the grass, quickly rolling away from the burning, charred wreckage of the Caprice. His face was bathed in a purple light. It was coming from a barely visible place—like the aura of a faintly discernible light from a candle.

Morehouse crawled farther away, dragging himself from the burning wreck. Morehouse was slumped on the ground, breathing shallowly, when a wave of heat inundated the field with flecks of burning metal and melted paint, and dozens of particles of smoke and ash.

Following the deafening noise, the other sounds, birds cawing and chattering, were barely audible. Morehouse's eyes climbed up the embankment until they were at road level. His body was overcome with a sickening flood of weakness. There were cuts on his arms and legs. He spotted the familiar yellow ribbons on the asphalt highway. The field was as hot as a burning star in a distant galaxy. His aching joints felt as if they were disconnected. He watched the grey cloud of smoke hanging in the air, growing dimmer with the dying fire in the engine compartment.

The sixteen-wheel truck was stopped on the gravel shoulder a long distance down the highway. The Caprice was on the side of the road down the embankment in the ditch. There were greasy tire smudges on the highway, and an aroma of gas and oil that burned through the tall grass just beyond the embankment.

Morehouse heard the car radio playing music. Then there was another burst of smoke from the engine compartment. Morehouse drifted into unconsciousness for a few minutes. When he opened his eyes, his head was buzzing and his ears were ringing.

Patches of the asphalt road and field, sprayed with gasoline were burning like an incinerator. Morehouse tasted the blood seeping through his teeth and over his lower lip, trickling down his chin. During the impact of the car crash, his head had bounced off the dashboard.

Paralyzed with fear, Morehouse initially took little notice of the vision. Then the ghostly image of a stranger, Marsden, grasping a double-gauged shotgun, came into focus. "You were in my way," Marsden said mechanically, as if he was in a trance. Morehouse smelled traces of a deathly stench coming from Marsden's clothing, and noticed his ruddy, textured cheeks.

With foggy eyesight and mind-numbing pain reaching across the hollow of Morehouse's injured skull, he had not recognized Marsden. Crimson blood trickled onto the blades of tall field grass, and the exposed flesh of Morehouse's hand looked like raw meat. Morehouse screamed in agony.

Along Morehouse's line of sight, stood the sheriff's deputy. *I must be hallucinating,* Morehouse told himself. *The shadow standing there can't be Deputy Balton.* "Approaching armed suspect, medium height," Balton shouted across the field, as if he was yelling into a walkie-talkie. With a blank expression on his face, Balton raised his deputy sheriff's revolver. He blew a hole through Marsden's stomach, his bloody intestines slithering out like snakes.

A combination of blood and vomit gurgled from Marsden's open mouth. He collapsed, his unmoving body making a small corridor in the tall field grass. Barely conscious and looking through half-closed eyes, Morehouse glowered at Balton from the ground. Then he dropped into unconsciousness.

There was a smattering of motorboats, schooners, trawlers and fishing vessels near the shoreline at Captain Moore's Boat Rental. The beach house resembled a besieged fortress. White caps rolled into the mouth of the marina, and the tranquility of the morning had passed.

A plume of black smoke drifted over the shoreline from the Caprice's burning wreckage. The smoke from the flaming metal shell of the car was visible from the lake. From the parking lot, Kevin and Justin gazed in the direction of Highway 46, which was in the forest and not visible from Captain Moore's. They saw the white flash, which resembled a fireball, in between the trees. Kevin guessed something bad had happened.

"There's a fire over there," Kevin said, pointing west. "Did you see that, Dad?" he asked.

Doug studied Kevin and the woods. "No, I don't see anything," his father responded.

"I think there is a fire taking place over there," Kevin continued, pointing.

Doug finally spotted the trail of black smoke rising out of the forest. "We'll drive that direction on the way back to our hotel room," Doug said. "If we see anything, we'll contact the sheriff's department. The smoke might be coming from a farmer burning leaves."

But Kevin suspected they would discover something bad had taken place.

A half hour later, Morehouse and Weaver leaned forward as the paramedics placed the stretcher on the ground. Doug, Kevin, Justin and the truck driver, Al Kirst, watched intently from the lip of the highway.

Morehouse winced when the paramedics moved his limp frame off the ground. They carried him on the stretcher, walking up a small incline in the field and ascending the steeper embankment leading back to the ambulance. Morehouse's heartbeat slowed down when he heard the familiar rumbling noise of the idling engine. The paramedics loaded him into the back of the ambulance.

"I didn't think it would be unsafe on the highway," Morehouse muttered. The ambulance left the ridge top and disappeared down the long ribbon of highway leading to Memorial Hospital in Centerville.

CHAPTER 19

When Morehouse woke up confined in his hospital bed, he felt like a prisoner, his aching head propped up on pillows, the pain on his left side neutralized by morphine and his back tender against the stiff mattress. The gashes and bruises on his body rebelled against his nervous system.

A cloud of worries whirled through his mind. When he had been sleeping, he experienced a fragmented nightmare in which he was shouting, "Wake me up!" But when the dream ended and Morehouse found himself in the hospital bed, his anxiety level went down.

Memorial Hospital was on the northern end of the medical complex, which was dotted with asphalt paths. The main entrance in the half-circle access driveway led into the eight-story, brick-and-glass structure. But Morehouse had been wheeled into the emergency entrance in the rear of the building.

He squinted into the glare of light from the hallway. The door was partially open, and hushed sounds from TVs, hospital staff and visiting relatives floated into the room.

There were four abrupt knocks on the door. The white uniform of the nurse, Rachel Elow, came into view. She had stringy blond hair tied in a bun and a look of concern on her face. She quickly flipped a wall switch, and the fluorescent light over the bed came on. Morehouse jerked up, still confused about what had happened on the highway and hoping the hospital staff could take care of him.

"That was some car crash you went through. I'm your nurse, Rachel Elow. I want to start by checking your pulse." Morehouse squinted at the brown name tag on her uniform, but he couldn't read it because his vision was blurry.

"How are you doing?" she asked.

"I'm pretty banged up," he responded. While the nurse pushed his wrist out from underneath the bedspread, the terrifying memories of the man in the pickup truck filtered into his conscious thoughts. Elow held his wrist in her hand and glanced at her watch, taking his pulse.

"You'll appreciate this," she said. "Your pulse is going down, returning to normal."

Morehouse relaxed on the bed. "What happened?" he asked. Elow held the clipboard of medical charts against her hip and studied Morehouse's red-rimmed eyes. "Don't you remember? You were in a serious car wreck."

Morehouse stared at her and looked away, toward the wall. "I think a pickup truck pushed my car into a tanker."

"Both you and the truck driver survived," the nurse said, hesitating. "His name was Al Kirst. He told the sheriff's department about the green pickup."

"The truck driver, Kirst, witnessed the accident?"

"Yes. Your Caprice was totaled," Elow continued. "You've been unconscious for awhile. You have minor cuts and contusions on your left side, hand, lower leg and head. Your condition is expected to improve in two weeks."

"What happened to the other people—the driver of the pickup truck and Deputy Balton?"

The nurse was confused. "Kirst pulled over on the side of the highway and called for an ambulance. The sheriff's deputies were at the scene yesterday. I don't know if Deputy Balton was there." A picture of the highway, and Morehouse pinned behind the steering wheel flashed through his mind. "That's all the information I have," Elow finished.

Startled, Morehouse shook his head. "A rugged-looking man was driving a green pickup truck. It looked like a Ford. He chased my car and ran it into the tanker. After I crawled away from the wreck, he cornered me in the field. Deputy Balton walked up behind him from out of nowhere. Balton pulled his gun out, and shot and killed him. His body was laying in the field."

Elow cleared her throat. "The general physician, Dr. Grant Nelson, will check up on you in the next hour. It's nine o'clock in the morning. I can schedule an appointment for you with the hospital psychiatrist, Dr. Henry Jensen. Would you like me to do that?"

"What do you mean? What happened to the man with the gun?"

Elow didn't say anything for a moment. "The hospital report stated you were in a bad car accident. It's possible the crash affected your memory. Although it's uncommon, it falls within the range of normality for a patient to experience memory loss."

"No, you're wrong. The man held a gun. Balton stopped him."

"I've read about Balton in the Observer," the nurse said. "Balton works as a deputy. The hospital staff and sheriff's deputies know about your car crash. I'll tell Dr. Nelson you're having problems. Have you seen a psychiatrist before?"

"No," Morehouse said.

"I'll schedule an initial evaluation for you with Dr. Jensen. You'll probably feel well enough to set up an appointment for this week. He'll just talk to you and ask you some brief questions. That's all the information I have."

The nurse walked out of the room, and through the haze of medication, Morehouse ruminated over the crash. During a period of hours, Elow assured Morehouse that Balton was okay. A sheriff's deputy telephoned his hospital room to verify his story that a pickup truck had caused the collision. Again, Morehouse mentioned the strange man in the hallucination. Morehouse spoke with the nurse about the crash twice. She asked Morehouse what he believed provoked the hallucination, and he did not have an answer. Finding no strong physiological evidence of severe mental duress prior to the highway accident, Elow concluded Morehouse's comments were caused by the concussion.

Morehouse didn't press the matter, realizing it was unlikely anyone would believe him.

The next morning, Kevin and Doug visited the hospital room. The idea of invading Morehouse's privacy bothered Kevin, but he wanted to check up on him. Without fanfare, they walked past the glass-walled nurses' station, down the hospital corridor and into Room 516. Once inside, Kevin sat down in a visitor's chair and Doug swung the heavy door closed.

In the drab, indigo hospital room, Morehouse was propped up in his bed on a tuft of pillows. A coarse contusion on the right side of Morehouse's head had resulted when he sustained a concussion. A band of white gauze circled around his forehead.

"How's everything going?" Doug asked.

"I just completed my last concert on a summer-long nationwide rock music tour," Morehouse joked. "My hangover should wear off by the end of the day."

The nurse tapped on the open hospital-room door and walked inside. She looked at Morehouse for a moment. "I have your test results. The scan turned up negative."

"Does that mean I don't have any broken bones?" Morehouse asked slowly.

"As far as we know. One more test is scheduled for this afternoon," the nurse said. The nurse cracked a joke: "The only other way to get out of here is to post bail." Doug giggled politely and the nurse left the room.

The nurse called the desk on the wall speaker and asked that breakfast be delivered to the room. A dressing table was near the window, which was situated above the metal heat register. Minor vibrations went through the glass as a city bus hummed down the street.

Sitting in bed, Morehouse shivered self-consciously under the covers. "I can hardly wait to get out of here," he said expectantly. "The main drink they serve is water."

"You mean they don't serve alcohol to patients?" Doug quipped. "What kind of hospital is this?"

"I've still got a headache," Morehouse yawned. "I guess alcohol might help." While contemplating his uncertain condition, Morehouse listened to the frenzied footsteps of nurses walking down the hallway.

Earlier in the morning, Morehouse had experienced a bad dream. It had resembled black-and-white news footage about a WWII concentration camp. He remembered a horrifying scene in which there were piles of prisoners' pale, emaciated bodies. The lifeless corpses had been dumped into bloody trenches. Their clothing and valuables had been looted, and their flesh rotted in the overflowing mass graves.

Prisoners were ordered to dispose of the dead bodies. Morehouse recalled the bodies were left in the open for expediency, and to destroy the spirit of resistance. Most were Jews who had been arrested in Germany and France by Nazi soldiers, and brought to the death camps by train.

Exhausted, Morehouse broke from the conversation, closed his eyes and drifted into a nap.

Dr. Nelson clutched the stethoscope in his right hand. Nelson was in his late forties. With a rounded jaw, serious-looking eyes, black skin and short, neatly trimmed jet-black hair, his expression exuded intensity. He had the confidence of a dedicated professional.

Using his hands, Dr. Nelson worked his way down Morehouse's midsection. He examined Morehouse's eyes, ears and throat with a miniature, tubular flashlight. He checked his heartbeat with the stethoscope. He performed a reflex test on his kneecaps and elbows.

"I'm finished with the examination," Dr. Nelson told Morehouse. When he lifted the stethoscope from around his neck, Morehouse was relieved. He glanced out the window toward the skyline.

"You're suffering from a concussion," Dr. Nelson said. "Following a crash of that nature, hallucinations aren't entirely uncommon. I'd like to complete an additional test."

Dr. Nelson held five fingers outstretched in front of Morehouse. "How many fingers do you see?" he enquired.

"Five."

Dr. Nelson pulled his thumb down. "Now how many are there?"

"Four."

"Good. Why don't we schedule an eye examination with Dr. Charles Underwood in Optometry? When the nurse returns, you can set up a convenient time."

"OK."

"Let me ask you a couple more questions. If you're north of the equator and the time is noon, in which direction is the sun located?"

Morehouse sifted through the fog on his brain. "Probably south."

"OK."

"Which of the following animals has a snout? A pig, a cow, a bird, a rabbit or a horse?"

Morehouse debated for a moment. "It's definitely not a horse. I'll say a pig."

"That's correct," he said. "I understand the nurse has set up an appointment with the staff psychiatrist. We'll learn more at that time. You're condition has stabilized. According to my charts, other than the injuries detected when you were admitted, there has not been additional trauma."

"What does that mean?"

"We have not found broken bones, internal bleeding, higher temperature or increased abdominal pain. The nurse reports you have experienced dizziness, fatigue, soreness from burns and gashes, and aches and pains."

Morehouse's limbs were like lead tree trunks. The hospital had monitored his pulse, blood pressure, sleeping habits, diet, exercise, skin pallor, bones, ears, eyes, teeth, throat and heartbeat.

Dr. Nelson pulled back the white hospital sheets over Morehouse's left leg. He sighed, and studied the leg without expression. He leaned forward and pointed to the rupture along the flesh in Morehouse's left leg. "As you can see, a large gash has erupted on the skin. We'll tape it up, and it should heal over the next several weeks."

"When will I be able to leave the hospital?"

Dr. Nelson pushed the sheets back into place and glanced furtively at Morehouse. "If you pass the remaining examinations, we can have you out of here by tomorrow morning. I expect a satisfactory recovery. You sustained a concussion during the crash. Other than various contusions, we've discovered no other evidence of shattered bones, internal bleeding and that sort of thing. We'll watch your condition closely. However, you're not the only patient on my schedule today. I have other appointments I must keep."

Dr. Nelson picked his clipboard off the night table. He left the room unceremoniously.

Confined to the bed by dizziness and soreness, Morehouse experienced a sense of frustration. He wanted to open the mirrored bathroom cabinet, and take two aspirin. He wanted to roll over. He wanted to rush down the hallway and leave the building.

Later, an orderly, Morgan Caine, listened to Morehouse tell him about the accident as he walked Morehouse around the hallway. With a beach tan, close-set eyes and golden brown hair, Caine possessed the muscular build of a soldier in a white hospital uniform. The walk gave Morehouse a chance to get out of the hospital room. The heavily-medicated patient, Morehouse, was suffering from delusions, Caine reasoned.

Morehouse couldn't shake the overwhelming sense of chaos surrounding the crash. When he wheeled into the hallway, in a delirious state, he told Caine he had been trapped in his burning automobile. "I can't recall clearly, but I remember running from the flames through the brush before I passed out."

Morehouse couldn't visualize the driver of the pickup truck. However, the images of the highway scene ran through his mind in slow motion.

At night and in the daytime, when he was laying in bed, Morehouse listened to the voices and footsteps in the narrow white hallway.

For instance, Caine had a gruff voice and used short words when talking to patients. Morehouse frequently recognized Caine speaking in the hallway, his voice squealing through the open doors.

Morehouse listened to a man's muffled voice from somewhere else in the building. There was another subdued sound as a TV was turned on. "If you touch me, you'll remember it for a long time." Morehouse heard a TV character say.

Morehouse reached over to the night table, where the light was burning steadily. He snatched the remote control and flipped the ceiling television on.

The camera shifted to a sandy-haired news anchorman. He said, "There appear to be few new developments in the tragic case of Jean Kirchner, the tourist who was found dead a week ago on the edge of the Waubeka National Forest near Highway 46. While Clayton County sheriff's officials have not released all the specific details, it is believed that, according to unconfirmed reports, Kirchner's boyfriend, Trent Purnell, will be charged with first-degree murder in Kirchner's death.

"Sources have told Channel Nine that Kirchner was likely murdered. The primary suspect, Purnell, is being held in custody for further questioning. Sheriff's officials are expected to provide additional information as soon as possible."

The anchorman swung around in his chair and the camera angle changed. "Coming up, a report on the impact of county population changes on Centerville's economy. What are economists at Clayton County College saying about the community? That will be coming up in a few moments."

Morehouse shut off the television. A headache was throbbing in his temples. He glimpsed sunlight streaming through the hospital window.

Adrienne had continued her workmanlike appearance on the job. Off the job, when she saw Morehouse, with the bandage around his head from the concussion, laying in the white pile of sheets and IV tubes in the hospital bed, she began crying.

But things could have turned out worse. Although the car had been totaled, doctors planned to release Morehouse tomorrow. He would keep the bandages on his head.

Adrienne realized her husband could have been killed. He had done everything from working the guest register to cleaning the kitchen at the Bay View. When Adrienne entered the cramped hospital room, she fell apart. They had been fixing up the resort complex, and now this, her husband involved in a collision on the highway.

Adrienne was relieved his injuries only amounted to a concussion and a banged up leg. But the Bay View, their home for years, had to be managed. It served as impetus for them to overcome Ray's highway accident.

"Are you OK, Ray?" Adrienne asked.

"I'm banged up. Bad concussion, bruised hand and damaged leg. Other than that, I guess I'm OK," Morehouse replied.

Adrienne kissed his cheek and tears streamed down her face. "I'm so sorry for you," she said.

As Morehouse's condition improved that night, he took a brief stroll through the hallway with the help of Elow. Morehouse saw a patient's relatives in one of the other rooms, Room 520, and the dim lights. He smelled the thick, pungent odor of medication wafting from the room. He heard buzzers, beepers and rubberized wheels on mobile hospital carts roll down the hallway past the door.

Morehouse's recovery from the accident continued. Most of his body functions would return to normal. For the time being, Morehouse's head was as heavy as his body, and drowsiness accompanied his headaches.

After Adrienne drove Morehouse home from the hospital the next morning, he officially returned to the casual side of his life at his bookcase.

Later, Adrienne drove him to a bookstore, where he purchased "*Savage Wilderness*" by Joe Kovach. He also read The Observer and a sports magazine to pass the time. Over a period of days, he would gradually gain strength in his injured arm and leg.

In the afternoon, he walked all the way down the access road to Highway 46. He planned to take a walk every other day. He talked to two friends of his on the phone, Ralph and Debra, and two of their friends whose names he couldn't remember, for a half hour in the evening.

A road construction crew was digging up part of a ditch due to recent storm flooding. Sizable pieces of cement pipe lined the roadway along the embankment. Long rectangles of black asphalt marked the spots where sewer line had been replaced. Amber lights flashed on the white-and-yellow road barriers.

When Morehouse walked down the road he experienced a bad headache and half-closed eyes. He drove a trunk of old junk to the town dump. He noticed the lawn crew had done landscaping work, replacing dead plants and flowers in front of the resort.

Morehouse, emerging from the shade of the Bay View Resort, hobbled to an outdoor beach chair near the swimming pool. He glanced at the neon sign that read, "Lodging Available". The sunshine was speckled with overflowing shadows from the hardwood trees. Sunset was several hours away, and Morehouse owed it to himself to take advantage of the quiet afternoon. He sank into the chair, closed his eyes and listened to birds chattering. In the distance, were the echoes of traffic moving down the highway, as well as an occasional plane overhead and a train each night. The background noise rose and fell, at times, in regular intervals. The rest would do him some good.

After going to the dump, he bought three videos at a video store. He mailed two postcards and a letter to friends. He sat down in a living room chair, and in between naps, skimmed over four books and jotted down notes. He remembered the nurse's advice that he should continue fighting against the ailments stemming from the car accident. When one of the tapes got caught in the VCR, he ripped it out and sliced it up with a scissors. It was a genre Satan movie, and the humidity caused it to become sticky, like a roll of Scotch tape. Morehouse was bewildered because he was accustomed to a DVD getting frozen on one frame in a scene. His tapes rarely snapped apart. When the videotape didn't work and he had a raging headache from his concussion, it was the last straw. He used the silver metal scissors to vent his hostility on it. A week ago, he had returned a rented DVD that didn't work to the video store, and on the way back, bought a camping magazine from a drugstore.

After work, Adrienne went grocery shopping for Morehouse. When he ran into Adrienne, he repeated his concerns about rude patrons at the library.

PART II

▼

THE PAST

CHAPTERS TWENTY THROUGH TWENTY-SEVEN

CHAPTER 20

The Past
The 1970s

For tonight, the "space ship" conspiracy against the Kellinger mining project was Vernon Stonehill's alibi. The plan was to simulate a mysterious UFO incident, to play off superstition, and most importantly, to ensure that no one ever learned the truth.

In his grey guard's uniform, Stonehill, with deep blue eyes and curly blond hair, made a superficially trustworthy, almost cautious, first impression. However, if law-enforcement authorities discovered what had really taken place, Stonehill would face a prison sentence for murder and robbery.

The conspiracy began with a small dot of light on the night horizon. It looked like a star in the dark sky. As it approached, it grew larger, like an airplane flying overhead.

When the craft was close, it cast a circular ball of glowing light over the rows of treetops. As the modified Apache helicopter became visible to Vernon Stonehill and the two other guards on duty at the mine that Friday night, they spotted a gun barrel jutting from an open window.

The presence of the private helicopter was an unusual and unforseen development to the two other guards, Ben Pachelle and Charlie Runningdeer. But not to Stonehill. For the past month, he had been telling stories about UFOs. He hadn't divulged anything about the appearance of an unidentified helicopter, especially when the mine was shut down after work.

When Stonehill mulled it over, the chopper, partially visible at night, did resemble the type of mysterious flying disk that was described in tabloids. The shaking helicopter was ribbed, like a sea shell, and the two shooters on board were armed with rifles.

The helicopter leveled off at two hundred feet above the ground and three-quarters of a mile from the lake. At that point, the mine was inundated with the artificial taped sounds of minors digging. The chopper hovered above the mine entrance, the illumination coming from the Apache's searchlights. Then the helicopter pulled away, circling back to the forest.

The confused guards were distracted by the ruckus. According to plan, after the helicopter searchlight had pointed the way, Stonehill ran to the spot in the woods where the electronic detonator for the planted dynamite charges was situated.

The central business office for the Kellinger Mining and Lumber Co. was closed for the night. The building, parking lot and access road were farther down the slope. Stonehill knew the location of the safe in the foreman's office. However, the plan hatched by his contacts on the helicopter hadn't included robbing the safe, so he left it untouched.

Hammering sensations were emitted by the speakers on board the helicopter. The recording simulated digging sounds made by picks when minors were working in the tunnel. It was intended to lure both guards into the cave-like mine shaft.

Stonehill hit the detonator button for the first explosion in a series of three. The initial blast shook the entire ridge, causing Pachelle to anxiously pick up his cabin lantern in one hand and his rifle in the other. Unaware of immediate danger, he charged toward the mouth of the mine, hoping to find out what had happened.

"I'm going to check this out," Pachelle yelled. "I'll be right back. Keep an eye on that...helicopter."

The day-shift minors had gone home. As far as Pachelle knew, no work was scheduled for that evening. And as far as he knew, the primary tunnel and an adjoining mine shaft that veered off the main tunnel were both empty.

For a few brief moments, Stonehill watched him fade into the gloomy shadows of the tunnel. Within thirty seconds, Pachelle reached the fork in the tunnel where Stonehill had planted another round of explosives. Stonehill pressed the detonator button again.

Suddenly, the rugged hillside leading to the top of the ridge cracked open thunderously. The jagged fissure that was barely visible after the first blast had given way to a full collapse. The mine shaft ruptured and caved in, taking Pachelle with it, while Stonehill listened to his screams of agony.

Through the drone of the helicopter's spinning blades, Stonehill followed with the third and fourth explosions, which sounded like depth-charges released from a WWII battleship. The ground shuddered again as an orange-and-black plume of flame screamed up the tunnel, which was the largest in the mining and lumber camp.

Waves of heat flowed over the site, and the final explosion ensured the totality of the purported cave-in.

Runningdeer watched the spray of light emitted from the "space ship" swirl over the ground. He was not able to fully fathom the unfolding raid, but he decided to fire his rifle in self-defense. His first shot missed the helicopter entirely and the second grazed the outer metal shell. Ping! He listened to the strident sound of the bullet striking the target. The helicopter clambered in an oval, like a delirious person struggling to stand on his own feet. The helicopter hesitated in flight, and the multicolored lights flickered on and off, as if it was indeed a spaceship that was losing power. Before Runningdeer could fire another round, the shooter on board pumped two bullets into his chest. Runningdeer fell to the ground, fatally slumped over his rifle.

In a matter of moments, the chopper landed and the shooter disembarked. He assisted Stonehill in placing Runningdeer's corpse onto the Apache.

Clayton County deputies and company officials later investigated the deathly incident. Three guards armed with .22 rifles had been on duty. Apparently, Mother Nature had disrupted the mining project, killing two guards and leaving one incapacitated, authorities concluded.

Stonehill was found unconscious, laying on the ground next to his .22 rifle. According to design, the shooter had clubbed Stonehill on the back of the skull with the butt of his rifle. This was to ensure that Stonehill would not be a serious suspect in the conspiracy to sabotage the mine. He was hospitalized for the night.

Frighteningly, Stonehill had been paid cash under the table and a drawstring bag of valuable minerals. Stonehill's story was the mine had collapsed, and two of the guards had died, their bodies buried deep in the rubble. Pachelle's body had been recovered. The coroner determined he had been killed in the collapse, in part, from severe trauma to the head, likely caused by cascading boulders.

Perhaps Runningdeer had abandoned the mining project and fled into the woods. Maybe he had sabotaged the mine. But it was more likely he had been killed underneath a landslide of rock and rubble, authorities surmised.

Thanks to Stonehill, his clandestine contacts on the helicopter made off with half a dozen drawstring bags filled with valuable minerals, worth almost $100,000. Stonehill had become a collector of mineral specimens. He had spotted the hardened sediment, streaked with silver and a variety of other colors, four months ago. Heat and pressure had hardened the minerals into the sediment.

Kellinger would have broken down the deposits if company officials had known about them. But Stonehill and his contacts had their own plans to blow the earthly luster apart and fly it out on the helicopter before starting the granulation process. Following directions, Stonehill had assembled the bags earlier that evening.

Stonehill's contacts hadn't just supplied him with inside information about Kellinger Mining. They knew where Stonehill and his family lived, in case he had ideas of keeping more than his allotment for himself. Moreover, the dynamite had been planted in positions difficult for investigators to locate. If discernible evidence existed, it was buried underneath a huge pile of crushed rock, soil and debris.

That was all that was down there. Even though Stonehill had gotten rid of the evidence, the violence that had transpired was in his memory.

Alone in the isolated wilderness, occasionally a miner, lumberjack or woodsman had exhibited strange behavior. In this case, Stonehill appeared to be delirious following the collapse. When he regained full consciousness, he said he had been struck on the head by a loose rock. And he believed both Pachelle and Runningdeer had been killed in the collapse.

And then he mumbled something that was hard to believe—that Runningdeer had fired at a flying saucer. Stonehill said he suspected the saucer had been on an extraterrestrial mining mission.

Sheriff's officials determined no rounds had been fired from the two rifles they recovered. Stonehill was probably suffering from severe hallucinations caused by the blow to the head, they concluded. With his fellow guards dead, Stonehill, in an irrational frame of mind, was clinging to a paranoid illusion.

Stonehill said he couldn't remember where the flying object went. He assumed it was damaged by gunfire from Runningdeer before it had crashed, causing the mine to cave in. When he was asked repeatedly by sheriff's officials and reporters, he admitted he didn't remember exactly what had transpired. Instead of crashing, the flying object might have proceeded south toward Centerville at a low elevation undetected by radar.

The story was intended to fool sheriff's officials from making Stonehill a serious suspect. How could a feeble-minded guard suffering from hallucinations destroy a mine? Stonehill's account of what had transpired brought his mental faculties into question. It not only damaged Stonehill's reputation within the community, but harmed his relations with his wife, Brenda, and his son, Nate.

Stonehill didn't think many folks would believe that a flying saucer had caused a mine to collapse. He was pleasantly surprised to learn that half the people in town who had heard about the mysterious incident agreed there must have been some truth in it.

With the bottom of the ship glowing brightly, he told his drinking pals and his son, Nate, the ship plunged into the tunnel. However, it had been losing control all along. The speed and distance were miscalculated, and it scraped along the sides of the mine shaft. Behind the force of a strong light ray, it continued to push earth out of its way, the mine becoming deeper and deeper. In the end, the crashed ship, plus Runningdeer's body and his rifle, lay buried at the very bottom of the collapsed mine shaft.

That story made Vernon Stonehill feel important, especially to his only son, Nate.

Some residents of Centerville objected to the far-fetched account, calling it an outright fraud. Others, studying the history of UFO incidents, suspected there might have been truth in it, even if Stonehill was an unreliable witness. After all, there was a long history of weird happenings connected to the woods.

Most people recognized that the mine collapse, and not Stonehill, was the important factor. They held the opinion that Stonehill had experienced delusions stemming from a concussion. Similar to other tragedies in the forest, the incident was followed by the usual gossip. Ghost stories about murders, greed, sexual lust and outsiders were retold. Authorities from the observatory and the local university did not rule out the possibility of electromagnetic disturbances creating the effect of flashing lights in the earth's upper atmosphere. According to one theory, in addition to Stonehill's hallucinations, the guards had fired at a flock of geese that had been disturbed.

Searching for tangible clues, officials representing both the Kellinger Mining and Lumber Co. and the Clayton County Sheriff's Department investigated Stonehill. They found his work application had included a bogus mining company he had never worked for. He had been cited twice for disturbing the peace in Centerville, and rumor had it that he had physically abused Nate.

A six-year veteran of Kellinger Mining, Stonehill was terminated. He returned to full-time work on his rural farm north of Centerville and south of Crater Lake on Highway 46.

Three months after the cave-in, forty minors and lumberjacks went on strike. One month later, under a revised agreement with management over long hours and unsafe working conditions, they went back to work. Following that, a lumberjack disappeared and was never seen again. Finally, Kellinger Mining was sold to a new owner.

Within two years after the collapse, the mine had failed to yield additional minerals. The land was sold for dirt-cheap prices, and Vernon Stonehill was among the minors and lumberjacks who bought a parcel from Kellinger Mining. The government assumed control over the remainder of the site.

At home, Stonehill retold the story of how a mysterious UFO had caused the cave-in.

CHAPTER 21

The Past
The 1970s

The short, bald man dressed entirely in a dark business suit and polished shoes walked timidly out of a back room toward the hotel's commodious guest check-in desk. Standing on the opposite side was a tall, shabby teenager with hair hanging down over his ears to his neckline. His name was Ray Morehouse, and he was actively looking for employment. Morehouse hadn't brought job-related paperwork, so he described his qualifications to the fidgety, clean-shaven hotel manager.

"I'm sorry.... um...sir, but we have no available jobs," the manager said.

"What are you talking about?" yelled Morehouse. "You have signs posted all over this hotel building that say 'Help Wanted'."

"Well...yes...but all those jobs have been filled. In fact, I was just about to take all those signs..."

"O-h-h-h, shut up!" Morehouse interrupted madly. With that, Morehouse, wearing a thick winter coat, grabbed his tattered stocking cap and gloves off the check-in desk and stormed out of the empty lobby.

Once outside, he marched down the marble steps of the Lexington Hotel to the concrete sidewalk. Again, as had been the case during previous days in his job hunt, he was in what he viewed as the claustrophobic urban confinement of a busy neighborhood in New York City. On his way back to his parents' home, which was three miles away from a metropolitan rescue mission, he could feel the cold winter air stinging his hands and face. Although the Big Apple lived up to its reputation for diversity, offering glamor and excitement, Morehouse didn't like the cheap gloves and stocking cap he was wearing.

He walked briskly to keep the blood circulating until finally the freezing, sub-zero wind-chill penetrated his flimsy clothes. He felt like a deer that might die in the frozen winter landscape. Morehouse hopped quickly into a heated municipal bus. Sitting in a window seat during the bumpy ride, Morehouse gulped nervously several times, as his cold throat thawed out. In ten minutes, the bus would drop him off at Art's Billiard Hall.

As a young child in the 1960s, Morehouse had lived in New York City, in a lower middle-class neighborhood, not far from impoverished downtown slums. It had always bothered Morehouse that he had grown up in an environment of poverty and substance abuse. Over the years, those kinds of descriptive terms reverberated through the inner recesses of Morehouse's mind like wind slapping against rocks in an empty cave.

At times, Morehouse found it hard to fathom—that he had survived his childhood in rundown urban areas where the street sounds were long lines of used, engine-chugging runners driven by high school kids, muggers' racing footsteps bouncing off alley walls, municipal buses charging up pot-holed streets and pedestrians flowing down sidewalks like fish in the ocean. In the poorer neighborhoods of major cities in the 1970s, confrontations with gang members, stealing and even killing were part of the daily rat race.

And, equally difficult to believe, Morehouse had received a street education in those unpleasant matters. When, as a fifteen-year-old, he had been angry, even filled with rage, he had spray-painted buildings, assured that the paint, unlike fingerprints, wasn't traceable. Filled with fear, his heart would pump wildly, as he ran from the scene of each spray-painting, wondering if the police's technological wizardry could nail one of the neighborhood's graffiti artists. It was a minor crime the cops weren't able to keep watch over. The police had been occupied investigating murder cases, drug busts and automobile theft, all of which had a more immediate impact on the community, and all of which Morehouse had read about in the newspaper when he was away from the bustling city streets.

After graduating from high school in 1974, Morehouse had decided he did not have enough money or patience to attend college. He perceived he had a quick mind, and would have liked to have enrolled in college. But it didn't work out that way. He knew he had to support himself, so he took up gambling. He was materialistic, he found gambling to be a challenge and he planned to earn money fast. Then he would have the freedom to do as he pleased—to continue working or to attend college.

When Morehouse was ten years old, his father had been unemployed and had disappeared for days at a time. Typically, he reappeared with booze on his breath, his cheeks flushed and his eyes like stones. When he was really drunk, his mother would toss him out the front door, and he would drive away in their used Ford Pinto, staying with his parents or friends of his.

As Morehouse later recalled, his sixty-six-year-old grandmother, Kathy, stayed with them when his mother needed help taking care of the kids—Ray and his brother, Derek. His mother was busy working first as a waitress at the Callerone Club, and several years later, as a secretary at Sunland Photo Finishing. Due to his grandmother's age, she couldn't hear very well, and she didn't believe in using hearing aids. Moreover, his mother and father weren't always home.

So on January 17, 1972, Morehouse, a high school sophomore, decided to add a little excitement to his day. After the bus dropped him off, he entered Art's Billiard Hall and ordered a Coke. When he took his eyes of his drink and turned around, he noticed two pool players wrapping up a game.

Looking at the old table, with its mint-green cloth and brown pockets idle under the effulgent hanging lights, he experienced an impetuous adolescent urge to begin playing. At this distance from the table, he could see through the smoky atmosphere.

As Morehouse walked to the table, he couldn't help calculating the probabilities of winning. They were about a hundred to one, he estimated. If he practiced, he might ultimately end up playing for big money. If nothing else, he could get away from the crude, self-indulgent talk at the bar.

Morehouse put four quarters down on the table, but would wind up losing the first game, primarily because he hadn't played pool in six months. In fact, it had been so long, he had forgotten the rules of eight-ball.

"My name is Ray," he said, shaking hands with a stranger.

The man introduced himself as Joey Carlson, an eighteen-year-old Brookline resident who had black hair and a pointed nose. "I don't want to play for money right away," he said tersely. He strode back to the table where his friends—two women and a man—were waiting.

Morehouse looked at the line of empty beer bottles on a wall shelf.

"I haven't played stripes and solids for a long time," Morehouse said absent-mindedly. "Do I have to hit my balls first?"

"Yeah," Carlson answered.

Morehouse deposited four quarters into the table's coin slot. Feeling self-conscious due to the likelihood of rookie screw-ups, he looked behind him to check if bar patrons were watching him. A few were, but most were not.

He lined up the balls in the plastic triangle with the eight-ball in the center. He picked the longest cue from the rack and chalked the tip. He went to the table where he had placed his whiskey sour, plucked it off the napkin and took a swig. He stalked back to the pool table, placed the white cue ball, balanced the cue between his fingers against the back rail and broke to open the game. His initial shot didn't do anything, and the table was full of billiard balls.

Morehouse walked over to the bar. "A TV station is supposed to be replaying a playoff football game," he told the bartender. He looked at the TV set. A rerun of Bonanza was on Channel 16. "It was one of the earliest Super Bowls. The Green Bay Packers against the Oakland Raiders."

"Oh," said the bartender. He didn't appear to be an avid sports fan. He flipped through the channels until the game appeared on Channel 29.

"See what I told you?" Morehouse shouted. "The Super Bowl is on."

From the rear of the bar, where the pool table was located, Morehouse heard, "C'mon, man, shoot the ball." It was Carlson.

"It's your turn," Morehouse shouted. He added: "I left the cue back there. What do think the cue is for?"

Carlson staggered forward. The cue was propped against the side of the table. His foot accidentally cut underneath the cue, sending it to the floor. "What did you say? I can't hear you?"

Morehouse repeated, "What do you think the cue is for?"

Carlson asked, "What cue?"

Morehouse scanned the billiards area. "The cue is laying on the floor behind you."

Carlson said, "Great, dude." He spun around, scooped the cue off the floor and chalked it up.

Carlson, who was a lefty, looked over the table. With his shorter cue, he pointed to a corner pocket and called the four-ball. The ball bounced off the cushion and fell into the pocket. Clunk! Morehouse was already losing. Again, Carlson surveyed the table's landscape and called the two-ball in the side pocket. The shot bounced off the rail.

It was Morehouse's turn. He checked the table and decided to try to hit the twelve-ball into the far corner pocket. After considering dissimilar shot possibilities, he determined he didn't have any clear shots other than a sideways angle on the twelve-ball. Solids were blocking straight-on shots at other stripes.

Morehouse sent the cue ball rolling and it skinned too much of the twelve-ball. The shot bounced off the cushion and missed the corner pocket.

Throughout the game, Morehouse ended up in parallel situations where he didn't have head-on angles to pockets because the opponent's balls were in the way. He either had to rely on bank shots or shots that were too long.

Although he ended up losing the game, he decided he would try again. It turned out to be the beginning of a repetitive cycle.

At first, Morehouse had told his relatives he was just shooting pool and playing cards with friends. His parents, busy arguing about the mortgage and bills, didn't pay attention. Between his father drinking, and his mother working, they didn't have much time. At one point, when his father was in a period of unemployment, which happened in between jobs selling shoes and men's clothing, he would stay awake at night, drinking beer, eating junk food and watching television.

While Morehouse and his brother, Derek, were in bed for school the next day, Todd, their father, was glued to the TV set. He must have memorized the lineup of late-night talk shows, situation comedies, reruns and old movies. When he was in this phase, pinned to a faded amber couch in the family room, he didn't fall asleep until 4 a.m. or wake up until 2 p.m. When Morehouse's mother returned from her daytime secretary job, she had to make dinner, do the laundry and grocery shopping, argue about utility and mortgage bills, and try to get her husband to stay sober. Ray didn't know how his mother and brother could stand it. He had to get out of there.

In his senior year, he accumulated enough money to buy a used 1968 Ford Pinto, new threads from Men's World and help his parents pay their mortgage bill. When Kathy was at the house, Morehouse told her he worked as a commissioned part-time salesperson at Men's World after school, on the second-shift. But she suspected he was also gambling on the side, since he seemed to have cash from sources other than a men's clothing store.

She hoped he wouldn't inherit his father's bouts with drinking, irresponsibility and laziness.

After time had passed, when it looked like his grandmother, who went through spells of senility, seemed relaxed, and when Morehouse was cool with his volatile world in their rundown house, he would mumble a couple sentences about working as he marched out the front door. He knew his combative parents weren't watching his every move, so he didn't have to keep a tight lid on what he told them. He had matters under control, he often repeated to himself.

To Morehouse, gambling meant playing cards with high school friends and placing piddling bets on high school football games. However, his obsession with wagering money grew worse. Where else would Morehouse have been getting his extra money from? Kathy reasoned.

When he was out of the house, Morehouse shot pool and played poker. With money from his clothing sales job, he also bet on high school games, sometimes up to $500 in a week. He was part of a pool of high school kids who routinely bet on professional football, as well. Not surprisingly, the Oakland Raiders, Dallas Cowboys and Green Bay Packers were popular picks.

When Morehouse left for Joey's one day, Kathy sensed a freak occurrence might take place. In terms of publicity from involvement in street crime, small-time drug users made the local news pages in mug shots and stories about drug-related shootings.

However, the incident that later unfolded and involved Derek didn't even get in a newspaper. Nevertheless, Kathy's instinct was correct. After leaving high school that day, walking home, Derek was almost struck by an irresponsible driver. Derek was carrying a bag of groceries home from the store and crossing a city street in the pedestrian walkway, when a car filled with four rowdy teenagers charged at him. He jumped out of harm's way just in time, but food was splattered on the street. Most of the groceries were destroyed. A few apples and oranges were carried from the street by poor people in the crowd of onlookers.

Morehouse, who had been talking to a group of friends thirty feet behind Derek, wended his way through the crowd. He and Derek were offended by the instance of reckless driving, as if it was part of a skirmish in a traffic war. During the screech of traffic returning to normal, Morehouse started to complain, and repeated his concerns to his friends and family for nearly a week.

With his father drunk part of the time and sporadic strife in his family, the fabric of Morehouse's emotions had worn down, and his gambling woes became worse. He shot pool and played poker. In 1972, when he was a sophomore, the stakes had started low—a dollar here, two dollars there. Over a period of years, the stakes grew higher until he was playing for one-hundred dollars, two-hundred dollars, $5,000 and even $10,000.

An habitual gambler tells himself he is in it for the money. But he deludes himself. He thinks he gambles for the profit, not for the thrill of gambling and not because he's inclined to wager money. Since he rationalizes that the money is the prize, he also anticipates that when he wins enough, he'll be able to stop. Without knowing his own motives, he has become addicted. He doesn't realize he's hooked and can't stop gambling, no matter how many times he has lost, no matter how much money is in his wallet. He doesn't admit how much money he has lost until he loses so much that he has to declare bankruptcy.

CHAPTER 22

The Past
The 1970s

Vernon Stonehill, the only survivor of the mine collapse, continued to see the white lights of the helicopter in his mind. Even though Vernon had made up the spaceship story, he almost believed it was true. He claimed the craft had been sent from Mars, and the charged electrical particles that had been left over from the crash had affected him, to say the least.

After Stonehill had regained consciousness at the hospital and returned home, he seemed even more abusive, even more inhuman, to his son, Nate, than he already had been. Vernon had been a moody, self-centered person to begin with, and now he appeared to be at a higher level of unpredictability.

When Nate was old enough, Stonehill had subjected him to variable periods of parental abuse. For instance, when Nate used profanity doing farm chores, as his father did, Vernon had punished him. When Nate complained to his parents about bad dreams, Vernon rebuked him, making him feel as if he was tied to his bed and locked into his nightmares.

One day, when Vernon wasn't able to come up with the money to pay a repair bill for his automobile, he grabbed Nate by the shirt collar and issued a series of swear words. That sent Nate up to his bedroom, where he was plagued by memories of Vernon intimidating him. After Stonehill's father abused him, images of each confrontation ran through Nate's mind and made him feel guilty, as if he was the cause of them. When Nate went awake throughout the night, he was exhausted the following day, his face ashen white and his limbs heavy with tension.

Vernon's temper had scared him. Although there was little to be gained by denying the naked truth, Stonehill didn't want to face up to the fact that his father was cruel. Stonehill figured his parents misbehaved, the same as other children's parents. But as he grew older, especially in high school, he realized his parents were much worse than others.

He wondered how Vernon had gotten Brenda to marry him. He must have seduced Brenda by playing undetectable tricks on her. As Nate grew older, he became a confused, alienated outcast.

Occasionally, he attended Sunday mass at the Holy Redeemer Church. When he did, the idea of getting even with his father went through his mind as he sat in the pews at the rear.

Once, when Stonehill was in a state of rage, he marched out of his parents' farm house and found a clearing in the woods. He sat and stared at the trees and clouds, imagining how happy he would be if he had better parents and lived on another farm.

He had begun going into the woods when he was twelve, and the pattern repeated, even into adulthood. The first time he walked away from home, he went past the clearing, to the spot where the mine had been, the place that had caused his father so much grief. He saw visions in his head and believed it was a spot where the dead surfaced. He learned Darwinism in school, and that added to his view that wickedness was genetically imprinted in his family.

Aside from getting away from his parents, his sojourns into the forest were a kind of cold-hearted survival test. If he was accidentally killed, there would be one less person in the world, he reasoned.

When he returned from the abandoned mine, he was usually inquisitive, and he once asked his father if the bodies of the dead miners were still buried underground. Vernon began repeating his exaggerated tale about the collapse, but lost his composure. Vernon rose from the dinner table and swung his hand into Nate's face. Containing his emotions, Stonehill got up from his chair and excused himself. He went to his bedroom, which was the room he liked best, in part, because he already had bad memories of the house. Sobbing, he curled up on his bed and buried his head in his pillow.

With most children, there was a healthy sense of curiosity, and, in some cases, even intellectual aggression. When Stonehill had asked his father a question, it was like a law had been violated.

Up in his bedroom, he was aided by the memory of the thing in the woods. Maybe it would take his side. When he looked around his bedroom, staring at the blank walls and the dirty fingerprints on the blue plaster, the house seemed no more welcoming than the abandoned mine.

Stonehill was confused. He didn't trust his parents nor the people in town. When he asked his impetuous father questions, he had to be disciplined. Sometimes, the punishment became the intellectually alluring part of his day. Why had Vernon slapped him? he wondered. Because he had interrupted his father's dinner, had asked him an impertinent question and had to be punished.

One day, when Stonehill came down from his room and returned to the kitchen table, where his mother was drinking coffee, he asked her a question. "Why did you marry Daddy?"

Brenda admitted, "When we first met, he was charming. I thought I knew him. He turned out different. Not what I expected." She hesitated. "He can be rough. But we'll make it."

Stonehill was beginning to doubt that. Whispering thoughts were telling him she was wrong. She was planning to run away, to desert Stonehill and his wicked father.

Brenda was tired by the time she and Stonehill finished supper. Tomorrow would be his first day in eighth grade. In six months he would turn 14. He and his mother, a dark-haired, fleshy woman who wore jeans and corduroys over her thick legs, were chatting about Vernon.

"So you think it was really all your father's fault," his mother said sternly. "You want to know what I think? You should follow your dad when he speaks to you. Do you understand?"

"Yes."

"Good."

The ruckus had started in the living room. Stonehill was sitting on the floor beside Brenda's rocking chair. She was knitting and playing with his hair, while they both watched TV. It was night, and Stonehill kept asking questions about school.

"Will daddy be happy if I get high grades this year?" Stonehill asked. "I'm going to study more."

"You don't have to worry about that," Brenda said. "The way you're going, I'd be surprised if you got high grades. But to answer your question, Nate, of course he would be pleased by a better effort."

"Will you help me with my homework?" Stonehill asked.

"Of course, Nate," Brenda said. "If you're having trouble, I can help you out."

"Will the teacher sock me if I ask her questions?"

Brenda, playing with his hair, twisted a strand tightly around her forefinger. "Not if you believe in the teacher," she said. "If you follow her teachings, it shouldn't matter what the teacher says or does. It shouldn't matter what Brenda says or does. It shouldn't matter what Daddy says or does."

As she spoke, she accidentally pulled several thick strands of Stonehill's hair into a tangled ball. There was a sharp, stinging pain, causing Stonehill to wince.

"You've got to get the teacher on your side, Nate. How do you think you do that?"

"I don't know," Stonehill said.

"You've got to follow all of the teacher's instructions," she finished. "And you should know that by now," she finished impatiently, waving her hand and fore-finger at him in admonishment.

"Mama, why can't you go to school with me?" Stonehill asked. She gave him a skeptical glance. She switched the knitting needle from her right hand, holding both needles and the blanket in her left hand. She slapped her right hand down on the wooden arm rest. He stared at her with trepidation.

"You're too old," she said mechanically.

"Why can't you go to school with me?" Stonehill repeated.

"You're too old," Brenda said. "I just told you that. What's making you worry about that? I take care of you when you're home, don't I?"

"Yes," Stonehill said uncomfortably, deciding to use diplomacy when talking to her.

"Yes, I do. I make you breakfast and send you off to school. I buy you clothing. I cleaned the whole house yesterday...dusted, vacuumed, washed the dishes, put the laundry out on the clothes line. Nobody ever did that for me. Isn't that right, Nate?"

Stonehill wasn't sure. "Yes," he blurted out nervously.

Brenda got out of her chair and waved her hand in front of Nate. "I treat you better than anyone does. You better remember that or I'll have your father give you a whipping. Do you understand that?"

Stonehill saw the intolerance in her eyes. "Yes," he said.

"Didn't they teach you anything in Sunday school?" she yelled.

"I never went to Sunday school," he said reflexively, not thinking much.

Brenda swung her right hand at him, striking him across the mouth. Tears welled up in his eyes. She studied his face. Stonehill grabbed her shirt collar and pushed her toward the wall.

As he held her, he felt a rivulet of blood dripping from his left nostril. He wiped it on the back of his hand and smeared it on Brenda's white blouse.

She screamed and pushed Stonehill away.

Stonehill heard the harsh sound of his father's approaching footsteps on the porch and the screen door creaking open menacingly. Vernon walked into the living room.

"This isn't my fault," Brenda said, a pleading look in her eyes.

"It isn't my fault, either," Stonehill said. "She started it."

"What's going on here?" his father asked, staring at the blood on Brenda's blouse. "Am I seeing things? That looks like blood."

"He threw me against the wall," Brenda said.

Stonehill was trembling. "She slapped my face," he pleaded.

"I don't care," Vernon said. "You should never strike a woman, especially your mother."

Vernon grabbed him by the shirt collar and forced him against the wall. "Don't you know how to get along with people?" he asked. He ran his fist into Nate's bleeding nose. Instinctively, Nate balled up his fist and landed a punch on Vernon's cheek.

He backed away from Vernon, moving toward the entrance hall and the screen door. "She's making this look like it's my fault," Nate said as he left the house.

Vernon waved his fist at him and yelled, "Where are you going? I'm not going to let my kid grow up among strangers. You're not good for anything. You don't cut wood, paint the barn or do anything around here."

Walking into the yard, Nate was still emotionally wound up. "It was her fault," he yelled.

Vernon kicked the screen door as it flapped on the rusty hinges. "When you get back, I'm gonna show you my belt," he threatened. "Your ass ain't gonna feel good for a month."

Vernon took a potted plant off the railing on the porch and hurled it at Nate. It landed five feet from him, smashing into pieces.

Dumbfounded, Nate couldn't think of anything to say. He ran toward the back of the house and the woods. He listened to a loud banging sound as his Vernon pounded the door closed. Stonehill made his way toward the clearing and the mine. As he ran, his heart pumped wildly. Eventually, he slowed down to a walk, and all that went through his mind was that things wouldn't be the same if he lived somewhere else.

When he reached the abandoned mine site, he sat down on the grass, catching his breath. Stonehill was a bubbling spring of ambivalent emotions—mostly anger, jealousy and depression. He was relieved to be out of the house, and he was shocked by the whole situation. He knew Vernon would never treat him fairly and would continually take his mother's side. Stonehill reasoned the night had been deflating for two reasons: The presence of his cruel father and mother, and whatever madness was controlling them.

He sensed he was near the spot where the guard's body had been fatally buried during the mine collapse years ago. His father had told him the story over and over. But overtly, the feeling that the cave-in stemmed from an unnamed evil wasn't what was troubling Nate. He knew he had never measured up to Vernon's expectations, and consequently, he considered himself to be a failure. And he suspected Vernon's bad experience at the Kellinger mine was one of the root causes of strife in their family.

Far below the pines that surrounded the site of the abandoned mine the thing that lurked underground had even more trouble in store for all of them, he surmised. It watched him in the woods and on the farm, and it knew Stonehill's repressed urges.

Because Nate reasoned it was partially responsible for controlling them, there was little they could do about it. Since his parents were good-for-nothings, anyway, he was doubly cursed. The farm wasted his time, he told himself. All he and Vernon did was lead a small herd of cows into a pasture and work the cornfield. But fortunately, Vernon went away periodically, looking for another job to supplement his low farm income.

As Nate sat there, his wrath burned him to the core. He didn't have the privilege of living under caring parents. His father was nothing like what a father is supposed to be, Stonehill told himself. And his mother was nothing like what a mother is supposed to be.

Stonehill bristled with indignation. He visualized tackling Vernon in the yard, dragging him to the old well and pushing him over the side. His father would fall and fall...down the dark hole. When Vernon landed wherever the bottom was, wherever the dead guard's skeletal bones rested, the alien evil down there would be morbidly pleased.

The world was supposed to be filled with big families and small communities, Stonehill reasoned. In his case, this theory was backward, and like his father, he presumed there was only one reality.

Vernon's story about the mine collapse crossed his mind. "Mars, mars, mars, mars, mars, mars," Stonehill chanted. His eyelids grew heavy in the tired isolation of the forest. He drifted off for a few hours.

When he woke up, he estimated the time to be in the lethargic hours before dawn. His father was probably sleeping.

Stonehill made his way back to the house. When he reached his family's property, he stopped. The lights were off. He walked cautiously up to the back door. Again, he halted at the door, looking around suspiciously. He heard only the nasal sounds of his own breathing. He waited a full minute, but no one seemed to be awake.

He snuck into the kitchen unobtrusively and made his way up the stairs to his bedroom. The clock showed it was 4 a.m., and he got undressed and slipped under the covers. As he began to doze, he felt a hand snake under the top blanket and the sheet underneath. It pulled the covers off his chest. He wanted to jump out of bed, but fatigue pulled him back.

The light on the night table next to his bed clicked on.

"I'll be damned," Vernon said, a belt in his hand. He pushed Nate's unresisting body onto his stomach, exposing his buttocks. An icy chill went up Stonehill's spine. His father made good on his promise, whipping him with the belt at least a half dozen times. He chewed him out, warning Stonehill to obey his parents. Stonehill felt like his limbs were chopped tree branches laying in a pile in the backyard, where they were waiting to be burned. The welts that had been raised up on his rear end would likely remain there for a month, as Vernon had said. Nate's head was throbbing feverishly, and tears streamed down his cheeks.

Swearing to himself, Vernon went downstairs to the kitchen and popped the tab off a can of beer. The screen door swung open and closed, and Nate heard sounds outdoors in the yard. Mama was snoring in the other bedroom.

Out in the dirt driveway, Vernon climbed into the pickup truck and drove away. With soreness in his body, Nate lapsed into sleep. His father spent the day at a friend's place, drinking and complaining about his kid. Stonehill spent most of the next day in bed. Listless, he fixed himself one meal at 3 p.m. Mama, who was camped out in front of the TV set, didn't talk to him.

His irascible father returned that night, drunk and swearing. He tumbled into bed and passed out. For a week, Stonehill wasn't able to do chores. Vernon took care of the cows and fields before he ordered Nate to pitch in. Vernon didn't say much that week. Then one morning he barged into Stonehill's bedroom, sweaty and greasy-looking, his skin red and weathered, even blistering in places.

"You expect to live here for free?" he asked Stonehill.

"No," he said.

All Vernon said was, "You better get out there and clean up the barn…or you'll get another whipping. You'll clean it up, won't you?" Stonehill noticed the maniacal gleam in his father's eyes, satisfied he was making his kid sweat.

"Yes," he answered.

"Good," Vernon said. He lifted the mud-crusted heel of his work boot and drove it hard into the side of the bed. The bed shook and vibrated, a board underneath the food-stained mattress fell on the floor, and the mattress followed shortly thereafter. After his father left the bedroom, Stonehill crawled around on the floor, pushing the mattress back on the metal frame and putting the board back in place. Then Stonehill got dressed and went downstairs to start his chores.

CHAPTER 23

The Past
The 1970s

The card players began arriving at the front door shortly before eight o'clock. A downpour had ended an hour ago, and the sultry evening air held the dank smell of rain. The storm had started in the southwest, the jagged clouds streaking across the city, and trailed off into the northeast, a shrinking ball on the horizon.

Ralph Farber hosted a private game every Thursday night in the study at his home. The players were drawn from a wide range of occupations, and it wasn't obvious what each one did for a living.

Morehouse didn't know most of the players. He had been invited to Farber's place once. Some of the players were white-collar professionals; most were just folks who liked to place wagers on poker.

Farber, for instance, worked in real estate development. He didn't tell most people specifically what type of real estate he sold. Farber had gotten started selling residential property, and somewhere along the line he had moved into commercial real estate. Morehouse read in the newspaper that Farber was behind a real estate sale that led to the construction of a new hotel in the neighborhood.

Another local celebrity was Byron Porter, a divorce attorney. He had short black hair around his ears and glasses that added an authoritative touch. His parents had emigrated to the United States in the 1930s from Warsaw, Poland, before WWII and the subsequent closing of the country's borders by the communist political system.

Porter liked to show that lawyers weren't always straight-laced. He once joked that the courtroom should be declared a crime scene by police and cordoned off with yellow tape. He thought an average lawyer in the United States should be taken to a hospital and have his brain x-rayed.

At the head of the pedestaled table was Farber, who delt the first hand. Farber had short, matted hair, light brown and parted on the left side. Although his waxy hair was pasted to his head, long cowboy sideburns slid down past the bottoms of his earlobes. He had round, marble eyes, and a thin poker player's face. He wore a dark lambskin jacket, worth $2,000, with the zipper open.

Another player was Reggie Underwood, an African American who wore silver men's earrings. He had a pencil-thin mustache and goatee, and a broad nose. He was wearing a dark-spotted tie and a white sports coat.

Then there was Michelle Braddock. Morehouse knew she did some type of bookkeeping and secretarial work in one of the departments of a motorcycle factory. She had frizzy brunette hair, a slender figure and brown eyes.

Finally, Morehouse sat at the far end of the table, across from the dealer.

The cards were kept in a red felt container embroidered with narrow silver sides. A gold Buick automobile emblem was enclosed by a circle and below was printed, "Roy Steepleton Buick". Each card in the deck featured a picture of a car, sedans through convertibles, painted on it.

Farber kept five decks on the square table. He peeled the clear wrapping paper off the first deck. He shuffled the cards, flipping and bridging them, in his fingers. His thin-knuckled hands dispersed the cards to the almost unseen players in the dim circle.

Morehouse held in his hands two queens, an ace, a three and a five. He would need another pair and suspected he might lose, so he decided to bet cautiously. He received two inconsequential cards—a six and an eight—and didn't win any money.

Four tricks later, the playing cards hit the table face down. While the dealer handed out the cards, Morehouse noted that he didn't have a particular feeling of intuition about his hand nor how he would fare over the course of the night. After he received all five cards, Morehouse calmly picked up his hand, revealing three kings, a five of diamonds and the ace of clubs.

Morehouse had a hunch he could possibly win the trick, and in the opening round of betting, placed a cool $500 in cash on the poker table.

He routinely discarded the five of diamonds and received another card, which turned out to be the ace of diamonds. Morehouse's full house was strong enough to top the competition and put him ahead by $3,000.

A half hour and several games later, Morehouse was still up by $3,000. When he flipped over his cards, and found that three were spades in sequential order—the ten, the jack and the queen—he decided it was an opportune time to take a calculated risk. For the past thirty minutes, he had been prudently towing the line, careful not to throw his winnings away.

He scrutinized the competing card players. Wearing poker faces, they didn't reveal much. Morehouse calculated which cards he had already seen, reviewing their white faces and black lettering on a mental TV screen. He analyzed the hands that he could remember had been played. He didn't recall having seen the king or ace of spades, two of the cards he was looking for.

He wanted to leave for the night and take his winnings with him. He wanted to make this his last serious bet. He thought it was the right moment. If he completed the royal flush, he intended to participate in two more tricks, bet modest amounts, and then get up from his cloth-backed chair and make a little-noticed exit.

On any given night, he was looking for one big win. Then he hoped the competition would forget about it.

Morehouse felt he might get a break. He bet $3,000. After turning over the king and the ace, he had completed a royal flush. The competition was stunned, and he took several gulps of his Miller. Instead of making it evident he had won a sufficient amount of money by excusing himself, he hung around for another half hour.

Finally, around 9 p.m., much earlier than he had anticipated, he excused himself. No one had been drinking heavily enough to give him trouble. He unpretentiously walked out the door with $10,540 in his pockets. Although he knew of another game taking place elsewhere, he decided to skip it and quit while he was ahead. Rotten memories of past games in which he had placed too many bets floated through his mind.

CHAPTER 24

The Past
The 1970s

It was Saturday, a bright, lazy June day in 1979. Stonehill, an eighteen-year-old senior at Centerville North High School, an alienated kid whose friends had nicknamed him Mars, was supposed to have rotated the tires on his father's car, a 1974 Buick Special. He had gotten carried away on Friday night, like other young people caught up in the glitz of the late 1970s, draining too many pitchers of beer and too many shots of whiskey, the alcohol circulating through his system like blood. To Nate's way of thinking, his father had been partly responsible. While Nate had contemplated staying home to avoid the twenty-five-degree temperature outdoors, his father set a drinking binge in motion. He had given Nate a stern lecture about the importance of automobile maintenance, creating in Nate a need to contact a friend and hit Roth's, one of Centerville's country bars.

A county sheriff's deputy, Roger Weaver, caught him staggering out of Roth's Bar at 2 a.m. with a friend of his, Jim Combs. During the night, Combs and Nate had staged a drinking contest, with Combs buying him half a dozen shots. Stonehill pounded them down, one after another. In contrast to his low grades in school, it was Nate's chance to shine.

Toward the end of the night, thirty patrons, clad in blue jeans and brown leather jackets, cheered frantically as Nate let drink number twenty, a shot of Tequila, burn down his throat.

After examining his empty wallet, Nate, along with Combs, tumbled down the cement steps of the bar. Walking down the sidewalk to Nate's car, which was parked on Main Street, they ran into Deputy Weaver. Combs explained to the deputy that his good friend, Nate, had gotten carried away, and rather than waste

Weaver's time, he would drive Nate home. He never mentioned that it was Nate's car he planned to drive home.

He smiled politely into the deputy's face, staying far enough back not to let the deputy catch a whiff of his breath.

At that moment, Weaver received an emergency call in his squad car. It was for a domestic dispute at the home of the Marvin Tyler family, 210 Barker Road. Following a loud husband-versus-wife argument in a series of roaring arguments known to neighbors, Marvin Tyler, had been spotted by a neighbor, Bert Mullen, retrieving a revolver from his car. The couple had been arguing profusely. Although no gun shots had been fired, the neighbor saw Tyler waving the gun at his wife through the picture window in the living room. Mullen reported hearing violent sounds such as doors slamming and glasses breaking.

Weaver determined he had to drive to Tyler's residence. Against his better judgment, he suggested Combs and Nate take their time, get some fresh air and have a couple of coffees at Marlene's Diner, a block down the street. Then Combs could drive Nate home in his car.

The situation reminded Nate of other encounters with school and sheriff's officials. The deputy had more important matters to attend to. Who the heck cared about Stonehill?

After the deputy left, Combs guided Nate into the passenger's seat. Then, he waffled around the back of the car, plopped down behind the steering wheel and ran the front of the car onto the curb. They both laughed, with Nate swearing at Combs to get him home before he vomitted.

Combs only struck one other curb in town and down Highway 46 on the way to Stonehill's house. He ran the car over ten feet of empty sidewalk at the corner of Jefferson Boulevard and 22nd Street. After dropping Nate off in the driveway, and watching Nate vomit in the front yard and stagger into the front entrance, Combs sped home in Nate's car.

When Nate woke up in a puddle of vomit in his bed at 10 a.m., his father was in his face. His meaty, middle-aged jowls were flaming red, and he was barking something about staying out too late. Nate had slept in his T-shirt and sweater. His father grabbed his sweater and lifted Nate's aching head off the pillow. Where the hell was his automobile? Was Nate mugged last night? Or had he sold the piece of junk?

In the midst of a wicked hangover, when Nate made out the words, he busied himself groggily pushing through the vomit-stained mound of white sheets and blue blankets on his bed. Then he remembered what had happened. He told his father that it was no big deal, nothing to worry about, that his friend, Combs, had needed the car last night for some reason, and Nate, overcome with feelings of charity, had let him borrow the car. Vernon yanked him off the bed and threw his alcohol-numb body onto the floor.

When Brenda saw the mound of vomit in the bed and learned Nate had lost track of Vernon's automobile, she understood the depth of Vernon's anger. In a fit of rage, she tossed Nate's messy sheets and blankets into the front yard, threw clean clothes at him and locked him out of the house. Even though Combs, who was in Nate's father's car, found him three hours later, walking down the highway, tired and depressed, and even though he returned the automobile to the farm, his mother and father kept him locked out of the house for the remainder of the weekend.

That was how Nate had learned to sleep in the barn and skip regular meals. Periodically, when Nate was banished from his parents' home, he thought of many things, including repaying Vernon for his "fun" childhood. In the barn, Nate fiddled with a buck knife and half a dozen pocket knives. During his high school years, he figured out how to swing an axe, and kept track of the location of shovels, pick axes and loose two-by-fours. They were part of a mental checklist of makeshift weapons.

Around his father, he often spoke with a nervous tremor. Periodically, insecurity swirled throughout their home, like dank mist rising from a swamp. Nate didn't know that eighteen years later, Vernon and Brenda would be gone. In a state of depression, Stonehill walked up the path to the front porch and sat down, napping in a whicker chair.

"That was back in sophomore year," Stonehill said, responding to a question from Deputy Weaver. "We don't have counselors at Centerville High," he said, a pleading tone in his voice.

Weaver considered this statement. He noticed Stonehill's anxious expression. As far as he knew, counselors who were available to students with disciplinary problems dated back to at least the 1970s.

"Why are you asking me this?"

"I'm trying to make connections with...problem students at the high school. I'm just checking parents and students around here to see if they know anything."

"I see," Stonehill said. "Ask and you shall receive," he added, smirking.

"The student body isn't always well-behaved, as you know. On Wednesday, we had a substitute teacher, Mrs. Thorn, for a sophomore history class. When the regular teacher, Judy Trenton, was sick, the other kids couldn't wait for a substitute to walk into the lion's den. Trenton missed school due to an ulcer. I thought Thorn's marbles were loose when I heard she was a substitute for the high school and not the grade school," Stonehill explained.

"Why was that?" Weaver asked.

"Thorn has a way with young children, they automatically like her. But that doesn't do her much good at Centerville North."

"What do you mean?"

Stonehill ground his teeth. "What I just told you," he snapped. "She was good for shit with high school kids."

Noticing Stonehill's irritation, Weaver continued. "How do you know that?"

"Look, I just know. Like through intuition, man. Some people's folks are good for…well, there not good with kids. Some people aren't cool around teen-agers. You have to fit in."

Weaver said, "Wait a minute. What do you mean by that? What do you mean by saying teachers have to be cool around high school kids. Who says so?"

Stonehill lost his temper. "I didn't say that," he yelled, raising his voice. "Nobody has to be cool around anybody." His smirk had turned sick-looking, as if his long mouth had been twisted sideways. "Know what I mean?"

Weaver assumed a stony expression, and continued to make comments that irritated Stonehill. "I don't know what you mean."

"What I just told you, stupid. Some people are cursed. They have bad parents. Their parents are like aliens from outer space." He laughed to himself. "They don't understand their own kids. They don't understand what things are about. I could see grade school kids took to Thorn. She was no good with high school kids."

Stonehill hesitated. "Thorn was invading somebody else's space. Even if she is a substitute, that high school crap is somebody else's job. It's Trenton' job. The students can see that. She looked like a grade school teacher, an idiot, wasting the high school students' time. She taught us dumb stuff about Angela Davis. That isn't her territory. That belongs in grade school—in eighth grade, like at other schools. Not tenth grade."

Stonehill pointed at the woods. "You see that? That's the deer's territory out there."

"I understand," Weaver said apologetically. "I know what you mean—that deer belong in the woods." Weaver sighed, and Stonehill heard him exhale. "Nobody wants to bother you, son. It's just that I have a few questions."

"Go ahead. Shoot."

"What happened in the class taught by the substitute?" Weaver enquired.

"She was late for her own class, like she normally is. An entire fifteen minutes late. The class was supposed to start at 1:55 p.m. She didn't drag herself into the room until 2:10."

Weaver added, "And that fifteen minutes can be an eternity for a high school kid."

Stonehill said, "Looking at the clock, school drags on forever. Anyway…the other students…some of the other students, Robby Berg, and Johnny Girard, started tossing paper airplanes around the classroom. The clock ticked, and the paper airplanes changed into pencils, then erasers, then chalk."

"And it was the fault of the other students—Berg and Girard?" Weaver asked.

"Yup."

Weaver said, "And when Thorn walked out of the room, to the principal's office, there was vulgar talk—profanity and sex jokes and that kind of thing. It offended her."

"Yeah, I remember that. She slapped open a thick modern history textbook and stared at it without saying anything for another ten minutes. Then she launched into her talk about Angela Davis. I'd already heard that talk another time she substituted. Many pupils already suspected that speech was useless, and wouldn't do them any good after they graduated and had to look for work."

Stonehill said, "When I applied at the Mobile gas station for a job, I didn't show the manager my textbook."

"I know what you mean. You don't want to look like a nerd," Weaver said. He changed the direction of the conversation. "From what I understand, Thorn earned her teaching degree in English from UW-Platteville in 1967. She's fifty-four years old. She made the dean's list in teaching college after getting an A minus grade-point average."

"She couldn't understand anything in the algebra textbook," Stonehill said. "She couldn't figure out enough of the questions or answers. Trenton left her directions. They were legible.

"She was looking for something in Thorn's desk. While she was flipping through desk drawers and pages, Girard took a paper airplane and squashed it into Berg's face. Watery blood began running out of his nostrils. It dripped over his puckered lips and onto his clean clothing. He got mad and rose from of his chair and slammed his fist off the top of Girard's head. Then Girard picked up his chair and started poking Berg with the legs.

"Soon, other students joined in the fracas, and desks were overturned and chairs went flying across the room. Before the class period ended, the school administrators, the principal and his right-hand man, an enforcer named Don

Zemler, cleared out the classroom. Most of the desks and chairs were scattered around the room. Pencils, erasers, books, notepads, and upended desks and chairs were all over the place."

"And all of that was because the teacher, Trenton, was sick with an ulcer? Is that what you're claiming?" Weaver asked.

"Uh-huh." There was silence. Weaver and Stonehill did not say anything.

CHAPTER 25

The Past
The 1970s

Morehouse sized up the shot, which looked challenging. The cue ball was touching the blue-striped ten-ball. After surveying the table, he realized there were no other balls he could sink. He didn't want to hit a safety, and there was a chance he could skin the side of the ten into the near corner pocket. Morehouse circled the table, studying the shot from three distinct angles. No matter how he visualized the projected shot, it looked like the cue ball would send the ten into the rail, rather than the pocket.

He leaned over the table, his left arm against the tabletop cloth. He took a dozen practice strokes. He extended the cue across the length of the table. Morehouse gently pushed the cue ball off the side of the ten. He got a break. The ten drifted toward the back of the table before it bounced off the eight-ball, which was touching the rail, and slid into the corner pocket.

Next, he faced another rough test. Again, he didn't have a wide selection of easy approaches. None of the potential shots involving stripes were at clear angles. The red-striped eleven was situated in the middle of the table, halfway between the two back pockets and the side pockets. It was at the top of the triangle where the balls are placed for the opening break.

The cue ball was near the back rail. The preceding shot had been so difficult for Morehouse he had forgotten to take the placement of the cue ball into consideration. The only opening Morehouse saw was to knock the eleven the length of the table into the far corner pocket to his left. He circled the table and pushed the cue through a series of practice strokes for a full five minutes before the eleven disappeared into the pocket.

Next up, was the nine-ball, which Morehouse intended to slap into the side pocket to his right. More confident and less deliberate, Morehouse lined up the shot. He drove the cue ball squarely into the nine-ball, listening to it drop into the side pocket.

When shooting pool, he tried to control the middle of the table. Playing for position, he wanted each shot to look like candy.

In this case, however, the cue ball was at the base of the table. The fourteen was hugging the left rail in front of the side pocket. Normally, Morehouse had little trouble making that type of moderately easy shot. He had to get the cue ball to strike the cushion and the fourteen simultaneously, giving the fourteen enough momentum to roll over the lip of the side pocket and down the rail into the corner. To Morehouse's way of thinking, it would turn out to be a simpler shot than what it appeared to be.

Morehouse bridged the fingers of his left hand on the table, holding the cue steady. He failed to aim carefully, and the fourteen bumped into the pointed opening in the cushion for the side pocket. He had missed the routine shot.

His opponent was Vernon Stonehill.

With the cue ball below the side pocket, Stonehill's shot to drive the six into the far corner was straight on. He held the cue steadily on the table and kissed the six into the corner.

The cue ball had rolled to the opposite end of the table. Stonehill lined up a pocketable shot—the object ball, which was the seven, halfway down the table, into the corner. Click! Click! Click! The seven dribbled imperfectly into the pocket.

Stonehill faced another length-of-the-table shot, with the object ball returning back to the other end. The cue was poised on top of the back of his hand, between his thumb and forefinger. He struck the cue ball with the tip of the cue. The three headed for the corner, scraped against the cushion and landed in the corner pocket.

With the cue ball at center table, he was left with a straightforward approach to the four ball in the corner. No sweat. The major obstacle would be the next shot.

The two-ball and thirteen-ball were touching each other near the side pocket. After sinking the four, Stonehill's only follow-up would be the two in the side. Then, somehow, he would have to put down the eight, likely in the opposite corner, depending upon where the cue ball ended up.

Stonehill analyzed the trajectory for several minutes.

Stonehill sent the four into the corner pocket. He had attempted to hit the cue ball very low in order to put enough English on it. His strategy had been to draw the cue ball backward into the two ball. Instead, he struck the cue ball too high, with little draw. It spun backward only two inches, not far enough to dislodge the two.

His best chance, at this point, was to sink the two ball in the side pocket. With forbearance, Stonehill undulated practice strokes at the cue ball for a full three minutes. Finally, he fired the shot and the two bounced off the rail, missing the side pocket.

Morehouse was jittery. He strode to the end of the table, and impatiently bridged the cue on the back of his left hand. He aimed for the corner, let the shot fly and the fifteen dropped right in.

He was relieved. Across the width of the table, the eight-ball was hanging innocently on the lip of the side pocket. A piece of cake. He sent the cue ball rolling and it tapped the eight into the side pocket.

Morehouse had won.

Not only had he taken the billiard game, but he had won the bet with Stonehill. Morehouse recalled Stonehill had said the land was located in between a place named Crater Lake and an old mine. Stonehill, who was wearing a leather jacket and corduroy pants, reached in his pocket, pulled out the deed and handed it to Morehouse.

Morehouse was the new owner of the vacant land, which he planned to sell relatively quickly.

He had been considering the offer to purchase the property since it was made two months ago, in November. Studying the map of Clayton County, where the land was located, his resolve to sell the vacant property had increased.

The undeveloped tract of land was overrun with wild grass. Two paths had been chiseled through the vegetation. The wire fence on the neighboring farm field to the south was electrified and the Waubeka National Forest ran along the eastern border.

Morehouse mailed copies of forms he filled out or obtained regarding the real estate sale between himself, grantor, and Norman J. Saffold, grantee.

About two weeks ago, Morehouse contacted the Register of Deeds for Clayton County. For three dollars, Clayton County mailed him the deed for E2717 Harbortown Beach, the property being sold to Saffold.

"They mailed me two copies of the real estate transfer tax return," Morehouse said, talking on the phone. "I've filled out ninety-five percent of the real estate transfer form. I'm mailing you a sample of the form, in case you fill out the official version for us, to save you time. Or in case I fill out the form myself, I can get additional comments from you."

Morehouse listened for a minute as Warren Kinney, the real estate agent, responded.

Morehouse said, "I spent between five and ten hours working on the form on Sunday and Monday." In phone calls on Monday, Morehouse received information for the form from Saffold and Clayton County.

Morehouse wanted Kinney to fill in a question asking about the buyer's financing. He assumed the buyer was paying in cash, but he wasn't sure. Anyway, for legal reasons, he wanted the real estate agent to fill in the proper box. "I left question forty-four, 'Grantee's Financing', blank at this time. After talking to a woman at the Register of Deeds office, I thought it would be best to include an attached photocopy of the deed for the property to add to the responses to questions fifteen through seventeen," Morehouse explained.

"From what I understand, your office will contact me when you receive the results of the title search for the undeveloped property. As far as I know, there are no liens on the property."

Morehouse listened, then resumed the conversation. "Just between you and me, Warren, I got the deed two weeks ago. The man who sold me the land, Stonehill, said he's owned it for years and hasn't made any improvements. He originally bought it from the Kellinger Mining Co., which, as I understand it, went out of business a long time ago."

Since Morehouse was familiar with the history of the property, he anticipated completing the sale in a timely fashion.

"When I contacted the woman at the Register of Deeds office, she said the only documents we needed were the real estate transfer form, the deed they mailed us and the check for $6,800 from Saffold. When I contacted your office, you indicated we should have a closing statement and your secretary mentioned another form relating to the deed. I have mailed you related forms I found at the public library and the Office Products World store that might satisfy these demands," he said.

"In any case, I'd like to complete the sale by January 13, as suggested on the offer-to-purchase agreement. You indicated you could complete the paperwork for us, if there is additional serious paperwork, at a cost no greater than $150. To assist you, I've mailed you the forms I filled out. Since I filled out ninety-five percent of the real estate transfer form, that should save you time. You can ask the buyer how to fill out the question about how he is financing the purchase."

Morehouse hung up the phone, both pleased and distressed. To begin with, he hadn't planned to hire a real estate agent.

Morehouse had exaggerated, and the parties he had contacted by phone hadn't detected anything amiss. In truth, Morehouse had won the lake property, which was probably a hillbilly dump located near a godforsaken place named Crater Lake, in a pool game. He had gotten the place from Stonehill, a stranger he had met while playing billiards.

When Stonehill lost the land, he had seemed uneasy, even frustrated. Stonehill wasn't able to retrieve the deed from Morehouse's hand because there were too many witnesses. Morehouse felt sorry for Stonehill. However, he had won the undeveloped parcel of land fair and square.

At least, he thought he had.

Morehouse didn't know that Stonehill had acquired the land for almost nothing by the standards of the real estate market. After tree-cutting crews had stripped the tract of land in question of all trees, Stonehill bought one of four available parcels for only $150, before Kellinger Lumber Co. sold the remainder to the government.

When Morehouse had sobered up the morning after he won the deed, laying in bed, he held the document in his hands, studying it. In the local economy of Morehouse's gambling world, he and his cohorts had judged the deed had a value of $2,000, based on Stonehill's description of the recreational setting.

He became the owner, and without even bothering to visit the vacant property, placed ads for it in local real estate guides. Within three months, Saffold, a retired shoe store owner, responded to Morehouse's ad asking for $8,500. Saffold bought the lot for $6,800.

Morehouse felt a tinge of guilt for having taken the land off Stonehill's hands.

Before letting the property go into the real estate ads, Morehouse spent an hour reading about Crater Lake. On a factual level, all Morehouse remembered was that the name stemmed from the Ice Age. Rock formations and basins of water had been molded into the earth's topography by massive sheets of ice, he recalled.

CHAPTER 26

The Past
1980

"Ray!" Ingrid Jacobs exclaimed, her cheeks rose-colored and a bubbly tone in her voice. "It's good to see you."

"It's good to see you, also," Morehouse replied.

Morehouse was glad to have been invited to the gathering of about fifty people at the home of his boss, Bill Jacobs. It was 1980 and President Jimmy Carter, like his recent predecessors, John Kennedy, Lyndon Johnson, Gerald Ford and Richard Nixon, was grappling with the federal government's budget issues. By the time the primaries had ended, Carter was running against Ronald Reagan and John Anderson.

Within a year of graduating from high school in 1974, Morehouse had worked his way from part-time salesman at Hawkins Clothing to store manager. Morehouse had earned twice as much on commission as the competition. He memorized where specific merchandise was located in the stock room and was glib around customers because he knew some of them from the neighborhood. When the preceding store manager was transferred to Pittsburgh, Hawkins Clothing followed its tradition of promoting young salesmen. After working with the regional sales manager off-and-on during the year, Morehouse was picked for the store manager slot.

Over five years as store manager, Morehouse had learned the business. He was patient with customers and fidgety with the sales staff. He passed along the management philosophy that salesmen needed to know all about the men's suits, shoes, sports clothes and casual wear they sold. If they didn't, they disappeared.

Morehouse was enthusiastic about arranging window displays for sidewalk customers, read manufacturers' newspaper ads, kept track of sales and spending, and stayed in close touch with Hawkins's management.

Off the job, Morehouse wasn't sure about anything. Hawkins's nearest competitor, Strickland Clothing, which was located a block down the street, had gone out of business in 1975. Morehouse figured Strickland hadn't gotten enough customers, and he also saw a threat from much larger national chains and department stores. Morehouse wanted to get out of the long hours on the retail floor.

As a single twenty-one-year-old, he continued to play poker and pool, mostly locally. It went with his drinking. Occasionally, he drove down to Atlantic City or flew to Las Vegas. The slick con men he met in those places were still too good for him, and from time to time he was snookered out of large sums of money. When he thought he was winning, he ended up losing. Yet he saw the inherent risks in gambling as the ultimate way out of the confinement of the day-to-day chores of retailing.

Then Morehouse got a break. From time to time, he had run into Tom Reddick, the public relations director for Jacobs Clothing Manufacturing. Like Morehouse, Reddick, in his late twenties, had never earned a college degree, and when the pair went out for a drink and the higher-ups weren't around, they railed about what a waste of time college was and how stupid some of the eggheads in business management seemed.

From Morehouse's perspective, Reddick had it made. Although his job title was director of public relations, he was, in actuality, one of the close right-hand assistants to Bill Jacobs, the affable fifty-five-year-old owner. After several years on the sales floor at Hawkins, Morehouse accepted the newly-created position as assistant to Reddick.

After six months of learning the ropes, something unanticipated took place. Reddick was walking around the Jacobs' clothing plant's back loading dock. He was taking photographs for the Jacobs Report, the firm's employee newspaper. Unexpectedly, as he was lining up a shot of workers unloading supplies from a truck, he slipped and fell, breaking his leg.

Like a football coach, Morehouse received an immediate injury report. Reddick was expected to be out of action and off his job for at least two months. Just like that, Morehouse was to take over as department manager, responsible for arranging business conferences and social gatherings, putting out the monthly employee newspaper, determining the department's budget and assisting Jacobs with errands that came up on a moment's notice.

Two weeks ago, Morehouse received written notice of a company gathering at Jacobs' mansion. Since Morehouse was new to the job, he wasn't expected to do much. Jacobs and his wife would take care of their party, as they did each year, and Morehouse was expected to attend. Morehouse had been working with Jacobs for half a year and had met Ingrid on several previous occasions.

She welcomed Morehouse to the party, and she told him about the guests. He added his comments. She became garrulous, telling him about her husband and children. She described the house and grounds.

There was a spacious outdoor patio in back and a full-sized swimming pool, which at fifty feet by one hundred feet could technically hold up to sixty occupants. Not far from the pool, connected to the house, was a blistering steam bath and a basic weight room, with a tread mill, arm and leg curls, a jump rope and barbells.

In addition to the front living room off the entrance hall, was the study with a wet bar and pool table. The room was L-shaped, with an open walkway connecting the bar and the study, where there was a long five-shelf bookcase, wall-mounted paintings and Jacobs' desk. Upstairs, the home, valued at four million dollars, contained eight bedrooms. The four-acre grounds included a circular entrance drive.

After fifteen minutes of chitchat, Ingrid asked Morehouse if he would like another gin and tonic. Morehouse agreed, and Ingrid insisted he follow her to the wet bar in the combination family room and study. Most of the approximately fifty guests were divided between the outdoor patio and pool in the back yard, the front entrance hall and the living room.

The bartender had been mixing drinks from a stand on the patio near the kitchen.

When they reached the multipurpose family room, Morehouse noticed two guests on the other side, in the study. Ingrid asked them if they needed a round, and they said no. They were preoccupied with their conversation, and in a very brief time, left the room.

Ingrid went behind the bar and stools. She seemed to like Morehouse and chatted with him as she fixed the drinks. She pulled out two glasses and filled them with ice. She went to the brown lacquered liquor cabinet, then she put an olive in her glass and poured a drink for herself.

She had been speaking to Morehouse about her husband's upcoming business trip. "Bill probably mentioned it to you?" she asked.

Morehouse wanted to draw out the conversation. "I don't know much about it," he said tactfully.

Ingrid described the trip to Miami, where Jacobs would be meeting two influential investors. Beautiful, Morehouse thought to himself. Jacobs will be out of town on business for a week. At the office, it will seem like a week of vacation.

As they sipped their drinks, Ingrid divulged more about her husband's trip. She was almost talking to herself, with Morehouse losing track of the conversation, becoming a figure in the background, like the other guests.

She blurted out, "Doesn't Bill realize that I have feelings, that I want to go to Florida, that I need to get away, on a trip, as much as he does."

She asked Morehouse if he would be interested in taking a tour of the house, and he said sure, as soon as they finished their drinks. Ingrid added that she could even fill up a couple more. Morehouse worried she might spill hers on the carpet, especially if they walked around the house and she bumped into another guest. He didn't want to spoil her good mood, so he didn't say anything.

Morehouse was becoming irritated. He viewed humoring Ingrid as a necessity, like filling out his name and address on a company form.

Ingrid expounded on her past trips to Florida. She had flown to Miami, driven down to the Florida Keys, toured Disneyland and visited friends up in Jacksonville, Orlando and Tampa Bay. She had vacationed in Florida at least a dozen times. She didn't like it as much as glitzy places such as Las Vegas, Acapulco and Paris.

But if Miami was all Bill Jacobs could arrange with his business contacts, then it would have to do. Then, as before, she began feeling sorry for herself and her husband. He had been working a lot. He was disciplined. He would get lonely down there unless...unless Ingrid went there with him. Then he would get his business deals completed.

Out of nowhere, Ingrid mouthed something almost incoherent about money and how much the trip would cost. She lost track of Morehouse, almost forgetting he was in the room. She strode to a portrait of Little Boy Blue on the north side of the room. Walking lightly, Morehouse followed.

It was an oil painting by an artist named J. Bellum. It depicted the fictional character dressed in blue silk leotards, a white cotton shirt with two-inch frills and a snug jacket. He held a rose in his hand and was sniffing its fragrant aroma.

She lifted the modest oil painting off the wall, exposing a safe. It was in between the bookcase and a window. Morehouse tried to keep his distance. He had helped Ingrid from behind the bar, taking her hand and holding her steady. He had been concerned she might stumble.

Though Morehouse held some respect for privacy, he couldn't keep himself from watching Ingrid spin the dial on the wall safe. The feeling returned that he was somebody who deserved more than he was getting. The feeling of unfairness reminded him of his gambling habits. At times, he still enjoyed wagering money and gambling, even if it was an old habit.

Morehouse didn't pay attention to the down side—that the urge to gamble may become a hidden illness that can lead to financial ruin. He had skipped a meal here and there to save money to finance his habit. He had begun borrowing money repetitiously, piling up debt on his credit cards and taking out a second mortgage on his home.

When he heard the tumblers click into place, it was as if the safe had a magnetic effect. He saw the combination—eight, twenty-seven and three—almost by accident. He couldn't help himself. He felt his primitive urges to steal the contents of the safe. Even from eleven feet away, he saw the stacks of green bills—twenties, fifties and hundreds—plus three glittering necklaces, two diamond rings, a handful of gold coins and some type of paperwork he couldn't see clearly, probably personal documents such as letters and deeds.

While Ingrid drunkenly studied the contents of the dark safe, Morehouse quietly padded back to the bar. A group of guests sonorously entered the room. Self-consciously, Ingrid swung the metal door closed and hung the portrait over the safe.

Later, she gave him the tour she had promised—the outdoor deck on the second floor, the eight upstairs bedrooms, and of course, the living room and other ground-level rooms he had already seen. After showing the house to Morehouse, her mood became even more casual. She trusted Morehouse.

As they partied, the night took on a slow-motion quality. Within two hours, Morehouse, his judgment impaired by alcohol, reached a decision. He owed money. He had been desperate, even paranoid. If he needed cash in a hurry, he had someplace to go.

Despite the crisp business suit Morehouse had worn to work that day and the watch on his wrist, he looked at the clock on the wall with nervous dread. He was looking for new income-generating activities other than perks and lawsuits, he thought sarcastically.

In a democratic society, the value of goods and services derives, in part, from the ethics and character of its people. School teachers emphasize following the rules, while professionals stress getting results. Maybe that was why Morehouse never earned outstanding grades in school, why he was more successful outside the classroom.

Morehouse sat at his desk, making computations of transactions he didn't report to the company. He hadn't been caught because he was extremely cautious, despite the detrimental impact, due to lost time, on his productivity and work effort. He was convinced he had to appear to others, on paper, as a worker who maximized profits.

Since there were periods when business was slow, he continued to place bets, sometimes big ones, when he had time on his hands.

After he returned home from work, he was periodically overcome with gambling fever. In a dozen instances, he used the proceeds from the second mortgage on his home to start his destructive gambling habit all over. This time, however, he determined the stakes had to be higher for him to bring in the massive income he needed.

During his year at Jacobs, he drained funds from his expense account. He rerouted money earmarked for public relations to his wallet, telling management his department was planning to put together an ad campaign, rather than just an ad. He used the money for gambling. When he was ahead, there was no problem. He grabbed his employer's money, won a profit and replaced the money without anyone at the company knowing about it.

If he ran low, he knew where to go. But there was a problem. When he had been working full-time at Hawkins, his math hadn't been too good. He had skipped more than a few commission sales the store management hadn't known about.

Off his job, his math hadn't been perfect either. At one point, he went on a losing streak, dropping money he thought he should have been winning. He believed he should have been ahead, but in his confused frame of mind, the real world refused to cooperate. He was $10,000 in the hole, a debt too steep for his clothing sales job. He plunged into his charge cards for cash, giving him more money to work with.

He had considered the possibility of selling marijuana to fund his gambling, but dealing drugs wasn't for him. He didn't know people in the drug business, and he wanted gambling money, not artificial highs.

He borrowed money from lenders he could trust and eventually from people he didn't know—loan sharks. They had heard about his exploits, and they were willing to fund his gambling habits. However, there was a price to be paid. The loan sharks charged him exorbitant interest, and if he didn't pay up on time, they weren't afraid to threaten him. At one point, he got a fist in his face, and explained to the folks at Jacobs that he bumped his eye moving furniture over the weekend.

As he got deeper into debt, he borrowed more and more from a variety of loan operations. Before he knew it, he owed $68,000, a staggering amount he couldn't pay back in twenty years. The spiraling interest climbed too high, and he didn't keep up with the promised payments. Morehouse worried about his reputation. If he didn't repay enough of the loan money on time, the lenders would go after him.

He didn't like thinking of his dead body having to be dredged out of a river.

Morehouse considered leaving the country. He knew the loan sharks were keeping track of him, possibly watching him. As public relations director, he only had two company accounts at Jacobs to dip into. If he fled to a foreign country—Switzerland, Canada or Mexico—the loan sharks would ultimately catch up with him, he reasoned.

There was nothing left for him to do, so he planned to rob the combination safe at Jacobs' opulent home. Well, not rob the safe. In his gambling-addicted state of mind, he contemplated lifting only $10,000 in cash from the safe. To well-to-do people like the Jacobs, that would be an insignificant sum of money. He would place several sure-thing bets while the Jacobs's were out of town, win $10,000, maybe even $20,000 or $30,000, and replace the cash before they even realized it was missing. Then his gambling-lame feet would be back on firm ground.

If Jacobs found out, he might even invest in Morehouse himself. That was overconfidence, and Morehouse knew it. And for the time being, that was too risky. He would continue to move money around in the company books. It was a risk, yet a safe one, he believed. A risk that looked similar to shooting pool, betting on football or playing poker. He would continue to use funds from the company's public relations budget and from his expense account.

Most of the time, when he had gambled, he had gotten something in return, he convinced himself. And he had been able to replace the money without anyone else at the firm noticing. Not Jacobs, not Reddick, not anyone.

Ostensibly, he was using the money to buy work materials for creating ads in local newspapers and placing them. The expense account funds were for meals with clients and motel rooms. Yet the money found its way to the poker table, and as long as Morehouse came out on top, it ended up back in his corporate public relations budget.

He had considered additional possibilities that he rejected. He looked into the amorphous construction budget, but decided taking money from that account would be too evident to company bookkeepers. As public relations director, he would have to invent a scenario that would be rejected by Jacobs himself as wasteful spending.

Though he had no proof, he assumed that over the years other employees had pilfered the account. He called upon his limited financial know-how to locate hidden pockets of money he was sure nobody was keeping close watch over. He didn't find many, so he diverted modest, little-noticed amounts of cash from his expense allotment and the public relations budget.

Even if he was caught red-handed, he suspected people like Jacobs weren't angels, and he could work out a repayment deal with them. He would explain he was experiencing emotional problems and his math wasn't so perfect.

But the loan sharks hadn't forgotten about him. They wanted immediate payments, wanted their money back, wanted the interest, and didn't care if Morehouse had gambling troubles. They didn't care whether he had a decent job. They didn't care whether he had a decent home in a middle-class neighborhood. They wanted their money back, plus the interest.

After Morehouse had worked at Hawkins for only a year, he was so efficient at his job he had been promoted to manager. After he had worked at Jacobs for only a year, he had been promoted to a position as a department head.

As for his debt, he was able to pay back $8,000 through his earnings from his public relations job at Jacobs. He dreamed up a modus operandi—that he was doing private consulting work. Because he was exploring other career avenues, Jacobs gave him a raise. He kept dabbling in the public relations budget and he made up a fictitious media event that he billed the company for.

Knowing Morehouse had been struggling for four years, the loan people gave him another break when they suspended the interest on his payments. Even though he had talked his way out of immediate interest payments, Morehouse was still paying them a significant portion of his annual earnings. One weekend, after he had been employed at Jacobs for two months, he had claimed $20,000 in winnings. To make sure he stayed out of trouble, he quickly shunted $15,000 to the loan sharks as a show of financial power. He had to display how fast he could pay up and that he was a profitable investment.

Morehouse just needed time to pay all the loan sharks' money, plus interest, back to them. He was easier to get along with than gun-toting bank robbers, zombie-like drug dealers and zealot-brained airline hijackers. But what he didn't know was that time and circumstances would catch up with him.

After eight months at Jacobs, he opened two additional personal accounts at his bank, hoping to conceal money the loan folks wouldn't know about. To solidify his standing at the company, he bought additional newspaper ads for the Jacobs brands. It was part of his long-range campaign for a bigger budget.

His income as public relations director was three times higher than his previous income as store manager at Hawkins.

Over time, Morehouse and Jacobs became friends. At least Morehouse thought so. He liked and trusted Jacobs. In fact, Morehouse believed he owed Jacobs something for giving him a new job and promoting him. His mind blocked out the broken leg Reddick had received. That was Reddick's tough luck. He also blocked out gambling losses and debts. As far as Morehouse was concerned, he was on a roll, especially when he went out to a nightclub after work.

He assumed Jacobs trusted him. It was the same arrogant mindset that led him to jump to the conclusion that he would gamble his way out of the need for daily employment. The truth was, Jacobs didn't necessarily trust anyone. Like other prudent businessmen, he placed just the right amount of trust in Morehouse to earn a profit as a clothing manufacturer.

Morehouse assumed Jacobs had it made. He had been pleasantly surprised when Ingrid showed him the house and the safe. They had ended up in conversation throughout most of the night, and she dropped her guard. Morehouse figured out she had grown accustomed to the cushy, upper-class lifestyle. She liked her expensive jewelry, enjoyed the comfort of her home and maid, and looked forward to traveling.

In Morehouse's judgment, Jacobs had been spending a significant amount of time out of the office, several months a year, away on business trips. However, it wasn't necessarily company business, Morehouse believed. Jacobs owned two apartment complexes in Arizona. He flew down there to check up on the tenants, grounds and apartment managers. Then he flew to California—Los Angeles, San Diego and San Francisco—to conduct company business, checking up on retail clothing trends.

However, Jacobs decided to show Morehouse just how trustworthy he really was. He had learned Morehouse owed money to investors in the community. He didn't know much about it. He didn't know how much Morehouse owed or the scope of his investments. Naively, Jacobs guessed his new public relations man had begun dabbling in the stock market. Jacobs hadn't learned from his sources that thousands of dollars were at stake, stemming from a hidden addiction to gambling.

Jacobs had kept his misinformation about Morehouse to himself. As he had done with other promising employees, he had hired a private investigator to check up on Morehouse, especially his personal habits. He knew Morehouse might have a future at Jacobs Clothing. If nothing else, he suspected Morehouse might work with Reddick and take part in building the company's client base through better public relations.

It was early in the morning, and the ringing phone resonated throughout Morehouse's house. Morehouse was getting ready to go to work and he picked up the phone.

"Hello," answered Morehouse.

"This is Bill Jacobs. You know those papers I gave you yesterday?"

"Yes," replied Morehouse.

"I want you to take them to my house. You see, I'm at the office right now and since you have them at your house, you can just take them to my house. It's the maid's day off, so just go straight in the front door and present them to my wife. Then I want you to pick up a couple sets of reports. They're both in black folders. I left them on top of my desk in the study."

With that, Jacobs quickly hung up the phone. In a hurry, Morehouse skipped breakfast. He remembered that Jacobs and his wife were planning to fly to Florida tonight. They had already made all the arrangements. Jacobs would be wrapping up other business at the office today, and wanted to go through company reports fast without wasting time.

Forty minutes later, Morehouse arrived at Jacobs' place. He greeted Ingrid over the intercom, and learned she was waking up and hadn't eaten breakfast yet either. He let himself in the front door, just as Jacobs had told him to do. Normally, he wouldn't just walk into anyone's house because he would be concerned about being accused of trespassing. So far, he had avoided putting a prison record on his resume. He thought of Jacobs as an affable executive and he assumed Jacobs considered him to be an amicable employee, even if it involved work-related diplomacy.

While he was waiting for Ingrid to come downstairs, he reached in his brief case to pull out the papers he was supposed to deliver. Instead, he felt like the inside of his head had been pulled out. He owed money. On the weekend, he might win more money than he earned. What was he doing standing there waiting for Ingrid like a delivery man?

He walked into the study and found Jacobs' desk. He popped open his briefcase and dropped the paperwork on the desktop. He anxiously scooped up the two black folders and deposited them in his briefcase.

Morehouse eyeballed the painting of Boy Blue. Behind it was at least $50,000, he estimated, and he was tempted to take all of it. He felt he deserved it. The necklace Ingrid was wearing the last time he had run into her must have been worth at least $10,000. Jacobs had talked about it often.

The whole world was crooked. Not just Morehouse or the loan sharks. The thief in him had risen up and taken control. He knew that if stole a fraction of the cash gathering dust in the safe, he could pay off some of his debts before Jacobs and his wife returned from their trip and noticed the money was missing. He guessed he could even leave the country, if the theft was discovered.

He held the picture in his hands, glanced at it momentarily, and put it down on the carpet, leaning the frame against the wall. He recognized the sounds of Ingrid leaving her bedroom and walking across the upstairs hallway leading to the stairs. He had memorized the combination—eighteen, twenty-seven and three. He turned the dial, flipped open the safe, studied the contents and quickly pulled out a pile of cash—five-hundred dollar and one-hundred dollar bills totaling $7,500.

He heard Ingrid walking down the stairway. He closed the safe and hung up the portrait, and as he did so, noticed something he hadn't anticipated. Standing next to the window, Morehouse scanned the grounds. He was stunned by the unmistakable shape of Jacobs' car approaching on the entrance drive. *What the hell is Jacobs doing here?* he asked himself. *I thought Jacobs was at the office.*

Morehouse was at his wit's end, mentally going over the amount of money involved, which he regarded as a comparatively small sum. There were other valuables in the house. If he was caught, the police might jump to the conclusion he had motives other than simply stealing money, that he harbored occupational resentment.

He had to think fast. Morehouse tried to stuff the money into an inside vest pocket in his sports coat, but all of the bills wouldn't fit. He flipped open the briefcase and tossed the cash inside. He snapped the briefcase shut.

He left the study. When he was halfway down the hallway, he listened to a voice talking into the intercom outside the entrance and heard the door opening. There was little doubt that it was Jacobs. *What is Jacobs doing here?* he repeated to himself. *I'm running an errand for Jacobs.*

Then the thought came to him. Maybe Jacobs had learned about his gambling debts. Maybe Jacobs had found discrepancies in his bookkeeping. Maybe Jacobs was on to something.

Jacobs' wife was descending the stairway and Jacobs was entering the hallway. Morehouse had the cash in his briefcase. Taking the money was a stupid thing to do, yet it was the decision he had made. How else would he pay off his gambling debts?

Jacobs had said initially he was planning to take a business trip to Miami tonight. Then he changed his mind. He informed Morehouse that he and Ingrid would fly to Florida tomorrow. Jacobs had told him that they had packed yesterday and were ready to go.

Morehouse didn't have a key to the house. The Jacobs planned to take a three-week vacation, giving Morehouse plenty of time to slip the money out of the safe, place a few bets he planned to win and return the cash—all without Jacobs knowing about it.

Jacobs had said he was going on a vacation with Ingrid. They would both be gone. What if Ingrid had decided not to go with him? They had already changed their plans once. They had decided to mix business and pleasure. What if one of them, or both of them, hung around the house and discovered money missing from the safe?

Suddenly Morehouse was facing Jacobs. "Hi, Bill," he said, struggling to appear innocent.

"Hi, Ray," Jacobs said. "Say, there's been a change of plans. I looked at my ticket packet from the travel agency and noticed I got the date wrong. The plane leaves tomorrow at 10 a.m., not tonight. I don't have to meet Ingrid at the airport this evening or go there straight from the office. I decided to slow down my schedule. I'm going to use the extra time to make a few additional preparations."

He continued talking. "I'm glad I ran into you. You can give me those papers I requested. You don't have to deliver them to the office."

Morehouse was bewildered. He looked skittishly at the chestnut leather Rolff's briefcase. He had made another stupid decision. The money was on top of the paperwork.

Morehouse exited the hallway and trudged into the study. He plopped onto the couch, placed the briefcase down on the coffee table, snapped it open hurriedly and yanked out the bookkeeping statements. Jacobs pulled up alongside of Morehouse as he closed the briefcase.

Morehouse didn't think Jacobs had seen the bundle of green bills.

"Before you head back to the office, Ray, why don't you take a break? I really appreciate your coming over here. How about a drink before you go to lunch?"

Morehouse handed the paperwork to Jacobs. He didn't want to look conspicuous.

"I'll have a whiskey sour," he said calmly, hoping he was covering his ass. Morehouse considered himself a poker-faced business associate of Jacobs, and now was the time to keep his guard up.

Jacobs said, "I guess you don't mind doing delivery work." He went behind the wet bar, retrieving the bottle of whiskey, soda and glasses.

"Most people complain about delivery work," he said as he stirred the drinks. "It makes them feel unimportant...like a dog fetching a bone."

Morehouse and Jacobs both laughed politely. With his square-looking head tilted sideways, Jacobs put the drinks down on napkins on the coffee table. His face was tinted with scarlet.

Ingrid strolled into the room.

"Was this your idea, Bill? Drinking alcohol at noon?" she asked.

"Well, I'm cutting back...in the daytime."

"I thought you were going to stop those lunch junkets."

"I'm getting there," he said.

"I see," Ingrid said, humoring him.

"You know those traveler's checks we've got stashed away?" Jacobs asked. "I don't remember where we put them. Last night, I looked through my desk drawers. I even checked inside the suitcase."

Ingrid was standing in the doorway. "Of course, you do, Bill." She looked self-consciously at Morehouse. "They're in the safe."

Jacobs gulped down a swallow of his drink. "Why don't we finally use those traveler's checks? I think they total at least $6,500. Let's get them in order today for tomorrow's flight. Then we can enjoy ourselves.

"Let's also do Ray a favor. Let's give him a tip for stopping in. Next time we need somebody we can trust, we can have Ray make a delivery."

As Ingrid strode across the room toward the safe, Morehouse planned to escape into the hallway. He was struck by the irony of his predicament. In thinking of Morehouse, Jacobs would help him into a prison cell. Morehouse didn't know what to do. Inside, he was a nervous wreck.

He jumped up from his chair and snatched the briefcase. "The tip won't be necessary," he said. "In fact, it's even demeaning. I have to get going."

Staring at the briefcase, Jacobs dumped his empty glass on the table. "That's a sharp-looking briefcase you've got there. It looks like a leather job. It's probably worth five hundred dollars. I've seen it at the office. Mind if I take a look at it sometime? Mine's getting old."

"No, not at all," said Morehouse calmly. "Not today, though. I've got a...meeting this afternoon. With someone. Out of the office. I've got to get going."

"You'll have to show it to me...at the office."

Morehouse plowed into the entrance hall. "Sure," he said, rushing to the front door.

After jumping into his car and leaving Jacobs' place in a rush, Morehouse contemplated dropping out of sight. He rejected the idea, figuring he was in enough trouble as it was. He wouldn't be able to get away. The police would track him down.

When he got home, he made a futile attempt to schedule an airplane flight out of New York. It was early in the afternoon when Morehouse picked up the phone and dialed the Behrens Travel Agency.

He listened to a recorded message asking him to wait until a travel agent was available. He looked at his watch, flipped open his briefcase, double-checked the money and waited for two minutes until a travel agent came on the line.

The man said, "Thank you for waiting. My name is Dean. May I help you?"

Morehouse said, "Yes. I'd like to get the next flight, as soon as possible, one seat, to Zurich, Switzerland."

"OK. Let me check the schedule. The next flight to Zurich leaves Friday at 9 a.m."

"That won't be soon enough," Morehouse said with agitation. "Do you have anything earlier?"

"No, sir."

"Can you tell me when the next flight leaves for Las Vegas?" Morehouse asked.

There was silence on the line for few moments. "Time of day?" Dean asked.

Morehouse stuttered, "Today. As soon as possible."

"One way or round trip?"

Morehouse took a long, frustrated breath. "One way."

"Next flight to Las Vegas, Northwestern flight number 248, departs from gate 60 at seven o'clock tonight."

Morehouse was overcome with a sense of defeat. He stared blankly into space.

"Will that be a charge or cash?"

"I don't think that flight leaves soon enough," Morehouse said. "Don't you have anything earlier?"

"No."

Morehouse hung up the phone.

After sitting in his living room and thinking matters over for twenty minutes, Morehouse never bothered to phone the airport or another travel agent. He reasoned it would be a waste of time. In one foolish moment, he had thrown away his career.

Within two hours after Morehouse had left Jacobs' mansion, two uniformed police officers knocked on his front door. They had a warrant for his arrest stemming from a complaint filed by Jacobs about $7,500 in cash missing from a wall safe in his study.

Jacobs and his wife had searched the house for an hour before realizing the missing hundred-dollar bills had been stolen. The police enquired about suspects, and Morehouse's name was the only one that popped into their heads. They were appalled. Underneath Morehouse's facade of goodwill and congeniality was a desperate thief.

Chapter 27

The Past
1996

The waitress, Sheryl Peterson, dumped the tray filled with plates on the Malone's Restaurant counter near the customers' stools. The place was busy at lunchtime, and her arms felt like led weights. She took a break before carrying all the dirty dishes back into the kitchen to the automatic dish washing conveyor belt. She could smell the baked potatoes and hear customers happily talking and eating.

The necklace Sheryl was wearing glinted in the sunlight. As she retrieved dirty dishes from a table, she felt the weight of a stranger's eyes on her, watching her.

She whirled around. A man sitting at a window-booth table, which was located five rows down, was gazing at her dress. She was wearing a brown-and-white cotton waitress uniform. The man looked down at his plate and resumed eating.

Sheryl didn't think she had forgotten anything. The man had ordered a chicken salad sandwich, a bowl of minestrone soup and a large Coke for lunch. He seemed quiet and was eating lunch alone. Sheryl sauntered down the aisle.

"Can I get you anything else?" she asked Stonehill. "A cup of coffee?"

"No," Stonehill responded.

Stonehill chatted with Sheryl for five minutes. Sheryl did not know Stonehill. He mentioned one of his friends, Trigger Terry, who was throwing a party on Friday night. Stonehill studied the name tag on Sheryl's waitress uniform. With a look of consternation on his face, he asked Sheryl if she wanted to accompany him to Trigger Terry's get-together.

Sheryl had never been a believer in mixing work and pleasure, nor in accepting invitations from strangers. She was dating Jason. She turned down Stonehill's invitation. She was expecting Jason to pick her up at 4 p.m., when her shift ended.

Sheryl had been working at Malone's during the summer of 1996 to save money for college. Jason worked at Kreggler Electric Supply, and always made time to give her a ride home. After a hard day at work, she welcomed Jason's familiar, amicable disposition.

Stonehill was scheduled to work the third shift as a security guard at the Biotech Medical and Research Complex.

After lunch, Stonehill went to a Mobile gas station and an Oscoe drug store. He bought a gallon can of gas, supposedly for his lawn mower, and lighter fluid and a lighter.

When he returned to the farm, he carried out his planned experiment. He had piled junk—an old mattress, a box of used paperback books and three unusable cardboard boxes from his basement—in the leaf-burning spot near the woods.

In the evening, Vernon and Brenda went to a friend's house. After years of parental manipulation, he hoped they would stay out of the house for a good long time. One of these days might be their last, Stonehill told himself, and they would never be seen on the farm again. Then Stonehill would have the pleasure of driving away. He would relish the memory of the rundown farmhouse engulfed in a ball of flames.

Stonehill threw lighter fluid and gasoline all over the junk. Fingers of fire rose up from the mattress, books and boxes. Stonehill's blood boiled. He embraced himself in a mixture of fear and triumph.

"Are you bringing anybody to the party at my house on Friday night?" Trigger Terry Stringer asked.

Stonehill hadn't planned to bring anyone. "I'm bringing a farm dog," he said, ignoring the crudeness of the joke. "I found it wandering around on the highway," he said.

"I don't think that's funny!" Trigger Terry protested. "Mars Stonehill. Mars must have been talking to his daddy's alien again."

Stonehill couldn't think of a follow-up for his churlish remarks. "I don't know," he said, becoming disturbed. "If you don't think that's funny, then don't waste your time listening to it."

"I demand nothing but the finest of jokes," said Darlene, Trigger Terry's girlfriend. She wrapped her arms around Trigger Terry's waist.

Larry Hall cut in. "I'm probably going to bring Barb to the party. I've been asking her about it for the past few days."

"A few days. That's the most patient you've been in a long time," Trigger Terry said.

"If you try to date a woman too fast, she ultimately won't trust you," Larry said.

"I guess you haven't been following advice from porn magazines," Trigger Terry said. "They don't recommend taking your time."

"I had to learn that the hard way," Larry said. "I've been rejected almost as much as Nate," he said, giggling.

"I don't think that's funny, either," Stonehill said. "I can't always think of anything to say. I'm not that glib on my feet."

"Even at this point in history, a lady still believes in formality," Larry continued. "You have to earn her trust."

"I see what you mean," Trigger Terry replied. "You don't want to press things."

"Except the cash register buttons at a porn shop," Larry interjected. They all laughed, except Stonehill.

"Nate, every now and then when you're shopping, just pick up a small pot of cheap flowers or a valentine's card," Trigger Terry said. "Women like that. It makes them think they're special. Either that or a bag of marijuana."

"I guess you must think I'm dumb," Stonehill protested. "With your advice, what you're saying is that you no longer try to take Darlene's panties off the night you run into her." He chuckled to himself.

"It sounds like you're putting the pieces of the puzzle together," Trigger Terry said.

"At the moment, we're interested in the museum," Darlene said. "Trigger Terry and I went there last night. We strolled through the exhibits—everything from dinosaurs to old historic Centerville."

Trigger Terry said, "I like the exhibit that portrays the quiet, noble plains Indians of the Nineteenth Century. It shows them riding buffalo herds over cliffs, surviving any way they can in the dust, grime and heat of the western plains. They built teepee villages in the orange sands, and lived underneath open skies and passing white clouds. They had to ride herd all day, forcing the buffalo to stampede toward a steep cliff face, driving them to plunge to their deaths on the desert floor hundreds of feet below. They killed the buffalo to collect their carcasses to fashion clothing, manufacture medicine and provide food."

"That sounds like a dangerous task—leading a herd of fierce buffalo over the edge of a steep drop-off," Stonehill said. "Indians died leading the buffalo to their deaths."

"Wrong," Larry said, waving his hands. "Probably there was a very low rate of Indian mortality during buffalo hunts. Despite their desperate circumstances, the Indians were remarkably proficient at surviving in the wilderness."

Stonehill gathered in this part of the conversation.

Larry said, "Even in Wisconsin, the Indians survived on patches of dry land. That's why the Dells is a popular tourist spot. Because the Indians believed it was cool to survive in a maze of desolate rock formations and fast-moving rivers. The Indians still entertain at the Dells, with Native American folk singing and dancing, performing shows amid the evergreens, pines, waterfalls and rock formations."

"You're full of shit," Stonehill objected indignantly. "The Indians made prisoners beg for mercy before torturing them and forcing them into slavery. Sheriff's deputies were volunteers. They didn't get paid."

"Wrong!" Trigger Terry barked. "John Q. Taxpayer fed them bribes before he trusted them with his tax money. Score a one-upper on Nate."

Stonehill pretended to laugh. Inside, he felt frustrated. Like the loose white string at the tail of a kite that gets swept away by a swift wind, he lost track of the conversation. He didn't show up for Trigger Terry's party on Friday night.

PART III

FINDING THE KILLER

CHAPTER 28

Jason, Sheryl and Morehouse were seated in office chairs on the opposite side of Weaver's large sheriff's desk.

For Jason and Sheryl, the meeting with Weaver and Morehouse would give them a chance to update two stories—the Kirchner death and Morehouse's highway crash. Oddly enough, they were not only covering the stories. Exchanging conversation, the reporters had made a discovery—the apparently anonymous person calling himself Marsden had written more than one threatening note. They all felt a sense of insecurity. After all, this was Centerville, the county seat, a place that was usually safe.

"Why does Marsden sign his name?" Sheryl wondered. "I don't get it."

"If you want my opinion," said Weaver, "he might be the type of poison-pen writer who does and doesn't want attention."

"What do you mean?" Jason asked, sounding confused.

"There is no one named Marsden living in Clayton County," Weaver said. "We checked the records. It might be an assumed name. It might be someone who is planning to take credit for a crime without giving away his real identity."

Morehouse was wearing white gauze across his head wound. Although he was lightheaded, he was generally feeling better. "Do you think there is a connection between the two Marsden notes and other crimes such as the murder?" Morehouse ventured.

Weaver appeared frustrated. "At the moment, we don't know. That's a possibility. There is a psychological personality type who wants to experience a sense of criminal power. He shirks responsibility, but in the back of his mind he feels guilty. He knows he's violated the law and he doesn't want to identify himself."

"Then maybe something is going on here," Jason sighed. He told Weaver there might be a connection between a pile of junk mail he had once reported to Balton and the two Marsden notes. In addition to that, Morehouse had been terrified by the pickup truck that had run his new car off the highway.

A motor vehicle exceeding the speed limit, even to the point of reckless driving, was a common phenomenon, Weaver indicated. Under the law, traffic officers must witness the incident unless there are overriding circumstances. Weaver needed evidence that the pickup incident was connected to other crime, if it was. "It sounds like you don't think it was an isolated case of road rage," Weaver said.

Over the past two decades, road rage had grown as a societal dilemma, Morehouse reminded Weaver. Dating back to the late 1980s, Morehouse, Jason and Sheryl were able to compose a list of various species of road rage: Motorists who were illegally tailgated. Vehicles in the oncoming lane driving too close to the unprotected body of a pedestrian taking a walk on the side of the road. Vehicles in the oncoming lane crossing the centerline and veering at other automobiles. Passing in the right-hand lane, and motorists cutting off other drivers from turning into parking lots for shopping centers. Occupants of motor vehicles yelling insults from open windows to tourists. Dozens of cars using U.S. Postal Service mailboxes on otherwise quiet streets. Strangers who accidentally drilled small dents into rear fenders and left the parking lot without identifying themselves.

Morehouse waved his hand at Weaver, asking for a chance to speak. He explained that the crash was deliberate, that it was caused by more than simply road rage. As Morehouse described the incident, which had been covered by the Observer, the others still expressed shock. Sheryl wrote in her notebook, a chance to do a follow-up story about Morehouse.

"The driver was likely someone who knew I had stumbled onto Kirchner's body," Morehouse suggested with emphasis.

"Then why didn't the pickup driver go after Fielding?"

Morehouse hesitated, then lifted his eyes to Weaver's. "The driver must have been someone who lives around here, someone who saw me Friday night or knows my identity."

"Was there anything else you saw that night?"

"Not that I can think of," Morehouse answered.

Weaver studied Jason. "On the phone, you mentioned something about receiving harassing mail. Can you fill me in?"

"Beginning approximately a year and a half ago," he said, "for reasons I don't understand, I received a great deal of junk mail, much of it from organizations I'm not familiar with, including both major political parties." And Jason had noticed something unusual—that on Mondays there was significantly more mail of all kinds in his mailbox.

Weaver lifted a cup of steaming coffee off his desktop and swallowed a mouthful.

"As a reporter trying to get a handle on the community," Jason explained, "I've even collected dozens of pamphlets about businesses such as the Bay View. One piece of mail, for instance, boasted that the Bay View is a quiet vacation retreat, that Crater Lake and the Marengo River are ideal for boating and canoeing."

"This was one pamphlet among hundreds?" Weaver asked.

"Yes." Jason described a sampling of the junk mail, things such as the weekly Warwick Press, the Hampton Job Fair, Joy Garden Center, the Oakland Warehouse, Dunbar Forklift Inc., Ace Construction, Roundy's, Pick 'N Save, National Trucking, Liberty Mutual Insurance, the National Law Enforcement Association, Geico, Time Magazine, First Weber Realty, Sears, Pet Mailer and Mr. Scratches' Used Furniture. Morehouse turned his head toward Weaver. "I send out mailings from time to time," Morehouse said. "Through Crossroads Marketing. The literature plays up the family atmosphere."

Before speaking, Jason paused. "I don't remember Crossroads Marketing. The last pamphlet I received mentioned a free day of golf. It included a picture of the main lodge and made reference to the Pine Knoll Golf Course."

Morehouse interjected, "That must have been a misprint. The Bay View offers golf packages, but not a free day. You'll have to show me the pamphlet."

Weaver asked Morehouse for more information. Morehouse told him his advertising emphasizes recreational activities on the lake, as well as live entertainment and economical dining at the Treasure Chest.

Jason told Weaver about the prank call to the newsroom. He had also received political literature claiming he was a grass-roots campaign worker, and additional contradictory correspondence saying he had contributed thousands of dollars to state and national races.

"The assertion that I'm a campaign worker," Jason explained, suddenly feeling stupid. "You know—reporters strive to be objective. Sheryl and I try to remain unbiased and unaffected by political opinions news sources may hold."

Morehouse snorted, "I take it you're not a political columnist, let alone a wealthy contributor."

Sheryl and Weaver both laughed.

"I couldn't meet the high standards of a political columnist," Jason responded. Jason had substituted for the editorial page editor when he was sick one day. It was one of Jason's most nerve-wracking experiences, he said. He couldn't erase more than two paragraphs from any column to get the damn thing to fit on the page because it altered the opinion in the piece too dramatically. Workers in the production department pointed that out to him at the deadline.

He could trim stories on news pages. They were easy to edit and were routinely moved from one part of a page to another part. Or even from one page to another one. Front-page stories were bumped back to the jump pages all of the time. That happened when a reporter walked into the news room with an important story at the deadline.

"In terms of unfolding news events, reporters at the Observer don't always know what will happen next," Jason said. Sometimes a building burns down or a ship sinks. Sometimes a person is stabbed or a bank is robbed. Sometimes a politician is picked up for drunk driving or an incumbent loses an election, he said.

Weaver wondered, "Regarding the junk mail and the prank call, do you think a practical joker at the Observer is responsible?"

Jason re-examined a parade of memories from a typical newsroom work day. One of the Observer's local photographers walked into the news room with three clear shots of a three-car crash on Main Street. The education reporter missed the deadline for a school board story, and he never phoned the news room to tell the editors where he was or why he didn't turn in his story. The local political reporter returned from the town council meeting five minutes before the deadline. He promised to work up a final, publishable version of the story about the budget meeting in twenty minutes. The AP photo of a bombed-out building in the Middle East was reduced to the wrong size and had to be re-shot.

Jason's memories reminded him of the serious atmosphere inside the newsroom. Was it likely the prankster was someone who worked for the newspaper?

"No," Jason answered. "One day, the mailman, or someone else, stuffed twenty pieces of mail, most of it pamphlets, into my mailbox."

Jason explained he had driven to the postal station on Main Street and asked, "What's the meaning of this?"

After he had calmed down and the postal clerk made sure he wasn't carrying a firearm in his coat pocket, he advised Jason to have his name and address removed from junk-mail advertising lists. Jason said he had refused, explaining he shopped through the mail and over the Internet on his computer. He made purchases from advertising pamphlets he received. It was just that, well, some of the mail, when there was too much mail, piled up in desk drawers and cardboard boxes around his house. It was a nuisance, Jason explained, and it distracted him from his quiet writing work at the newspaper.

In May, Jason had mentioned this matter to Deputy Balton. Jason told Balton that he was "struggling with his mail", to which Balton responded he should throw it away without opening it.

Jason did just that, and received fewer pamphlets. He hadn't even mentioned them to Sheryl until several months ago. As a curious journalist, he opened the correspondence in cycles, and threw some of it away.

Jason also told a neighbor last summer he had received animal-rights literature. Jason had not covered animal-rights issues. As Jason recalled, he received the animal-rights mailings for several years before they ended on their own.

Moreover, from 1995 to 2000, Jason received about one hundred pieces of mail for Virginia Bates. She was a neighbor of his in Centerville who lived on Bone Bluff Road. Jason reported this to the U.S. Postal Service at their station in 1995 and 1996. Jason also talked to his mailman twice. He continued to receive Bates' junk mail until April 2000. Jason and Sheryl had put Bates' mail in Postal Service mailboxes over the period of five years. They had gotten used to it, and even made jokes about the unobservant mailman.

Listening to Jason ramble on about the inescapable drawbacks of newspaper work, solidified Weaver's opinion that Jason's profuse junk mail may have been a threat. "There's a possibility someone has printed up bogus mail," Weaver said.

"Why?"

"At this point, I'm not sure. Do you know of anyone who has a vendetta against you, a sinister person likely to use scare tactics."

"No." Jason hesitated, then joked, "One reader wrote to the editor that the county courtroom should be declared a crime scene and cordoned off with yellow tape."

"Jason, that isn't funny," Sheryl warned. "You don't have to mention letters to the editor."

Even though he was a small-town reporter, Jason didn't paste bumper stickers on his car. This was because when the election ended, he didn't know how to get the sticky paper off the fender. He tried a political sticker once, and had to peel it off with his finger nails. Jason didn't post lawn signs because they had to be prearranged with the competing political parties. It was illegal in Centerville to post signs that were not approved by the town hall. And Jason didn't resort to wearing pins advertising political candidates because they left holes in the fabric of his cotton shirts. He wasn't going to ruin a twenty-five-dollar shirt with a metal pin.

Jason had been in this predicament before, he explained. When he was in college, he had covered a meeting of a radical political party at the student union for a journalism school feature-writing class. Jason had been required to sign his name and phone number on a guest register as a requirement of the journalism school. A young college man from the radical party, someone who claimed he was from Centerville, phoned his apartment, and Jason described how he was writing about the meeting for a class. The zealous phone solicitor did not believe Jason, and contacted his apartment once a month for six months before finally giving up. Although he had felt sorry for the man, whose name he couldn't remember, Jason never took him seriously, never talked to him much and never joined a one-dimensional political party.

"Do you know anyone in Centerville who might have been the caller?" Weaver enquired.

Jason searched his memory, while Sheryl sat silently. "No," he said.

Working as general assignment reporters at the Observer, Jason and Sheryl were on-call, jumping from assignment to assignment. They covered board meetings for the town and school district, and spent much of their time drumming up feature stories. Editors and reporters, especially inexperienced ones in the early stages of their careers, often considered themselves busy, even harried.

Weaver told Jason to bring mail he had saved to the sheriff's department. "We'll check it for prints," Weaver said.

CHAPTER 29

Deputy Balton knocked on Weaver's office door. After Weaver greeted him, he slid into an office chair across from Weaver's desk.

Balton told Weaver he was following up on rumors of two missing persons, Jenkins and Stonehill. He wasn't sure if they held a connection to the Kirchner death. He wasn't even sure if Jenkins and Stonehill were actually missing.

Weaver was the type of sheriff who didn't know if brainstorming was always useful. For the time being, he sought Balton's opinion.

"I'm going out on a limb," Balton admitted. "I don't think Purnell's our guy. He's not a good suspect."

"What about the possibility the couple had argued?"

The couple had likely panicked over being lost, Balton said. It was reasonable to assume they had bickered, possibly even staged a full-blown argument. Yet both Weaver and Balton agreed that after questioning Purnell further, he didn't seem to possess the viciousness necessary to have attempted to strangle his girlfriend, then push her into a mass of boulders.

Weaver had more information, possibly, from a second interrogation of Purnell. "I contacted Angel's, the brand-new hair salon. An irate customer was waiting for a trim the day of the murder. He insulted Kirchner while the stylist was working on Purnell in the chair."

"Do you have a description?"

Weaver said, "Purnell didn't get a good look at him, but he remembered the man had dark hair and was wearing grey corduroys. The customer didn't sign in and stormed out of the shop."

Weaver had worked over the phone, and suggested Balton check the hair salon, when it fit his schedule. Balton indicated he would stop in at Angel's after he did field work on the Stonehill and Jenkins reports. As usual, he had been researching files at the courthouse, and he wanted to learn whether there was a link between the gossip and the murder.

"How do we know Jenkins, or someone like him, didn't have something to do with Kirchner's murder? Away from home, out of the community's purview, he may have run into Kirchner. People like Jenkins don't always behave when they're away from home."

Weaver flipped through an open folder. "I can't imagine Jenkins getting that out of control."

"Maybe he needed the money. Maybe he flipped his lid, like Chalker," Balton suggested.

"You did a good job in stopping Chalker," Weaver credited. "This case doesn't have enough legitimate leads."

If it turned out Jenkins was simply drunk again, probably in a tent or near a waterfall, they had to make sure he got home safely. Regarding Stonehill, Weaver planned to phone around about unreported illness, engine trouble and that type of problem. At the moment, Balton could work in the field, while Weaver handled the office. Weaver reminded the deputy to keep him posted as to his whereabouts.

Weaver didn't want to go the wrong way in Purnell's case, yet he wanted to ensure no more bodies turned up. Weaver wanted to be both careful and aggressive, striking a fine line. In his twenty-plus years in the department, he believed this was why he'd seen the homicide rate drop.

A long-drawn-out case had to be avoided. Nowadays the professional resumes of officers in law enforcement included community relations, as well as the ability to react quickly in dangerous situations. Not to mention cursory knowledge of anything and everything.

"At least we don't have another Orlick case," Balton pointed out.

In 1996, the Orlick brothers, Craig and Dan, cold-bloodedly killed a deputy and a pedestrian during a chase following a bank robbery. After being apprehended, it came to light they had killed four additional people in a string of thirteen bank robberies over a period of four years.

Neighbors heard the Orlicks conducting target practice on a secluded farm property with what they assumed were hunting weapons, Weaver recalled. It turned out they had been using semiautomatic guns during the bank robberies.

"Somewhere there's evidence we haven't uncovered," Weaver lamented. "Leads we've missed."

As sheriff, Weaver wasn't exclusively an investigator. Over a period of hours, he slogged through the case in his mind while working, outwardly at least, on other sheriff's matters in his office. He mentioned his concerns to the sheriff's staff—the dispatcher and deputies. Weaver sometimes took his investigative skills for granted. Much of the case was common knowledge in the media.

Like other law enforcement authorities, Weaver didn't know if brainstorming with deputies was always propitious. But he wanted to pass information on to them, as he had done for other authorities such as the mayor and state troopers. For instance, he e-mailed a copy of the initial deputies' report on Kirchner to the sheriff of neighboring Stark County. He sought to learn more about the sheriff's observations on the matter. He also sent a copy to the office of the district attorney.

He had competition. Deputy Balton had been known to be such a true believer in law enforcement that he read sheriff's reports out loud to other deputies at staff meetings. He knew Balton compulsively browsed through cases at the county courthouse, and saved notes at his house.

Weaver tried to be more efficient, and throw extraneous paperwork away in a timely fashion so it wouldn't clog up his office. A desk piled high with forms would make him look irresponsible to deputies, he had concluded. Too much paper-pushing could interfere with an investigation.

In his judgment, Balton's approach was professional, even dedicated. However, at times, Balton followed his own tangents. Weaver believed Balton rationalized he was saving time, when, in fact, he may have spent too much time reading police files.

Although Weaver strove to remain open-minded, Balton was an unorthodox deputy. If deputies were all the same, they would have "Made In China" stamped on their foreheads. Must sheriff's officials follow a repetitive system? Probably not all of the time, Weaver reflected. He could let a deputy like Balton operate alone at times, even if his work routine didn't perfectly make sense to Weaver.

Weaver had saved several books about the Lawrencia Bembenek murder case. Bembenek was found guilty of murdering a police officer's wife in a love triangle in the 1980s. Bembenek claimed, as a female police officer, she had been victimized by unfairness in the Milwaukee Police Department.

Weaver was not an expert on the Bembenek case, nor did he possess any inside knowledge about the matter. In performing his sheriff's research duties, he had read several nonfiction, true crime books about the Bembenek court trial. In his opinion, these books had shed new light and greater depth on what had actually taken place. But the hard evidence in them didn't nail down a perfect resolution of the question of the degree of guilt of Bembenek, if she was, in fact, the killer.

The few books Weaver had skimmed over seemed to sympathize with Bembenek, indicating that whether she committed the murder or not, there may have been extenuating circumstances—such as gender and ethnic biases—for the court to have taken into consideration at the time the trial was held. Factors such as ethnic heritage (Polish), gender (female) and occupation (police officer) may have affected the outcome of the court case.

As Weaver had mentioned in letters and comments to law enforcement officials at state sheriff's meetings over the years, he had witnessed some level of bias—intellectual, personality, racial and ethnic—during his twenty years of work for the sheriff's department. It was possible this perceived bias had an impact on the society, including court cases. Among convicted criminals, certain social classes and racial and ethnic backgrounds appeared to be better represented than others. In general, Weaver enjoyed reading detective novels and police books about different countries around the world, different cultures and nationalities, different races and religions, different intellectual levels, and different occupations. For instance, he noticed it was very difficult to find books that describe countries such as Poland and Germany that were not written in the context of World War II. It was Weaver's understanding those two countries offered things unrelated to military conflicts such as farms, forests, mountains and manufacturing plants.

A subtle example of people's attitudes toward national heritage, crime and violence could, in Weaver's opinion, be detected in the editorial comments on tapes such as the nonfiction WWII videocassette, "From Beyond Hitler". The narrator claimed that the Polish military was easily defeated by Germany due, in part, to "antiquated" war equipment such as horse-drawn carriages. That might have been true. But he did not mention other factors such as the numbers of soldiers fighting for each country, for instance.

If Weaver was not mistaken, the current economies of Germany and Poland ranked ahead of many others around the world. Numerous American citizens of the Polish and German ethnic heritages had ancestral familial relations who have lived in the United States since before WWII. It was difficult for video watchers and book-reading library patrons to find nonfiction material that objectively described the cultures of European countries such as Poland and Germany when they were not engaged in war. It also was difficult to imagine that these attitudes did not have a negative impact on the reasoning behind decisions made by law-enforcement officers, judges and attorneys.

As in his other sheriff's cases, Weaver wanted to make sure he had the right suspect locked up. He wanted to make certain that, subconsciously, he was not reaching police decisions based on biases. Was Purnell guilty, or was he even a likely suspect? Weaver had to be sure.

Yet, as a sheriff, an integral member of the law-enforcement community, Weaver faced uncertainties all of the time. In determining guilt or innocence in the course of charging a suspect, not every case was black and white. Weaver believed there were degrees of guilt and innocence, depending on the specific circumstances in each case.

Were some criminals programmed to commit crime, as a branch of philosophy known as determinism implied? Or were the actions of people voluntary, not predetermined and not affected by the society?

In answering these philosophical questions, Weaver fell into the grey middle ground. He realized the arguments for determinism were complex and formidable. Yet they were suspect to much questioning and criticism. It seemed perfectly reasonable to assume that all actions were caused and that determinism was inconsistent with the idea of an individual assuming moral responsibility.

Historically, many philosophers have accepted these two parts of the philosophy of determinism. The major objection to this argument was against the assertion that because every act was caused it was, therefore, determined.

Idealism was part of Weaver's mind set. He believed that just because an act was caused didn't mean that it would necessarily occur. Certainly it was possible to imagine a situation in which the same set of antecedents could produce two different occurrences.

This is a situation similar to the example presented by the famous philosopher William James. A man walking home reached a fork in the road and had to decide which way to take home. The first path was shorter and faster. The second path was longer and less dangerous. According to determinists, one of these two possible alternatives was nothing more than an illusion, while the other was the only path the man in James' example could really have taken.

In other words, the fictitious man didn't really have a choice. His "selection" was predetermined. For whichever route the man decided to take, determinists argue that it was the only road that he could have chosen, and they could sight specific causes that lead to the man's decision. However, to nondeterminists, this argument was ambiguous since there were clearly antecedents for both alternatives.

Obviously, the man could only choose one path. But how could it necessarily have been predetermined which one he chose? According to determinists, there was only one alternative that was actually available. Yet the same antecedents supported two different possibilities.

The idea of determinism was in some ways convincing. However, in Weaver's opinion, it was not completely plausible. He doubted that any philosopher could prove to the satisfaction of all that determinism was the force behind every human action or decision. Yet it was a relevant factor, nonetheless. There was no doubt in Weaver's mind that this issue would be a source of controversy for a long time to come.

Weaver held the opinion that the Kirchner case was more brutal than controversial. And he knew that real-world cases were more brutal than cute children's stories about cops-and-robbers crimes and supernatural cases. They usually involved crimes such as theft, assault, sexual abuse, murder and dismemberment. The distinctions between belief in the supernatural in various forms and practical explanations of crime were blurred.

In the course of doing background research off his job, Weaver had inadvertently stumbled upon vague similarities to other cases in library books. The questions Weaver had were these: Was he imagining coincidences involving dreams and books about crime? Why were there embedded comments in literary works that appeared to relate to real-world crimes? Were missing persons situations more common than what he would have liked to have believed?

A citizen who studied at public libraries or a movie fan who watched entertainment videotapes could take an educated guess at the likely outcome of the unresolved case. Centerville residents at Maxi's Coffee Shop did that all of the time. In other words, when the term "woods" was used in this type of fatal situation, it could be interpreted figuratively rather than literally, meaning a person could approximate an admittedly questionable answer to unsolved cases by sorting through piles of books in high-profile cases.

High school and college students have made references to Europe, the setting for historical fiction and fairy tales about crimes such as murder, kidnapping and robbery, which have taken place in forests. While students are not always able to articulate further, these references reminded law-enforcement officers such as Weaver of historical conflicts between social classes, intellectual levels, regions of the world, genders, and ethnic and racial heritages.

Historically, even the Pilgrims coldly cast out some of the ill, diseased or alienated members of their founding colonies. Far away from the protection of law enforcement, the wilderness occasionally became an arena for brutality and wrongdoing.

CHAPTER 30

Sprawled along Highway 46, Hector Lowell's farm was located near Crater Lake and down the road from the Bay View Resort. Lowell's farm paralleled Stonehill's property, except it was on the opposite side of Elm Road, an access road to the forest. It was the same road Hilton had driven down house-hunting for a summer place.

Work on the farm added up to at least six hours a day, sometimes twelve, depending on the season. With wheat and corn crops, Lowell earned enough to support his wife, Tanya, and his son, Todd.

The steady reverberation of a hammer pounding nails into a wooden wall was coming from the back of the barn. Since no one was around, the methodical pounding did little to disturb the rhythmic patterns of nature, of niggling robins and harmless raccoons. Lowell was boarding up gaps in his barn wall.

With sweat dripping into the cloth of Lowell's T-shirt and his blue jeans mud-crusted, he took a break. Lowell, who had sandy hair and thick jowls, walked casually to the family picnic table underneath an oak tree. Brightly bleached daylight surrounded the patch of shade.

Lowell had been working on the repairs to the pockmarked barn wall, when his left arm began aching. He rubbed it with his other hand. He trudged back to his farmhouse, where he checked the temperature on the mercury thermometer. The reading was eighty-six degrees.

Lowell heard the wind whispering down the neat rows of corn stalks.

From time to time, he heard a loud noise coming from Stonehill's neighboring farm. It was usually Stonehill's pickup truck. Occasionally, there was a popping sound, like a hunting rifle. Squinting his eyes, he watched a strange-looking man, Stonehill, carrying supplies from the back of his pickup truck. Sometimes, Lowell saw Stonehill return from the forest and put on farm overalls for work.

He wondered about his neighbor, Stonehill. Over the years, most of Stonehill's land had been sold. It was now occupied by a modest cornfield, a small pasture for four dairy cows and a converted barn. It was a one-man operation, and Lowell believed Stonehill might want to give up farming due to the low income. He knew Stonehill worked in town in the winter. Beyond that, he didn't know much about Stonehill, other than that he was a reclusive person by nature.

Lowell felt as if he had spent enough time contemplating the matter. He planned to get more repair work done before heading back from the barn to his farmhouse. Lowell visualized a sack in Stonehill's pickup truck. He had been in the sunshine for a long time.

Lowell went into his barn. He climbed over the bales of hay. Through the opening in the double doors, he glanced at the herd of cows in the pasture. One heifer at the end of the field, chewing grass, swung its muzzle around, staring blankly.

Tomorrow, Lowell would wash the floor of the barn. Eventually, in August, he intended to resurface the asphalt portion of the entrance drive to his farmhouse and to repair a loose door on a metal equipment storage shed.

The farmer walked back toward his house after an industrious morning of making repairs to the barn. As he stepped onto the front porch, a Clayton County sheriff's cruiser pulled up. Lowell didn't know why Deputy Balton was in the driveway.

Balton had been assigned to the investigation, and had driven to the Lowell farm. He did not have much evidence, and he remembered the old credo: Get the facts. Campbell had reminded him to avoid conjecture.

Lowell met Balton on the front porch. Balton said, "Hello. I'm Deputy Dennis Balton, with the sheriff's department. As you probably know, we're investigating a murder. Jean Kirchner."

"A tourist," Lowell said quickly. "I heard about that."

"We've been asking questions," Balton said. "We need some information. Do you know about suspicious activity of any kind?"

"Not really. Just some noise at night. No big deal."

"What do you mean."

Lowell said, "One of the neighbors, the Stonehills, own a pickup. There's traffic out at night, on the highways and back roads, and either Nate or Vernon, one of them is probably driving somewhere late at night."

"Do you know the make and model?"

"I think it's a green Ford Ranger."

"Have you seen Vernon around lately?"

"Now that you mention it, I haven't," Lowell answered.

"Have you seen Nate around?"

"Yes."

"Have you ever heard Stonehill threaten anyone—his relatives, for instance, or strangers?" Balton asked.

"Not recently," Lowell said. "Over the years, I've heard gossip that Stonehill and his parents didn't get along. That he was an only child."

Lowell continued. "Everybody threatens his parents in high school. I haven't heard much from Stonehill. Just talk. That outsiders—city people—are no good. Trying to steal people's jobs and bringing crime with them from the city. That they're wrecking the town."

"Where did you hear this?"

"I've seen Stonehill from time to time at the Treasure Chest and Malone's. Places like that."

"Do you know Stonehill very well?" Balton asked.

"I'm not a friend of his, if that's what you mean," Lowell responded. "I've only talked to him three times this year. I guess he was disciplined down at the school in Centerville. That was about twenty years ago."

"What do you mean?"

"You don't know what I'm talking about?" Lowell asked.

"Not really," Balton answered.

"There was a story circulating, back there, twenty years ago, that his father supposedly punched him after he lost his job at the mine. He locked Nate out of the house at night in high school. I guess Nate slept in the barn a few times. I heard the Stonehills staged awful arguments, yelling and fighting about bills. Used to tell their kid about discipline and money. Probably took out their frustration over the rundown farm on Nate. Same old story. The place is too small to earn a living. Vernon and Nate both took seasonal jobs."

Lowell paused. "You don't suspect him of anything, do you?"

"We have to investigate," Balton said. "You can't trust anybody. I'm familiar with the fact that Stonehill isn't very visible around here. That he's reclusive."

Lowell interrupted, "I don't think of him as a serious threat, if that's what you mean. It would be shocking to discover that he had committed murder. Has he ever been charged with a serious crime?"

"No," Balton answered. "The sheriff's office is investigating. Have you ever seen anything out of the ordinary—guns, suspicious people at his farmhouse, a stolen car?"

"I don't keep track of him."

"Are you sure you haven't seen anything"

"Just the vehicle on the highway at night a few times. When he worked odd jobs, his farm wasn't kept up.

"After he graduated from high school, his mother was gone. She ran away, left the farm. From what I heard, she never got along with Vernon, his father. Over the years, Vernon mellowed a little. One of Nate's cousins lived there for a while."

"Do you remember his cousin's name?"

"Dell Stonehill. I met him once at the Treasure Chest. He seemed OK. Like Nate, he kept pretty much to himself. I guess he drove in from Waldwick and stayed overnight, sometimes, and commuted other times. His wife got pregnant, they had a son and he went back to his home in Waldwick."

"When was that?"

"About a year ago," Lowell answered. "Stonehill lost his part-time janitorial job in town."

"When did he leave the job?" Balton asked.

"I don't remember exactly," Lowell said.

"What was it you said about him hanging around his barn?" Balton asked.

"I've seen him kicking the door. It's probably broken. And I've seen him going off at night in his pickup," Lowell said.

Todd, wearing baggy shorts down to his knees, walked up behind him at the front door. "My son, here, Todd, has seen Stonehill in his farmyard. I don't think he's seen much that is suspicious."

"I saw him the other day on the way to my summer classes," Todd said. "At the technical college in Centerville. I drove there with my dad. We were in a hurry because I was late for school," Todd said.

He shrugged. "I did not see much cattle in the farmyard. The hill, the crops and the trees were blocking my view," he continued. "He has a small place. Just six cows and one cornfield. I glanced casually through the windshield at the corn crops rolling along the highway. Up the dirt-packed entrance drive, I saw Stonehill walking purposefully toward the deteriorating barn, as if he had important chores to perform. Other people—his cousin and father—have worked the fields."

Balton held a quizzical expression on his face. "Do you remember how he was dressed?"

Lowell answered. "He was dressed in dusty blue-jean overalls with suspenders. He was wearing a T-shirt."

"Did you actually see him?" Balton asked.

"I got a clear look at him through the passenger's window," Lowell said.

Todd cut in. "When he reached the barn door, he kicked the heel of his boot against it, like he wanted to make sure the latch wouldn't pop open."

Balton's eyes widened slightly, yet he still appeared skeptical. "That's no big deal—a farmer kicking a barn door to make sure it's closed."

"The other folks around here don't normally check the barn door by kicking it," Todd said.

"Have you been on Stonehill's property recently?"

"I don't go over there. I haven't visited their farm in years. Like I said, they've had money problems. I've seen him loading and unloading his pickup truck. There must be a lot of old junk on his property."

"Have you seen him near a dumpster?" Balton enquired.

"You mean to dump a body?" Todd said asked rhetorically. "No," he said.

Balton wrapped up the interview.

After Balton left, Lowell ate lunch.

Then Lowell went back to work in the fields. He got on his tractor and circled the cornfield counterclockwise. With this type of equipment, Lowell harvested the field, as if the stalks of wheat and corn had been lined up with a giant ruler. The tractor banked to the left as it taxied around the field.

Lowell, wearing denim blue jean overalls, killed the engine. The tractor stopped. From the distant lake, he heard the sound of loons squawking. Lowell stepped off the tractor and picked up debris, negligible pieces of metal, in front of his tractor in the corn field.

Instead of slowing the pace of the work, clearing debris saved the farmer the time involved in repairing a damaged blade. In this case, he spent a few minutes examining the metal pellets.

He put the charred, corroded pieces of metal in his pocket. Rocking the tractor back and forth, Lowell jumped onto the seat. There was the harsh noise of the engine cranking up. He pulled the throttle into forward and resumed working the corn field.

The next morning, the scene at the Lowells' farmhouse was a cheerfully decorated yellow-colored kitchen with a counter extending into the middle of the room, resembling a pier.

To the left of the counter was a series of hanging wall cabinets for dishes, drawers for silverware, a dishwasher, a sink, and the refrigerator. There was a tea kettle whistling on the stove, which was against the left wall. There was a window above the sink, which was located toward the center of the kitchen, and two other windows on the right wall next to the dinner table.

As Tanya entered the kitchen, she widened the curtains above the sink. Forgotten over years due to lack of use, was a shade rolled up above the window. Tanya, with blond hair tied in a bun over her cotton blouse, scurried about the kitchen preparing breakfast. She set the table for Todd, who was upstairs in his bedroom.

"Todd, come on, you'll be late for work." Todd, who would be a freshman in college next fall, was scheduled to go to his summer job at Duram Manufacturing.

"Don't worry. I've got plenty of time, Mom," Todd yelled from upstairs. "I'll be right there." Todd entered with a newspaper in his hand and sat down at the table, reading the newspaper. He put the newspaper down, and hurriedly buttoned his upper shirt. He returned to the paper, while Tanya served breakfast.

Tanya said, "Todd, do you think I should wake up your dad?"

"No, don't bother him," Todd said. "Not after the day he put in yesterday. He repaired the wall on the barn yesterday morning. He has to take care of his health," Todd said.

"Did you read about the murder?" Todd asked, holding the newspaper behind the table.

"I heard about it," his mother said.

"I feel so weird about it," Todd said. "I mean, knowing that Purnell's girlfriend was murdered just the night before last. We've been out in the woods fishing dozens of times."

Tanya said, "That's one of the more gruesome things that's ever happened in this area."

"What kind of a person would do such an ugly thing? The killer must be nuts," Todd said.

Tanya said, "Todd, if the sheriff arrested the right person, he's sick, very sick. Maybe he'll get help."

Todd cut her off. "Don't be foolish! How can you say that? Don't you care about the victim?"

"Of course, I do."

"If Purnell's the murderer, he's not a human being," Todd protested.

"Oh Todd!" Tanya said. "Don't become hysterical."

Hector entered the kitchen and sat down at the table. After he started eating breakfast, he looked at his watch. "Hey, big guy, it's eight o'clock. You better hurry up or you'll be late for your summer job."

Todd said, "Right, dad. I'm on my way."

Todd rushed out the door, then returned and ran through the kitchen. "Sorry, but I had to come back because I forgot my lunch." He pulled a lunch bag out of the refrigerator.

"By, son," Hector said.

"By."

Hector ate breakfast and read the paper, while Tanya washed the dishes.

Hector said, "According to the paper, the murderer chased the woman through the woods. He must not have been after money. If it was Stonehill, and not Purnell, he could have snuck in through our back door and killed one of us."

Tanya said, "Oh, Hector! I know Stonehill isn't friendly, but I'd be surprised if he killed anybody."

"I'm just trying to make you understand that the murderer is a real creep," Hector said.

Tanya said, "Hector. Just think. Todd and I were right here over the weekend, while you were visiting your relatives."

"That's what I've been trying to tell you—that it isn't likely this place will turn dangerous. The sheriff has a suspect in jail."

"This talk of death is upsetting," Tanya said. "Maybe we should drop it for awhile."

Hector looked through the kitchen window near the table. "I hope the person who killed the tourist has no intention of coming here."

"I don't know what to think," Tanya said.

"You wouldn't have to worry if those sheriff's deputies would do their jobs," Hector said.

"Hector, it takes the sheriff's department time to find a killer," Tanya said.

"Why not?" Hector asked indignantly. "Purnell has already had enough time to contact an attorney. If those deputies got the wrong man, and they keep wasting time talking to people like us, they'll give the killer another chance to strike again."

"But, Hector, let's suppose Purnell didn't commit the crime. How can sheriff's deputies catch the guilty party without investigating, and without knowing what he looks like?"

Hector chuckled to himself. "All those goons look alike. If it's not Purnell, it's likely a drunk-as-a-skunk booze hound living in a dump downtown."

Tanya said, "Don't be ridiculous. All the suspects aren't goons. Where do you get that stupid vocabulary? Get with it! It's the year 2000. The police must have clues, a description of the guy, or something. You don't necessarily know what he looks like. He could be anybody, even a farmer like Stonehill."

Chapter 31

On Friday afternoon, Deputy Balton slid into the front seat of his squad car. He turned the ignition key and the squad's engine revved up. The sheriff's radio crackled with tin-sounding conversation, much of it directions from the dispatcher.

Through experience, Balton had learned to keep track of the police chatter in case there was an emergency. In the Kirchner case, Balton suspected there might be a connection to Morehouse's car accident. Since Morehouse had been at the scene of the murder and had been placed in the newspaper, the killer had at least two ways of learning his identity. However, the killer's motive wasn't apparent. Morehouse may have seen something that disturbed someone.

A green pickup truck. There were dozens of green pickups in Clayton County. Yet it was a lead for Balton to work on. Lowell had mentioned a neighbor, Stonehill, who owned a green pickup.

As Balton drove, he noticed the gray ribbon of highway disappearing underneath the front hood of his squad car. Dried mud was crusted onto the floor of the driver's seat.

Over the years Balton had been taken to task for not being careful enough in fitting the details of cases together, especially during important investigations. He had exhibited a tendency to jump to conclusions, and when he compensated, he was accused of not working carefully. It was a case of damned if you do and damned if you don't.

Despite Balton's suspicion that there was an increasing need to uncover the killer's identity, care obviously had to be taken to follow departmental procedures. Every few years, it seemed, the newspaper ran an editorial criticizing the sheriff's department for wasting time and money, and for relying on outdated equipment and procedures. Too much or too little manpower. The media had been concerned about changes in personnel and staffing.

Ironically, when a high-profile case was completed, other cases surfaced to take its place. Although a typical deputy grew accustomed to the repetitive cycles of crime, he was not always sure what would happen next.

Deputy Balton supported the department's policies—most of them, but not all of them. He wanted to hire additional deputies, in part, to solidify his own position in the sheriff's office. His line of thought was that necessity demanded that the sheriff's office continually modernize police tactics, combining the useful qualities of both country and urban crime-fighting. On occasion, the media agitated law-enforcement authorities into making errors, he concluded. On other occasions, he thought it was the top brass in the department playing games with the deputies. And sometimes he recognized it was the deputies themselves, one deputy undermining the other.

Deputy Balton had followed the Kirchner case with enough attention to become emotionally involved in it. He thought he would scream if he didn't find more convincing, concrete evidence. He knew, for instance, that there was a significant difference between the scenario he described to Campbell and Campbell's analysis.

Balton wanted enough proof to satisfy department rules. He believed the victim had been murdered, and the perpetrator had displayed unusual ire. Yet describing that to fellow deputies without choosing his words carefully would make him appear almost as if he was callous.

For the time being, he would tell other deputies only the most believable aspects of the Kirchner case. What if they caught him missing a few points? They would deduce he had drawn no firm conclusions. It was better to leave comments that might be misconstrued roll around his head, than to admit he didn't have plausible answers for the case, he reasoned.

A green pickup truck.

The images of missing persons—Jenkins and Stonehill—quickly popped into the back of his head, and then just as swiftly, evaporated. He lifted his foot off the gas pedal, as he approached the old Stonehill farm. Balton decided that Stonehill was someone he needed to have a talk with.

Located at the end of the dirt entrance drive leading to Highway 46, Stonehill's farmhouse and barn were both tucked far back into the gloomy hillside. The wide doors at the entrance to the barn faced Stonehill's farmhouse and the long side of the building was pointed south toward the highway. There was darkness behind the barn, revealing only the old-fashioned pump well with peeling paint.

Balton scanned the property and walked toward the dilapidated home. The garage door was open, and from a distance, Balton made out the rear storage compartment of a Ford Ranger and a Dodge Dakota. Then he saw Stonehill, who was almost in slow motion and wearing blue-jean overalls, walking out the front screen door.

"What's the problem, Deputy Balton?" Stonehill asked.

Balton stepped up onto the white wooden porch, then halted. "You remembered my name," he said.

Stonehill's head lolled on his shoulders. "I think I've read your name in the newspaper and I've run into deputies before," he said in a reedy voice. "A few times."

Balton acted surprised, recalling records at the courthouse. "Now that I think about it, I remember the sheriff questioned you back in high school."

'That's right."

Balton mentioned a neighbor and an agricultural agent had asked about Vernon and hadn't seen him for awhile. He drove a red van.

"How's Vernon doing?" Balton wondered.

"He's all right."

The deputy asked Stonehill if Vernon had left Centerville, if he was missing. No, Stonehill replied. As far as he knew, Vernon wasn't missing. Everything was OK.

Switching to a different subject, Balton said, "I don't know if you're aware of this. There was a murder that took place in the forest Friday night, not far from here. A tourist named Jean Kirchner. She was vacationing at the Bay View Resort with her boyfriend, Trent Purnell. I've been talking to your neighbors. I was wondering if you've seen any suspicious activity?"

Dumbfounded, Stonehill didn't answer immediately. "I don't remember anything real suspicious. There are always a few tourists around…at rest stops, gas stations, that type of thing."

"Real suspicious? What do you mean? What tourists?" Balton asked impetuously. It was late in the afternoon and Balton was becoming edgy.

Stonehill looked flustered. "There were a couple of tourists at the scenic overlook."

"When was that?"

Stonehill hesitated, acting as if he didn't fully recall. "I guess that was Friday night."

"About what time?"

"I don't know...probably around nine o'clock," Stonehill responded.

"Do you know their names?" Balton enquired.

Stonehill considered the question. "They said they worked for a newspaper."

"What were you doing talking to them?"

Stonehill felt as if he had been pricked by a needle. "They looked tired. I thought their car was stalled."

Balton remembered that Purnell had said the engine on his rental boat wouldn't start. He didn't recall anything about a stalled automobile. Maybe it was a coincidence, but he didn't trust Stonehill's answers. Stonehill had been in trouble before. Then something popped into Balton's head. *I believe Stonehill committed the murder, Balton thought to himself. I believe he committed the murder, Balton repeated to himself. Sheriff's records indicate he's only a petty troublemaker. Perhaps they're wrong. He could be something much worse.*

"Was their car stalled...at the overlook?" Balton asked.

"No."

"Did they say anything about a boat being stalled?"

An expression of confusion masked Stonehill's beneath-the-surface anger. "No," he said hesitantly, a feeling of being trapped creeping over him. "I don't know what you're talking about."

Balton noticed a tinge of mistrust in Stonehill's eyes, and simultaneously, Stonehill was conscious of Balton's suspicion.

Balton's right wrist bumped against his holstered sheriff's revolver, a sign he was becoming jittery. "Has anything been stolen from your property recently?"

Again, Stonehill was surprised by the question. "Not that I know of. Stonehill began to crack. "Are you saying there's a thief on the loose? Or a murderer?"

"Have you found any pieces of metal, possibly spent shotgun shells, on your property?" Balton asked.

Stonehill stumbled. "I don't think so."

Balton said to himself, *If I challenge him, he might tell me something.* "You don't think so! What were you doing in the woods on Friday night?"

"Is it a crime to go out on Friday night?" Stonehill lost his temper. "What do think I was doing?" he barked.

"I don't know. If I knew what you were doing, I wouldn't ask. What were you doing?" Balton asked in a thick voice.

"I was driving home...from a day of fishing," Stonehill said.

Balton decided to trust his hunch, rather than follow police procedures. It was Balton who had decided to question Stonehill. And it was Balton who was responsible for getting a result. He fingered his sheriff's revolver.

"Driving home from a day of fishing at nine o'clock on Friday night, huh? Where was that?"

Looking shocked, Stonehill tripped over his own words. "You're accusing me of…I don't know what you're talking about. I don't know why you're asking me these questions. I was someplace…on Crater Lake."

For a passing moment, Balton hesitated. He whirled around and studied the property—the dilapidated farmhouse, the pickup, the pair of abandoned autos and the aging barn. He didn't see a fishing boat or fishing rods. He studied the green pickup truck. "Where's your fishing boat and trailer?"

Balton began lifting the sheriff's revolver out of the leather holster. *I don't have time to contact the sheriff's department,* he told himself. *I don't need help. I've got the situation under control.*

As Balton turned around, he realized Stonehill had been acting. Stonehill's fist was clenched. He cocked his arm back and connected with Balton's jaw. Simultaneously, Balton raised his gun, fired and hit Stonehill in the left shoulder. Balton tumbled onto the wooden porch. With the fury of a desperate animal, his arms outstretched, his hands together, Stonehill lunged at Balton. He yanked the police revolver out of the deputy's hand. Stonehill didn't give the deputy a chance. He fired a round directly into the left side of Balton's chest, near the heart, and the deputy shrieked in pain.

Balton made an effort to grab the gun back, but he was too weak. His insides trickled through tiny slits in the grey wooden planking.

With blood oozing from his left shoulder, Stonehill was suddenly in a hurry. He heard a loud noise, probably the police radio in Balton's squad car. Stonehill had to work fast. He had to follow his plan. Disoriented, he tried to push his hand into the tight pocket of his blue jeans. He wanted the keys for his pickup, but the world around him wasn't making sense. He felt hot pain from the bullet wound creep up his shoulder and into his skull, spinning him with fear. He slid his hand down his pants and missed the pocket again.

Sinking to his knees, he put the gun down. He groped around Balton's unmoving body for what seemed like a long time, until he located the keys for the squad car and the deputy's wallet. Dripping blood, he picked up the gun and trotted lamely to the squad. He heard the dispatcher saying Weaver was headed to the farmhouse. He plunged into the front seat, fumbled for the ignition and pounded his foot onto the gas pedal. The squad car whirled around, the tires screeched down the dirt driveway and Stonehill raced recklessly down the highway.

For a moment, Balton believed he was in a car wash. The car was in neutral, slowly moving forward through the dimly lit garage. It shook back and forth, jet sprays of soapy water pounding the metal frame from both sides. Then, like magic, the gleaming car was standing clean, washed and waxed, in the stark sunshine.

In the bleak, subconscious recesses of his mind, Balton watched his body floating down a long, black tunnel. He was being pulled helplessly away from the world, from his friends and family, his neighborhood and home of twenty years, and his deputy's work at the office. He coughed up blood.

Balton visualized Weaver calling a group of deputies to gather around his body, staring at him. Stars swam through Balton's field of vision. Helplessly, he looked at the circle of deputies and closed his eyes, his body dead and unmoving.

CHAPTER 32

Gasping and shrieking in pain from the bullet wound to his left shoulder, Stonehill steered the squad car, primarily with his right hand. Although Balton had blown a bloody hole in Stonehill's shoulder, he followed the dispatcher's chatter on the sheriff's radio. Weaver had been headed his direction, to the farmhouse, but Stonehill had pulled off Highway 46, successfully evading the sheriff.

Almost delirious, Stonehill couldn't think straight. *Grabbed deputy's gun,* he thought to himself. *Shot Balton. Probably dead. Weaver approaching farmhouse now. Deputies will begin searching for Balton's squad car.*

Things aren't always like this, he lamented to himself. *Balton started it. He tried to arrest me. Balton fired bullet into left arm. Painful as hell and bleeding.*

To evade Weaver, Stonehill had been forced to take County Trunk C. He was approaching the city limits. In the front seat of the squad car, Stonehill made out the beginnings of a residential neighborhood. His right side leaned into the steering wheel, while blood trickled onto the seat from his shoulder.

He pressed his foot on the pedal and the sheriff's car sped erratically down the blacktop.

As the engine droned, Stonehill yanked the steering wheel to the right, and Balton's cruiser rocked insanely. As Stonehill's vision grew cloudy, he lost his grip. He groped for the steering wheel and slammed his foot on the brakes.

The squad car screeched across the road, spun in an arc, careened off a tree trunk and rolled to a stop. Stonehill pushed open the door and staggered onto the street.

Escaped from deputy's squad car, Stonehill repeated to himself. *Argued with Balton. Dizzy and lightheaded.*

Ripped wallet out of pocket. Deputy Dennis Balton. Sixty dollars in wallet. Examined charge cards.

Jumped in squad car. Lost grip. Car spun out of control. Lost touch again. Climbed out of squad.

Ran. Several pedestrians down the street on the left. Potential witnesses. Buildings on right. To apartment building. Ran into parking garage. Afraid when going down stairway. Heart pumping like locomotive. Heard sirens. Heard door close. Didn't hear lock snap into place.

Need water, bandage, aspirin.

His brainsick eyes floundered like driftwood on a river.

The woods has legs. The woods has guns. The woods has voices.

The building's basement was what Stonehill had expected—supplies in wooden crates and cardboard boxes. Not only was it chilly and damp, but it smelled of dust, musty papers and water pipes.

Although supplies were kept on shelves, Stonehill was located in what was primarily a messy underground storage room. An oversized furnace unit hummed efficiently in the east corner. There were cobwebs hanging between the duct work, pipes and metal beams suspended on the ceiling.

Overall, the basement room could have been tidier.

He groped in the darkness along on of the walls until he found a mounted flashlight. He slipped it out of the metal prongs and it flicked on.

He swung his head around suspiciously, holding the gun and studying the dark basement. Aside from the heat blasting from the metal furnace unit, the basement was cold and wreaked of mildew. In Stonehill's deteriorating condition, it was difficult for him to grasp how much junk could be stored in a basement, everything from piles of books to electric drills.

Intruders should not look at other people's things, Stonehill said to himself. His eyes were fixed on a mound of junk in the corner. There were boxes of toys gathering dust and a used chair, which was too tattered to donate to a charity. Stonehill sat down on it.

He thought he saw a figure move in the shadows. He called out, "Father, is that you?"

He thought he heard the words, "Yes, it's me." But it was his disturbed imagination. He leaped up from the chair and charged into the shadows, accidentally bumping his work boot into a black-and-white soccer ball, sending it across the floor.

Stonehill found a pile of blankets in a wide-open cardboard box. They were wrapped neatly in plastic, and he jerked the first blanket out of the open end of the bag. With his good arm and hand he scrounged around inside the box, wincing in pain and unwrapping three more blankets. He spread them on the floor in the corner, turned off the flashlight and passed out in his makeshift bed.

CHAPTER 33

During his long career, the sheriff had witnessed murders he detested, but Deputy Balton's death came as a terrible shock, even to a veteran like Weaver. He felt guilt and anger over his inability to protect the deputy.

For Balton, there was no tomorrow. He had been devoted to police work. Weaver had not only lost a dedicated deputy, but a longtime partner, as well. Cruelty and banality were sometimes part of law enforcement.

After stumbling upon Balton's body on the porch, Weaver recognized the deputy's gun and squad car were missing. Since no one was in the farmhouse, Weaver realized Balton's investigation had clearly turned up evidence that unnerved Stonehill, causing him to resist arrest.

Sheriff's authorities had discovered the abandoned squad car on the north side of Centerville. While deputies canvassed the neighborhood where Balton's car was dumped, Weaver had quickly searched Stonehill's farmhouse.

Experiencing an even greater sense of distaste, Weaver entered Stonehill's plain-looking bedroom. With available deputies searching for Stonehill, Weaver looked cautiously behind his back, as if he had been followed through the doorway. No one was there.

Weaver lifted his eyes, scanning the bedroom. On one side was Stonehill's bed, and on the other, was oak furniture—a dresser, a bureau and a desk.

Weaver lifted his eyes from the bed. He glanced at the solemn grey walls of Stonehill's bedroom, which were smudged with grime and fingerprints. Flimsy cotton curtains and plain blue shades covered the windows overlooking the old farm property outdoors.

Across the room from the bed was Stonehill's oak desk. Two sliding drawers were loose and crooked, not properly attached to the inch-wide metal tracks. On the desktop was a cheap wooden clock. The batteries were dead and the hands had stopped at 3:16, not clear if it was a.m. or p.m. Behind the clock was a porcelain lamp, with the brown shade tilted unevenly. On the opposite side, next to a clear plastic cup containing an assortment of pens, were black metal bookends holding half a dozen folders.

Curious, Weaver stepped over to the desk. He pulled a red folder from the rack, browsing through the contents, which looked disorganized. Weaver studied a clump of charge-card statements, for Stonehill's Mastercard. Sheriff's authorities could save them as evidence of Stonehill's whereabouts, at least in terms of shopping and spending. Stonehill had also ripped pages out of a paperback true-crime book, *"Who Was The Real Jack The Ripper?"* by Kent Connally. They were held together by a rubber band.

Weaver removed one of several typewritten letters from the pocket, and began reading it. Stonehill had received a speeding ticket from a state patrol officer. Although Stonehill had been ordered to pay the fine, he had objected to the citation. If Stonehill had run Morehouse's Caprice off the highway, Weaver held in his hands additional evidence.

The letter read:

Clerk of Courts, Traffic Division
Stark County Courthouse
520 S. Main Street
Hamilton, WI 53549

Dear Law-Enforcement Official:

As you can see from the attached information, I am being forced to pay a speeding fine of $180.30. I had pleaded not guilty through the mail, yet you sent the wrongful guilty verdict to my house.

I still have a number of concerns about the citation, which I expressed to the State Patrol officer, B.V. Kipp. They revolve around the fact that when law-enforcement officials run into me, they are placed in very confusing situations.

As I mentioned to the State Patrol officer, I am a citizen who believes he has been cheated by people in Centerville. I am the victim of unlawful behavior that has caused me to live on a low farm income. Many people, especially "educated" citizens from "higher" social classes, are in the habit of treating me in a fashion that is at the same time cruel and inhumane.

I am a lifetime resident of this state, and an experienced farm worker. Although I suspect I have as strong an IQ as an educated person, a degreed college professor or writer, I have suffered a tremendous number of individual setbacks, which obviously has an impact on related matters, such as driving my car. Since graduating from high school, I have earned a meager average annual income because I don't have a college degree or big-city connections.

In terms of a social life, my home has been harassed by outsiders, and I have had my constitutional rights violated. In terms of the speeding ticket, I informed the state traffic officer that I was driving to my home from Hamilton. I had been planning to attend a high school baseball game with my cousin in Waldwick. The Observer, which employs idiot reporters, printed the wrong date, Thursday night.

I ended up in Hamilton, my first visit to the county seat in ten years. I visited the college campus, and watched a band perform outdoors, next to the student library. I walked by my cousin's old dorm building, and saw many arrogant students, who were dressed like sex pots and hippies from the 1960s. Before leaving, I stopped into two motels, and neither had a vacancy. I did not have a reservation, and all the local motels appeared to be filled, so I decided to return to my home, a trip of 70 miles.

After I was pulled over by an unmarked police car at about 3 a.m., I informed the patrol officer that I was not speeding and that my vehicle had been singled out unfairly. In the daytime, tourists drive much faster.

Let me give you an example of what I'm talking about. In 1997, a car with two young women inside flipped upside down on Highway 46, just west of my house. Another motorist telephoned 9-1-1. I ran outside to see if I could help. As the two women were assisted from the overturned vehicle, they refused to touch my skin, look at me or acknowledge that I and other neighbors had been concerned.

Let me add that in the northern part of the county, where I live, tourists typically drive 20 miles per hour over the speed limit and traffic police can hand out speeding tickets all day long. Moreover, it's my understanding that the police are not supposed to anger citizens by issuing speeding tickets to victims.

Cordially,

Nate Stonehill

So Stonehill had a human, emotional side after all, Weaver realized. If Stonehill had used Marsden as an assumed name, the speeding ticket and traffic incidents had angered him enough to bring him out of his assumed identity. Of course, since his name was on Kipp's citation, his cover, in that case, had come close to being exposed, anyway.

Next to the desk was a wooden crate with clothing draped over it—a pair of grey pants, black cotton shorts and a yellow sports shirt. Weaver remembered the description of the irate customer at Angel's.

He pushed the clothing aside and pulled the lid off. Books, newspapers and pamphlets. Weaver plunged his hands inside, exposing the contents. At the bottom was a cardboard box of envelopes and a small nondescript wooden box, which turned out to be filled with shotgun shells.

Weaver went to the bed, and on impulse pulled the sheets back. For a brief moment, an image of a bloody corpse flashed through his head. And just as quickly as it had materialized, it disappeared.

Weaver's throat felt constricted, yet despite this, he quickly turned away from the waterbed. Time was running out. His last memory before he stalked out of Stonehill's bedroom was that he should immediately warn Campbell and the other deputies that Stonehill was a homicidal maniac.

Sheryl had driven to Stonehill's farmhouse with the hope that she could put together a serious story about the sheriff's search. Due to reduced manpower at the newspaper on the weekend, she hadn't taken the time to wait for an assignment. In addition to calling Jason, she had left a message on Merteau's answering machine telling him what she was up to. Normally, she would have asked for the city editor's permission to write a story and take photographs at the property of a murder suspect.

She had been so busy she had forgotten to telephone Jason. Sheryl had visited Jason's country home enough times to remember he had said he was fixing up his yard. When he had time in between writing stories, Jason planned to chop down an overgrown elm tree that was tangled up in power lines. Sheryl anticipated phoning him later to learn how the yard work was coming along.

Sheryl turned off Highway 46 and pulled into the entrance to Stonehill's farmhouse. She saw Weaver's sheriff's car in the driveway and Stonehill's pickup truck in the garage.

Sheryl didn't notice other reporters present. No one else was available, she reasoned, and the newspaper needed photographs and background information. After she took some photos, she could interview Weaver.

She drove her car halfway down the dirt entrance road and walked the remaining half. She was concerned about the isolated location of the farmhouse. She snapped half a dozen photos of the house, but she needed to get closer for a front-page photograph.

As she walked toward the farmhouse, she was vaguely aware of sounds coming from inside, likely from sheriff's officials.

Suddenly Weaver emerged from the front door. He talked to Sheryl for several minutes, filling her in. He asked her not to go in the house. Without explaining in great detail, Weaver had found sufficient evidence to conclude Stonehill had likely murdered Kirchner and Balton. And Stonehill's father was still missing.

If Sheryl could hold off until 1 p.m., Weaver would give the media complete information at that time. Sheryl agreed. That would give her plenty of time to make the Observer's midnight deadline for the Sunday edition.

Chapter 34

For Stonehill, childhood brought back fearful memories of his brutal childhood. It was a resentful cognizance that left him feeling incomplete, as if he had missed everything that was fun. For Morehouse, childhood left recollections of the inner city and gambling. And for Kevin, childhood was still a mysterious and mirthful place, with the worries of the adult world lost somewhere in the future.

When Kevin was younger, and wasn't hanging around his friends, he pretended his identity had changed. He imagined he was a spy in Nazi Germany in World War II.

Kevin once explained this to his parents:

"Sometimes, when I get bored around the house, I pretend I'm a spy for the allies in WWII who has been captured. As a spy, I was trying to break out of my jail cell.

"I took a screwdriver off my father's garage workbench and hid it in the bedroom. If the Nazis conducted an on-the-spot search, they wouldn't find it. My plan was to fool the Nazis, to unscrew the screen on the bedroom window, climb down to the ground with a rope and slip out of the concentration camp under the cover of the night."

"Late one night, I amended my escape plan. I headed downstairs and picked a screen on the dining room window. Since I was able to pry the screen open with the screwdriver and snap it back into place, the Nazi patrols were none the wiser. Interrogating my parents did no good, because I had completed a legendary escape.

"My next problem was how to escape from Nazi Germany, which, in WW II, was an industrialized nation with modern communications and police tactics.

One way was to time-travel into the future. Otherwise, the next step was to infiltrate the German intelligence network, acquire military identification, pass myself off as an undercover spy and stow away on a German submarine."

"Let me correct that," his father had said. "You don't mean a German WWII U-boat. You'd have to explain why you were wearing civilian clothing. You'd have to take over the submarine and steer it into Allied waters. Then you'd have to raise the sub to the surface, climb out of the hatch and tell the allies you're not the enemy."

Kevin had said, "If I could travel back in time, here's how I would do it: I would get dressed in a scuba-diving suit, leave a time bomb on the submarine, swim to the ocean surface and watch the aquatic fireworks. Then I would use a flare gun to signal allied warships patrolling the area from an inflatable raft. It would be an amazing rescue.

"I would be freed from the clutches of the Nazis and provide the allies with military geographic coordinates showing the location of the prison camp. Meanwhile, the Nazis would search the cell and discover that it was unoccupied."

"It would take a degree of cleverness to arrange this. From my photographic memory, I would re-create a blueprint of the prison camp and a map of the surrounding countryside. The distrusting guards would crack down on the remaining prisoners, but the allies would arrive just in time to liberate the camp."

Doug had replied, "What I meant to say was, you would have to stow away on a freight ship. Then you would have to disembark when no one was looking."

"OK," Kevin had said, leaving it at that.

Those were the abstract images that ran through Kevin's mind as his father hunted for real estate. Doug drove down the dirt road. He was wrapped up in conversation with Morehouse about buying a summer place. He seemed unaware of possible problems, Kevin thought. What if the summer house burned down? What if the seller cheated him and didn't own the property? What if he bought a ramshackle cabin and it was haunted?

Doug had already been involved in a futile attempt to arrange a meeting with the owner of the unoccupied house near Stonehill's farm. He would have to make another appointment and return another time.

Although he had been undecided, he was leaning toward buying the property. Doug mentioned repairing a leak in the roof. He watched a grey chipmunk crawl out of a hole in the brick chimney and scurry from the shingled roof to the curved branches of an oak tree.

Hilton continued to drive back to the Treasure Chest. As they drove down Highway 46, they went through a heavily wooded area where the forest and highway intersected. From the highway, Kevin noticed a couple properties that apparently contained abandoned houses.

"Why are those houses in that dilapidated condition?" he asked.

"The owners are probably holding the land to see if they can sell it without making further improvements," Morehouse said. "That looks like they want the new owners to fix up the places."

Doug said, "The new owner can arrange a summer house the way he wants. He can pay a cheaper price. But he has to go through the work of renovating or tearing down the existing building and putting up a new home. With land values at their present levels, I guess that's what potential buyers are looking for."

"I see," Kevin said. He looked out the window, listening to the clicks of the wheels rolling over the asphalt highway.

"It must be freezing around here in winter," Kevin said, trying to make conversation like an adult.

"It can get very cold," Morehouse responded. "With the wind chill, the temperature can fall below zero."

Doug interrupted. "Not today. Looks like it will be in the eighties."

Doug steered the car onto a gravel driveway. He parked in front of a lake cottage. It was bordered by a bed of roses and a dirt path that led to the front porch. Kevin heard the waves lapping against the shoreline.

"What do you think of the cabin?" Morehouse asked.

"Looks like a fine place," Doug said.

"There's a fishing beach down there," Morehouse said. "There's a boathouse in the hillside down at the beach. You can't see it from here. I think there are several boats in there."

A silver metal fishing boat was propped upside down off the ground on two wooden saw horses. There was a tangle of rope nearby on the ground. A white wooden pier extended twenty feet from the shoreline.

The lake cabin was on a slightly wooded lot. It had a kitchen, a living room, two modest bed rooms, a utility room and a basement. It was about 2,500 square feet.

There was a "For Sale" sign on the property that read: "Wagner Realty. Call Debbie. 939-0045."

"It looks like it has a decent view of the lake, through the trees," Doug said. "How long has the property been up for sale?"

Morehouse scratched his chin. "Now that I think about it, I haven't seen anybody here for several years. I think the woman who owns the land has been ill. She hasn't been up here for years. Nobody has used the boats or cottage. She likely planned to spend weekends here. She has been undergoing treatments for cancer. Her husband died ten years ago.

"They used to have a lawn crew clean the property up in summer. Years before that, there was an elderly man, Russell Lopez, who was sort of a caretaker. He would check the locks on the doors and windows.

"I haven't seen a lawn crew or caretaker around here for at least the past three years. That's why the grass and bushes are overgrown. I know the 'For Sale' sign went up recently, but the property has been on the market longer than that.

"The woman who owns the property, Jessica Henderson, likely telephoned the real estate firm."

"Yea, I found the ad in a real estate booklet," Doug said. "As I recall, it mentioned something about the view of the lake. The cottage and real estate property look like they have something to offer. I'd have to put a lot of work into the place, fixing it up and that type of thing.

"Do you see the garage back there?" Doug asked, pointing behind the spot where they were standing.

"Yes," Morehouse said.

"Do you see the shingled roof?" He didn't wait for an answer. "If you look closely, there's a hole a few feet from the apex. I bet it was made by a raccoon. They have sharp teeth and claws."

"Yes, I see what you mean," Morehouse said.

"We'll have to contact the real estate agent," Doug said. "She can give us keys, and we can get inside the garage and lake house. We can take a look and determine what condition they are in."

"OK. That's what we'll do. I think you're right. I wouldn't be surprised if a raccoon is hiding out in the garage," Morehouse said.

"There is another place I wanted to look at," Doug said. "It's just off Highway 46 and next to a farm. It's on Orchard Road."

"That sounds familiar. I think I know the place," Morehouse said. "Let's get going. It's not far from here."

The house was down the road and next to a meadow. Across the meadow and down the road, was a summer campground. The entire area was bordered by the lake and the forest.

Unaware of the developing news story about Stonehill, Morehouse, Doug and Kevin looked at the house. Afterward, they drove to Centerville, where Kevin planned to spend the day with an old friend of his. Morehouse dropped Kevin off at Justin's house, and he and Doug returned to the resort.

"I didn't know he faked his death," Kevin said.

"Yes he did," said Justin, who had curly light brown hair trimmed neatly over his ears. "The alien faked his death so he could surprise the humans in his quest to take over the world. So they would let their guard down."

"How did he fake his death?" Kevin asked.

Justin said, "He hid in a space ship deep in the forest where no one could find him. The Air Force believed he died when the space ship was destroyed in a crash."

"And then what happened?"

"The alien impregnated a human, kidnaped the offspring, returned to his space ship and flew back into outer space," Justin explained. "He got what he came for."

Kevin sighed. "What do you mean?" he asked.

"He got the offspring—a half-human, half-alien creature."

Kevin laughed. "That was a funny story, but it needs something new. I've heard that one before."

"That's not a funny story," Justin said, glaring at Kevin's grin. "Morehouse hikes into the forest with a camcorder all the time."

Kevin said, "He's video taping nature—the birds, the trees, the lake, the tourists. He wants to get away from his job at the resort."

Justin said, "He's smarter than you think. He's on an alien hunt, searching for a being who might kidnap a human. Morehouse knows no one will believe him unless he brings back evidence."

"So that's why we've got a camera, binoculars and a knapsack," Kevin said. "When we spot the alien, we can tell him to say 'cheese' and bring back the photographic proof. Then nobody can doubt us, argue with us or laugh at us. We'll have conclusive evidence."

Kevin held the thirty-five-millimeter camera in his hands. Justin carried the knapsack on his back with the binoculars strapped around his neck.

"We forgot something," Kevin said.

"What's that?"

"We should have brought a tape recorder. Photographs won't be good enough," Kevin said.

"It's too late to go back for a tape recorder," Justin remarked. "Alien hunts are all about remembering things. We've got to move on without the tape recorder. At least we know our way around the area. Let's get going. We're running out of time. We have to find the alien before it gets dark."

Kevin nodded.

They saw the faint outline of the house in the late-afternoon twilight. In a few hours, the stars would become visible. As the earth became overpopulated, astronauts and robotic space probes would be called upon to continue exploring them, Kevin thought. There were many things human beings didn't understand about outer space.

So what was the big deal about exploring the neighborhood, the woods, and now the summer house? Doug had warned Kevin and Justin to be careful, and not to wander into the woods without an adult around. Doug and Morehouse had driven off to take a look at the property on Orchard Road.

Scientists explored all the time, Kevin reasoned. They experimented on laboratory mice. They studied animals, such as monkeys, in the wild. The drudgery of reading could not explain everything. What would each day be like without challenge and excitement?

So, out of curiosity, they decided to explore the neighborhood. For a few hours, at least, before Doug and Morehouse returned. After working their way down the beach, they had ended up back at the lake house Doug and Morehouse had looked at earlier.

They were still searching for the alien. Kevin was wearing his lucky ring on his left hand and Justin had donned the crucifix chain around his neck his parents had given him.

Kevin snapped a photograph of the front of the lake house. He had forgotten to bring his camera earlier when they had looked at the place with Doug and Morehouse. Kevin could show the snapshot to Doug. If he was interested in buying the property, he could return with the real estate agent. If Justin and Kevin spotted an alien, they would have evidence.

Justin glanced at the whitecaps on the lake. He said, "If we spot the alien, we can hijack that silver fishing boat and make a getaway on the lake. Aliens don't swim."

"We shouldn't be here," Kevin warned. "We're trespassing."

"Let's check the place out," Justin said. "We're not trespassing. Don't forget the "For Sale" sign for visitors. Don't be a scaredy cat."

Kevin surveyed the lake house. It was at the end of a gravel road along the lakefront. Bordered by the woods, it was the last house on the road, several hundred feet from a neighbor. At two hundred feet from the shoreline, it was surrounded by a wooden fence. The front door was under a canopied porch.

Kevin aimed his thirty-five millimeter at the canopied front porch and snapped a photo he could give to Doug. Justin unzipped his knapsack and pulled out a flashlight he was planning to shine through a window. They walked through the gates and started down the entrance path.

Kevin saw multicolored flowers near the porch. He couldn't remember most of the official names from school classes used to describe them. Some were called daffodils and buttercups, but he felt stupid not knowing the terms to describe them.

As they approached the front door, Kevin spotted the empty clothing first. The boys hesitated, their instincts telling them to head back to the resort. Almost involuntarily, they walked onto the porch.

"You can't beat that," Justin joked. "The alien shed his skin on the porch."

"Shut up!" Kevin said, with irritation. "What is that?" he remarked excitedly.

They were both standing over a filthy woodsman's jacket and a sweat-stained plaid shirt. Streaked with mud, the shirt and jacket were sprawled across the wooden porch. Behind the screen door, the front door was open a crack, even though it had been locked in the morning. A hole had been ripped through the screen. Another hole had been smashed into the glass window on the door and the doorknob appeared to have been yanked loose. Sticking out from the door, the amber knob was tilted at an angle.

"A man's jacket and shirt!" Kevin yelled. "So much for your alien theory. But there is something strange going on."

Justin approached the bay window, investigating with his flashlight. The flimsy cloth curtains were partially open.

"What are you doing?" Kevin asked.

"The action is this way." Justin flipped the flashlight on, and both boys peered through the grimy window. Their eyes were filled with apprehension as Justin sprayed the flashlight beam over the living room, which was shrouded in darkness.

The flashlight beam exposed the back wall, which displayed a prodigious hanging portrait over a grimy-looking fireplace. Four bookshelves were filled with musty volumes, including fishing and travel guides. A hallway off the living room extended to the kitchen, and a stairway lead to the two upstairs bedrooms.

Suddenly they saw the eyes gleaming, white and black in the shadows. The pair of animal eyes spotted Kevin and Justin in the window. They disappeared and the shape scurried across the floor like a rabid dog. A loud banging noise punctured the silence as the thing slammed through the screen door, which swung wildly on the rusty hinges. Self-consciously, the raccoon flashed a frozen stare at Kevin and Justin. It scurried across the porch, through the overgrown grass in the yard and vanished in a clump of bushes.

"A raccoon!" Justin exclaimed. "The alien sent it to frighten us."

"We're both going to get in trouble," Kevin said.

They heard a stranger's voice, coming from the direction of the screen door. "I won't cause any trouble," the tired-sounding voice said. "Come here."

Justin and Kevin went to the front door and pushed it open. As they entered, Justin scanned the musty-smelling room with his flashlight. Through the particles floating in the dusty living room, they made out the dim outlines of furniture—a couch, a coffee table and two chairs. There were two mounted deer heads on the wall above the couch.

The flashlight beam caught the dust-covered glass ceiling lamp. The light didn't work because the fixture held a clump of dead flies. Justin could make out the puddle of black flies and rainwater in the glass fixture. There were thin jagged cracks and brown water stains running across the ceiling.

"I ain't done nothin' wrong," the voice said.

Kevin and Justin felt a wave of cold air and heard heavy, shallow breathing. Shards of broken glass crunched under Justin's shoes.

"I ain't done nothin' wrong," the voice repeated.

Justin pointed the flashlight toward the direction the voice had come from, swinging the beam down the wall and onto the couch. In the darkness, the boys made out a head and a body laying on the couch. It looked like a shabby old man, with greasy, unkempt hair. Visible rivulets of sweat were dripping from Jenkins' T-shirt.

Laying on his back on the couch, Jenkins appeared to be in a semiconscious state. Both Kevin and Justin looked astonished at the sight of the exhausted woodsman. As Jenkins moved his tired limbs, with a delirious expression on his face, Justin swung around and pushed Kevin through the door. Both boys tumbled onto the porch.

"I ain't done nothin' wrong," Jenkins repeated, in a rasping voice.

Knowing little about empty homes, they had decided to explore the old lake house out of a sense of curiosity. They did not know they would run into anyone. As Kevin and Justin ran past the pine trees, tulips and berry plants, down the gravel road, it was as if the terrifying image of Jenkins, ragged and tuckered out, had become frozen in their minds.

When they knocked on a neighbor's door and the sheriff's department was contacted, they felt a sense of relief wash over them. When they saw Deputy Campbell cart Jenkins to the hospital, they felt even less consternation.

Chapter 35

Stonehill woke up in darkness. He didn't know if it was day or night. He lay on an old mattress, underneath a mess of dusty blankets that were rank with the distinctive smell of his body odor and blood from his injured shoulder. The clear, crusty ooze coming from the crease where Balton's bullet had pierced his shoulder emitted a foul stench.

His breathing shallow, he didn't have the steam to get out of his makeshift bed..

Staring out the basement window well, he watched the pitch darkness. He heard a car transmission shutting off in a nearby parking lot and the sounds of diesel truck motors straining on the highways. It must be night, he thought.

In a criminal frame of mind, he came to a twisted realization: Outsiders would begin working earlier the next morning than traveling salesman. Motels were empty at night, except for outsiders. Traveling salesmen had become extinct. For breakfast, the outsiders would dine on coffee and pastry in the motel lobby, and gaze through the picture windows at the empty indoor swimming pool. They would pour coffee into Styrofoam cups from black plastic spigots on metal coffee makers. Then, the outsiders would dress in faded blue jeans and drab long-sleeve work shirts, even monotonous body uniforms, jump into vans and drive to plumbing calls, power outages, residential landscaping jobs and construction sites. Armies of outsiders, Stonehill thought. His idle thoughts repeated over and over—outsiders replacing salesmen, going to work from motel rooms—until a heavy weight like gravity fell over his body.

He drifted back to sleep.

Two hours later, he heard a person in the lobby. He left the basement and checked. He found an Observer laying on the floor underneath a tenant's mailbox. He took it with him back to the basement.

With his flashlight, he skimmed over news stories on the front page. The gastrointestinal juices inside his system ate his stomach lining. He didn't care. He could read. Barely. He couldn't assimilate much. The evil wouldn't let him. *It's the enemy,* Stonehill told himself. *It's against me and never takes my side.*

His thought processes were frozen, but he made out bits and pieces of sentences, the stuff reporters spend their time putting in stories and headlines. *Sheriff's deputies investigate farm. No sign of Stonehill. Cache of guns and explosives found.* A sense of perverted pride surged through Stonehill, and his blood veins swelled and ached.

Balton killed in escape yesterday. The inside of Stonehill's head felt as if it might implode. *Deputies continue search. Stonehill dangerous. Citizens worried. Streets near sheriff's office look deserted overnight.* He read the reporter's byline over one of the front-page stories. Sheryl Peterson. *The lazy bitch won't make it to the sheriff's office for another story,* Stonehill predicted. *I'll be ready. If I don't get her, I can hit another one. They're interchangeable, like bowling pins. Bowling for victims,* Stonehill thought.

Stonehill had undergone spells of vertigo before, and attributed them to stress stemming from his circumstances. His problem was worse in the summer, especially in the predawn darkness. Within a few hours, it would be breakfast time.

More acrimony went through Stonehill's brain. *Notes for her story. Information for the story. Where's Jason? Conspirator. Criminal. They're all criminals. All the deputies. All the traveling salesmen. All the outsiders. All the reporters. All criminals. First, the citizens of the United States should progress beyond the state of watching terrible crimes committed and seriously weigh the possibility of doing something more about them. But they won't. They never do.* Stonehill giggled to himself. *Second, the story about Balton's death will be televised on TVs throughout the country, not just in Centerville.* Once again, Stonehill giggled to himself. *Third, each deputy and outsider and reporter will look at his wristwatch every fifteen minutes.*

Now, in the midst of the rat race, he would outwit the other rats in their good-for-nothing motel rooms. He would take a hostage. Earlier in the night he had heard the reporter in the hallway. He had heard her door close. According to the newspaper, she had been trespassing on Stonehill's property. She must have forgotten to lock the door. He hadn't heard the lock snap into place.

The last time Stonehill was in trouble, he figured out a way to distract the deputy. He used the deputy's own line of thought. Now he needed protection. He needed a hostage to stop other deputies from killing him. Who the hell was he? He was nobody. He needed a hostage for insurance. Not just anyone. Someone the deputies couldn't touch. Someone who was important.

The reporter would do. Stonehill liked seeing his name in big headlines, but he knew the newspaper was run by cold-hearted back-stabbers. The media sliced people up like knife-wielding assailants. They were part of the figurative monster that had wrecked his life.

The hostage was now the answer. The hostage would solve his problems. The hostage was like money in the bank. The deputies would have to think twice before they shot at him. He had a plan for them.

Stonehill thought: *People are exactly the same as tools on a basement workbench. Just figure out what each tool is good for, figure out how to use him, figure out how to threaten him, figure out how to control him and figure out what commands to give him. Exactly the same as pounding a hammer, pushing and pulling a saw, or swinging an axe.*

Stonehill thought: *Using a tool is exactly the same as training a pet dog. Tell the dog to sit, tell the dog to hold still, tell the dog to come here, tell the dog roll over, tell the dog to jump up and down, tell the dog to go outside, tell the dog to take a leak, tell the dog to take a shit, tell the dog to eat the dog food, tell the dog not to bark so loud, tell the dog to shut up, tell the dog not to bite strangers, tell the dog to jump in the car, tell the dog to fetch the bone, tell the dog your name, tell the dog his name, tell the dog to stay on your property. Yes, dogs and people, exactly alike.*

Without the master's voice, without the voice from the workbench, all people did was argue and complain and waste each other's time, pretending they were people, when, in fact, they were dogs running aimlessly in circles. People were like the dumb animal eyes in dogs, growing grayer and dimmer and older and less trusting and more distant and more unimportant each and every day.

Stonehill's wrathful contemplations were interrupted. He saw the reporter in the hallway. Stonehill flipped his flashlight off. But in his mind, Stonehill could still see the alien being's marble eyes and feel the forest's collective heartbeat palpitating erratically. He backed away from the basement door, never losing sight of the marble eyes glowing in the darkness. With a self-imposed pang of terror, he lifted the deputy's gun.

No response. Not yet.

She didn't know he was watching. She didn't know he was waiting.

CHAPTER 36

Worrying about Jason, Sheryl awoke from a fitful sleep. The last time she saw him at the newspaper, their conversation had ended in an argument. Despite her tight news reporting schedule, Sheryl had wanted Jason to accompany her shopping after work. Jason said he would meet Sheryl at her place to accompany her to the Centerville Mall. After waiting an hour, Sheryl gave up and drove to the mall herself, intending to buy a new pair of slacks. By the time, she got there, it was too late and the mall had closed.

When she returned to her apartment, she finally reached Jason by phone. He told her he had gotten carried away with the news story about Stonehill's escape. Before leaving the newspaper, Sheryl had written a story about the sheriff's search at Stonehill's farmhouse.

Jason admitted that he had worked late, he forgot to drive to her place, and he should have called and apologized. That wasn't the first time Jason had undergone a memory lapse. They bickered on the phone for half an hour before Sheryl lost her temper and hung up. When Jason immediately phoned back, she swore at him and hung up again.

When she had heard the phone ring again, she hadn't bothered to answer. It was getting too late, and she had to get to bed in time for work tomorrow.

As Sheryl slipped off her indigo peignoir and got dressed, she wondered if squabbling with Jason had hurt his feelings too much. She doubted it because Jason was resilient. At times, both she and Jason came across as insensitive reporters. Yet deep down, they were anything but uncaring. It wasn't the first time she had hung up on him. Both of them had been putting in long hours at work, and

Sheryl knew it wouldn't be the last time he would become immersed in a news story.

In the end, they would affectionately make up, anyway, as they always did. Sometimes a stifling argument leads to an answer, Sheryl thought. Perhaps she had been too hard on Jason.

Stonehill had been watching Sheryl, waiting for the opportune moment. In his callousness, Stonehill was inclined to believe he had found an easy escape route, and a soon-to-be captive, as well.

He had rationalized he should have had a better occupation so he could afford all of the things he wanted. He was jealous of reporters and deputies, of salesmen and outsiders, because they earned more money than he did, because they had more freedom then he had.

There would never be a place for an oddball like him, he reasoned. He was one of those unlucky victims who was cheated from the day he was born.

Every time the citizens of Centerville turned their heads up, they would have something to worry about. Because the person who died in the mine collapse, and the guard who disappeared, who died an unreported death, had now become the thing that had been lurking at the bottom of the mine shaft, which was using him for its sinister revenge, just as his abusive parents had used him for their own ends.

He knew the evil was real. Like Kevin, he saw it, feeling a mixture of aggravation and panic wash over him. He believed the tentacles of wickedness stretched everywhere, confronting the forces for justice. Vernon had warned him when he was a little boy that the world was filled with monsters, and that he had no chance, no chance at all, of escaping from this grim reality.

He watched Sheryl.

When she flipped on the wall switch in the bedroom, she could have sworn she heard someone breathing. She had been worrying too much, and the noise she heard was likely the wind playing a trick on her stressed-out mind.

As Sheryl looked around the dusky living room, her contemplations returned to Jason. Unless he was upset, why would he be here at this time of night?

"Jason, is that you?" she asked.

In the obscure light filtering from the bedroom lamp into the living room, she made out the blurry shape of Stonehill. His left arm was limp and its movement restricted. He was holding an L-shaped object that Sheryl couldn't see clearly.

When Sheryl walked into the living room, a frightening heaviness crept into the pit of her stomach. It was the same kind of feeling she experienced when she was writing a story and suddenly realized she had missed the deadline.

Even in the deficient light, Stonehill managed to clamp his right hand over Sheryl's mouth. Sheryl struggled against what felt like a snake coiled around her head. Her attempt to scream for help was muffled.

Stonehill pushed Sheryl across the living room into a chair he had retrieved earlier from the kitchen. With his right hand, he threw her forcefully.

For a moment, Stonehill's hand disappeared. "Hey, what is this? Jason…is that…"

Before Sheryl was able to resume talking, the intruder fastened a cloth snugly around her mouth. To taunt the hostage, and to taunt the alien in his head, Stonehill placed the gun down on the living room carpet. Then he picked it up.

A shiver of terror came over Sheryl. Oh God! This must be a dream, a figment of my imagination! she thought. But it wasn't a dream. Sheryl's heart was beating faster than ever. She considered screaming for help, but Stonehill pointed the gun at her.

"It's about two o'clock in the morning so I doubt your neighbors will hear you, anyway," Stonehill threatened.

"I want to be released," Sheryl mumbled from underneath the gag.

Stonehill held a firm grip on the sheriff's revolver. "I'm afraid that's not possible. You're a hostage now."

"I've got a boyfriend," Sheryl announced.

"I know," Stonehill said, despite his paranoid condition. "Where are his clothes?" Stonehill asked rhetorically, with a tinge of desperation. Sheryl couldn't help noticing the flowery blood stain seeping through his shirt.

Stonehill looked around the apartment, the beaded sweat dripping down from his forehead. From the living room, Sheryl made out the mound of tangled blankets on her bed. She saw her bathrobe and pajamas draped over the side of the dresser chair next to her bed, where she had left them when she had gotten dressed.

Holding the gun, Stonehill pushed Sheryl into the bedroom closet and closed the door. Sheryl heard him pulling drawers out of her dresser. She noticed that Jason had left two sports shirts and a pair of blue jeans hanging in the closet. His gym bag was sitting in the living room next to the couch.

Angrily, Stonehill spilled the contents of a dresser drawer onto the bedroom floor. Sheryl knew he was becoming frustrated. He pulled open the closet door and spotted Jason's jeans and shirts. He held the pants to his hips. Then he walked to the mirror over the dresser and held them against his waist. He estimated Jason's clothes, even if they didn't fit perfectly, would cover up his identity.

Threatening Sheryl with the gun, he put the jeans on, and although they were too large, decided to stay in them. The yellow sport shirt was also baggy. Then Stonehill got a break. He was going to brag to Sheryl about evading sheriff's officials. When he walked into the living room, he spotted the grey gym bag next to the couch. He dug through it and fished out Jason's tennis shoes. They fit, and as Stonehill tied the laces, he laughed to himself with a premature sense of triumph.

As he ordered Sheryl to return to the living room, reeking of sweat and blood, he resembled an astronaut in a baggy space suit.

Sheryl's eyes glanced at the front door.

"You made a mistake. You forgot to lock it," Stonehill said. "Don't you like me watching over you, taking care of you?"

"Not at all," Sheryl responded defiantly, saliva spilling onto the gag. "You broke into my apartment. You're invading my privacy."

"You've got that backward, bitch," Stonehill asserted. "You've put my name in the newspaper, once again destroying my family's reputation. Stonehill was in newspaper headlines long ago. What would my father think? You've upset him. You understand, don't you? I'll have to stay out of the house for the night...in the woods...with that thing. Don't you understand how awful that is?"

"I guess so," Sheryl mumbled despondently.

"You guess so?" Stonehill questioned angrily.

Stonehill studied Sheryl in the corner of the living room, and saw the questions in her eyes, as his parents had seen the questions in his eyes, when they told him the world was no good. His parents had said the world was evil, and had invested their time and what little money they had in raising him on the farm. The hostage would understand what he meant when he said the world was a bad place.

Stonehill noticed Sheryl crying, several tears tumbling over the gag. He seldom experienced pity for other people, even Sheryl. Stonehill stood in the hollow shaft of moonlight seeping through the window. Sheryl looked at him. In contradiction to her harrowing circumstances, she experienced a small amount of sympathy for Stonehill.

Stonehill wiped the beads of perspiration off of the oily skin on his forehead onto his bloody arm. The sport shirt Stonehill had put on was already becoming stained with blood and sweat.

"Don't worry," Stonehill said, his voice breaking the silence. Sheryl could see Stonehill's crazy-looking face in the shadows. "There's nobody else around," he said. "There's nothing they can do to help you, anyway."

She had finished crying.

"I'm getting even against folks around here. I have to atone for the errors of my parents...and you...and the people in the community. They took advantage of my family for generations. They have been getting away with murder. I saw that at the farm, I saw that in the woods, and I saw that here in town."

It was not difficult for Sheryl to believe Stonehill had committed murder. His blasphemous tirade amounted to a description of a bad childhood. Like his father, he had experienced trouble keeping a series of seasonal jobs and running the small farm. It didn't take him long to realize each job was another dead end in an unrelenting series of dead ends. And too many neighbors and residents had learned about his antisocial behavior.

Stonehill repeated more derogatory comments about his "good-for-nothing father". And he exhibited one of the classic symptoms of schizophrenia—he blamed convenient scapegoats for his failures.

He recalled the nominal amount of positive attention his parents had given him. They hadn't allowed him much autonomy. His parents had warned him to avoid lazy degenerates, yet his father had been a binge drinker and his mother had disappeared. That was either their fault or the world's fault or both. Stonehill didn't care, just as long as he had convenient targets around to make up for his parents.

Stonehill reasoned that anybody and everybody owed him a debt. There were no distinctions between individuals. His father had once described the townspeople as a horde of grubby fools who hadn't bought his flying saucer story.

"I never liked snoops and back-stabbers, at the newspaper or anywhere else," Stonehill ranted. "Big mouths. I have always hated them. When your around big mouths, confrontation is inevitable.

"The police, teachers and politicians are just as bad as big mouths. They're all back-stabbers," he continued. "People are corrupt, yet they are not purposefully corrupt. Therefore, they forgive themselves. This is ridiculous. The system is mad."

For a moment he paused, taking a break from his ranting commentary. His eyebrows were knitted together in confusion. Now Sheryl held a better understanding of Stonehill's resentment toward anyone and everyone in Centerville. Sheryl could hear sounds of traffic outside the building. The putrid smell coming from Stonehill's wound was growing profusely. The odor choked Stonehill's throat, and he grabbed his neck with his hand.

"The people in this town are like narrow-minded fanatics. Each one sticks with his own kind—his own intellectual level, his own personality type, his own occupation. In short, they are a bunch of assholes," he yelled.

Stonehill smirked, and quickly erased his twisted grin. "If I were running Centerville and you were covering the story, the residents wouldn't be allowed to go anyplace—not to school, not to work, not home, not any place. Not without my permission."

Sheryl couldn't contain herself. "You're joking, aren't you? That would be cruel to treat them that way."

The fluorescent numbers showing the time on the front of the digital clock on the wall across the room slid quietly into place. "They're the ones who are cruel. Not me. Most people cover up their cruelty."

This self-conversational diatribe continued, and at one point, Stonehill said: "The news anchorman uses the climactic part of crime as a major news event on his show every night. It's cruel to repeat violence on the news every evening. It's cruel because there's none left over for people like me, who have the right to use violence."

He hesitated. "My parents are gone now. Kellinger Mining and Lumber Co. needed workers. My parents were supposed to have been prosperous years ago, and here my mother went and took off and disappeared, and my father...and before that, he was going to kill me...and then, I should have killed the whole town. My father was desperate. He didn't care about the law. On the farm, he could make mistakes, terrible ones, and get away with them. Hardly anybody knew."

He stopped talking. "Nobody believes me."

"What do you intend to do to me?" Sheryl asked, wincing uncontrollably.

"I don't need a reporter snooping around here. Not with the deaths. I think you're in good enough shape to travel."

He steered her to the front door, but left the gag in place. She felt the cold barrel of the gun against her temple.

"Don't make a sound," he said. "Let's go."

He led Sheryl through the door, into the deserted hallway and down the stairwell. Stonehill pushed her into the front driver's seat of her car. The parking garage was eerily silent. Sheryl started the ignition, and with Stonehill sitting next to her and holding the gun, pulled out of the parking lot.

CHAPTER 37

Clayton County Sheriff Roger Weaver faced the greatest challenge of his career. People he was responsible for had unexpectedly turned up dead or missing. Balton was dead. He had been murdered viciously by Stonehill at the farmhouse. Right under Weaver's nose. A harmless tourist was dead. Not just dead, but murdered brutally by a psychopathic stranger. Again, Weaver was responsible. She had come to the lake for a vacation, to escape her humdrum life in the city.

And then something even more unpredictable took place. Morehouse had talked about a nightmare in which the victim, a woman, likely Kirchner, was running through the woods, desperately struggling to escape the attacker, who was presumably Stonehill. The sheriff had also experienced an unusual dream. And deputies had told Weaver about Balton's theories, especially his belief that an angry outcast had mercilessly stalked Kirchner and ruthlessly killed her.

Weaver reviewed the facts. Morehouse had a prison record and had served his time. He had admitted to having gone through an obsession with gambling. And he had stumbled onto an unconscious man. In the middle of the night, sitting up on the pillows on his bed, he had phoned Weaver to tell him about a nightmare.

That was unusual. Most folks don't phone the sheriff's office to describe nightmares.

Weaver had heard the gossip, and had called the hospital to double-check. Morehouse had told the nurse, Elow, and the psychiatrist, Nelson, that following the car crash on the highway, Morehouse had experienced vivid hallucinations.

Morehouse had sustained a severe blow to the head. He complained to the hospital psychiatrist he had seen phantoms in his head. At the time, he believed they were real. The doctor, nurse and psychiatrist assured Morehouse they had been caused by the injury to his head.

How many deaths had been connected to the woods and the lake over the years? Weaver asked himself. No one knew the exact number.

Weaver had to cover a lot of ground fast. Having worked overtime studying files at the courthouse, Balton may have known how many deaths were connected to the forest. But Balton was dead. And judging from the apparent struggle that had taken place, Kirchner knew an assailant was chasing after her. And she was dead. And Morehouse…Morehouse had been seen at the library, reading about the forest. Morehouse might be able to tell him about the unexplained violence.

On the surface, Weaver was supposed to be a problem-solver, especially in terms of preventing death and stopping crime. But below the surface, he questioned himself about his own competence. Why couldn't he figure out what was transpiring in the Stonehill case?

He had received even more bad news when Jason told him that Sheryl, an ambitious reporter, was missing. Jason and Sheryl had become embroiled in an argument Saturday at the newspaper. At some point, she had hung up on him. When he called repeatedly, she failed to answer the phone. When he went to Sheryl's apartment Sunday, he found the door half open. Sheryl wasn't there and wasn't at the newspaper working on the Stonehill story. Her car was missing from the parking garage and Deputy Campbell had found a trail of blood stains leading to the basement storage room.

Jason believed a doll was missing from Sheryl's bedroom. He told Weaver she had complained about hearing noises in her apartment. When they had visited the scenic overlook, the same night Kirchner was murdered, she had been worried about violence.

Weaver had to have concrete evidence. Normally, Weaver didn't put much faith in opinions about suspects. But the way things were going, it might only be a matter of time before he did.

Weaver pondered Stonehill. Following a rotten childhood, Stonehill, a reclusive, isolated farmer, appeared to be bent on revenge. He murdered Deputy Balton and had almost certainly killed Kirchner. Vernon Stonehill, Nate's father, was still missing. Stonehill's mother hadn't been seen since the 1970s, when she reportedly fled the farm for New York or Las Vegas. And Vernon had even gone to New York to look for her.

Weaver considered the questions this raised. What was the explanation for the miserable human monster that Stonehill had become? His childhood? Why had Morehouse and Kevin experienced visions warning them of Stonehill's attacks?

Sheryl didn't know Morehouse or Kevin very well. Even though she was a newspaper reporter, she had admitted to feeling watched. Jason and Sheryl had been in the general vicinity of the spot where Kirchner was murdered. They covered the sheriff's department for the newspaper, and they had run into more trouble than they had bargained for.

Both Stonehill and Jenkins had been missing for several weeks. Justin and Kevin had stumbled onto Jenkins in a summer cottage. Once again, he had gotten lost, and had made his way back to civilization. However, he told Campbell he had been too afraid to sleep in the woods, too frightened of something he couldn't put his finger on. Overall, Weaver's instincts argued against making serious decisions based upon vague warnings. Yet he had to find Stonehill as fast as possible.

Weaver went into the dispatcher's office. The dispatcher, Janet Stewart, was at her work station behind the glass partition, talking to Deputy Eric Upton. At twenty-five years of age, Upton, a budding, white-collar crime specialist, recognized the importance of stopping Stonehill as much as Balton had.

Weaver said, "We have to do a better job of canvassing the town and farms. We don't know what happened to Stonehill…or where he is."

"Balton already tried to arrest him at his farmhouse once," Upton said. "I'd be surprised if he tried to return there. That would be too obvious, even though it's a possibility."

"Wherever we find Stonehill, I'm expecting him to be armed and dangerous," Weaver said. "We'll have to call on our experience. We can't let him get away again."

Weaver approached the dispatcher's desk and flipped on the radio. "This is Weaver at dispatch calling Deputy Jones."

"This is Jones," came the reply.

"I want you posted at Stonehill's farmhouse," Weaver barked into the microphone. "He might try to return to his home."

"I'm near Highway 46," Jones radioed back. "I'll get there in 10 minutes."

"Ten-four," Weaver said. Next, Weaver contacted the state troopers' headquarters for assistance with a search throughout Clayton County. Earlier, he had put out an all-points-bulletin for Stonehill. Weaver didn't know how to express his real opinions about Vernon Stonehill's disappearance, or the dreams connected to the deaths of Balton and Kirchner.

Weaver backed away from the dispatcher's console.

"He might be en route out of the county," Upton interjected. "Why would he hang around Centerville?"

"Because of his malicious desire to kill and cause trouble," Weaver said. "Because he has no place to go. He's injured. In a psychopath's confused state of mind, killing and evading the authorities might seem like necessities. He may want to cause more trouble. We don't know where he is. We have to figure out a way of exposing his whereabouts.

"When the troopers arrive, I want a neighborhood-by-neighborhood search of Centerville," Weaver said.

With a look of concern on his face, Deputy Campbell walked up to Weaver.

"We had no way of knowing," he said, a sound of distress in his speech. "Balton's mood shifts, the edginess...that Balton would go there...that Stonehill is a killer...Balton suspected someone other than Purnell all along."

"Why was that?" Weaver asked.

Campbell said, "The courthouse sheriff's records...and the woods...must have affected him somehow...in his mind...like the stories that have been circulating. Other than Stonehill's bad reputation, that's all I can think of."

"Affected Balton? I guess at this point, I'm starting to believe that's a possibility," Weaver said.

"Do you remember that phone I got from Morehouse out at the resort? He called me at the sheriff's office to report a bad nightmare in which a terrified woman, someone like Kirchner, was murdered. It kept him awake half the night and sounded like it frightened him."

"I heard about that," Campbell said.

"I think these nightmare theories have some truth in them. That they contain warnings about the future."

There was a stony silence.

"I don't know exactly how to put this," Weaver said. "I had a nightmare one night, a vivid one. Balton and I worked as prison officials. The sheriff's office here was a maximum security prison complex. An inspector arrived to check up on the place. I had to leave. The inspector wanted to learn where the inmates were located. He and Balton went on a perilous hike down a dirt access road in the woods to some type of abandoned building...and a graveyard."

Weaver halted his speech, trying to select his words more carefully. "I think the nightmare was a warning!" Weaver exclaimed.

Campbell shrugged his ample shoulders. "That is hard to swallow! You and Balton worked in a prison."

Weaver said, "The prison setting was different from the old Stonehill place. However, there was a parallel—the fact that Stonehill was going to be driven to the county jail."

"Do you remember Kevin's fears?" Campbell asked sheepishly.

"Yeah," Weaver replied. "His father is an old friend of Ray's. We went fishing together."

"I understand that when he was at Morehouse's place, he fell off the pier and believed he was drowning. His father didn't bother to contact the sheriff's department. Anyway, Kevin told Hilton and Morehouse he had a vision in the water, like your dream. He thought he saw something mysterious in the lake."

"I'm familiar with that," Weaver said. "A pattern of dreams and coincidences."

"One thing we know for sure: At this point, Stonehill is our man," Campbell said. "He's really out to get us."

"All murder investigations are about pressure and doing our jobs when it counts. We can't ignore the facts. But we don't have to fully explain everything we don't understand to the state troopers. If there is someone or something behind the deaths other than Stonehill, we'll have to cross that bridge when we get to it. For now, follow standard procedure," Weaver finished.

"You mean treat Stonehill like…an insane person?" Campbell asked.

"Yes," Weaver said. "Whatever we do, we don't want any more one-on-one showdowns with Stonehill. He's too much for any one of us."

"How do we explain the nightmares?" Campbell asked.

"We don't," Weaver answered. "At least not right away. Like you said, we've got more than enough evidence that Stonehill is our man."

CHAPTER 38

Sheryl studied the twelve-gauge shotgun propped against a narrow stack of wooden crates next to the wall. She was tied to an uncomfortable wooden chair toward the middle of the nondescript room. She swallowed hard and closed her eyes. With all her might, Sheryl pulled her wrists and ankles against the rope, yet she was unable to break free.

Along the wall to her left was a maple computer console holding a battery-powered laptop, which was on. Next to that was a long, rectangular wall closet. It was partially open, revealing half a dozen rifles and handguns propped against the back wall. No doubt Stonehill also had ammunition in storage. Hanging on a rack next to the guns were long medical IV tubes, syringes and plastic bags containing powdered drugs.

On the other side of the room, beakers, test tubes and burners sat on a Formica lab table. The table was located near a white porcelain sink that smelled of formaldehyde. Next to the sink was a visored helmet.

Strewn about the floor were cigarette butts, fast-food wrappers, beer bottles and styrofoam coffee cups. Against the back wall near the shotgun were empty cardboard boxes and plastic packaging, a few rusted workbench tools, and a pile of lidless metal cooking pots and frying pans.

Sheryl called for help, but there was no answer. Looking through the dust-stained window, she could see the rows of trees in the woods.

Stonehill entered the room. He lifted the shotgun in his hands and slammed the butt off the wooden wall. A ball of loud noise echoed through the empty building.

Sheryl flinched. She couldn't speak through the knot of tension in her throat. Her eyes were closed in fear. When she opened them, the scene was the same.

"There is no possibility of escaping from here," Stonehill taunted. "I knew you were thinking of running away. That is a hopeless illusion," he said.

Despite his pronouncement that it was useless to try to run away, Sheryl regarded Stonehill as a deluded crackpot who could be outwitted. Yet at this stage of her captivity, she wasn't sure how to confront him.

Stonehill smirked at her. Blood trickled in rivulets from the foul-smelling crevices of the bullet wound in his left shoulder. Underneath his sometimes glowering countenance, she sensed his brainsick malice.

Stonehill launched into another zealous speech. "The plot here is predictable," Stonehill explained. "An angry madman is out for revenge because his head was screwed up...by his parents and by the thing in the mine."

Stonehill's hostility was not waning. His body jerked upward in frustration, like a human version of an exclamation mark.

"You have trouble understanding people. To compensate, you work as a reporter so you can pry into bullshit you can't figure out. I don't bother to read the newspaper because I already know everything."

He derided the society as if he was a foreign being observing humanity from a black forest. Terror scurried through her blood veins, and her palpitating heartbeat accelerated in the fashion of a speeding driver pressing his foot against the gas pedal.

Only yesterday, she had been writing in the newsroom, following the rules of print journalism and working on a computer tube. Outside the newspaper building, when she had finished talking to other reporters on the sidewalk, she entered her car to drive home. She didn't remember why she hadn't informed the city editor she was working on the story about the search at Stonehill's house. Judging from Stonehill's seething temperament, he had read Sheryl's and Jason's stories about the case.

With a nauseating feeling in the pit of her stomach, she listened to the doorjamb creak and looked at Stonehill. There was scraggly stubble around his chin and over his chirlish lips. He was dressed similar to a soldier, wearing army-green pants and a grey work shirt.

Stonehill picked up a plastic tray filled with screws. He swung the tray in a half-arc toward his back and flung the screws around the room like a lawn sprinkler spraying water. He picked up an empty beer bottle and smashed it off the floor. He sat down at the table and pulled out a leather wallet, removed the paper money and counted the bills. Then he put the wad back into the billfold.

Stonehill's weathered, expressionless face was a rubbery mask. He started another insolent lecture, and when he talked, the tone of his voice was bitter. "As a reporter, you should be aware that the quality of the news media has been growing worse for decades. As a writer, you should be aware that the stature of literature has been deteriorating for centuries. Misinformed citizens believe that's a current trend and not a historical trend," he said.

"Some argue this is caused by tensions between the social classes. Other people think it's immorality, the corrupt media and dependence on modern technology, creating people who are like aliens, who use the new technology without much restraint."

Stonehill held a crazy look in his eyes, almost talking to himself.

"That's all entirely incorrect. That situation has existed for centuries. Shakespeare was obviously a better writer than Charles Dickens. Charles Dickens was a better writer than Mark Twain. Mark Twain was a better writer than Edgar Allen Poe. Edgar Allen Poe was a better writer than Sir Arthur Conan Doyle. Sir Arthur Conan Doyle was a better writer than Ernest Hemingway. Ernest Hemingway was a better writer than F. Scott Fitzgerald. F. Scott Fitzgerald was a better writer than John Steinbeck. John Steinbeck was a better writer than the best contemporary authors. I can see there is a path of historical progression. The farther we go back in literary history, the more sensitive the intellect of the writer, the higher the degree of dedication to the profession, the greater the level of appreciation among readers."

Stonehill said, "Today, students, like reporters, are spread thin throughout a massive institutional educational system. They wade through the fallout of information from the population explosion of the 1980s. They don't have time to concentrate on any one subject for very long."

Stonehill continued. "What would you think about an explosion?" Stonehill asked laconically. "A little ole' explosion," he repeated. "That would cause this whole place to collapse. Then I would be important and you would be unimportant."

The air was cool, like a hard mantle over a fireplace, and it carried the smells of junk food and body odor. The yellowing wallpaper was old and ugly, faded in places, and covered with a film of dust.

Sheryl's gaze returned to the shotgun on the wooden crate.

Closing her eyes, she visualized beams of gentle light, waves of pure energy, cleansing the inherent evil from inside her, circling around her like sunshine. The rejuvenating light would flow from her hands, penetrating her enemies and defending justice.

As long as she kept her eyes closed, the light would flow from her fingertips. She held her eyes closed for a moment longer before opening them. Although it was dim, she observed that Stonehill had disappeared.

She saw the doll propped up in the corner, its unmoving plastic face staring coldly at her. Somehow, Stonehill's twisted reasoning had led him to bring the doll along.

Although she was numb with a headache, the doll's eyes glinted red in the darkness. She stared at them. Dead eyes. Plastic eyes. Doll's eyes, which she believed the breeze in her apartment had blown open and closed.

She continued to glower at them, realizing they were simply doll's eyes.

Groggy, she glanced across the empty room to the opposite side. There was a portable TV quietly sitting on a low brass stand. Outdoors, the branches hanging over the window shifted with the wind.

Under duress, Sheryl swivelled her head around, hoping Jason was in the room. No one was there. Then an illogical thought went through her head. Maybe like the doll in her apartment, Stonehill's face would become Jason's familiar, reassuring visage.

She wished she hadn't gotten mad at Jason. She would tell him about her terrifying experience with Stonehill. She wanted to return to her bed, hugging the doll, then hugging Jason.

Stonehill seemed to be accustomed to having lost his grip on reality, yet Sheryl did not entirely accept her misery.

Suddenly the abandoned room whirled slowly in tiny circles and later in wide hallucinatory arcs—a dizzying, mawkish version of a merry-go-round at an amusement park. It was like floating through orbit in a space ship that was traveling farther and farther away from Earth.

After hovering on the brink of sleep and wakefulness, feeling her anatomical shell of flesh and bones, Sheryl passed out. As she slipped away, she dreamed. Sheryl was in a place that was too bright. She was unable to move her arms and legs, and was floating in a circle of light—pink, green, blue and white. She was in a hypnotic, trance-like state in which she felt cognizant of her bodily actions, but unable to control them.

Through the patches of shadow and light in the thin slits of her mostly unopened eyes, she could barely make out the dark outlines of a circular bank of computer keyboards and screens. Bright lights were pointed at her, with even more lights overhead.

Her frame of mind was like a bad dream. An unidentified person, probably Stonehill, was chasing her and she was unable to get away. It was as if the motor control in her body had turned off with the flip of a switch, and she was locked inside unmoving flesh and bones.

She tried to call for help, but her vocal chords didn't work. Her neck was sore and aching, as if the arteries were swollen and infected. Her head throbbed and her breath came in trembling gasps.

When she tried to make contact with whoever was in the room, no words issued from her throat. She swallowed nervously, the swallow freezing for a moment in the back of her throat. The world swam around her and she was dizzy.

She tried to stop worrying about her dilemma and focused her attention on her surroundings. Through a haze of multicolored partitions of light and shadow, she traced the outline of a dark figure. It was an alien being that Stonehill claimed was behind his violent actions and bad behavior. Tubes of tinted light from the creature's red eyes cut through the mist. Sheryl squinted and recognized the shape of a bulbous head. Like an inverted triangle, the cranium was hideously bloated. Black, sunken circles surrounded its eyes and its arms were thin and distended.

Sheryl sensed the being probing her like a laboratory specimen. The idea of being treated as less than human made her flinch. Sheryl closed her eyes momentarily, wishing she could escape.

She heard a brand of cruel laughter, and after that, barely audible voices. They brought Sheryl to the realization that they were not spoken and were coming from the being. The inside of the dream creature's head was a liquid pool of sounds. She heard fragments of its memory. It was angry because it had been forced to come here decades ago. It had traveled across space, and it viewed humans as its enemies. It hadn't had sexual intercourse with its own kind for decades. It had never mated and had no offspring.

Hearing the confusing maelstrom of its inner thought processes, Sheryl concluded it was similar to Stonehill—scared and alienated. Its body contained no vocal chords. Sheryl didn't understand how it communicated other than through the vague concept of telepathy. She was sure she heard chattering voices, like the kind that come from a garbled radio in another room.

She opened her eyes and was in the room again. The being she had glimpsed while unconscious was not there.

Sheryl felt ruddy and haggard. Where was Jason? she asked herself. Where was Weaver?

CHAPTER 39

Where exactly was Stonehill? And more importantly, why had he kidnapped Sheryl?

Morehouse hypothesized that criminals such as Stonehill experience difficulty thinking, talking and writing. A psychopath might blame the impediments to expressing what's on his mind. He reacts with fear and hysteria to change in the society—to immigrants from foreign countries, to tourists, to new residents, to shifts in the workforce, and to the altering of conventional boundary lines between social classes.

That was what Morehouse told Weaver and Jason when he and Doug met them at the sheriff's office.

Question: Why are certain perceptions more noticeable than others? People see what they want to see, even when it is not there. Are these honest mistakes, tactics or philosophical opinions? Why do people believe in things that are not visible? Why do they fail to see things that are visible? In the darkness or the blinding light, they can hear things they can't see. So they can perceive things, which as far as their eyes tell them, are not there.

There was little doubt in Morehouse's mind that Stonehill's paranoid outlook toward the community was what had prompted him to attack Kirchner.

"A cold-blooded killer may not react emotionally because he doesn't admit his role in murdering his victims," Weaver said. "He doesn't hold the perception of how unfair and horrible the crime of murder is."

"Secretly, the villain's aware of his violent deeds, but he acts as if he's not responsible for them," Weaver added. "At least, that's what I think."

"When you put a partition between two people, it is a barrier that separates them," Morehouse told Weaver, Jason and Doug. "It makes them communicate without seeing each other, talking across the partition. If you remove the partition and replace it with a table, the people at the table can see each other."

Jason, worried about Sheryl, was noticeably tense. "What is this leading up to?" he enquired impatiently.

Morehouse said in order to figure out where Stonehill might have taken Sheryl, he needed to analyze why he kidnapped her.

For instance, Morehouse explained that people's conscious and unconscious, voluntary and involuntary, body movements are a way of communicating without words. To go a step further, he said, scholars have described this means of communication, talking subconsciously in voices in the brain, as kinesics.

"Layman have called this a psychic telephone—a flat, horizontal, invisible plane on which people communicate without talking," Morehouse said. "Some people have described this as a barely detected mode of communication similar to an ancient ceremonial dance attempting to make contact with spirits. Others have described this situation as hearing your own thoughts—or thinking out loud.

"Whatever desperately sick situation Stonehill is in, I think he is trying to make a point, that he is trying to communicate his hostility to us," Morehouse said.

"What do you mean?" Weaver asked.

"Look, I'm not an expert," Morehouse answered, with irritation in his voice. "I don't know exactly what I mean. I've just been reading about it."

Jason returned to his reporter's objective mindset. "You think there is a psychic telephone connecting unexplained events—your traffic accident, the murder in the woods, the vision Kevin described at the lake and Sheryl's disappearance," Jason said. "Is that what you're saying?"

"We use words to communicate,' Morehouse said. "From what I've been reading, I've learned that there are methods of communication beyond words. I think there is something else at work here that isn't obvious."

"On a practical level, what you're getting at is that Stonehill doesn't have the compassion to talk to us on our own human terms," Weaver said. "In his psychotic frame of mind, he wrongly believes there are too many partitions and too many enemies. And unfortunately, this leads him to the use of ruthless violence. And you think this follows a pattern of killers blaming victims?"

"Yes, residents think of their property as land they own, yet recognize it is part of the neighborhood and community," Morehouse said. "A pernicious killer thinks of the farm, the woods and the town as places to cause trouble, giving him destructive control over his victims."

"Why here?" Weaver asked.

"I don't know," Morehouse answered. "When I'm in a heavily populated city, I have the feeling that there is a giant glass dome, like a greenhouse, around everything. I don't like to think of Centerville that way."

Jason ventured an opinion. "It sounds like you think Stonehill doesn't like it here or anyplace else, for that matter. When we were at the scenic overlook on Friday night, Sheryl described the woods as scary—like she got a premonition of impending danger. Since I grew up around here, I don't like to dwell on the ugly side of the woods."

"Which is?" Weaver asked.

"Mother Nature and survival of the fittest," Jason said. "The opportunities for criminals like Stonehill to commit murder."

"Stonehill may have seen Sheryl that night," Doug interjected.

Jason's eyes widened. "Now that you mention it, Stonehill was the man in the pickup truck! He pulled over and asked us if my car was stalled. Sheryl was right. We were in danger and didn't even know it. How could I have been so insensitive? Now Stonehill might kill her."

"Don't blame yourself," Doug responded. "For a couple, a girlfriend and boyfriend, a relationship should be a bridge. You can trust me on that. I've been married for sixteen years. You shouldn't have to worry about crime all of the time," Doug pointed out.

"I contact many sources for my reporting work," Jason said. "I don't entirely trust anybody."

"For now, we have to find Sheryl and Stonehill," Weaver said. "We have to separate the facts from the conjecture."

"I don't think things are bad in Centerville," Morehouse said. "Stonehill thinks we're his enemies. He thinks things around here are bad enough to kill his enemies."

"If he doesn't like Centerville, why doesn't he just leave?" Jason asked indignantly.

Morehouse studied Jason, observing the worried expression on his face. "Stonehill is sick in the head. He's afraid to leave. He isn't able to leave because he doesn't know how. It's like he's locked in a jail cell all of the time."

"That doesn't help us much," Jason objected. "Stonehill must have someplace to hide, someplace where he doesn't feel confined."

"Wait a minute," Weaver said. "Stonehill came from a bad home. When his father kicked him around too much, he disappeared."

"The last time Sheryl and I were at the scenic overlook, she sensed trouble," Jason said.

"Ray, when you were taping that night, was there any reason why Stonehill would have selected that part of the forest?" Weaver asked.

"All that's around there is the old Kellinger Mine and Timber Co. buildings—the abandoned mine site. Aside from the overlook, the wildlife, the scenery and the highway, there isn't much else around that neck of the woods. There were stories...decades ago that a space ship crashed."

"That's right!" Weaver exclaimed. "They were attributed to Stonehill's father, Vernon. After the mine collapsed, he was fired from his job as a security guard. Folks thought he made up the spaceship story to deflect attention from the job loss, the catastrophe at the mine and the fact that he didn't get along with his wife and kid. Years later, she supposedly fled from home, leaving Nate alone against his tyrannical father."

"The worst battles are fought in the home," Morehouse said. "I think you're on the right track. Stonehill likely blames his father and the spaceship story for his bad childhood. An empty building in the woods sounds like the place a psychopath might go."

"We don't have much time," Weaver said. "Jones is at Stonehill's place. We must stop Stonehill before he kills again. We'll drive to the Kellinger site. You folks better come along."

CHAPTER 40

Weaver gave directions to Campbell over his squad's radio. "If Morehouse's hunch turns out to be correct, we've got to pinpoint Stonehill's precise location," he barked. "He's likely holed-up in one of the abandoned office buildings or mine shafts. Wherever I go, I'm going to need backup."

Weaver, who planned to meet Upton at the Kellinger site, had his squad's emergency lights flashing as he sped down Highway 46. Doug and Morehouse, who were riding with Weaver, were armed. Jason rode in Campbell's car, directly behind Weaver's.

From the squad's window, Doug watched the terrain roll by. From his past, he remembered how the terrain leading to the heavy forest was a progression of residential homes to farms to wooded hills. Along the highway there were distant farmhouses and barns, not to mention two campgrounds, the golf course, and a smattering of abandoned buildings, complete with gaping holes in the walls and caved-in roofs.

"What had happened to the family that used to live there?" Doug asked, recognizing too late that it wasn't an appropriate time to bother the others. Doug waited for a response, but nobody said anything.

"Continue patrolling the town," Weaver yelled over the radio, "in case the son-of-a-bitch tries to walk in the daylight."

Doug realized the other deputies were tied up watching Centerville in case Stonehill wasn't holed-up at the Kellinger site. Even though Doug was queasy and felt only a vague familiarity with the surroundings, he knew the Marengo River wound through the woods south to the Centerville Dam.

In 1992, there had been a bad drought that lasted the entire summer. That had been a factor in the additional deterioration of Stonehill's farm. Stonehill's farm and neighboring properties had also been damaged by indiscriminate flooding from the river during rainstorms. Over the years, lumber supplies from river barges that had spilled out of control added to their woes.

Normally, farmers didn't like to interfere with each other's operations. However, when the weather turned bad and their land was damaged, they had disputed property lines, and had argued at town council meetings about written statements in the law about spilled timber.

On Highway 46 they passed the broken mailbox in front of Stonehill's farm. During the drive, Doug told Morehouse he still planned to buy a summer place, despite the deaths attributed to Stonehill. He hadn't picked one out yet, he said. Living out of a hotel room for the past two weeks had been motivation enough for finding a permanent vacation retreat.

As they neared the abandoned site, Weaver and Campbell both slowed to a stop, taking nothing for granted and exercising caution. Upton's deputy's squad also arrived on time. Kirchner and Balton had been killed. With Sheryl missing, Weaver and Morehouse had to believe their calculations were on the money.

"This better be the right place," Weaver told Morehouse. "Deputy Campbell and I will check the main office building. Upton's headed to the closest mine shaft. I want the rest of you to stay back here, near the cars, in case there is trouble."

As soon as Jason heard Weaver's directions, he suspected he wouldn't have the patience to follow them. For one minute, he tried to stay back, but ended up sprinting after Weaver and Campbell to the Kellinger building. He knew it was important to let Weaver take charge. However, he held a special link to Sheryl, and sensed she was nearby someplace, probably in the old building, certainly in terrible danger.

They reached the entrance, with Weaver gripping his sheriff's revolver in both hands. When Weaver saw Jason directly behind him, he was startled. He didn't have a chance to argue with Jason, who was apparently going to follow him. He didn't want Stonehill to know he was at the front door. He ordered Campbell to circle the outside of the building and block the rear exit. If Stonehill was inside, they would converge from opposite directions.

Weaver flung the door open and headed down the main hallway. It was dark, and Jason was trailing behind Weaver. There were four corridors, and with their flashlights shining, they split up, each one selecting a separate hallway.

After proceeding a short distance down a corridor, Weaver saw Stonehill. He was about forty-five feet away. He was in a room at the end of the passage directly to Weaver's right.

Suddenly a bullet whizzed by Weaver at a very high velocity. Judging from the speed of the bullet, Stonehill must have been using a military-style assault rifle, Weaver reasoned.

Weaver ran ten feet down the hallway into Stonehill's threat. Stonehill fired a second shot, and Weaver dove into the nearest open doorway, which tapered off into a deteriorating room.

Weaver surveyed the dim corridor. Stonehill's body was not completely obscured by the door he was hiding behind. Weaver lifted his sheriff's revolver, and fired two shots, one of which sliced through the middle of the door. For a moment, Weaver saw one of Stonehill's shoes on the floor. Weaver charged down the hallway, figuring one of the shots might have hit Stonehill.

Stonehill saw the sheriff's dark figure approaching. With his left shoulder still in pain and bleeding, Stonehill lifted his assault rifle and poured three shots into the hallway. Weaver landed on the floor hard and crawled through another open doorway. He estimated he was only twenty-five feet from Stonehill. From his spot on the linoleum floor, Weaver aimed carefully, with both hands clasped on the butt of his gun, and drilled another shot into the door.

Laughing and mimicking Weaver, Stonehill also aimed carefully and fired two more rounds toward Weaver. However, Stonehill's injury hampered his mobility, and his military-style rifle recoiled, sending waves of pain into his shoulder. Stonehill screamed as loudly as an alarm.

"I can see you clearly," Stonehill yelled defensively into the hallway. "You're an easy target."

Weaver knew better, and sent another round directly at Stonehill, forcing him to jump away from the open doorway. Stonehill retreated, making his exit into a side passage extending to the back of the building.

At the same time as Weaver and Stonehill were engaged in the gun battle, Jason, with his flashlight and gun, worked his way down a corridor on the left side of the building.

Suddenly, Jason's flashlight beam caught Sheryl, her face frozen in terror.

Sheryl sensed the flashlight scanning over her body, suspecting Stonehill had returned. Sheryl flinched before she realized the beam came from Jason's flashlight. Through her grogginess, Sheryl squinted and recognized Jason's familiar face.

Jason yelled out, "Sheryl, it's Jason. Are you all right?"

The world tilted around her. "Jason, be careful," she called out. "Stonehill is around here someplace. I don't know where he is. This might be a trick. There might be a booby trap, a bomb, in the building set to go off!"

Sheryl repeated, "Don't come in here. It's a trap. Stonehill is crazy. He hates the newspaper, the sheriff's department, the whole town."

"I'll be careful," Jason responded, adrenaline rushing through his system.

Jason swallowed hard, and the muscles in his throat instantly tightened and then relaxed. This shouldn't be too difficult, he said to himself. Jason couldn't help noticing how the contents of the room reflected Stonehill's malicious nature. He glanced at the maple computer console supporting the laptop and the half-open wall closet revealing half a dozen rifles. He saw large cardboard boxes filled with old newspaper stories about the mine collapse, among other headline topics. The unmistakable pages of decades-old Observers were yellow and brittle. And like Sheryl, he fixed his eyes on the small pile of letters near the laptop, the unplugged portable printer and the unopened packages of blank Kodak paper. On the floor was another box filled with bogus junk mail. Next to that was a stack of three wooden crates.

Jason rushed up to Sheryl, who was still tied to the chair. Standing over her, he quickly uncoiled the rope. Sheryl cried out, gasped and flopped out of the chair. Jason caught her in his arms, clasped her hands, hugged her and led her out of the room.

Though Jason and Sheryl were still curious about the morbid contents of the room, they were in desperate circumstances. "Despite the violent junk in this place, we'll have to get the hell out as fast as possible," Jason said.

"Where's the gunfire coming from?"

"Probably Weaver?" Jason replied.

Both Jason and Sheryl scrambled away from the chair. As they pulled each other along, out of the room, Jason remembered Sheryl's words of warning: *Stonehill is around here someplace...a trick...a bomb set to go off!* Now Jason's sole purpose was to make sure he got Sheryl safely out of the building.

Running through the doorway and down the hallway, pulling Sheryl with all his might, Jason heard a thud followed by a ticking sound—click, click, click. As Sheryl warned, Stonehill had planted a bomb in the building. Maybe he had attached a timing mechanism to the chair. Or possibly, Jason, in his haste, may have pulled Sheryl across a tripwire. Or Stonehill may have set the bomb manually. Jason was sure of one thing: It was an impending threat that had created a high degree of trepidation in both he and Sheryl. Jason could almost feel waves of deadly electric current flowing through the building.

Weaver heard Jason and Sheryl shouting to him and felt the building begin to shake. He recognized their voices, telling him there was a bomb, that the building was rigged, that it was a diabolical trap, that the madman wanted to get into the headlines, that they had to get out immediately. Campbell was stationed at the rear. Weaver raised his pistol and fired another shot at Stonehill. He listened to the muffled echo of the bullet in the vacuous building.

He won't get away, Weaver told himself.

Weaver raced down the corridor toward the main hallway, which veered left. To the best of his memory, that was the direction he had come from. Weaver prayed that he, Jason and Sheryl would reach the exit safely.

All of them noticed a slight movement, and then heard and felt a sharp thud. In just a brief moment, a matter of seconds that seemed like eternity, they were dangling in space, off balance, like a broken light fixture coming loose from the ceiling mount. A few more seconds later, Weaver, Jason and Sheryl felt a primal, instinctive panic set in.

The structure of the building—the beams and supports—rattled. The explosion triggered currents of flame that later reduced much of the old Kellinger Mining and Lumber Co. to burning rubble. The deafening explosion rippled from the core of the building, with one wave of fire-induced humidity and smoke following another one.

Fire rolled across the body of the structure. Flames spewed in all directions, metal pipes melted with heat and smoke seeped through broken windows. Within a matter of minutes, plaster shattered, furniture crawled across the floor and walls collapsed. The sheer power of the explosion had compressed the air into balls of pressure that prickled the skin.

Like turbulent weather, rows of flame traveled across the empty corridors of the structure. The explosion rocked the concrete foundation, the steel framework and the walls, leaving the first floor bubbling with fire. The second and third stories of the building swayed overhead, with tangles of electric wiring erupting in the fire.

There were two other doors, east and south, and Jason picked the east door quickly. He went to the insulated door and looked down the hallway. A cloud of thick black smoke pushed him back. When he spotted an opening in the cloud, he led Sheryl down the corridor along the wall, tracing his path from memory.

In the murky smoke, they clambered down the treacherous corridor as fast as possible.

Weaver tripped over a slow-moving body sprawled across the middle of the floor. It was Jason. With Sheryl a few feet away, Jason groped for Weaver's hand,

and the sheriff lifted him up. There were virtually out of time. The three dark figures continued running down the smoke-shrouded corridor and charged out of the exit door.

Although stars swam in front of Sheryl's eyes, she and the others were incredibly relieved because they had made it out safely. Inch-thick ashes and chunks of flaming wood rained down.

Weaver endured labored breathing, yet staggered to his feet, realizing their ordeal wasn't over. An indistinct fear crept over him as he heard the sounds of bullets whizzing.

Light from gunfire flickered momentarily on the other side of the rapidly disintegrating building. Weaver ran toward the back. From a distance, he could see Morehouse chasing Stonehill with his gun. Campbell had been guarding the rear exit, but to Weaver's amazement, Stonehill had smashed a window open and climbed out.

Bleeding from his bullet wound and other injuries, Stonehill spilled onto the ground, gasping from a chemical odor among the fumes. Weaver, Campbell, Upton and Morehouse charged up to the spot where Stonehill had dropped from exhaustion.

"You're under arrest, asshole," Weaver shouted, keeping his gun trained on Stonehill.

The smoke-filled structure was engulfed in flames and smoke. Down the gravel entrance drive, Jason, Sheryl and Doug watched the fire rise into the sky, the flames leaping from the broken windows, the roof collapsing into the smoking walls and the mound of rubble steaming.

The sounds changed drastically. The steady crackling of fire carried by the wind was replaced by the screaming sirens of fire engines and squad cars speeding up the entrance road. A wave of relief washed over everyone.

Jason followed Weaver as they made their way along the eastern edge of the mass of rubble, then turned the corner and walked along the northern edge of the site. Weaver hesitated, awed by the extent of the wreckage. He studied the half-empty ruins where the intact building had stood.

Firefighting equipment was scattered near the smoldering, debris-cluttered site. The dirt road at the fire's edge was crisscrossed with firefighters, stretching water hoses. Amid the thick haze, the firemen held hoses pointed at the fire. They shouted comments and instructions to each other, and sprinkled water over the ashes.

Flames amid piles of debris glowed orange. As firemen jockeyed around upright walls and beams, they were careful to avoid inhaling smoke. Several studied large pieces of debris laying in the ruins.

The spread of flames across the wooded property ceased near the forest's edge, moving tentatively toward the perimeter of the woods, then stopping. When firemen had arrived, they chopped apart a thicket of trees and brush, successfully blocking a full-scale forest blaze.

Bryan Pollard, a fireman, gathered up the thick fire hose and sprayed the contents of a water truck into the smoldering ruins. Beneath the shroud of smoke and flames, he breathed air up from the tank through his mask.

As the tense moments wore on, the fire gave up, groaning and belching into nothing, the sickening aroma of melted plaster and rubber spreading around the site. In the dim twilight, the expressions on the firemen's faces reflected relief that the ordeal had ended.

Chapter 41

Above the waterline of Crater Lake, a flock of gulls were heard squawking over a county sheriff's vessel. While the wind whistled and dairy cows grazed idly in a pristine farm pasture along the cool shoreline, Mitch Camber, a sheriff's scuba diver and former Centerville High School swimming champion, conducted another grim search.

Below the choppy surface, slanting toward the cold floor of the lake, the sheriff's scuba diver swung his head around. Camber stared at the horrible sight of the dead man suspended in the bottom of the sunken boat. One of Vernon Stonehill's mangled arms and part of his bloody right leg were visible underneath a pile of rocks and boulders Nate had used to sink the boat. The diver felt fear and trembling rise from the pit of his stomach.

Camber swam as deep as he could for closer inspection. Lettering on the hull read "Captain Moore's Boat Rental". It was the boat Purnell and Kirchner had rented. After fatally hacking Vernon to death with an ax, Stonehill had attached his bloody corpse to the motor boat. And after stealing "Allison" an expensive recreational vessel, Stonehill had transported the lightweight boat to the center of Crater Lake. Riddled with holes and cracks from bullets and a heavy-duty construction drill, weighted down with rocks and cement blocks, Stonehill had sunk the disabled boat to the bottom of the lake.

Now Camber heard the tranquil sounds of water trickling and flowing around his mask. The incapacitated vessel and Vernon's waterlogged corpse swayed in the slow, thick currents.

Vernon had been missing for at least two weeks before anyone other than Nate had noticed. A county agricultural agent and a farm neighbor had asked about Vernon a week before the gossip had reached Balton. Now authorities had an explanation for Vernon's whereabouts and Kevin's visions. It wasn't a surprising explanation, that Nate had gone berserk, in light of the fact that his freedom had hinged on his tyrannical father.

Stonehill's eyes were burned out, like uncleaned ashtrays containing a film of gritty dust. He was dog-tired and his head was aching. He rubbed the palm of his left hand against his forehead, fingering oily pockmarks, remnants of an attack of acne when he was a teenager. He closed his eyes and pinched the eyelids. Stonehill remembered his abusive father, and asked himself why he was cursed with so much bad luck.

He listened to the voices of patients and nurses drifting down the hallway into his hospital room. He heard the emphatic sounds of deputies engaged in conversation just outside his door. And he listened to the TV weatherman giving a report: "Be careful driving because there is a fifty-five percent chance a storm system might cause slippery patches along streets and highways. A fast-moving Midwestern rain storm may hit the area in three hours. Be ready to bring out your umbrella."

A flash flood, waves of muddy rainwater rolling down the streets, seeping into basements and clogging storm pipes, would be more interesting, Stonehill told himself.

The hubbub outside Stonehill's hospital room aggravated him. From his standpoint as a prisoner, he fantasized about free citizens out on the streets—pedestrians talking and laughing, children riding bikes and parents mowing lawns, shrill motorcycles and heavy trucks, and dashboard stereos blasting from passing automobiles. He listened to a sheriff's walkie-talkie.

Sooner or later, Stonehill realized, the racket would stir up malicious demons in his head. Stonehill's entire body ached, especially his blown-out left shoulder, and in exasperation, he released the warped chuckle of a lunatic.

He looked at his Clayton County wristband, which was underneath the cloth of his hospital blankets. A permanent misfit, always under the control of the corrupt society, he repeated to himself. Someone who should be ignored. He shifted his heavy feet and twisted sideways in bed, releasing a shriek of pain.

Some sheriffs would have given up, but not Weaver. After Stonehill was arrested and taken to Memorial Hospital, Weaver decided to stay after his first-shift schedule officially ended. He needed more information.

Weaver deduced Stonehill had struggled with Balton before he killed the deputy. Soon after Stonehill was examined by Dr. Nelson, deputies relayed an immediate report to the sheriff.

The results of the cursory examination showed the skin on the hole Balton had blown into Stonehill's shoulder contained patches of purple and red discoloration. Ironically, Weaver reflected, this was similar to the appearance of the horrendous gash running across Kirchner's head, not to mention the bruise-colored marks on her neck. Stonehill also had a reddish skin condition resembling sunburn, possibly from working alone in the small cornfield at his farm, according to Dr. Nelson. Of interest to Weaver, the condition also included the foreskin on Stonehill's penis. Although he admitted only to pain from the bullet wound, there appeared to be noticeable discomfort in his penis, as well.

Weaver received additional information from the hospital. Stonehill had made a previous appointment with a skin doctor a year earlier. The preceding doctor had checked Stonehill's pelvis and observed the skin irritation causing the discoloration. The doctor suggested a skin sample be taken, which Stonehill turned down. Instead, the doctor removed three warts from Stonehill's right foot. A wart on his left foot, Stonehill said, receded on its own before the doctor saw it. Stonehill did not make another appointment.

At the time of the doctor's appointment, Stonehill had not mentioned emotional feelings of anger and panic, and the hospital staff had seen no reason to have him evaluated by a psychiatrist. In short, patches of Stonehill's skin appeared to have been burned, including the skin on his penis. The doctor assumed the problem was not self-inflicted. Because Stonehill hadn't been to a dentist in a long time, he also had bleeding gums and two rotting teeth.

Weaver had listened to Balton's comments about how it was known that Stonehill had grown up in an abusive home. He also knew that the onset of mania stemming from accumulated resentment and isolation, and even the ultimate possibility of sexual dysfunction, might cause a pensive, solitary individual like Stonehill to turn into a psychopath.

Chapter 42

The next day, Weaver led an animated conversation about the case. It was held behind the brick walls and glass windows of the county administration building, inside the sheriff's office.

"I understand why Stonehill resorted to an assumed identity," Jason said. "He used the Marsden name to sign me up for a boatload of mailing lists."

Sheryl cocked her head toward Jason. "Now we're certain where those threatening messages and Jason's pile of junk mail came from," Sheryl said.

"More importantly, Stonehill's assumed identity helps explain how he acquired weapons and developed explosives," Weaver interjected.

Weaver turned his head. "After the bomb went off, I couldn't believe it," he said. "Stonehill had the building wired. In part, that's why he waited to take a hostage—to manipulate us to his makeshift armory."

"It's too bad his parents, especially his father, never placated him," Campbell said.

Weaver understood. "That was certainly a contributing factor," he agreed.

"Vernon's weakness became the community's problem," Morehouse pointed out. "Now he's dead and his son is locked up. At least the villain turned out to be an ordinary human," he giggled.

Sheryl leaned forward, listening. At the moment, she didn't mention the vision she had seen in captivity. She didn't want to taint her image as a level-headed journalist. Morehouse also downplayed the hallucination he saw after the highway crash.

They agreed it was frightening to think a stranger had chosen Sheryl to be the victim of a plot as senseless as it was terrifying.

"No one recognized the fact that a murderer was among us, and that he despised everyone," Sheryl said.

"He never developed his own identity," Jason said. "He didn't live like a free person. It turned out to be a case of us versus him."

"Thank God we have such wonderful neighbors," Morehouse pointed out.

"Such decent folks," Weaver chimed in.

They were talking from opposite sides of Weaver's office when Upton stopped in the open doorway. He barked instructions to Upton. Among them, he wanted a full investigation of whether Stonehill had weapons contacts. If nothing else, he wanted deputies to check gun purchases.

According to Jason and Sheryl, Stonehill kept at least twenty rifles at the abandoned building. Based on one lead, he was likely responsible for the theft of ten weapons from a Centerville gun shop a month ago. In addition to repaying Vernon for his oppressive childhood, Stonehill looked like the type of dangerous criminal who was on the verge of launching a career in bank robbery.

"The extent of the explosion at the Kellinger building indicates Stonehill had amassed a sizable munitions stockpile," Weaver said.

"He didn't buy those bombs at a porn shop," Jason quipped.

"He sure as hell didn't," Morehouse chimed in. "Or that laptop."

"Stonehill's a remarkable catch," Upton said. "The son-of-a-bitch is going to spend a long, long time behind bars. Although that's little consolation for Deputy Balton's family or the other folks Stonehill killed."

Campbell waited to comment. "He didn't even thank us," he said.

"For what?" Weaver asked.

"For not putting him out of his misery," Campbell said with exasperation.

"In groups, distinctions are made between individuals," Morehouse hypothesized. "When an alienated person such as Stonehill, or Marsden, as he wanted to be known, watches a group from a distance, his seething temper stops him from distinguishing one person from another one."

"Hmmm. Crime is stupid," Weaver said.

Upton swung around. "We're not going to forget this...Stonehill...and Balton's death. Because it happened in our jurisdiction." Emotional pain and sympathy was evident in his strained voice.

It was clearly obvious that Balton's faithful service would be missed. "At least, the principles for which Balton sacrificed his life, justice and liberty, are still alive," Weaver said. "I'll sure miss him."

Following Sheryl's explanation about the laptop, mail bearing the name Marsden, the accumulated stash of junk mail, guns, explosive devices and detonators at Stonehill's makeshift hideout, Weaver ordered a heightened search in case they had missed anything. So far, Vernon's body was the only one that had been found.

Sheryl and Jason verified they had seen boxes of bogus pamphlets. In addition to stalking Sheryl at her tranquil apartment complex, Stonehill admitted under questioning to using his laptop to manufacture his own peculiar junk mail. Sheriff's officials had located an inkjet printer and a variety of correspondence, some of it threatening, in the family room of Stonehill's house.

In the basement, deputies found four wide cardboard boxes filled with newspaper clippings and old Observers. Seventy-two stories Stonehill had clipped out of the newspaper were under the bylines of Jason and Sheryl. At the bottom of the musty box were dozens of photocopies of stories about the cave-in at the Kellinger mine. In one case, a single story giving Vernon's account of the tragedy had been photocopied fifty-two times.

Underneath the stairwell were six old-fashioned suitcases loaded with ammunition. Two of the suitcases were locked shut and the keys were missing. The remaining mud-crusted suitcases contained scuff marks and broken buttons and zippers.

Across the dark basement against the north wall was a metal cabinet containing two blaze orange hunting outfits, two military uniforms, a dozen maps of the forest, a pair of fishing boots, and a box of hunting and fishing knives. On a rusty ping pong table was a coil of rope, a pile of cloth and rags, a box of paramilitary magazines, four flares, two boxes of cigars and a half dozen electrical cords.

In his bedroom, Stonehill had kept a list of names and addresses, some of them folks he didn't like, such as Jason and Sheryl. He also had lists of 1-800 phone numbers and a box of junk mail.

When Weaver had started the search, he discovered a skull had been carved into the trunk of the elm tree on Stonehill's farm. Perhaps the fact that Stonehill's father had been labeled as missing was what had caused him to carve the skull. It was Stonehill's morbid way of giving deputies a clue as to his father's whereabouts. That may have been why he owned paraphernalia, such as rings and caps bearing human skulls, Weaver surmised.

Behind the peeling paint and ruddy walls of Stonehill's barn, deputies uncovered two handguns, in addition to a half dozen boxes filled with old newspapers and books. However, there was no one left on the farm who would miss the madman, Nate Stonehill, and his morbid exploits, Weaver realized.

CHAPTER 43

Morehouse watched his boat, which was tied securely to the pier, floating on the buoyant lake current. Considering the flabbergasting trauma all of them had been through, it was understandable that Morehouse was anxious to double-check the boat's condition.

Adrienne joined Morehouse, and they strolled down the rock-strewn beach, looking at the beautiful lake and tenderly holding hands. The sun was rising, a bright gold sphere of flame climbing over the radiant, blue water.

Birds were celebrating the new morning.

"If we told a guest the grim story about Stonehill's destructive vengeance, he might not want to take a vacation at the Bay View. Or at least he would want to be careful to avoid dangerous criminals," Adrienne said.

Morehouse gazed at his wife and said, "You're exactly right. Stonehill's unfortunate fascination with destruction might affect the tourist trade."

As they strolled down the beach, an ivory cormorant with black wings landed in the sand. The bird glanced blankly at Morehouse and Adrienne. Then it scanned a smattering of sunbathers, as well as some footprints and tire tracks in the sand.

Waves were rolling ashore, but his attention also was drawn to the beach. Morehouse spotted a black shiny oval that was buried just underneath the surface of the sand. He bent down and picked it up. It appeared to be a ring that was broken. The band for the finger was partially missing, and on the body of the ring was a weathered skull.

Morehouse held it in his hand and examined it.

Adrienne pushed her sunglasses up onto her forehead. "What is that?" she enquired.

"I don't know exactly," he responded. "It has a jagged edge and half a dozen grooves, like a seashell." He cocked his arm and almost tossed it back onto the beach. Then he changed his mind, and studied it more carefully, observing the skull face.

"It looks like our friend, Stonehill, might have been here," Morehouse said. "Or somebody like him was here."

He displayed the broken ring to Adrienne. "Oh my!" she exclaimed. "You better show that to Weaver."

"That's exactly what I'll do," said Morehouse, dropping the ring into his pocket.

After trudging a little further down the beach, they reached a square sign indicating they were leaving the designated swimming area. A men's Schwinn ten-speed was leaning against the wooden shaft, underneath the black lettering on the sign.

"It looks like a tourist parked here," Morehouse said. Sunbathers were scattered on the sand, some behind slanted beach umbrellas.

The portion of the beach that was not used by swimmers stretched 1800 feet from the spot where the sign was posted to the slanted wooded hills and bluffs leading into the forest. Interspersed with an occasional meadow, the tract was covered with oak, pine, spruce and elm trees.

"Even though this region has been thoroughly settled, there's a remarkable level of wildlife," Morehouse informed. "Much of the land remains in a fairly natural condition."

"Temperate forests still produce useful lumber," Adrienne said. "Not to mention protecting all the different species of plants, trees and wildlife."

On their way across the beach, Adrienne accidentally stepped on a shell. It exhibited a rough-hewn beauty, and she didn't want to just leave it sitting there. She scooped it off the sand, planning to take it home. "Finders, keepers," she said.

CHAPTER 44

Despite the Stonehill case, Kevin had enjoyed his visit with Justin and Morehouse.

When he had unfastened his eyelids early in the morning, he eagerly anticipated his jet flight back to his home in Skokie. With his dad along, he didn't have to go through the monotony of flying alone.

"You have been such a wonderful sweetheart to travel with your Dad," his mother had said on the phone. She told him it's invigorating to ride around the northern forests, farms and towns.

Kevin took vivid memories of nature with him: The shrill chirping of birds and restless willow trees in the sunny corners of Morehouse's yard. And of course, he recalled raccoons skulking around garbage containers, rainstorms tearing leafy branches off trees, and the tall ears of a rabbit poking out of an underground warren.

In a matter of hours, Doug and Kevin would be landing at O'Hare Airport in Chicago. But if Doug ended up buying a summer place, they would visit every year.

Doug said, "I bet when the stewardess flings the exit door open and you walk into O'Hare, you'll be relieved the trip is over. Maybe the next time you visit, you could bring a good book with you."

After the airplane had taken off, Kevin gazed through the open window. From the aerial point of view of a passenger, the topography surrounding the airport during take-off resembled a map. When the plane reached its predetermined altitude, the pilot banked hard to the right and followed the route to O'Hare.

Behind the drone of the jet's powerful engines, the vapor they expelled pushed the plane through the rippling turbulence like a diesel engine pushing a large, sixteen-wheel truck down a highway. From inside the cockpit near the nose, the pilot maneuvered the wings and rudders on the tail.

While the airplane skittered above the clouds, Kevin pulled out a letter he had received on vacation. It was from Jill Compton, his eighth-grade teacher. He had been so busy, he hadn't had time to look at it. He began reading it.

Dear Kevin:

I hope you enjoyed your vacation. Sounds fun to go out on Crater Lake or to take a sightseeing tour through the forest. After you get back, tell me about your fishing trip.

When a tourist travels, he learn things. For instance, I flew to Des Moines, Iowa, a couple years ago. I read in a travel book that Iowa is known for its outstanding potato crop. While I was there, I tried a variety of potato dishes. I imagine the resort where you stayed overnight must have offered tasty fish dinners.

There are many farms around Centerville, as is the case in towns and cities throughout the Midwest. Farm communities include agricultural colleges and businesses geared to farmers such as family-owned country grocery stores. Farm stores are plainly furnished.

It must have been very heartwarming to spend part of the summer vacation with your father. Golf courses, sandy beaches, a lake voyage, scenic rock formations, amusement parks, a vacation escape—sounds like a good time. You probably felt like a pirate, standing on a lake pier, leaning against the metal railing and gazing down upon the blue waters.

Centuries ago, seafaring ships were constructed from timber harvested in forest lumber camps. There was great beauty in the forest, but trees had to be chopped down. White, puffy clouds hung over each lumber camp, like the ivory sails hanging from the vast wooden rigging of an 18th century ship.

When a tourist is far away from his urban home, he can observe the stars with well-defined clarity. A stargazer can witness outer space phenomena such as an aurora. That is why scientists have called human beings children of the Mother Earth. Even cave men knew the stars in the night sky represented a vast outer world.

How was your vacation? Did you enjoy it? What was the name of the resort hotel? Did you meet other guests?

Hope you had a good time. I look forward to hearing from you.

Cordially,

Jill Compton
Eighth-grade teacher

Chapter 45

Before the murders, Sheryl felt like she and Jason had been running in circles. Since then, their budding romance had gained more momentum.

Wearing black pants and a yellow denim jacket, he resembled the reassuring Jason whom Sheryl had met in college. He certainly looked better than he had during the gunfight with Stonehill.

"Ready to go?" he asked Sheryl.

"Yes."

Sheryl's eyes found Jason's. Sheryl stood up and placed her hands on Jason's shoulders.

"Jason, something beneficial came out of the gunfight with Stonehill. I had a chance to see you in a distinctly positive light and to get a clear view of your good side. You were calm under pressure and brave," Sheryl said.

Jason sat beside her on her living-room couch. She was the woman he had looked on as her own, who had done so much to help him with his reporting work and his career. She had survived Stonehill's madness with great fortitude.

There was much more that Sheryl meant to say, but not much more that she needed to know about Jason's compassionate emotions. Suddenly her lips were pressed against his and her arms were around his neck.

"I just want to show my appreciation, Jason," she whispered softly in his ear. "Thank you for always being there when it mattered."

Jason rubbed his fingertips against her jaw and cheek, and traced the outline of her face.

"I remember the last time we were together, and we were talking and we thought there was so much ahead of us in the future," Sheryl said. "I believed we had important things to work out."

In the back of their minds, maybe they had known all along that everything would turn out all right, Sheryl realized.

"This was all so hard to understand," Sheryl said smoothly. "We know one thing. We weren't just reporting the story. We helped the sheriff's department solve the case."

"That's right. We were part and parcel of the effort to eradicate crime," Jason said proudly.

"Jason, we still have work to do at the newspaper."

Jason glowered momentarily. "I guess so. I don't really want to concentrate on that right now. It was a pain to go through journalism school in college."

Sheryl started to feel like herself again. Taking her hand gently, Jason lifted her moist lips to his a second time. She innocently closed her eyes and let Jason kiss her, tracing his muscular shoulders with her hands.

Suddenly Sheryl buried her face in her hands. Thin tears of relief slid down her cheeks. "I hope we never run into a psychopath like Stonehill again."

Jason quickly moved closer to Sheryl, and they pulled together in a passionate embrace. "I hope Stonehill rots in hell," Jason said, the anger and tension rising in his voice.

Sheryl snorted through the tears and a sob wrenched up from her chest. She lifted her head off his shoulders.

"He was a terrible person," Sheryl agreed. She paused and asked, "Jason, are you sure we're safe with Stonehill in jail?"

Trying to avoid looking presumptuous, Jason hugged Sheryl again. "Stonehill was arrested at the fire," he said. Jason flashed a warm smile. "Weaver said Centerville is safe. Things should return to normal around here."

Glancing at Sheryl from the corner of his eye, Jason said, "The next time we have a chance, let's rent a skiff and spend a day on the lake."

"You're absolutely right, Jason," Sheryl said incredulously. "We only get to live once."

Jason explained that, in terms of percentages, it wasn't likely the Stonehill case would repeat for a long time. If he was a gambler, he would bet against it, he said.

"All the work he put into his makeshift compound leads me to wonder why Stonehill didn't just proceed with his own date life," Sheryl pointed out.

Sheryl added, "Instead of terrorizing Centerville, he could have been seeing his girlfriend."

"I don't think the haunting memory of his abusive father let him get that far," Jason said.

"If Stonehill had received psychiatric help, there was an outside chance the doctor might have predicted his violent behavior, and his victims would be alive today," Jason said. "When I saw the rope tied around you, if I'd had the chance, I would have smashed the maniac's face inside-out."

Since Sheryl had undergone the nightmare of being kidnapped, Jason had been acting like quite the gentleman. For instance, he had bestowed a number of gifts upon her. Since it wasn't her birthday, she didn't know exactly why, but her days had certainly been more frighteningly chaotic than romantic. Jason's thoughtfulness and his gifts left her feeling appreciated.

For Jason, the intimate celebration with Sheryl was a welcome break. At the newspaper, they had both been occupied almost exclusively with their work. He had been writing the first draft of a story on a notepad. Sheryl was in the early stages of gathering information for a story, and was lining up leads and jotting down rough notes.

"I'm glad you received the two medical thrillers I ordered through AOL," Jason said.

He had ordered the books two weeks ago from amazon.com, and Sheryl received them in her mailbox today. It was perfect timing, but Jason wasn't done. He held in his hands more gifts.

She was determined to love whatever gifts Jason gave her.

Sheryl removed the wrapping paper and ripped the cardboard box open. After it was unraveled, she pulled out the unconnected glass container for a kitchen blender. Below that, in the box, was the metal unit with the control keypad and motor.

"I hope it's OK."

"It's great," Sheryl exclaimed. "What a wonderful present. I'm sure we need more dinners and time together."

"You can take canned fruit, such as Del Monte pears, and mix them together with ice cream for a milk shake," he explained.

Sheryl replied, "A moderate diet that places the emphasis on variety. Sounds like a good idea."

Jason handed Sheryl another gift-wrapped box. She unraveled the beige masking tape and parted the cardboard flaps. "A crock pot! How wonderful," she said. Sheryl understood Jason's gifts fit their plans to one day buy a home.

"Use it for slow-cooking during the day, when you're busy at the newspaper. I got it at Hembel's Department Store for twenty-five dollars. Now they won't get bought by a national chain," Jason quipped.

Jason switched the subject. "How is Morehouse doing?"

"Quite well, as far as I know. He had difficulties sleeping after the concussion. He finished the current round of doctor's checkups for the head wound. He looks better."

"Now that the doctors are finished with him, we might stop in," Jason suggested.

"That's a strong possibility," Sheryl said. "It should be the idyllic place to spend a weekend."

Jason fastened his arms around her in a tight embrace, probed the dark strands of her hair with his free hand and brushed his dry lips hungrily across her cheek.

Sheryl said, "What a trying summer this has been, Jason. I hear birds chirping early in the morning now. I didn't appreciate them so much before. Why don't we go to a movie together after dinner? There's a movie showing at eight o'clock tonight."

"OK."

Sheryl had saved a box of birthday cards she had received and another filled with letters they had exchanged over the years. She sauntered to her desk and retrieved the boxes. She showed Jason cards she had received from friends and relatives. She pulled out a touched-up color photograph of Jason done by a professional portrait studio and showed it to him. It had been taken when he was in college.

Sheryl went into the kitchen and refilled their wine glasses. She returned and they sat on the couch. The evening light slanting through the window played on her attractive facial features. They clinked their wine glasses together in a toast.

Normally, Jason didn't care to waste time, especially at work, and occasionally, in his social relations. But Sheryl noticed an awkwardness about him. Holding her hand, he placed the wine glass down on the table.

"Jason, don't you have anything to say?" Sheryl asked.

"When the summer started, I suspected I was in love with you," Jason blurted out. "Now I'm certain we should stay together."

"So am I," Sheryl said. "Deep down, I always knew you were the right person."

Jason stammered. "Why don't we start making plans...for setting a marriage date? Possibly next fall?"

Sheryl felt dizzy. Was it true that Jason had finally asked her to marry him? When Sheryl gazed at him, she realized he must have been considering the subject of marriage for a long time.

Sheryl said, "Oh, Jason! That's just what I wanted to hear. That's a very good idea."

Experiencing warm feelings, she took Jason's hand and patted it. They pondered the reality of marriage and living in their own home.

"Just think, when we buy our own place, we won' have to go out on Friday night," Jason said. "Not unless we really want to."

Sheryl felt the depth of Jason's love. "And you won't have to drive back to your parents' home," Sheryl said. Once they were married, Sheryl would no longer have to return to an empty apartment. Jason had always supported her, especially in the most trying circumstances. Jason boosted her career and lifted her spirits. He was loving and reliable. He was Jason.

Perhaps nothing would get in their way.

EPILOGUE

In the 1970s, when Stonehill was young, the small farm and its surroundings consisted primarily of the mine, a gas station, a few farms that lined the highway, and a shabby tavern called "Tilly's", which was torn down.

Stonehill had despised growing up in a place he viewed as a nauseating mud hole. Back in Stonehill's past, Centerville had been built around the county building, several truck stops and gas stations, a few taverns, various factories and a bank. Stonehill had blamed strangers, yet he had always disliked living in the area, and hated the emotional abuse he had suffered in childhood at the hands of his hostile father.

Safely behind bars, it was unlikely anyone would have to face Stonehill's wrath again. Nobody would have to listen to his self-centered grumbling about his childhood.

Most citizens who wrote to the Observer described Stonehill as a deplorable maniac who should have sought psychiatric help. His personal hatred against his parents should not have been unleashed on the community. The sheriff's department had done what it could, successfully rescuing a kidnap victim from a violent stalker.

Yet, as Stonehill remembered, his father worked as an insignificant farmer who accomplished nothing. Showing little remorse for the death and destruction he had caused, those were among complaints he expressed to law enforcement authorities. Stonehill and his parents could not have been suitably trained for other work, he claimed.

Outside the county law-enforcement building, pedestrians, including Morehouse and Weaver, walked across the downtown avenues of Centerville. Having left the sheriff's office, Morehouse and Weaver went into Dawson's, a busy drugstore.

"I thought the name was familiar, but I wasn't sure," Morehouse said, talking to the baldheaded figure standing in front of the counter. It was Sam Dawson, the 83-year-old proprietor of the original general store. Morehouse asked him for prescription medication for his head injury, while Weaver expressed gratitude that Dawson had recognized him. Following his retirement from full-time employment at the store, Dawson spent much of his spare time at home. Weaver hadn't run into him behind the counter in two years.

"Here's your medication," said Sam, pushing the white stapled pharmacy bag across the counter. "You're the same healthy person, Ray," Dawson said.

"What are you doing at the store?" Weaver offered.

"I came back today because I heard about Ray's injury. Normally, Bob, our pharmacist, would have taken care of him."

Dawson adjusted his glasses. "I read about that bum, Stonehill, in the newspaper, about his arrest and Deputy Balton's death. Our customers, people all around town, have been buzzing about it."

"It won't be long before he's tried and shipped off to prison," Weaver said.

"I remember Vernon back there, what was it, twenty-five years ago, or thereabouts? He was an ornery bastard, and his son turned out the same."

"I didn't live here then, but I remember Vernon's crazy story about the supposed collapse of the mine shaft," Morehouse said.

"After the Kellinger site was robbed, it was eventually shut down," Dawson reminded them. "The farmers returned to their farms and the workers returned to town. They couldn't get nobody to run the place properly, so they just shut it down. The same thing will happen at Stonehill's farm."

Morehouse interrupted, "As far as Stonehill is concerned, I can't say I feel entirely bad about the whole mess. Thanks to the courageous efforts of the sheriff, we've got him safely locked up."

"That's the truth, all right," Dawson agreed. "He'll get what he deserves, a long prison sentence. It's bad enough he was drinkin' at bars around here, just like law-abidin' folks. I read all that crap in the newspaper about how his father didn't treat him fairly. Maybe our justice system will put some sense into him."

"I realize that with new residents moving in, the town is quite a bit different than it used to be," Morehouse reasoned.

Dawson looked at Weaver. "You just can't let dangerous folks run around loose, sheriff, thinking that they're citizens."

"You're right about that, old-timer," Weaver said. "You don't have to worry about anything. Stonehill ended up where he belongs."

Morehouse picked up the bag, and he and Weaver began walking away from the druggist's counter toward the front exit. "We'll see you, Sam," they said in unison.

"Smile, when you take that medication," Dawson said.

"I will," Morehouse said.

Strolling down the sidewalk to Weaver's office, gazing at the modern restaurants, gas stations and banks that had sprung up over the years, they both agreed the community had undergone noticeable improvements.

The End

0-595-33137-8

Printed in the United States
R909200001B/R9092PG24288LVSX00012B/43-45